THE ART OF WAR

DAVID WINGROVE is the Hugo Award-winning co-author (with Brian Aldiss) of *Trillion Year Spree: The History of Science Fiction*. He is also the co-author of the first three MYST books – novelizations of one of the world's bestselling computer games. He lives in north London with his wife and four daughters.

CHUNG KUO

THE ART OF WAR

CHUNG KUO

BOOK 5

DAVID WINGROVE

CORVUS

The Art of War was first published as The Broken Wheel in Great Britain in 1990
by New English Library.

This revised and updated edition published in special edition hardback, trade paperback,
and eBook in Great Britain in 2013 by Corvus, an imprint of Atlantic Books Ltd.

10 9 8 7 6 5 4 3 2 1

A CIP catalogue record for this book is available from the British Library.

Hardback ISBN: 9 780 85789 070 2
Trade paperback ISBN: 978 0 85789 071 9
E-book ISBN: 978 0 85789 423 6

Printed in Great Britain by the MPG Books Group.

Corvus
An imprint of Atlantic Books Ltd
Ormond House
26–27 Boswell Street

CONTENTS

THE ART OF WAR

Book Five

'Keep away from sharp swords,
Don't go near a lovely woman.
A sharp sword too close will wound your hand,
Woman's beauty too close will wound your life.
The danger of the road is not in the distance,
Ten yards is far enough to break a wheel.
The peril of love is not in loving too often,
A single evening can leave its wound in the soul.'
—Meng Chiao, 'Impromptu', 8th century AD

For Rose and Ian
'A new sound from the old keys.'

INTRODUCTION

Chung Kuo. The words mean 'Middle Kingdom' and, since 221 BC, when the First Emperor, Ch'in Shih Huang Ti, unified the seven Warring States, it is what the 'black-haired people', the Han, or Chinese, have called their great country. The Middle Kingdom – for them it was the whole world; a world bounded by great mountain chains to the north and west, by the sea to east and south. Beyond was only desert and barbarism. So it was for two thousand years and through sixteen great dynasties. Chung Kuo *was* the Middle Kingdom, the very centre of the human world, and its Emperor the 'Son of Heaven', the 'One Man'. But in the eighteenth century that world was invaded by the young and aggressive Western powers with their superior weaponry and their unshakeable belief in Progress. It was, to the surprise of the Han, an unequal contest and China's myth of supreme strength and self-sufficiency was shattered. By the early twentieth century China – *Chung Kuo* – was the sick old man of the East: 'a carefully preserved mummy in a hermetically sealed coffin', as Karl Marx called it. But from the disastrous ravages of that century grew a giant of a nation, capable of competing with the West and with its own Eastern rivals, Japan and Korea, from a position of incomparable strength.

By the turn of the twenty-second century, Chung Kuo, the Middle Kingdom, had come to mean much more. For more than a hundred years the Empire of the Han had encompassed all the world, the Earth's bloated population of thirty-six billion contained in vast, hive-like cities of three hundred levels that spanned whole continents. The Council of Seven – Han lords, T'*ang*, each more powerful than the greatest of the ancient emperors

– ruled Chung Kuo with an iron authority, their boast that they had ended Change and stopped the Great Wheel turning. But war, famine and political instability, thought to be things of the past, returned to Chung Kuo with a vengeance.

A new generation of powerful young merchants – Dispersionists, formed mainly of *Hung Mao*, or Westerners – challenged the authority of the Seven, demanding an end to the Edict of Technological Control, the cornerstone of Han stability, and a return to the Western ideal of unfettered progress. In the face of assassination and counter-assassination, something had to give, and the destruction of the Dispersionist starship, *The New Hope*, signalled the beginning of 'the War-that-wasn't-a-War', an incestuous power struggle fought within the City's levels. The Seven won that War, but at a price they could ill afford. Suddenly they were weak – weaker than they had been in their entire history, four of their most experienced members having died in the space of six short years. In their place, the new T'ang were young and inexperienced, while the older T'ang had lost the confidence, the certainty, they had once possessed.

In the long years of peace before the War it had seemed inconceivable to challenge the Seven. But now...

For the Dispersionists, too, it was a costly war. Five years of struggle found them with most of their major leaders dead and more than two thousand of their number executed. One hundred and eighteen of their great Companies had ceased trading – their assets and holdings confiscated by the Seven – while many more, numbering hundreds of thousands, had been demoted 'down the levels' for being sympathetic to their cause.

But the War was merely the first tiny sign of the great disturbances to come, for down in the lowest levels of the City, in the lawless regions 'below the Net' and in the overcrowded decks just above, new currents of unrest – darker and deeper than those expressed by the War – have awoken. Currents which, inflamed by the ever-mounting burden of population pressures, threaten to tear Chung Kuo itself apart...

PROLOGUE **THE SOUND OF JADE**

SUMMER 2206

'At rise of day we sacrificed to the Wind God,
When darkly, darkly, dawn glimmered in the sky.
Officers followed, horsemen led the way;
They brought us out to the wastes beyond the town,
Where river mists fall heavier than rain,
And the fires on the hill leap higher than the stars.
Suddenly I remembered the early levees at Court
When you and I galloped to the Purple Yard.
As we walked our horses up Dragon Tail Way
We turned and gazed at the green of the Southern Hills.
Since we parted, both of us have been growing old;
And our minds have been vexed by many anxious cares;
Yet even now I fancy my ears are full
Of the sound of jade tinkling on your bridle-straps.'
—Po Chu-I, 'To Li Chien' (AD 819)

CHUNG KUO

I t was night and the moon lay like a blinded eye upon the satin darkness of
the Nile. From where he stood, on the balcony high above the river, Wang
Hsien could feel the slow, warm movement of the air like the breath of
a sleeping woman against his cheek. He sighed and laid his hands upon
the cool stone of the balustrade, looking out to his right, to the north,
where, in the distance, the great lighthouse threw its long, sweeping arm
of light across the delta. For a while he watched it, feeling as empty as the
air through which it moved, then he turned back, looking up at the moon
itself. So clear the nights were here. And the stars. He shivered, the bitterness flooding back. The stars...

A voice broke into his reverie. 'Chieh Hsia? Are you ready for us?'

It was Sun Li Hua, Master of the Inner Chamber. He stood just inside the
doorway, his head bowed, his two assistants a respectful distance behind
him, their heads lowered. Wang Hsien turned and made a brief gesture,
signifying that they should begin, then he turned back.

He remembered being with his two eldest sons, Chang Ye and Lieh Tsu,
on the coast of Mozambique in summer. A late summer night with the
bright stars filling the heavens overhead. They had sat there about an open
fire, the three of them, naming the stars and their constellations, watching
the Dipper move across the black velvet of the sky until the fire was ash and
the day was come again. It was the last time he had been with them alone.
Their last holiday together.

And now they were dead. Both of them, lying in their coffins, still and
cold beneath the earth. And where were their spirits now? Up there? Among

the eternal stars? Or was there only one soul, the *hun*, trapped and rotting in the ground? He gritted his teeth, fighting against his sense of bitterness and loss. Hardening himself against it. But the bitterness remained. Was it so? he asked himself. Did the spirit soul, the *p'o*, rise up to Heaven, as they said, or was there only this? This earth, this sky, and Man between them?

Best not ask. Best keep such thoughts at bay, lest the darkness answer you.

He shivered, his hands gripping the stone fiercely. Gods but he missed them! Missed them beyond the power of words to say. He filled his hours, keeping his mind busy with the myriad affairs of State; even so, he could not keep himself from thinking of them. *Where are you?* he would ask himself on waking. *Where are you, Chang Ye, who smiled so sweetly? And you, Lieh Tsu, my ying tao, my baby peach, always my favourite? Where are you now?*

Murdered, a brutal voice in him insisted. And only ash and bitterness remained.

He turned savagely, angry with himself. Now he would not sleep. Bone-tired as he was, he would lie there, sleepless, impotent against the thousand bitter-sweet images that would come.

'Sun Li Hua!' he called impatiently, moving the curtain aside with one hand. 'Bring me something to make me sleep! *Ho yeh*, perhaps, or *tou chi*.'

'At once, *Chieh Hsia*.'

The Master of the Inner Chamber bowed low, then went to do as he was bid. Wang Hsien watched him go, then turned to look across at the huge, low bed at the far end of the chamber. The servants were almost done. The silken sheets were turned back, the flowers at the bedside changed, his sleeping robes laid out, ready for the maids.

The headboard seemed to fill the end wall, the circle of the *Ywe Lung*, the Moon Dragon, symbol of the Seven, carved deep into the wood. The seven dragons formed a great wheel, their regal snouts meeting at the hub, their lithe, powerful bodies forming the spokes, their tails the rim. Wang Hsien stared at it a while, then nodded to himself as if satisfied. But deeper, at some dark, unarticulated level, he felt a sense of unease. The War, the murder of his sons – these things had made him far less certain than he'd been. He could no longer look at the *Ywe Lung* without questioning what had been done in their name these last five years.

He looked down sharply. Five years. Was that all? Only five short years? So it was. Yet it felt as though a whole cycle of sixty years had passed since

The New Hope had been blasted from the heavens and war declared. He sighed and put his hand up to his brow, remembering. It had been a nasty, vicious war; a war of little trust – where friend and enemy had worn the same smiling face. They had won, but their victory had failed to set things right. The struggle had changed the nature – the very essence – of Chung Kuo. Nothing would ever be the same again.

He waited until the servants left, backing away, bowed low, their eyes averted from their lord's face, then went across and stood before the wall-length mirror.

'You are an old man, Wang Hsien,' he told himself softly, noting the deep lines about his eyes and mouth, the ivory yellow of his eyes, the loose roughness of his skin. 'Moon-faced, they call you. Maybe so. But this moon has waxed and waned a thousand times and still I see no clearer by its light. Who are you, Wang Hsien? What kind of man are you?'

He turned, tensing instinctively, hearing a noise in the passageway outside, then relaxed, smiling.

The three girls bowed deeply, then came into the room, Little Bee making her way across to him, while Tender Willow and Sweet Rain busied themselves elsewhere in the room.

Little Bee knelt before him, then looked up, her sweet, unaffected smile lifting his spirits, bringing a breath of youth and gaiety to his old heart.

'How are you this evening, good Father?'

'I am fine,' he lied, warmed by the sight of her. 'And you, Mi Feng?'

'The better for seeing you, my lord.'

He laughed softly, then leaned forward and touched her head gently, affectionately. Little Bee had been with him six years now, since her tenth birthday. She was like a daughter to him.

He turned, enjoying the familiar sight of his girls moving about the room, readying things for him. For a while it dispelled his previous mood; made him forget the darkness he had glimpsed inside and out. He let Little Bee remove his *pau* and sit him, naked, in a chair, then closed his eyes and let his head fall back while she began to rub his chest and arms with oils. As ever, the gentle pressure of her hands against his skin roused him. Tender Willow came and held the bowl with the lavender glaze while Sweet Rain gave him ease, her soft, thin-boned fingers caressing him with practised strokes until he came. Then Little Bee washed him there and, making him stand, bound him up in a single yellow silk cloth before bringing a fresh sleeping garment.

He looked down at her tiny, delicate form as she stood before him, fastening his cloak, and felt a small shiver pass through him. Little Bee looked up, concerned.

'Are you sure you are all right, Father? Should I ask one of your wives to come to you?'

'It's nothing, Mi Feng. And no, I'll sleep alone tonight.'

She fastened the last of the tiny, difficult buttons, looking up into his face a moment, then looked down again, frowning. 'I worry for you, *Chieh Hsia*,' she said, turning away to take a brush from the table at her side. 'Some days you seem to carry the whole world's troubles on your shoulders.'

He smiled and let her push him down gently into the chair again. 'I am Seven, Mi Feng. Who else should carry the burden of Chung Kuo?'

She was silent a moment, her fingers working to unbind his tightly braided queue. Then, leaning close, she whispered in his ear. 'Your son,' she said. 'Why not make Ta-hung your regent?'

He laughed shortly, unamused. 'And make that rascal friend of his, Hung Mien-lo, a T'ang in all but name?' He looked at her sharply. 'Has he been talking to you?'

'Has who been talking to me, Father? I was thinking only of your health. You need more time to yourself.'

He laughed, seeing for himself how free from subterfuge she was. 'Forget what I said, Mi Feng. Besides, I enjoy my duties.'

She was brushing out his hair now, from scalp to tip, her tiny, perfectly formed body swaying gently, enticingly beside him with each passage of the brush. He could see her side on in the mirror across the room, her silks barely veiling her nakedness.

He sighed and closed his eyes again, overcome by a strange mixture of emotions. *Most men would envy me*, he thought. *And yet some days I think myself accursed. These girls... they would do whatever I wished, without a moment's hesitation, and yet there is no joy in the thought. My sons are dead. How could joy survive such heartbreak?*

He shuddered and stood up abruptly, surprising Little Bee, making the others turn and look across. They watched him walk briskly to the mirror and stand there, as if in pain, grimacing into the glass. Then he turned back, his face bitter.

'Ta-hung!' he said scathingly, throwing himself down into the chair again. 'I was a fool to let that one be born!'

There was a shocked intake of breath from the three girls. It was unlike Wang Hsien to say such things. Little Bee looked at the others and nodded, then waited until they were gone before speaking to him again.

She knelt, looking up into his face, concerned. 'What is it, Wang Hsien? What eats at you like poison?'

'My sons!' he said, in sudden agony. 'My sons are dead!'

'Not all your sons,' she answered gently, taking his hands in her own. 'Wang Ta-hung yet lives. And Wang Sau-Leyan.'

'A weakling and a libertine!' he said bitterly, not looking at her; staring past her into space. 'I had two fine, strong sons. Good, upstanding men with all their mother's finest qualities. And now...' He shivered violently and looked at her, his features racked with pain, his hands gripping hers tightly. 'This war has taken everything, Mi Feng. Everything. Some days I think it has left me hollow, emptied of all I was.'

'No...' she said, sharing his pain. 'No, my lord. Not everything.'

He let her hands fall from his and stood again, turning away from her and staring at the door that led out on to the balcony.

'It is the most bitter lesson,' he said fiercely. 'That a man might own the world and yet have nothing.'

Little Bee swallowed and looked down. She had seen her master in many moods, but never like this.

She turned, realizing there was someone in the chamber with them. It was Sun Li Hua. He stood in the doorway, his head bowed. In his hands was the lavender glaze bowl that Tender Willow had taken out to him only moments earlier.

'*Chieh Hsia?*'

Wang Hsien turned abruptly, facing the newcomer, clearly angered by the interruption. Then he seemed to collect himself and dropped his head slightly. He looked across at Little Bee and, with a forced smile, dismissed her.

'Good night, *Chieh Hsia*,' she said softly, backing away. 'May Kuan Yin bring you peace.'

*

Sun Li Hua stood there after the maid had gone, perfectly still, awaiting his master's orders.

'Come in, Master Sun,' Wang Hsien said after a moment. He turned away and walked slowly across the room, sitting down heavily on his bed.

'Are you all right, *Chieh Hsia*?' Sun Li Hua asked. He set the bowl down on the small table at the bedside, then looked up at his master. 'Has one of the maids done something to upset you?'

Wang Hsien glanced at his Master of the Inner Chamber almost without recognition, then shook his head irritably. 'What is this?' he said, pointing at the bowl.

'It is your sleeping potion, *Chieh Hsia*. Lotus seeds mixed with your own life elixir. It should help you sleep.'

Wang Hsien took a deep, shuddering breath, then reached out and took the bowl in one hand, sipping from it. The *ho yeh* was slightly bitter to the taste – a bitterness augmented by the salt tang of his own yang essence, his semen – but not unpleasant. He drained the bowl, then looked back at Sun Li Hua, holding out the empty bowl for him to take. 'You will wake me at five, yes?'

Sun Li Hua took the bowl and backed away, bowing again. 'Of course, *Chieh Hsia*.'

He watched the old T'ang turn and slide his legs between the sheets, then lower his head on to the pillow, pulling the covers up about his shoulders. *Two minutes*, he thought; *that's all the good Doctor Yueh said it would take.*

Sun Li Hua moved back, beneath the camera, waiting in the doorway until he heard the old T'ang's breathing change. Then, setting the bowl down, he took a key from inside his silks and reached up, opening a panel high up in the door's frame. It popped back, revealing a tiny keyboard and a timer unit. Quickly he punched the combination. The timer froze, two amber lights appearing at the top of the panel.

He counted to ten, then touched the EJECT panel. At once a thin, transparent card dropped into the tray beneath the keyboard. He slipped it into his pocket, then put its replacement into the slot at the side and punched SET.

'Good,' he said softly, closing the panel and slipping the key back inside his silks. Then, taking a pair of gloves from his pocket, he stepped back inside the bedchamber.

Six floors below, at the far end of the palace, two soldiers were sitting in a cramped guardroom, talking.

The younger of them, a lieutenant, turned momentarily from the bank of screens that filled the wall in front of him and looked across at his captain. 'What do you think will happen, Otto? Will they close all the companies down?'

Captain Fischer, Head of the T'ang's personal security, looked up from behind his desk and smiled. 'Your guess is as good as anyone's, Wolf. But I'll tell you this, whatever they do there'll be trouble.'

'You think so?'

'Well, think about it. The volume of seized assets is so vast that if the Seven freeze them it's certain to damage the market badly. However, if they redistribute all that wealth in the form of rewards there's the problem of who gets what. A lot of people are going to be jealous or dissatisfied. On the other hand, they can't just give it back. There has to be some kind of punishment.'

The lieutenant turned back to his screens, scanning them conscientiously. 'I agree. But where do they draw the line? How do they distinguish between those who were actively against them and those who were simply unhelpful?'

Fischer shrugged. 'I don't know, Wolf. I really don't.'

They were discussing the most recent spate of Confiscations and Demotions, a subject never far from most people's lips these days. In the past eighteen months more than one hundred and eighty thousand First Level families had been 'sent down' and all their material goods confiscated by the Seven as punishment for what had been termed 'subversive activities'. A further five thousand families had simply vanished from the face of Chung Kuo – to the third generation as the law demanded – for active treason against the Seven. But now, with the War in its final stages and the clamour for peace growing daily, the Confiscations had become a delicate subject and a major bone of contention between those who wanted retribution and those who simply wanted to damp down the fires of resentment and bitterness that such retribution brought in its wake.

The lieutenant turned, eyeing his captain speculatively. 'I hear there's even talk of reopening the House.'

Fischer looked back at his junior officer sternly, his voice suddenly hard. 'You would do best to forget such talk, Lieutenant.'

'Sir.' The lieutenant gave a curt bow of his head, then turned back to his screens.

Fischer studied Rahn's back a moment, then leaned back, yawning. It was just after two, the hour of the Ox. The palace was silent, the screens empty of activity. In an hour his shift would be over and he could sleep. He smiled. That is, if Lotte would let him sleep.

He rubbed at his neck, then leaned forward again and began to catch up with his paperwork. He had hardly begun when the door to his right crashed open. He was up out of his seat at once, his gun drawn, aimed at the doorway.

'Sun Li Hua! What in Hell's name?'

The Master of the Inner Chamber looked terrible. His silks were torn, his hair dishevelled. He leaned against the doorpost for support, his eyes wide with shock, his cheeks wet with tears. He reached out, his hand trembling violently, then shook his head, his mouth working mutely. His voice, when he found it, was cracked, unnaturally high.

'The T'ang...'

Fischer glanced across at the screen that showed Wang Hsien's bedchamber, then back at Sun Li Hua. 'What is it, Master Sun? What's happened?'

For a moment Sun Li Hua seemed unable to speak, then he fell to his knees. A great, racking sob shook his whole body, then he looked up, his eyes wild, distraught. 'Our master, the T'ang. He's... dead.'

Fischer had known as soon as he had seen Sun Li Hua; had felt his stomach fall away from him with fear; but he had not wanted to know – not for certain.

'How?' he heard himself say. Then, seeing what it meant, he looked across at his lieutenant, pre-empting him; stopping him from pressing the general alarm that would wake the whole palace.

'Touch nothing, Wolf. Not until I order you to. Get Kurt and Alan here at once.'

He turned back to Sun. 'Who else knows, Master Sun? Who else have you told?'

'No one,' Sun answered, his voice barely audible. 'I came straight here. I didn't know what to do. They've killed him. Killed him while he slept.'

'Who? Who's killed him? What do you mean?'

'Fu and Chai. I'm certain it was them. Fu's stiletto... '

Fischer swallowed, appalled. 'They knifed him? Your two assistants knifed him?' He turned to his lieutenant. 'Wolf, take two copies of the surveillance tape. Send one to Marshal Tolonen at Bremen. Another to General Helm in Rio.'

'Sir!'

He thought quickly. No one knew anything. Not yet. Only he and Wolf and Sun Li Hua. And the murderers, of course, but they would be telling no one. He turned back to his lieutenant. 'Keep Master Sun here. And when Kurt and Alan come have them wait here until I get back. And, Wolf...'

'Sir?'

'Tell no one anything. Not yet. Understand me?'

Wang Hsien lay there on his back, his face relaxed, as if in sleep, yet pale – almost *Hung Mao* in its paleness. Fischer leaned across and felt for a pulse at the neck. Nothing. The flesh was cold. The T'ang had been dead an hour at least.

Fischer shuddered and stepped back, studying the body once again. The silk sheets were dark, sticky with the old man's blood. The silver-handled stiletto jutted from the T'ang's bared chest, the blade thrust in all the way up to the handle. He narrowed his eyes, considering. It would have taken some strength to do that, even to a sleeping man. And not just strength. It was not easy for one man to kill another. One needed the will for the job.

Could Fu have done it? Or Chai? Fischer shook his head. He could not imagine either of them doing this. And yet if not them, then who?

He looked about him, noting how things lay. Then, his mind made up, he turned and left the room, knowing he had only minutes in which to act.

The board lay on the desk in front of DeVore, its nineteen by nineteen grid part overlaid with a patterning of black and white stones. Most of the board was empty: only in the top right-hand corner, in *ch'u*, the west, were the stones concentrated heavily. There the first stage of the battle had been fought, with black pressing white hard into the corner, slowly choking off its breath, blinding its eyes until, at last, the group was dead, the ten stones taken from the board.

It was an ancient game – one of the ten games of the West Lake, played by those two great masters from Hai-nin, Fan Si-pin and Su Ting-an, back in 1763. He played it often, from memory, stopping, as now, at the fifty-ninth move to query what Fan, playing white, had chosen. It was an elegant, enthralling game, the two masters so perfectly balanced in ability, their moves so exquisitely thought out, that he felt a shiver of delight contemplating what was to come. Even so, he could not help but search for those small ways in which each player's game might have been improved.

DeVore looked up from the board and glanced across at the young man who stood, his back to him, on the far side of the room. Then, taking a wafer-thin ice-paper pamphlet from his jacket pocket, he unfolded it and held it out.

'Have you heard of this new group, Stefan – the Ping Tiao?'

Lehmann turned, his face expressionless, then came across and took the pamphlet, examining it. After a moment he looked back at DeVore, his cold, pink eyes revealing nothing. 'I've heard of them. They're low level types, aren't they? Why are you interested?'

'A man must be interested in many things,' DeVore answered cryptically, leaning forward to take a white stone from the bowl, hefting it in his hand. 'The Ping Tiao want what we want, to destroy the Seven.'

'Yes, but they would destroy us just as readily. They're terrorists. They want only to destroy.'

'I know. Even so, they could be useful. We might walk the same path a while, don't you think?'

'And then?'

DeVore smiled tightly. Lehmann knew as well as he. Then there would be war between them. A war he would win. He looked down at the board again. The fifty-ninth move. What would he have played in Fan's place? His smile broadened, became more natural. How many times had he thought it through? A hundred? A thousand? And always, inevitably, he would make Fan's move, taking the black at 4/1 to give himself a temporary breathing space. So delicately were things balanced at that point that to do otherwise – to make any of a dozen other tempting plays – would be to lose it all.

A wise man, Fan Si-pin. He knew the value of sacrifice: the importance of making one's opponents work hard for their small victories – knowing that while the battle was lost in ch'u, the war went on in shang and ping and tsu.

So it was now, in Chung Kuo. Things were balanced very delicately. And one wrong move... He looked up at Lehmann again, studying the tall young albino.

'You ask what would happen should we succeed, but there are other, more immediate questions. Are the Ping Tiao important enough? You know how the media exaggerate these things. And would an alliance with them harm or strengthen us?'

Lehmann met his gaze. 'As I said, the Ping Tiao are a low level organisation. Worse, they're idealists. It would be hard to work with such men. They would have fewer weaknesses than those we're used to dealing with.'

'And yet they are men. They have needs, desires.'

'Maybe so, but they would mistrust us from the start. In their eyes we are First Level, their natural enemies. Why should they work with us?'

DeVore smiled and stood up, coming round the desk. 'It's not a question of choice, Stefan, but necessity. They need someone like us. Think of the losses they've sustained.'

He was about to say more – to outline his plan – when there was an urgent knocking at the door.

DeVore looked across, meeting Lehmann's eyes. He had ordered his lieutenant, Wiegand, not to disturb him unless it was vitally important.

'Come in!'

Wiegand took two steps into the room then came sharply to attention, his head bowed. 'I've a call on the coded channel, sir. Triple-A rated.'

DeVore narrowed his eyes, conscious of how closely Lehmann was watching him. 'Who is it?'

'It's Stifel, sir. He says he has little time.'

'Stifel' was the code name for Otto Fischer in Alexandria. DeVore hesitated a moment, his mind running through possibilities, then nodded.

'Okay. Switch it through.'

It was a non-visual, Fischer's voice artificially distorted to avoid even the remote possibility of recognition.

'Well, Stifel? What is it?'

'The moon is down, sir. An hour past at most.'

DeVore caught his breath. 'How?'

'Eclipsed.'

DeVore stared across at Lehmann, astonished. He hesitated a moment, considering, then spoke again.

'How many know about this?'

'Three, maybe four.'

'Good. Keep it that way.' He thought quickly. 'Who's guarding our fallen moon?'

'No one. A camera...'

'Excellent. Now listen...'

He spelt out quickly what he wanted, then broke contact, knowing that Fischer would do exactly as he'd asked.

'Who's dead?'

DeVore turned and looked at Lehmann again. His face, like the tone of his words, seemed utterly devoid of curiosity, as if the question were a mere politeness, the answer a matter of indifference to him.

'Wang Hsien,' he answered. 'It seems he's been murdered in his bed.'

If he had expected the albino to show any sign of surprise he would have been disappointed, but he knew the young man better than that.

'I see,' Lehmann said. 'And you know who did it?'

'The agent, yes, but not who he was acting for.' DeVore sat behind his desk again, then looked up at Lehmann. 'It was Sun Li Hua.'

'You know that for certain?'

'Not for certain, no. But I'd wager a million *yuan* on it.'

Lehmann came across and stood at the edge of the desk. 'So what now?'

DeVore met his eyes briefly, then looked down at the board again. 'We wait. Until we hear from Stifel again. Then the fun begins.'

'Fun?'

'Yes, fun. You'll see. But go now, Stefan. Get some rest. I'll call you when I need you.'

He realized he was still holding the white stone. It lay in his palm like a tiny moon, cold, moist with his sweat. He opened out his fingers and stared at it, then lifted it and wiped it. The fifty-ninth stone.

The game had changed dramatically, the balance altered in his favour. *The moon was down. Eclipsed.*

DeVore smiled, then nodded to himself, suddenly knowing where to play the stone.

The dead T'ang lay where he had left him, undisturbed, his long grey hair fanned out across the pillow, his arms at his sides, the palms upturned. Fischer stood there a moment, looking down at the corpse, breathing deeply, preparing himself. Then, knowing he could delay no longer, he bent down and put his hand behind the cold, stiff neck, lifting the head, drawing the hair back from the ear.

It was not, physically, difficult to do – the flesh parted easily before the knife; the blood stopped flowing almost as soon as it had begun – yet he was conscious of a deep, almost overpowering reluctance in himself. This was a T'ang! A Son of Heaven! He shivered, letting the severed flesh fall, then turned the head and did the same to the other side.

He lowered the head on to the pillow and stepped back, appalled. Outwardly he seemed calm, almost icy in his control, but inwardly he quaked with an inexplicable, almost religious fear of what he was doing. His pulse raced, his stomach churned, and all the while a part of him kept saying to himself, *What are you doing, Otto? What are you doing?*

He stared, horrified, at the two thick question-marks of flesh that lay now on the pillow, separated from their owner's head, then steeled himself and reached out to take them. He drew the tiny bag from inside his jacket and dropped them into it, then sealed the bag and returned it to the pocket.

Wang Hsien lay there, regal even in death, indifferent to all that had been done to him. Fischer stared at him a while, mesmerized, awed by the power of the silent figure. Then, realizing he was wasting time, he bent over the corpse again, smoothing the hair back into place, hiding the disfigurement.

Nervousness made him laugh – a laugh he stifled quickly. He shuddered and looked about him again, then went to the doorway. There he paused, reaching up to reset the camera, checking the elapsed time against his wrist timer, then moved the camera's clock forward until the two were synchronized. That done, he pressed out the combination quickly. The lights at the top changed from amber to green, signifying that the camera was functioning again.

He looked back, checking the room one final time, then, satisfied that nothing was disturbed, he backed out of the room, pulling the door to silently behind him, his heart pounding, his mouth dry with fear, the sealed bag seeming to burn where it pressed against his chest.

Wang Ta-hung woke to whispering in his room and sat up, clutching the blankets to his chest, his mind dark with fear.

'Who is it?' he called out, his voice quavering. 'Kuan Yin preserve me, who is it?'

A figure approached the huge bed, bowed. 'It is only I, Excellency. Your servant, Wu Ming.'

Wang Ta-hung, the T'ang's eldest surviving son, pulled the blankets tighter about his neck and stared, wide-eyed, past his Master of the Bed-chamber, into the darkness beyond.

'Who is there, Wu Ming? Who were you whispering to?'

A second figure stepped from the darkness and stood beside the first, his head bowed. He was a tall, strongly built Han dressed in dark silks, his beard braided into three tiny pigtails, his face, when it lifted once again, solid, unreadable. A handsome, yet inexpressive face.

'Excellency.'

'Hung Mien-lo!'

Wang Ta-hung turned and glanced at the ornate timepiece beside the bed, then twisted back, facing the two men, his face twitching with alarm.

'It is almost half two! What are you doing here? What's happened?'

Hung Mien-lo sat on the bed beside the frightened twenty-year-old, taking his upper arms gently but firmly in his hands.

'It's all right, Ta-hung. Please, calm yourself. I have some news, that's all.'

The young Prince nodded, but it was as if he was still in the grip of some awful dream; his eyes continued to stare, a muscle in his left cheek twitched violently. He had been this way for eighteen months now, since the day he had found his two brothers dead in one of the guest bedrooms of the summer palace, their naked bodies grey-blue from the poison, the two maids they had been entertaining sprawled nearby, their pale limbs laced with blood, their eyes gouged out.

Some said that the pale, wasted-looking youth was mad, others that it was only natural for one of his sickly disposition to suffer after such a discovery. He had never been a strong boy, but now...

Hung Mien-lo stroked the young man's shoulder, comforting him, knowing the delicacy of what lay ahead – that what must be said might well send him deeper into madness. He spoke softly, reassuringly. 'It is your father, Ta-hung. I am afraid he is dead.'

For a moment it didn't register. There was a flicker of disbelief. Then, abruptly, the Prince pulled himself away, scrambling back until he was pressed up against the headboard, his eyes wide, his mouth open.

'How?' he said, the words the tiniest, frightened squeak. 'How did he die?'

Hung Mien-lo ignored the question. He spoke calmly, using the same reassuring tone as before. 'You must get dressed, Ta-hung. You must come and bear witness to what has happened.'

Wang Ta-hung laughed shrilly, then buried his head in his arms, shaking it wildly. 'No-o-o!' he cried, his voice muffled. 'No-oh! Gods, no, not again!'

Hung Mien-lo turned and clicked his fingers. At once Wu Ming bustled off to get things ready. *Yes*, Hung thought, *he at least understands. For now that the old T'ang is dead Ta-hung is T'ang in his place, mad or no. Indeed, the madder the better as far as I'm concerned, for the more Ta-hung relies on me, the more power lies within my hands.*

He smiled and stood, seeing how the young man cowered away from him, yet how his eyes beseeched his help. *Yes, indeed*, Hung Mien-lo thought; *my hour has truly come; the hour I waited for so long as companion to this young fool. And now I am effectively first man in City Africa. The shaper. The orderer. The granter of favours.*

Inwardly he felt exultation, a soaring, brilliant joy that had lit in him the moment he had been told; yet this, more than any other moment, was a time for masks. He put one on now, shaping his face towards sternness, to the expression of a profound grief. Satisfied, he went over to the young Prince and lifted him from the bed, standing him on his feet.

'It was so cold,' the youth murmured, looking up into his face. 'When I touched Chang Ye's shoulder, it was like he had been laid in ice. The cold of it seemed to burn my hand. I...'He hesitated, then looked down, turning his hand, lifting the palm to stare at it.

'That's done with, Ta-hung. You must get dressed now and see your father. You are the eldest now, the Head of your family. You must take charge of things.'

Ta-hung stared back at him, uncomprehendingly. 'Take charge?'

'Don't worry,' Hung said, unfastening the cord, then pulling the Prince's sleeping silks down off his shoulders, stripping him naked. 'I'll be there beside you, Ta-hung. I'll tell you what to do.'

Wu Ming returned and began at once to dress and groom the Prince. He was only part way through when Ta-hung broke away from him and threw himself down at Hung Mien-lo's feet, sobbing.

'I'm frightened, Mien-lo. So frightened!'

Hung glanced at Wu Ming, then reached down and hauled the Prince roughly to his feet. 'Stop it! You've got to stop this at once!'

There was a moment's shocked silence, then the young Prince bowed his head. 'I'm sorry, I...'

'No!' Hung barked. 'No apologies. Don't you understand, Ta-hung? You are T'ang now. *Seven*. It is I who should apologize, not you, *Chieh Hsia*.'

Chieh Hsia. It was the first time the words of imperial address had been used to the young man and Hung Mien-lo could see at once the effect they had on him. Though Ta-hung still shivered, though tears still coursed freely down his cheeks, yet he stood straighter, slightly taller, realizing for the first time what he had become.

'You understand, then? Good. Then remember this. Let none but a T'ang touch you without your permission. And let no man, not even a T'ang, speak to you as I spoke then. You are T'ang now. Supreme. Understand me, *Chieh Hsia*?'

Ta-hung's voice when he answered was different, almost calm. 'I understand you, Mien-lo. My father is dead and I am T'ang now.'

'Good. Then, with your permission, we will go to see your father and pay our respects, neh?'

The slightest shudder passed through the young man's wasted frame, the smallest cloud of revulsion momentarily crossed the sky of his face, then he nodded. 'As you say, Mien-lo. As you say.'

*

Wang Sau-leyan heard their voices coming nearer – the rustle of silks and the sound of their soft footsteps on the tiled floor – and slid the door open, slipping out into the dimly lit corridor. He pulled the door to quietly, then turned, facing them. They came on quickly, talking all the while, not seeing him until they were almost on top of him. He saw the look of surprise on Hung Mien-lo's face, heard his brother's gasp of fear.

He smiled and gave the slightest bow. 'I heard noises, Ta-hung. Voices calling softly but urgently in the darkness. What is happening, brother? Why do you wander the corridors at this early hour?'

He saw how Ta-hung looked to his friend, at a loss, his face a web of conflicting emotions, and smiled inwardly, enjoying his brother's impotence.

'I'm afraid there is bad news, Wang Sau-leyan,' Hung Mien-lo answered him, bowing low, his face grave. 'Your father is dead.'

'Dead? But how?'

He saw how Hung Mien-lo glanced at his brother and knew at once that Ta-hung had not been told everything.

'It would be best if you came yourself, Excellency. I will explain everything then. But excuse us, please. We must pay our respects to the late T'ang.'

He noted how pointedly Hung Mien-lo had emphasized the last two words; how his voice, while still superficially polite, was a register of how he thought things had changed. Wang Sau-leyan smiled tightly at Hung, then bowed to his elder brother.

'I will get dressed at once.'

He watched them go; then, satisfied, slid the door open again and went back into his rooms.

A voice from the bed, young, distinctly feminine, called softly to him. 'What was it, my love?'

He went across to her and, slipping off his robe, joined her, naked beneath the sheets.

'It was nothing,' he said, smiling down at his father's third wife. 'Nothing at all.'

Wang Ta-hung stood in the doorway of his father's room staring in, fear constricting his throat. He turned and looked at Hung Mien-lo beseechingly. 'I can't...'

'You are T'ang,' Hung answered him firmly. 'You can.'

The young man swallowed, then turned back, his fists clenched at his sides. 'I am T'ang,' he repeated. 'T'ang of City Africa.'

Hung Mien-lo stood there a moment, watching him take the first few hesitant steps into the room, knowing how important the next few minutes were. Ta-hung had accustomed himself to the fact of his father's death. Now he must discover how the old man died. Must learn, firsthand, the fate of kings.

And if it drove him mad?

Hung Mien-lo smiled to himself, then stepped inside the room. Kings had been mad before. What was a king, after all, but a symbol – the visible sign of a system of government? As long as the City was ruled, what did it matter who gave the orders?

He stopped beside the old man's chair, watching the youth approach the bed. Surely he's seen? he thought. Yet Ta-hung was too still, too composed. Then the young T'ang turned, looking back at him.

'I knew,' he said softly. 'As soon as you told me, I knew he had been murdered.'

Hung Mien-lo let his breath out. 'You *knew?*' He looked down. There, beneath him on the cushion, lay the T'ang's hairbrush. He leaned forward and picked it up, studying it a moment, appreciating the slender elegance of its ivory handle, the delicacy of its design. He was about to set it down when he noticed several strands of the old T'ang's hair trapped amongst the darkness of the bristles; long, white strands, almost translucent in their whiteness, like the finest threads of ice. He frowned then looked back at Wang Ta-hung. 'How do you feel, *Chieh Hsia?* Are you well enough to see others, or shall I delay?'

Wang Ta-hung looked about him, then turned and stared down at his father. He was still, unnaturally calm.

Perhaps this is it, thought Hung. *Perhaps something has broken in him and this calmness is the first sign of it.* But for once there seemed no trace of madness in Ta-hung, only a strange sense of dignity and distance, surprising because it was so unexpected.

'Let the others come,' he said, his voice clear of any shade of fear, his eyes drinking in the sight of his murdered father. 'There's no sense in delay.'

Hung Mien-lo hesitated, suddenly uncertain, then turned and went to the door, telling the guard to bring Fischer and Sun Li Hua. Then he went back inside.

Wang Ta-hung was standing at the bedside. He had picked something up and was sniffing at it. Hung Mien-lo went across to him.

'What is this?' Ta-hung asked, handing him a bowl.

It was a perfect piece of porcelain. Its roundness and its perfect lavender glaze made it a delight to look at. Hung turned it in his hands, a faint smile on his lips. It was an old piece, too, *K'ang Hsi* perhaps... or perhaps not, for the colouring was wrong. But that was not what Ta-hung had meant. He had meant the residue.

Hung sniffed at it, finding the heavy, musky scent of it strangely familiar, then turned, hearing voices at the door. It was Sun Li Hua and the Captain.

'Master Sun,' he called out, 'what was in this bowl?'

Sun bowed low and came into the room. 'It was a sleeping potion, *Chieh Hsia*,' he said, keeping his head lowered, addressing the new T'ang. 'Doctor Yuch prepared it.'

'And what was in it?' Hung asked, irritated by Sun's refusal to answer him directly.

Sun Li Hua hesitated a moment. 'It was *ho yeh*, for insomnia, *Chieh Hsia*.'

'*Ho yeh* and what?' Hung insisted, knowing the distinct smell of lotus seeds.

Sun glanced briefly at the young T'ang, as if for intercession, then bent his head. 'It was mixed with the T'ang's own yang essence, *Chieh Hsia*.'

'Ah...' He nodded, understanding.

He set the bowl down then turned away, looking about the room, noting the fresh flowers at the bedside, the T'ang's clothes laid out on the dresser, ready for the morning.

He looked across at Fischer. 'Has anything been disturbed?'

'No... Excellency.'

He noted the hesitation and realized that though they knew how important he had suddenly become, they did not know quite how to address him. *I must have a title*, he thought. *Chancellor, perhaps. Some peg to hang their respect upon.*

He turned, looking across at the open door that led out on to the balcony. 'Was this where the murderer entered?'

Fischer answered immediately. 'No, Excellency.'

'You're certain?'

'Quite certain, Excellency.'

Hung Mien-lo turned, surprised. 'How so?'

Fischer glanced up at the camera, then stepped forward. 'It is all on tape, Excellency. Sun Li Hua's assistants, the brothers Ying Fu and Ying Chai, are the murderers. They entered the room shortly after Master Sun had given the T'ang his potion.'

'Gods! And you have them?'

'Not yet, Excellency. But as no one has left the palace since the murder they must be here. My men are searching the palace even now to find them.'

Ta-hung was watching everything with astonishment, his lips parted, his eyes wide and staring. Hung Mien-lo looked across at him a moment, then turned back to Fischer, giving a curt nod. 'Good. But we want them alive. It's possible they were acting for another.'

'Of course, Excellency.'

Hung Mien-lo turned and went to the open door, pulling back the thin, see-through curtain of silk and stepping out on to the balcony. It was cool outside, the moon low to his left. To his right the beam of the distant light-house cut the darkness, flashing across the dark waters of the Nile delta and sweeping on across the surrounding desert. He stood there a moment, his hands on the balustrade, staring down into the darkness of the river far below.

So, it was Fu and Chai. They were the hands. But who was behind them? Who beside himself had wanted the old man dead? Sun Li Hua? Perhaps. After all, Wang Hsien had humiliated him before his sons when Sun had asked that his brothers be promoted and the T'ang had refused. But that had been long ago. Almost three years now. If Sun, why now? And in any case, Fischer had said that Sun had been like a madman when he'd come to him, feverish with dismay.

Who, then? *Who?* He racked his brains, but no answer sprang to mind. Wang Sau-leyan? He shook his head. Why should that no-good wastrel want power? And what would he do with it but piss it away if he had it? No, Ta-hung's little brother was good only for bedding whores, not for intrigue. Yet if not him, then who?

There was an anguished cry from within the room. He recognized it at once. It was Ta-hung! He turned and rushed inside.

Ta-hung looked up at him as he entered, his face a window, opening upon his inner terror. He was leaning over his father, cradling the old man's head in the crook of his arm.

'Look!' he called out brokenly. 'Look what they've done to him, the carrion! His ears! They've taken his ears!'

Hung Mien-lo stared back at him, horrified, then turned and looked at Sun Li Hua.

Any doubts he had harboured about the Master of the Inner Chamber were dispelled instantly. Sun stood there, his mouth gaping, his eyes wide with horror.

Hung turned, his mind in turmoil now. *His ears! Why would they take his ears?* Then, before he could reach out and catch him, he saw Ta-hung slide from the bed and fall senseless to the floor.

'Prince Yuan! Wake up, your father's here!'

Li Yuan rolled over and sat up. Nan Ho stood in the doorway, a lantern in one hand, his head bowed.

'My father?'

A second figure appeared behind Nan Ho in the doorway. 'Yes, Yuan. It's late, I know, but I must talk with you at once.'

Nan Ho moved aside, bowing low, to let the T'ang pass, then backed out, closing the door silently behind him.

Li Shai Tung sat on the bed beside his son, then reached across to switch on the bedside lamp. In the lamp's harsh light his face was ashen, his eyes red-rimmed.

Li Yuan frowned. 'What is it, Father?'

'Ill news. Wang Hsien is dead. Murdered in his bed. Worse, word of it has got out, somehow. There are riots in the lower levels. The *Ping Tiao* are inciting the masses to rebellion.'

'Ah...' Li Yuan felt his stomach tighten. It was what they had all secretly feared. The War had left them weak. The Dispersionists had been scattered and defeated, but there were other enemies these days; others who wanted to pull them down and set themselves atop the wheel of State.

He met his father's eyes. 'What's to be done?'

Li Shai Tung sighed, then looked aside. 'I have spoken to Tsu Ma and Wu Shih already. They think we should do nothing. That we should let the fires burn themselves out.' He paused, then shrugged. 'Tensions have been high lately. Perhaps it would be good to let things run their course for once.'

'Perhaps.'

Li Yuan studied his father, knowing from his uncertainty that this was a course he had been talked into, not one he was happy with.

The T'ang stared away broodingly into the far corner of the room, then turned, facing his son again.

'Wang Hsien was a good man, Yuan. A strong man. I depended on him. In Council he was a staunch ally, a wise counsellor. Like a brother to me. The death of his sons... it brought us very close.'

He shook his head, then turned away, suddenly angry, a tear spilling down his cheek. 'And now Wang Ta-hung is T'ang! Ta-hung, of all the gods' creations! Such a weak and foolish young man!' He turned back, facing Li Yuan, anger and bitterness blazing in his eyes. 'Kuan Yin preserve us all! This is an ill day for the Seven.'

'And for Chung Kuo.'

When his father had gone Li Yuan got up and pulled on his robe, then crossed the room and stood there by the window, staring out into the moon-lit garden. It was as his father said, the Seven were made much weaker by this death. Yet Wang Hsien had been an old man. A very old man. They would have had to face the consequences of his death some day or other, so why not now? Wang Ta-hung was weak and foolish, that was true – but there were six other T'ang to lead and guide him. That was the strength of the Seven, surely? Where one might fall, the Seven would stand. So it was. So it would always be.

He turned and looked down. There, on the low table by the window, was his bow, the elegant curve of it silvered by the moonlight. He bent down and lifted it, holding the cool, smooth surface of the wood against his cheek a moment. Then, abruptly, he spun about, as he'd been taught, the bow suddenly at his waist, the string tensed, as if to let fly.

He shivered, then felt himself grow still, looking back.

He had not thought of it in a long time, but now it came clear to him, the memory released like an arrow across the years. He saw himself, eight years old, sitting beside Fei Yen in the meadow by the lake. He could smell the faint, sweet scent of jasmine; see the pale cream of her sleeve – feel once more the shudder that had run through him as it brushed deliciously against his knees. Across from them sat his brother, Han Ch'in, his booted feet like two young saplings rooted in the earth, his hands placed firmly on his knees.

Wang Sau-leyan... Yes, he remembered it now. Fei Yen had been talking about Wang Sau-leyan and how he had been caught in his father's bed. Ten years old, he'd been. Only ten, and caught with a girl in his father's bed!

Li Yuan frowned, then swallowed, his mouth suddenly dry, remembering how Fei Yen had laughed, not shocked but amused by the tale. He recalled how she had fanned herself slowly; how her eyes had looked briefly inward before raising her eyebrows suggestively, making Han guffaw with laughter. Fei Yen. His brother's wife. And now his own betrothed. The woman he would be marrying, only weeks from now.

And Wang Sau-leyan? Yes, it all made sense. He remembered how Wang Hsien had exiled his youngest son; had sent him in disgrace to his floating palace, a hundred thousand li above Chung Kuo. And there the boy had stayed a whole year, with only the T'ang's own guards for company. A year. It was a long, long time for such a spirited child. An eternity, it must have seemed. Long enough, perhaps, to break the last thin ties of love and filial respect. What bitterness that must have engendered in the boy – what hatred of his captors.

Li Yuan looked down at the bow in his hands and shivered violently. That day with Fei Yen. It had been the day of the archery contest – the day she had let his brother best her. And yet, only two days later, Han Ch'in was dead and she a widow.

He shuddered, then saw her smile and tilt her head, showing her tiny, perfect teeth. And wondered.

Sun Li Hua, Master of the Inner Chamber, stood by the door, watching as the doctors examined the body. He had made his statement already, sat beneath the glaring lights of the Security cameras while monitors tested his vital body signs for abnormalities. He had passed that test and now only one thing stood between him and success.

He saw them mutter amongst themselves, then Fischer turned and came across to him.

'It tests out, Master Sun,' he said, making a small bow. 'The *ho yeh* was pure.'

'I did not doubt it,' Sun answered, allowing a slight trace of indignation to enter his voice. 'Doctor Yueh is a trusted servant. He had served the T'ang for more than forty years.'

'So I understand. And yet men can be bought, can they not?' Fischer smiled tightly, then bowed again and walked on, leaving the room momentarily.

Sun watched him go. *What does it matter what he suspects?* he thought. *He can prove nothing.*

He turned, then went across to where the doctors were busy at their work. One cradled the T'ang's head while a second delicately examined the area where the ear had been cut away. They would make new ears from the T'ang's own genetic material – for a T'ang must be buried whole. But as to where the originals had gone, there was no sign as yet, just as there was no sign of Fu or Chai.

A mystery...

Sun Li Hua stared down into the old man's vacant face and took a deep breath, filled suddenly with a sense of grim satisfaction. *Yes, old man,* he thought, *you humiliated me once, before your sons. Refused to promote my brothers. Held down my family. But now you're dead and we will rise in spite of you. For another has promised to raise the Sun family high; to make it second family in all of City Africa.*

He turned away, smiling beneath the mask of grief. It had been so easy. Fu and Chai – what simpletons they'd been! He thought back, remembering how he had drugged them and taped them murdering the copy of the T'ang. But they knew nothing of that, only that they were being sought for a crime they had no memory of committing.

Trust. It was a fragile thing. Break it and the world broke with it. And Wang Hsien had broken his trust in him some years ago.

He glanced across and saw himself in the wall-length mirror opposite. *Do I look any different?* he wondered. *Does my face betray the change that's taken place in me? No. For I was different that very day, after he'd spurned me. It was then I first stuck the knife in him. Then. For the rest was only the fulfilment of that first imagining.*

He turned and saw Fischer standing there, watching him from the doorway.

'Well, Captain, have you found the murderers?'

'Not yet, Master Sun, but we shall, I promise you.'

*

Fischer let his eyes rest on Sun a moment longer, then looked away. It was as DeVore said: Sun Li Hua was the murderer. While Sun had been in his office Fischer had had his lieutenant take a sample of his blood under the pretext of giving him a sedative. That sample had shown what DeVore had said it would show: traces of CT-7, a drug that created the symptoms of acute distress.

His shock, his overwhelming grief – both had been chemically faked. And why fake such things unless there was a reason? And then there was the camera. There was no way of proving it had been tampered with, but it made sense. Apart from himself, only Sun Li Hua knew the combination; only Sun had the opportunity. It was possible, of course, that they had simply not seen Fu and Chai go into the room, but his lieutenant was a good man – alert, attentive. He would not have missed something so obvious. Which meant that the tape of the murder had been superimposed.

But whose hand lay behind all this? Hung Mien-lo? It was possible. After all, he had most to gain from Wang Hsien's death. Yet he had seen with his own eyes how fair, how scrupulous, Hung had been in dealing with the matter. He had let nothing be rushed or overlooked – as if he, too, was anxious to know who had ordered the T'ang's death.

As he would need to. For he would know that whoever killed a T'ang might kill again.

No. *Would* kill again.

'Captain Fischer...'

He turned. It was Wang Ta-hung. Fischer bowed low, wondering at the same time where Hung Mien-lo had got to.

'Yes, *Chieh Hsia*?'

'Have you found them yet?'

He hesitated. It had been almost thirty minutes since they had begun searching for Sun's two assistants and still there was no trace of them.

'No, *Chieh Hsia*. I'm afraid...'

He stopped, astonished. A man had appeared in the doorway at Wang Ta-hung's back, his hair untidy, his clothing torn. In his hand he held a bloodied knife.

'Wang Sau-leyan!'

Ta-hung spun round and cried out, then took two faltering steps backward, as if he feared an attack. But Wang Sau-leyan merely laughed and threw the knife down.

'The bastards were hiding in my rooms. One cut me, here.' He pulled down his *pau* at the neck, revealing a thin line of red. 'I stuck him for that. The other tried to take my knife from me, but he knew better after a while.'

'Gods!' said Fischer, starting forward. 'Where are they?'

Wang Sau-leyan straightened up, touching the wound gingerly. 'Where I left them. I don't think they'll be going far.'

Fischer turned and looked across at the doctors. 'Quick now! Come with me, *ch'un tzu!* I must save those men.'

Wang Sau-leyan laughed and shook his head. He was staring at his brother strangely. 'Do what you must, Captain. You'll find them where I left them.'

Fischer turned, facing the new T'ang. '*Chieh Hsia*, will you come?'

Wang Ta-hung swallowed, then nodded. 'Of course.'

They met Hung Mien-lo in the corridor outside.

'You've found them, then?'

Fischer bowed, then glanced at Wang Sau-leyan. 'The Prince found them, in his quarters. He has incapacitated them, it seems.'

Hung Mien-lo glared at Wang Sau-leyan, then turned away angrily. 'Come, then. Let's see what the Prince has left us, neh?'

Wang Sau-leyan sat on a footstool in his bedroom, letting the doctor dress the wound at his neck. Across from him Fischer was moving about the bathroom suite, examining the two corpses.

'Why?' Hung Mien-lo asked him again, standing over him almost threateningly. 'Why did you kill them?'

He looked up, ignoring Hung Mien-lo, his eyes piercing his elder brother. 'They were dangerous men. They killed our Father. What was to stop them killing me?'

He smiled tightly, then looked back at the bathroom. He saw Fischer straighten up, then turn and come to the doorway. He had been searching the dead men's clothing, as if for something they had stolen.

'Where are they?' Fischer asked, looking directly at him.

Wang Sau-leyan stared back at him, irritated by his insolence. 'Where are what?' he asked angrily, wincing as the doctor tightened the bandage about his shoulder.

'The ears,' said Fischer, coming out into the room.

'Ears?' Wang Sau-leyan gave a short laugh.

'Yes,' Fischer said, meeting the Prince's eyes. 'The ears, my lord. Where are the great T'ang's ears?'

The Prince rose sharply from his stool, pushing Hung Mien-lo aside, his broad, moon face filled with disbelief. He strode across and stood there, glowering at Fischer, his face only inches from his.

'What are you suggesting, Captain?'

Fischer knelt, his head bowed. 'Forgive me, my lord. I was suggesting nothing. But the murderers took your father's ears, and now there is no sign of them.'

Wang Sau-leyan stood there a moment longer, clearly puzzled, then whirled about, looking directly at his brother.

'Is this true, Ta-hung?'

'*Chieh Hsia*...' Hung Mien-lo reminded him, but Wang Sau-leyan ignored him.

'Well, brother? Is it true?'

Wang Ta-hung let his head fall before the fierceness of his younger brother's gaze. He nodded. 'It is so.'

Wang Sau-leyan took a shuddering breath, then looked about him again, his whole manner suddenly defiant, his eyes challenging any in that room to gainsay him.

'Then I'm glad I killed them.'

Hung Mien-lo stared at the Prince a moment, astonished by his outburst, then turned and looked across at Wang Ta-hung. The contrast was marked. Tiger and lamb they were. And then he understood. Wang Sau-leyan had dared to have his father killed. Yes! Looking at him he knew it for a certainty. Sun had had access to the T'ang and motive enough, but only Wang Sau-leyan had had the will – the sheer audacity – to carry through the act.

It took his breath. He looked at the Prince with new eyes. Then, almost without thinking, he stepped forward and, his head bowed in respect, addressed him.

'Please, my Prince, sit down and rest. No blame attaches to you. You did as you had to. The murderers are dead. We need look no further.'

Wang Sau-leyan turned, facing him, a smile coming to his lips. Then he turned, facing Fischer, his face hardening again.

'Good. Then get the bodies of those vermin out of here and leave me be. I must get some sleep.'

PART TEN   **THE ART OF WAR**

SUMMER 2206

Though the enemy be stronger in numbers, we may
prevent him from fighting. Scheme so as to discover
his plans and the likelihood of their success. Rouse
him, and learn the principle of his activity or inactivity.
Force him to reveal himself, so as to find out his
vulnerable spots. Carefully compare the opposing army
with your own, so that you may know where strength
is superabundant and where it is deficient.
—Sun Tzu, *The Art of War* (5th century BC)

Chapter 43

THE FIFTY-NINTH STONE

It was dawn on Mars. In the lowland desert of the Golden Plains it was minus one hundred and fourteen degrees and rising. Deep shadow lay like the surface of a fathomless sea to the east, tracing the lips of huge escarpments, while to the north and west the sun's first rays picked out the frozen slopes and wind-scoured mouths of ancient craters. Through the centre of this landscape ran a massive pipeline, dissecting the plain from north to south: a smooth vein of polished white against the brown-red terrain.

For a time the plain was still and silent. Then, from the south, came the sound of an approaching craft, the dull roar of its engines carried faintly on the thin atmosphere. A moment later it drew nearer, following the pipeline. Feng Shou Pumping Station was up ahead, in the distance – a small oasis in the billion-year sterility of the Martian desert – discernible even at this range from the faint spiral curve of cloud that placed a blue-white smudge amidst the perfect pinkness of the sky.

The report had come in less than an hour ago: an unconfirmed message that an unauthorized craft had been challenged and brought down in the Sea of Divine Kings, eighty li north-west of Feng Shou Station. There was no more than that, but Karr, trusting to instinct, had commissioned a Security craft at once, speeding north from Tian Men K'ou City to investigate.

Karr stared down through the dark filter of the cockpit's screen at the rugged terrain below, conscious that, after eight months of scouring this tiny planet for some sign of the man, he might at last be nearing the end of his search.

At first he had thought this a dreadful place. The bitter cold, the thin, unnatural atmosphere, the closeness of the horizon, the all-pervading redness of the place. He had felt quite ill those first few weeks, despite the enjoyable sensation of shedding more than 60 per cent of his body weight to Mars's much lower surface gravity. The Han Security officer who had been his host had told him it was quite natural to feel that way: it took some while to acclimatize to Mars. But he had wondered briefly whether this cold, inhospitable planet might not be his final resting place. Now, however, he felt sad that it was coming to an end. He had grown to love the austere magnificence of Mars. Eight months. It was little more than a season here.

As the craft drew nearer he ordered the pilot to circle the station from two li out.

The five huge chimneys of the atmosphere generator dominated the tiny settlement, belching huge clouds of oxygen-rich air into the thin and frigid atmosphere. Beneath them the sprawl of settlement buildings was swathed in green – hardy mosses that could survive the extreme temperatures of the Martian night. Further out, the red sands were rimed with ice that formed a wide, uneven ring of whiteness about the station. The generator itself was deep beneath the surface, its taproots reaching down towards the core of the planet to draw their energy. Like thirty other such generators scattered about the planet's surface, it had been pumping oxygen into the skies of Mars for more than one hundred and fifty years. Even so, it would be centuries yet before Mars had a proper atmosphere again.

Karr made a full circle of the settlement, studying the scene. There were four transports parked to the east of the pipeline, in an open space between some low buildings. At first, in the half-light, they had seemed to form one single, indistinct shape – a complexity of shadows – but through the resolution of field glasses he could make out individual markings. One was a craft belonging to the settlement, another two Security craft from out of Kang Kua in the north. The fourth was unmarked. A small, four-man flier, the design unlike anything he had seen before on Mars.

He leaned forward and tapped out that day's security code, then sat back, waiting. In a moment it came back, suitably amended, followed by an update.

Karr gave himself a moment to digest the information, then nodded to himself. 'Okay. Set her down half a li to the south of those craft. Then suit up. I want to be ready for any trouble.'

The young pilot nodded tersely, setting them down softly on the southern edge of the settlement. While the pilot suited up, Karr sat there, staring out at the settlement, watching for any sign that this might yet be a trap.

'Ready?'

The young man nodded.

'Good. Wait here. I'll not be long.'

Karr took a breath then released the hatch. As he climbed out, systems within his suit reacted immediately to the sudden changes in temperature and pressure. It was cold out here. Cold enough to kill a man in minutes if his suit failed.

There were five buildings surrounding the craft: three domes and two long, flat-topped constructions, the domes to the left, the flat-tops to the right. The pumping station itself was the largest of the domes, straddling the pipeline like a giant swelling, one of eight similar stations – situated at two-hundred-li intervals along the pipeline – that pumped water from the sprawling Tzu Li Keng Seng generating complex in the south to the three great northern cities of Hong Hai, Kang Kua and Chi Shan.

Karr walked towards the huge hemisphere of the station, the tiny heat generator in his suit clicking on as he moved into the shadow of the giant pipeline. As he came nearer a door hissed open and unfolded towards the ground, forming steps. Without hesitation he mounted them and went inside, hearing the door close behind him.

He went through the airlock briskly and out into the pressurized and heated core of the station. Two Security men were waiting for him, at attention, clearly surprised that he was still suited up. They looked at him expectantly, but he went past them without a word, leaving them to follow him or not, as they wished.

He took a left turn at the first junction into a corridor that bridged the pipeline. As he did so an officer, a fresh-faced young Han, hurried down the corridor towards him.

'Major Karr. Welcome to Feng Shou. Captain Wen would like...'

Ignoring him, Karr brushed past and turned off to the left, taking the narrow stairwell down to the basement. Guards looked up, surprised, as he came down the corridor towards them, then stood to a hurried attention as they noticed the leopard badge of a third-ranking officer that adorned the chest of his suit.

'Forgive me, Major Karr, but the Captain says you must...'

Karr turned and glared at the junior officer who had followed him, silencing him with a look.

'Please tell your captain that, as his superior officer, I've taken charge of this matter. And before you ask, no, I don't want to see him. Understand me?'

The young soldier bowed deeply and backed off a step. 'Of course, Major. As you say.'

Karr turned away, forgetting the man at once. These stations were all the same. There was only one place to keep prisoners securely. He marched down the narrow, dimly lit passageway, then stopped, facing a heavy, panelled door. He waited as one of the guards caught up with him and took a bunch of old-fashioned metal keys from inside a thick pouch, then, as the door swung inward, pushed past the man impatiently.

Hasty improvisation had made a cell of the small storeroom. The floor was bare rock, the walls undecorated ice, opaque and milky white, like a blind eye. The four men were bound at wrist and ankle.

Berdichev was sitting slumped against the wall. His grey uniform was dusty and dishevelled, buttons missing from the neck, his face thinner, gaunter than the Security profile of him. He hadn't shaved for a week or more and he stared back at Karr through eyes red-rimmed with tiredness. Karr studied him thoughtfully. The horn-rimmed glasses that were his trademark hung from a fine silver chain about his neck, the lenses covered in a fine red grit.

He had not been certain. Not until this moment. But now he knew. Berdichev was his. After almost five years of pursuit, he had finally caught up with the leader of the Dispersionists.

Karr looked about the cell again, conscious of the other three watching him closely, then nodded, satisfied. He knew how he looked to them. Knew how the suit exaggerated his size, making him seem monstrous, unnatural. Perhaps they were even wondering what he was – machine or man. If so, he would let them know. He lit up his face plate, seeing how the eyes of the others widened with surprise. But not Berdichev. He was watching Karr closely.

Karr turned, slamming the door shut behind him, then turned back, facing them again.

He knew what they expected. They knew the laws that were supposed to govern an arrest. But this was different. They had been tried in their absence and found guilty. He was not here to arrest them.

'Well, Major Karr, so we meet up at last, neh?' Berdichev lifted his chin a little as he spoke, but his eyes seemed to look down on the giant. 'Do you really think you'll get me to stand trial? In fact, do you even think you'll leave Mars alive?'

If there had been any doubt before, there was none now. It was a trap. Berdichev had made a deal with the Captain, Wen. Or maybe Wen was in another's pay – a friend of Berdichev's. Whatever, it didn't matter now. He walked over to where Berdichev was sprawled and kicked at his feet.

'Get up,' he said tonelessly, his voice emerging disembodied and in-human through the suit's microphone.

Berdichev stood slowly, awkwardly. He was clearly ill. Even so, there was a dignity of bearing to him, a superiority of manner, that was impressive. Even in defeat he thought himself the better man.

Karr stood closer, looking down into Berdichev's face, studying the hawk-like features one last time. For a moment Berdichev looked aside, then, as if he realized this was one last challenge, he met the big man's stare unflinchingly, his features set, defiant.

Did he know whose gaze he met across the vastness of space? Did he guess in that final moment?

Karr picked him up and broke his neck, his back, then dropped him. It was done in an instant, before the others had a chance to move, even to cry out.

He stepped away, then stood there by the door, watching.

They gathered about the body, kneeling, glaring across at him, impotent to help the dying man. One of them half rose, his fists clenched, then drew back, realizing he could do nothing.

Karr tensed, hearing noises in the corridor outside. Captain Wen and his squad.

He took a small device from his belt, cracked its outer shell like an egg and threw the sticky innards at the far wall, where it adhered, high up, out of reach. He pulled the door open and stepped outside, then pulled it closed and locked it. His face-plate still lit up, he smiled at the soldiers who were hurrying down the corridor towards him as if greeting them, then shot Wen twice before he could say a word.

The remaining four soldiers hesitated, looking to the junior officer for their lead. Karr stared from face to face, defying them to draw a weapon, his own held firmly out before him. Then, on the count of fifteen, he dropped to the floor.

The wall next to him lit up brightly and, a fraction of a second later, the door blew out.

Karr got up and went through the shattered doorway quickly, ignoring the fallen men behind him. The cell was devastated, the outer wall gone. Bits of flesh and bone lay everywhere, unrecognizable as parts of living men.

He stood there a moment, looking down at the thermometer on the sleeve of his suit. The temperature in the room was dropping rapidly. They would have to address that problem quickly or the generators that powered the pumps would shut down. Not only that, but they would have to do something about the loss of air pressure within the station.

Karr crossed to the far side of the room and stepped outside, on to the sands. Debris from the blast lay everywhere. He turned and looked back at the devastation within. *Was that okay?* he asked silently. *Did that satisfy your desire for vengeance, Li Shai Tung?* For the T'ang was watching everything. All that Karr saw he saw, the signal sent back more than four hundred million *li* through space.

He shrugged, then tapped the buttons at his wrist, making contact with the pilot.

'I'm on the sands to the west of the pipeline, near where the explosion just happened. Pick me up at once.'

'At once, Major.'

He turned back and fired two warning shots into the empty doorway, then strode out across the sands, positioning himself in a kneeling position, facing the station.

Part of him saw the craft lift up over the massive pipeline and drop towards him, while another part of him was watching the doorway for any sign of activity. Then he was aboard, the craft climbing again, and he had other things to think of. There was a gun turret built into the side of the station. Nothing fancy, but its gun could easily bring down a light two-man craft like their own. As they lifted he saw it begin to turn and leaned across the pilot to prime the ship's missiles, then sent two silkworms haring down into the side of the dome.

A huge fireball rose into the sky, rolling over and over upon itself. A moment later the blast rocked the tiny craft.

'*Kuan Yin!*' screamed the pilot. 'What in hell's name are you doing?'

Karr glared at the young Han. 'Just fly!'

'But the station...'

The big dome had collapsed. The two nearest domes were on fire. People were spilling from the nearby buildings, shocked, horrified by what they saw. As Karr lifted up and away from the settlement, he saw the end of the fractured pipeline buckle and then lift slowly into the air, like a giant worm, water gushing from a dozen broken conduits, cooling rapidly in the frigid air.

'*Aiya!*' said the young pilot, his voice pained and anxious. 'It's a disaster! What have you done, Major Karr? What have you done?'

'I've finished it,' Karr answered him, angry that the boy should make so much of a little water. 'I've ended the War.'

Four hundred million *li* away, back on Chung Kuo, DeVore strode into a room and looked about him. The room was sparsely furnished, undecorated save for a flag that was pinned to the wall behind the table, its design the white stylized outline of a fish against a blue background. At the table sat five people: three men and two women. They wore simple, light blue uniforms on which no sign of rank or merit was displayed. Two of them – one male, one female – were Han. This last surprised DeVore. He had heard rumours that the *Ping Tiao* hated the Han. No matter. They hated authority, and that was good enough. He could use them, Han in their ranks or no.

'What do you want?'

The speaker was the man at the centre of the five: a short, stocky man, with dark, intense eyes, fleshy lips and a long nose. His brow was long, his thin grey hair receding. DeVore knew him from the report. Gesell was his name. Bent Gesell. He was their leader, or at least the man to whom this strange organization of so-called 'equal' individuals looked for their direction.

DeVore smiled, then nodded towards the table, indicating the transparent grid that was laid out before Gesell. 'You have the map, I see.'

Gesell narrowed his eyes, studying him a moment. 'Half of it, anyway. But that's your point, isn't it, Shih Turner? Or am I wrong?'

DeVore nodded, looking from face to face, seeing at once how suspicious they were of him. They were of a mind to reject his proposal, whatever it might be. But that was as he had expected. He had never thought this would be easy.

'I want to make a deal with you. The other half of that map – and more like it – for your co-operation in a few schemes of mine.'

Gesell's nostrils dilated, his eyes hardened. 'We are not criminals, Shih Turner, whatever the media says about us. We are Ko Ming. Revolutionaries.'

DeVore stared back at Gesell, challenging him. 'Did I say otherwise?'

'Then I repeat. What do you want?'

DeVore smiled. 'I want what you want. To destroy the Seven. To bring it all down and start again.'

Gesell's smile was ugly. 'Fine rhetoric. But can you support your words?'

DeVore's smile widened. 'That packet your men took from me. Ask one of them to bring it in.'

Gesell hesitated, then indicated to the guard who stood behind DeVore that he should do so. He returned a moment later with the small, sealed package, handing it to Gesell.

'If this is a device of some kind...' Gesell began.

But DeVore shook his head. 'You asked what proof I have of my intentions. Well, inside that package you'll find a human ear. The ear of the late T'ang of Africa, Wang Hsien.'

There was a gasp from the others at the table, but Gesell was cool about it. He left the package untouched. 'Half a map and an ear. Are these your only credentials, Shih Turner? The map could be of anything, the ear anyone's.'

He's merely playing now, thought DeVore; *impressing on the others how wise he is, how cautious. Because he, at least, will have had the map checked out and will know it is to the Security arsenal at Helmstadt Canton. Likewise with the ear. He knows how easy it is to check the authenticity of the genetic material.*

He decided to push. 'They might. But you believe otherwise. It must interest you to know how I could get hold of such things.'

Gesell laughed. 'Perhaps you're a thief, Shih Turner.'

DeVore ignored the insult, but stored it in memory. He would have his revenge for that.

'The ear is easy to explain. I had Wang Hsien assassinated.'

Gesell's laughter was harder; it registered his disbelief. 'Then why come to us? If you can have a T'ang murdered so easily, what need have you for such...' he looked about him humorously '...small fish as we *Ping Tiao*?'

DeVore smiled. 'I came here because the War has entered a new phase. And because I believe I can trust you.'

'*Trust* us?' Gesell studied him closely, looking for any trace of irony in the words. 'Yes. Perhaps you could. But can we trust you, *Shih* Turner? And should we even consider trusting you? I mean, what are your real motives for coming here today? Is it really as you say – to ally with us to bring down the Seven? Or do you simply want to use us?'

'I want to share what I know with you. I want to fight alongside you. If that's using you, then yes, I want to use you, *Shih* Gesell.'

Gesell's surprise was marked. 'How do you know my name?'

DeVore met his stare openly. 'I do my homework.'

'Then you'll know we work with no one.'

'You used not to. But those days are past. You've suffered substantial losses. You need me. As much as I need you.'

Gesell shrugged. 'And why *do* you need us? Have your Above backers pulled out, then, *Shih* Turner?'

He feigned surprise, but he had known Gesell would raise this point. Had known because he himself had passed the information on to his contact inside the *Ping Tiao*.

Gesell laughed. 'Come clean, *Shih* Turner. Tell us the real reason why you're here.'

DeVore stepped forward, appealing suddenly to them all, not just Gesell; knowing that this was the point where he could win them over.

'It's true. The War has taken many whose funds supported my activities. But there's more to it than that. Things have changed. It's no longer a struggle in the Above between those in power and those who want to be. The conflict has widened. As you know. It's no longer a question of who should rule, but whether or not there should be rulers at all.'

Gesell sat back. 'That's so. But what's your role in this? You claim you've killed a T'ang.'

'And Ministers, and a T'ang's son...'

Gesell laughed shortly. 'Well, whatever. But still I ask you: why should we trust you?'

DeVore leaned forward and placed his hands on the edge of the table. 'Because you have to. Alone, both of us will fail. The *Ping Tiao* will go down into obscurity, or at best earn a footnote in some historical document as just another small, fanatical sect. And the Seven...' He heaved a huge sigh and straightened up. 'The Seven will rule Chung Kuo for ever.'

He had given them nothing. Nothing real or substantial, anyway. As Gesell had so rightly said, all they had was half a map, an ear. That and his own bare-faced audacity in daring to knock on their door, knowing they were ruthless killers. Yet he could see from their faces that they were more than half-convinced already.

'Unwrap the package, *Shih* Gesell. You'll find there's something else beside an ear inside.'

Gesell hesitated, then did as DeVore had asked. Setting the ear aside, he unfolded the transparent sheet and placed it beside its matching half.

'I have three hundred and fifty trained men,' DeVore said quietly. 'If you can match my force we'll take the Helmstadt Armoury two days from now.'

Gesell stared at him. 'You seem very sure of yourself, *Shih* Turner. Helmstadt is heavily guarded. It has complex electronic defences. How do you think we can take it?'

'Because there will be no defences. Not when we attack.'

Quickly, confidently, he spelled out his plan, holding back only the way he had arranged it all. When he'd finished, Gesell looked at his colleagues. He had noted what DeVore had said, in particular the part about the high-profile media publicity the *Ping Tiao* would gain from the attack – publicity that was sure to swell their ranks with new recruits. That, and the prospect of capturing a significant stockpile of sophisticated weaponry, seemed to have swung the decision.

Gesell turned to him. 'You'll let us confer a moment, *Shih* Turner. We are a democratic movement. We must vote on this.'

DeVore smiled inwardly. *Democracy, my arse. It's what you want, Gesell. And I think you're clever enough to know you've no option but to go along with me.*

Giving the slightest bow, he went out, and sat there. He had only to wait a few minutes before the door opened again and Gesell came out. He stood, facing the Ping Tiao leader.

'Well?'

Gesell stared at him a moment, coldly assessing him. Then, with the smallest bow, he stepped back, holding out his arm. 'Come in, Shih Turner. We have plans to discuss.'

The girl was dead. Haavikko sat there, distraught, staring at her, at the blood that covered his hands and chest and thighs, and knew he had killed her.

He turned his head slightly and saw the knife, there on the floor where he remembered dropping it, then shuddered, a wave of sickness, of sheer self-disgust washing over him. What depths, what further degradations, lay ahead of him? Nothing. He had done it all. And now this.

There was no more. This was the end of that path he had set out upon ten years ago.

He turned back, looking at her. The girl's face was white, drained of blood. Such a pretty face it had been in life: full of laughter and smiles, her eyes undulled by experience. He gritted his teeth against the sudden pain he felt and bowed his head, overcome. She could not have been more than fourteen.

He looked about the room. There, draped carelessly over the back of the chair, was his uniform. And there, on the floor beside it, the tray with the empty bottles and the glasses they had been drinking from before it happened.

He closed his eyes, then shivered violently, seeing it all again – the images forming with an almost hallucinatory clarity that took his breath. He uttered a small moan of pain, seeing himself holding her down with one hand, while he struck at her frenziedly with the knife, once, twice, a third time, slashing at her breasts, her stomach, while she cried out piteously and struggled to get up.

He jumped to his feet and turned away, putting his hands up to his face. 'Kuan Yin preserve you, Axel Haavikko, for what you've done!'

Yes, he saw it all now. It all led to this. The drinking and debauchery, the insubordination and the gambling. This was its natural end. This grossness. He had observed his own fall, from that moment in General Tolonen's office to this... this finality. There was no more. Nothing for him but to take the knife and end himself.

He stared at the knife. Stared long and hard at it. Saw how the blood was crusted on its shaft and handle, remembering the feel of it in his hand. His knife.

Slowly he went across, then knelt down, next to it, his hands placed either side of it. End it now, he told himself. Cleanly, quickly, and with more dignity than you've shown in all these last ten years.

He picked the knife up, taking its handle in both hands, then turned the blade towards his stomach. His hands shook and, for the briefest moment, he wondered if he had the courage left to carry the thing through. Then, determined, he closed his eyes.

'Lieutenant Haavikko, I've come...'

Haavikko turned abruptly, dropping the knife. The pimp, Liu Chang, had come three paces into the room and stopped, taking in the scene.

'Gods!' the Han said, his face a mask of horror. He glanced at Haavikko fearfully, backing away, then turned and rushed from the room.

Haavikko shuddered, then turned back, facing the knife. He could not stand up. All the strength had gone from his legs. Neither could he reach out and take the knife again. His courage was spent. Nothing remained now but his shame. He let his head fall forward, tears coming to his eyes.

'Forgive me, Vesa, I didn't mean...'

Vesa. It was his beloved sister's name. But the dead girl had no name. Not one he knew, anyway.

He heard the door swing open again and footsteps in the room, but he did not lift his head. *Let them kill me now*, he thought. *Let them take their revenge on me. It would be no less than I deserve.*

He waited, resigned, but nothing happened. He heard them lift the girl and carry her away, then sensed someone standing over him.

Haavikko raised his head slowly and looked up. It was Liu Chang.

'You disgust me.' He spat the words out venomously, his eyes boring into Haavikko. 'She was a good girl. A lovely girl. Like a daughter to me.'

'I'm sorry...' Haavikko began, his throat constricting. He dropped his head, beginning to sob. 'Do what you will to me. I'm finished now. I haven't even the money to pay you for last night.'

The pimp laughed, his disgust marked. 'I realize that, soldier boy. But, then, you've not paid your weight since you started coming here.'

Haavikko looked up, surprised.

'No. It's a good job you've friends, neh? Good friends who'll bail you out when trouble comes. That's what disgusts me most about your sort. You never pay. It's all settled for you, isn't it?'

'I don't know what you mean. I...'

But Liu Chang's angry bark of laughter silenced him. 'This. It's all paid for. Don't you understand that? Your friends have settled everything for you.'

Haavikko's voice was a bemused whisper. 'Everything... ?'

'Everything.' Liu Chang studied him a moment, his look of disgust unwavering, then leaned forward and spat in Haavikko's face.

Haavikko knelt there long after Liu Chang had gone, the spittle on his cheek a badge of shame that seemed to burn right through to the bone. It was less than he deserved. But he was thinking about what Liu Chang had said. Friends... What friends? He had no friends, only partners in his debauchery, and they would have settled nothing for him.

He dressed and went outside, looking for Liu Chang.

'Liu Chang. Where is he?'

The girl at the reception desk stared at him a moment, as if he were something foul and unclean that had crawled up out of the Net, then handed him an envelope.

Haavikko turned his back on the girl, then opened the envelope and took out the single sheet of paper. It was from Liu Chang.

Lieutenant Haavikko,
Words cannot express the disgust I feel. If I had my way you would be made to pay fully for what you have done. As it is, I must ask you never to frequent my House again. If you so much as come near, I shall pass on my record of events to the authorities, 'friends' or no. Be warned.
Liu Chang

He stuffed the paper into his tunic pocket then staggered out, more mystified than ever. Outside, in the corridor, he looked about him, then lurched over to the public drinking fountain, inset into the wall at the intersection. He splashed his face then straightened up.

Friends. What friends? Or were they friends at all?

Liu Chang knew, but he could not go near Liu Chang. Who, then?

Haavikko shivered, then looked about him. Someone knew. Someone had made it their business to know. But who?

He thought of the girl again and groaned. 'I don't deserve this chance,' he told himself softly. And yet he was here, free, all debts settled. Why? He gritted his teeth and reached up to touch the spittle that had dried on his cheek. Friends. It gave him a reason to go on. To find out who. And why.

DeVore took off his gloves and threw them down on the desk, then turned and faced his lieutenant, Wiegand, lowering his head to dislodge the lenses from his eyes.

'Here.' He handed the lenses to Wiegand, who placed them carefully into a tiny plastic case he had ready. 'Get these processed. I want to know who those other four are.'

Wiegand bowed and left.

DeVore turned, meeting the eyes of the other man in the room. 'It went perfectly. We attack Helmstadt in two days.'

The albino nodded, but was quiet.

'What is it, Stefan?'

'Bad news. Soren Berdichev is dead.'

DeVore looked at the young man a moment, then went and sat behind his desk, busying himself with the reports that had amassed while he was away. He spoke without looking up.

'I know. I heard before I went in. A bad business, by all accounts, but useful. It may well have alienated the Mars settlers. They'll have little love for the Seven now, after the destruction of the pipeline.'

'Maybe...' Lehmann was silent a moment, then came and stood at the edge of the desk looking down at DeVore. 'I liked him, you know. Admired him.'

DeVore looked up, masking his surprise. He found it hard to believe that Stefan Lehmann was capable of liking *anyone*. 'Well,' he said, 'he's dead now. And life goes on. We've got to plan for the future. For the next stage of the War.'

'Is that why you went to see those scum?'

DeVore stared past Lehmann a moment, studying the map on the wall behind him. Then he met his eyes again.

'I have news for you, Stefan.'

The pink eyes hardened, the mouth tightened. 'I know already.'

'I see.' DeVore considered a moment. 'Who told you?'

'Wiegand.'

DeVore narrowed his eyes. Wiegand. He was privy to all incoming messages, of course, but he had strict instructions not to pass on what he knew until he, DeVore, authorized it. It was a serious breach.

'I'm sorry, Stefan. It makes it harder for us all.'

The Notice of Confiscation had come in only an hour before he had gone off to meet the *Ping Tiao*, hot on the heels of the news of Berdichev's death. In theory it stripped Lehmann of all he had inherited from his father, making him a pauper, but DeVore had pre-empted the Notice some years back by getting Berdichev to switch vast sums from the estate in the form of loans to fictitious beneficiaries. Those 'loans' had long been spent – and more besides – on constructing further fortresses, but Lehmann knew nothing of that. As far as he was concerned, the whole sum was lost.

Lehmann was studying him intently. 'How will it change things?'

DeVore set down the paper and sat back. 'As far as I'm concerned it changes nothing, Stefan. All our lives are forfeit anyway. What difference does a piece of paper bearing the seals of the Seven make to that?'

There was the slightest movement in the young man's ice-pale face. 'I can be useful. You know that.'

'I know.'

Good, thought DeVore. *He understands. He's learned his lessons well. There's no room for sentimentality in what we're doing here. What's past is past. I owe him nothing for the use of his money.*

'Don't worry,' he said, leaning forward and picking up the paper again.'You're on the payroll now, Stefan. I'm appointing you lieutenant, as from this moment. Ranking equal with Wiegand.'

Yes, he thought. *That should take the smile from Wiegand's face.*

When Lehmann had gone he stood and went across to the map again. In the bottom left-hand corner the carp-shaped area that denoted the Swiss Wilds was criss-crossed with lines, some broken, some solid. Where they met or ended were tiny squares, representing fortresses. There were twenty-two in all, but only fourteen of them – boxed in between Zagreb in the south-east and Zurich in the north-west – were filled in. These alone were finished. The eight fortresses of the western arm remained incomplete. In four cases they had yet to be begun.

Money. That was his greatest problem. Money for wages, food and weaponry. Money for repairs and bribes and all manner of small expenses. Most of all, money to complete the building programme: to finish the network of tunnels and fortresses that alone could guarantee a successful campaign against the Seven. The Confiscations had robbed him of many of his big investors. In less than three hours the remainder were due to meet him, supposedly to renew their commitments, though in reality, he knew, to tell him they had had enough. That was why Helmstadt was so important now.

Helmstadt. He had wooed the *Ping Tiao* with promises of weapons and publicity, but the truth was otherwise. There would be weapons, and publicity enough to satisfy the most egotistical of terrorist leaders, but the real fruit of the raid on the Helmstadt Armoury would be the two billion *yuan* DeVore would lift from the strongroom. Money that had been allocated to pay the expenses of more than one hundred and forty thousand troops in the eight garrisons surrounding the Wilds.

But the *Ping Tiao* would know nothing of that.

He turned away from the map and looked across at his desk again. The Notice of Confiscation lay where he had left it. He went across and picked it up, studying it again. It seemed simple on the face of it: an open acknowledgment of a situation that had long existed in reality – for Lehmann's funds had been frozen from the moment Berdichev had fled to Mars, three years ago. But there were hidden depths in the document. It meant that the Seven had discovered evidence to link Stefan's father to the death of the Minister Lwo Kang, and that, in its turn, would legitimize Tolonen's action in the House in killing Lehmann Senior.

It was an insight into how the Seven were thinking. For them the War was over. They had won.

But DeVore knew otherwise. The War had not even begun. Not properly. The Confiscations and the death of T'angs notwithstanding, it had been a game until now; a diversion for the rich and bored; an entertainment to fill their idle hours. But now it would change. He would harness the forces stirring in the lowest levels. Would take them and mould them. And then?

He laughed and crumpled the copy of the Notice in his hand. Then Change would come. Like a hurricane, blowing through the levels, razing the City to the ground.

Major Hans Ebert set the drinks carefully on the tray, then turned and, making his way through the edge of the crowd that packed the great hall, went through the curtained doorway into the room beyond.

Behind him the reception was in full swing, but here, in the T'ang's private quarters, it was peaceful. Li Shai Tung sat in the big chair to the left, his feet resting on a stool carved like a giant turtle shell. He seemed older and more careworn these days, his hair, once grey, a pure white now, like fine threads of ice, tied tightly in a queue behind his head. The yellow cloak of state seemed loose now on his thin, old man's frame and the delicate perfection of the gold chain about his neck served merely to emphasize the frail imperfection of his flesh. Even so, there was still strength in his eyes, power enough in his words and gestures to dispel any thought that he was spent as a man. If the flesh had grown weaker, the spirit seemed unchanged.

Across from him, seated to the right of the ceremonial *kang*, was Tsu Ma, T'ang of West Asia. He sat back in his chair, a long, pencil-thin cheroot held absently in one hand. He was known to his acquaintances as 'The Horse', and the name suited him. He was a stallion, a thoroughbred in his late thirties, broad-chested and heavily muscled, his dark hair curled in elegant long pigtails, braided with silver and pearls. His enemies still considered him a dandy, but they were wrong. He was a capable, intelligent man for all his outward style, and since his father's death he had shown himself to be a fine administrator; a credit to the Council of the Seven.

The third and last man in the anteroom was Hal Shepherd. He sat to Tsu Ma's right, a stack of pillows holding him upright in his chair, his face drawn and pale from illness. He had been sick two weeks now, the cause as yet undiagnosed. His eyes, normally so bright and full of life, now seemed to protrude from their sockets, as if staring out from some deep inner darkness. Beside him, her head bowed, her whole manner demure, stood a young Han nurse from the T'ang's household, there to do the sick man's least bidding.

Ebert bowed, then crossed to the T'ang and stood there, the tray held out before him. Li Shai Tung took his drink without pausing from what he was saying, seeming not to notice the young major as he moved across to offer Tsu Ma his glass.

'But the question is still what we should do with the Companies. Should we close them down completely? Wind them up and distribute their assets among our friends? Should we allow bids for them? Offer them on the Index as if we were floating them? Or should we run them ourselves, appointing stewards to do our bidding until we feel things have improved?'

Tsu Ma took his peach brandy, giving Ebert a brief smile, then turned back to face his fellow T'ang.

'You know my feelings on the matter, Shai Tung. Things are still uncertain. We have given our friends considerable rewards already. To break up the one hundred and eighteen Companies and offer them as spoils to them might cause resentment amongst those not party to the share-out. It would simply create a new generation of malcontents. No. My vote will be to appoint stewards. To run the companies for ten, maybe fifteen years, and then offer them on the market to the highest bidder. That way we prevent resentment and, at the same time, through keeping a tight rein on what is, after all, nearly a fifth of the market, help consolidate the Edict of Technological Control.'

Ebert, holding the tray out before Hal Shepherd, tried to feign indifference to the matter being discussed, but as heir to GenSyn, the second largest Company on the Hang Seng Index, it was difficult not to feel crucially involved in the question of the confiscated Companies.

'What is this?'

Ebert raised his head and looked at Shepherd. 'It is Yang Sen's Spring Wine Tonic, Shih Shepherd. Li Shai Tung asked me to bring you a glass of it. It has good restorative powers.'

Shepherd sniffed at the glass, then looked past Ebert at the old T'ang. 'This smells rich, Shai Tung. What's in it?'

'Brandy, kao liang, vodka, honey, gingseng, japonica seeds, oh, and many more things that are good for you, Hal.'

'Such as?'

Tsu Ma laughed and turned in his seat to look at Shepherd. 'Such as red-spotted lizard and sea-horse and dried human placenta. All terribly good for you, my friend.'

Shepherd looked at Tsu Ma a moment, then looked back at Li Shai Tung. 'Is that true, Shai Tung?'

The old T'ang nodded. 'It's true. Why, does it put you off, Hal?'

Shepherd laughed, the laugh lines etched deep now in his pallid face. 'Not at all.' He tipped the glass back and drank heavily, then shuddered and handed the half-empty glass to the nurse.

Tsu Ma gave a laugh of surprise. 'One should sip Yang Sen, friend Hal. It's strong stuff. Matured for eighteen months before it's even fit to drink. And this is Shai Tung's best. A twelve-year brew.'

'Yes...' said Shepherd hoarsely, laughing, his rounded eyes watering. 'I see that now.'

Tsu Ma watched the ill man a moment longer then turned and faced Ebert. 'Well, Major, and how is your father?'

Ebert bowed deeply. 'He is fine, *Chieh Hsia*.'

Li Shai Tung leaned forward. 'I must thank him for all he has done these last few months. And for the generous wedding gift he has given my son today.'

Ebert turned and bowed again. 'He would be honoured, *Chieh Hsia*.'

'Good. Now tell me, before you leave us. Candidly now. What do you think we should do about the confiscated companies?'

Ebert kept his head lowered, not presuming to meet the T'ang's eyes, even when asked so direct a question. Neither was he fooled by the request for candour. He answered as he knew the T'ang would want him to answer.

'I believe his Excellency, Tsu Ma, is right, *Chieh Hsia*. It is necessary to placate the Above. To let wounds heal and bitterness evaporate. In appointing stewards the markets will remain stable. Things will continue much as normal, and there will be none of the hectic movements on the Index that a selling-off of such vast holdings would undoubtedly bring. As for rewards, the health and safety of the Seven is reward enough, surely? It would be a little man who would ask for more.'

The old T'ang's eyes smiled. 'Thank you, Hans. I am grateful for your words.'

Ebert bowed and backed away, knowing he had been dismissed.

'A fine young man,' said Li Shai Tung, when Ebert had gone. 'He reminds me more of his father every day. The same bluff honesty. Tolonen's right. He should be general when he's of age. He'd make my son a splendid general, don't you think?'

'An excellent general,' Tsu Ma answered him, concealing any small qualms he had about Major Hans Ebert. His own Security reports on Ebert revealed a slightly different picture.

'Now that we're alone,' Li Shai Tung continued, 'I've other news.'

'What's that?' Tsu Ma asked, stubbing out his cheroot in the porcelain tray on the *kang* beside him.

'I've heard from Karr. Berdichev is dead.'

Tsu Ma laughed, his eyes wide. 'You're certain?'

'I've seen it with these eyes. Karr was wired up to transmit all he saw and heard.'

'Then it's over.'

Li Shai Tung was silent a moment, looking down. When he looked up again his eyes seemed troubled. 'I don't think so.' He looked across at Shepherd. 'Ben was right after all, Hal. We've killed the men, and yet the symptoms remain.'

Shepherd smiled bleakly. 'Not all the men. There's still DeVore.'

The old T'ang lowered his head slightly. 'Yes. But Karr will get him. As he got Berdichev.'

Tsu Ma leaned forward. 'A useful man, Karr. Maybe we ought to mass-produce the fellow. Give Old Man Ebert a patent for the job.'

Li Shai Tung laughed and lifted his feet one at a time from the turtle stool. 'Maybe.' He pulled himself up and stretched. 'First, however, I have another idea I want you to consider. Something Li Yuan has been working on these last few months. I'm going to introduce it in Council tomorrow, but I wanted to sound you out first.'

Tsu Ma nodded and settled back with his drink, watching the old T'ang as he walked slowly up and down the room.

'It was an idea Li Yuan had years ago, when he was eight. He was out hawking with Han Ch'in when one of the hawks flew high up in a tree and refused to come down to the lure. Han Ch'in, impatient with the hawk, took the control box from the servant and destroyed the bird.'

'Using the homing-wire in the bird's head?'

'Exactly.'

Tsu Ma took a sip, then tilted his head slightly. 'I've never had to do that, myself.'

'Nor I,' agreed Li Shai Tung. 'And it was the first I had heard of the matter when Li Yuan told me of it six months back. However, until then Li Yuan had not realized that the birds were wired up in that way. It made him wonder why we didn't have such a thing for men.'

Tsu Ma laughed. 'Men are not hawks. They would not let themselves be bound so easily.'

'No. And that is exactly what Li Yuan told himself. Yet the idea was still a good one. He argued it thus. If the man was a good man he had no fear of having such a wire put into his head. It would make no difference. And if the man was a bad man, then he *ought* to have the wire.'

'I like that. Even so, the fact remains, men are not hawks. They like the illusion of freedom.'

Li Shai Tung stopped before Hal Shepherd and leaned forward a moment, placing his hand on the shoulder of his old friend, a sad smile on his face, then turned back, facing Tsu Ma.

'And if we gave them that illusion? If we could make them think they *wanted* the wires in their heads?'

'Easier said than done.'

'But not impossible. And Li Yuan has come up with a scheme by which the majority of men might do just that.'

Tsu Ma sat back, considering. 'And the technicalities of this?'

Li Shai Tung smiled. 'As ever, Tsu Ma, you anticipate me. There are, indeed, problems with creating such a control system. Men's brains are far more complex than a hawk's, and the logistics of tracking forty billion separate individuals through the three hundred levels of the City are far greater than the problems involved in tracing a few hawks on an estate. It is fair to say that Li Yuan has made little progress in this regard. Which is why there is a need to invest time and money in research.'

'I see. And that's what you want from the Council tomorrow? Permission to pursue this line of enquiry?'

Li Shai Tung inclined his head slightly. 'It would not do for a T'ang to break the Edict.'

Tsu Ma smiled. 'Quite so. But rest assured, Shai Tung, in this as in other things, you have my full support in Council.' He drained his glass and set it down. 'And the rest of your scheme?'

Li Shai Tung smiled. 'For now, enough. But if you would honour me by being my guest at Tongjiang this autumn, we might talk some more. Things will be more advanced by then and Li Yuan, I know, would be delighted to tell you about his scheme.'

Tsu Ma smiled. 'It would be my great honour and delight. But come, talking of Li Yuan, we have neglected your son and his new wife far too much already. I have yet to congratulate him on his choice.'

Both men pretended not to see the flicker of doubt that crossed the old T'ang's face.

'And you, Hal?' Li Shai Tung turned to face his old friend. 'Will you come through?'

Shepherd smiled. 'Later, perhaps. Just now I feel a little tired. Too much Yang Sen, I guess.'

'Ah. Maybe so.' And, turning sadly away, Li Shai Tung took Tsu Ma's arm and led him out into the gathering in the Great Hall.

Karr leaned across the desk and, with one hand, pulled the man up out of his seat, the front of the man's powder blue silk tunic bunched tightly in his fist.

'What do you mean, "*Can't*"? I'm leaving today. By the first craft available. And I'm taking those files with me.'

For a moment the man's left hand struggled to reach the summons pad on his desk, then desisted. He had heard what a maniac Karr was, but he'd never believed the man would storm into his office and physically attack him.

'Don't you know who I *am*?' he screeched, his voice half-strangled. 'I'm Governor of Mars. You can't do this to me!'

Karr dragged the man across the desk until he was eye to eye with him. 'You're a fine one to lecture me on what can and can't be done, Governor Schenck. You were ordered to give me full assistance, but you've been nothing but obstructive since I came back to Tian Men K'ou City.'

The Governor swallowed painfully. 'But... the investigation... Feng Shou

Station's destroyed, the pipeline badly damaged.'

'That's your concern. Mine is to report back to my T'ang at the earliest opportunity, and to take back with me all relevant information. You knew that. You had your orders.'

'But...'

Karr leaned back across the desk and threw Schenck down into his chair, then slammed his fist down on the summons pad.

'Do you want war with the Seven?'

'What?' Schenck's face blanched.

'Because that's what you'll get if you take any further measures to keep me here. By a special Edict of the Seven I was authorized to do as I saw fit to bring the traitor Berdichev to justice and to reclaim any files or documents relating to that same person. That I have done. Now, tell me, *Shih* Schenck, what has your investigation to do with me?'

'I...' he began, then saw the door open behind Karr.

Karr turned at once. 'Bring the Berdichev files. At once.'

The underling looked past Karr at Governor Schenck. 'Excellency?'

Karr turned back to Schenck. 'Well? Will you defy the Seven and sign your own death warrant, or will you do as I request?'

Schenck swallowed again, then bowed his head. 'Do as he says. And while you're at it, prepare Major Karr's clearance for the *Tientsin*. He leaves us this afternoon.'

'At once, Excellency.'

'Good,' said Karr, settling his huge frame into the tiny chair, facing Schenck. 'Now tell me, Governor, who ordered you to keep me here?'

Back on Chung Kuo, DeVore looked up from the files and stared hard at his lieutenant. 'Is this all?'

Wiegand bowed his head. 'For now, Excellency. But our contacts have promised us more. You'll know all you need to know about these scum before you meet with them again.'

'Good. Because I want to know who's good at what, and who's responsible for what. I want to know where they came from and what they ultimately want. And I want no guesses. I want facts.'

'Of course, Excellency. I'll see to it at once.'

Wiegand bowed low, then turned and went. *A good man*, thought DeVore, watching him go. *Intelligent and reliable, despite that business with Lehmann and the Notice.*

He got up and came round his desk, then stood there, studying the huge, blown-up photograph of the five *Ping Tiao* leaders that Wiegand had pinned to the wall.

The simple black and white image was clear and sharp, the life-size faces of the five terrorists standing out perfectly, Gesell in their centre. It had been taken ten or fifteen seconds into the meeting, the tiny lens cameras activated when he'd nodded to indicate the half-map on the table in front of Gesell. His intention had been merely to get images of the other four *Ping Tiao* leaders so they could be traced through his contacts in Security, yet what the picture captured most clearly was the intense, almost insane suspicion. DeVore smiled. He had sensed something of it at the time, but had been too engrossed in his own scheme to make anything of it. Now, seeing it so vividly – so physically – expressed, he realized he had missed something of real importance.

They were scared, yes, but it was more than that. They were on the run. Their cockiness was merely a front. Gesell's bluster masked a general fear that someone would come along and simply wipe them out. They and everything they stood for. They had suffered too many setbacks, too many betrayals by their own kind. They were paranoid, afraid of their own shadows.

But that was good. He could use that. It would give him the whip hand when they met in two days' time.

He went through what he knew. The Han male to the far left of the picture was Shen Lu Chua, a computer systems expert, trained as a mathematician. He was in his mid-thirties, his clean-shaven face long and drawn. Beside him was a rather pretty-looking woman with finely chiselled features – a *Hung Mao*, though her dark, fine hair was cut like a Han's. Her name was Emily Ascher and she was an economist, though of more interest to DeVore was the fact that she was Gesell's lover. On the other side of Gesell – second from the right in the photo – was the Han female, Mao Liang. She was an interesting one. The fourth daughter of a quite prominent Minor Family, she had been raised and educated at First Level, but had rebelled against her upbringing in her late teens and, after a year of arguments at home, had vanished into the lower levels, surfacing only now, five years on, amongst the *Ping Tiao*.

Last of the five – on the far right of the photo – was Jan Mach. He was a tall, broad-shouldered man of thirty-three with dark, shoulder-length braided hair and a thick growth of beard. He worked for the Ministry of Waste Recycling as a maintenance official. It was a good job for a *Ping Tiao* member, allowing him quick and legitimate passage between the levels, but Mach had the further advantage of being a volunteer in the Security Reserve Corps, licensed to carry a firearm. In the circles in which he operated it provided the perfect cover for his *ko ming* activities.

Mach, alone of the five, was looking away from DeVore in the picture, his eyes lowered to a writing pad on the desk before him. On the pad – in neatly formed pictograms that could be read quite clearly – was written, '*Jen to chiu luan lung to chiu han.*' Too many people bring chaos; too many dragons bring drought.

The detail was interesting. If Gesell was the leader, Mach was the power behind the throne. He was the one to watch, to influence, the ideologue of the group.

There was a sharp knock on the door.

'Come in!'

Lehmann stood there in the doorway. 'Our guests are here, sir.'

DeVore hesitated, noting how well the albino looked in uniform, then nodded. 'Good. I'll be down in a short while. Take them to the dining room, and make sure they're well looked after.'

Lehmann bowed and left.

DeVore turned and had one last brief look at the life-size picture of the five terrorists. 'As one door closes, so another opens.'

He laughed softly, then went across to his desk and pressed out the code to link him to the landing dome. His man there, Kubinyi, answered at once.

'Is everything in hand?'

'As you ordered, Excellency.'

'Good. I want no foul-ups. Understand me?'

He cut contact before Kubinyi could answer, then reached across and took the file from the drawer. He paused, looking about his office, conscious of the significance of the moment. Then, with a sharp laugh of enjoyment, he slammed the drawer shut and went out.

New directions, he told himself as he marched briskly down the corridor towards the lift. *The wise man always follows new directions.*

They turned as he entered the room. Seven of them. First Level business-men, dressed in light-coloured silk *pau*.

'Gentlemen,' he said, deliberately – ironically – avoiding the normal Han term, *ch'un tzu*. 'How good to see you all again.'

He saw at once how tense they were; how they looked at each other for support. They were afraid of him. Afraid of how he might react to the news they brought. News they thought he was unaware of. But he saw also how resigned they were. A spent force. The Seven had routed them thoroughly. The Confiscations, the arrests and executions – these had shaken them badly. They saw now the true cost of their involvement.

So it is, he thought. *And now your time has passed.*

He went amongst them, shaking hands, making small talk, his style and manner putting them at ease. He left Douglas until last, taking the old man's hand firmly, warmly, and holding his shoulder a moment, as if greet-ing the best of friends. Douglas was leader of the Dispersionists now that Berdichev was dead. Leader of a broken party, unwilling even to whisper its own name in public.

The news of Berdichev's death had been broken publicly only two hours back. While they were meeting, no doubt, finalizing what they would say to him this afternoon. The shock of that lay on them too. He could see it in Douglas's eyes.

'It's a sad business,' he said, pre-empting Douglas. 'I had nothing but respect for Soren Berdichev. He was a great man.'

Douglas lowered his head slightly. The news had affected him badly. His voice was bitter and angry, but also broken. 'They killed him,' he said. 'Like a common criminal. One of their animal-men – some GenSyn brute – did it, I'm told. Snapped his back like a twig. No trial. Nothing.' He met DeVore's eyes. 'I never imagined...'

'Nor I,' said DeVore sympathetically, placing an arm about his shoulder. 'Anyway... Come. Let's have something to eat. I'm sure you're all hungry after your flight here. Then we'll sit and talk.'

Douglas bowed his head slightly, a wistful smile on his lips softening the hurt and anger in his eyes. 'You're a good man, Howard.'

Little was said during the meal, but afterwards, with the plates cleared and fresh drinks poured all round, Douglas came to the point.

'The War is over, Howard. The Seven have won. We must plan for the long peace.'

The outer blast shutters had been drawn back and through the thick, clear glass of the wall-length window could be seen the sunlit valley and the cloud-wreathed mountains beyond. The late afternoon light gave the room a strangely melancholy atmosphere. DeVore sat at the head of the table, his back to the window, facing them, his face in partial shadow.

'Ai mo ta yu hsin ssu.'

Douglas gave a slow nod of agreement. 'So it is. Nothing is more sorrowful than the death of the heart. And that is how we feel, Howard. Weary. Heartbroken. More so now that Soren is not with us.'

'And?' DeVore looked from one to another, noting how hard they found it to look at him at this moment of surrender. They were ashamed. Deeply, bitterly ashamed. But of what? Of their failure to dislodge the Seven? Or was it because of their betrayal of him? Only Douglas was looking at him.

When no one spoke DeVore stood and turned his back on them, staring out at the mountains. 'I'm disappointed,' he said. 'I can't help it, but I am. I thought better of you than this. I thought you had more...' He turned, looking at them. 'More guts.'

'We've lost,' Douglas said, sitting back, suddenly defensive. 'It's an unpleasant fact to face, but it's true. Things have changed drastically, even in the last few months. It would be suicide to carry on.'

'I see.' DeVore seemed surprised. He turned slightly aside, as if considering something unexpected.

'Surely you must have thought about it, Howard? You must have seen how things are. The arrests. The Confiscations. The Seven are riding high. Anyone who shows even the slightest sign of opposing them is crushed. And no half-measures.' He paused, looking about him for support. 'That's how it is. I can't change that, Howard. None of us can. We failed. Now it's time to call it a day.'

'And that's how you all feel?'

There was a murmur of agreement from around the table.

DeVore sighed heavily. 'I thought as we'd come so far...'

They were watching him now. Wondering what he would do.

DeVore tapped the file, suddenly more animated, his voice holding the slightest trace of anger. 'I had plans. Schemes for new campaigns. Ways to finish what we had so successfully begun.'

'Successfully?' Douglas laughed sharply. 'I'm sorry, Howard, but in that you're wrong. We lost. And we lost heavily. Berdichev, Lehmann and Wyatt. Duchek, Weis and Barrow. They're all dead. Along with more than two thousand other, lesser members of our "revolution". One hundred and eighteen Companies have ceased trading – their assets and holdings confiscated by the Seven. And the Seven are still there, stronger than ever, more dominant than ever.'

'You're wrong. The Seven are weak. Weaker than they've been in their entire history. The Council has lost four of its most experienced members in the last six years. The new T'ang are young and inexperienced. Not only that, but the older T'ang have lost the confidence, the certainty, they once possessed. Once it was considered inconceivable to challenge the Seven. But now...'

'Now we understand why.'

DeVore shook his head, then, resignedly, sat again.

Douglas watched him a moment, then looked down. 'I'm sorry, Howard. I know how you must feel. You were closer to it all than we were. The fortresses. The campaigns. These were your projects – your children, if you like. It must be hard to give them up. But it's over. We would just be throwing good money after bad if we continued to support it all.'

DeVore lifted his head, then smiled and shrugged. His voice was softer, more reconciled. 'Well, as you say, old friend. But you're still wrong. We shook the tree. Can't you see that? It almost fell.'

Douglas looked away, his disagreement implicit in that gesture. 'What will you do?'

DeVore stared down at the two files, as if undecided. 'I don't know. Wind it all down here, I guess.'

'And after that?'

DeVore was still staring at the folders, his hunched shoulders and lowered head indicative of his disappointment. 'Go to Mars, maybe.'

'Mars?'

He looked up. 'They say it's where the future lies. The Seven have a weaker hold out there.'

'Ah...' Douglas hesitated a moment, then looked about him once more.

'Well, Howard. I think we've said all we came to say. We'd best be getting back.'

DeVore stood up. 'Of course. It was good seeing you all a last time. I wish you luck in all your ventures. And thank you, gentlemen. For all you did. It was good of you.'

He embraced each one as they left, then went to the window, staring out at the jagged landscape of rock and ice and snow. He was still there, watching, as, ten minutes later, their craft lifted from the hangar and slowly banked away to the right. For a moment its shadow flitted across the escarpment opposite, then, with a sudden, shocking brightness, it exploded. The shock of the explosion struck a moment later, rattling the empty glasses on the table.

He saw the fireball climb the sky, rolling over and over upon itself; heard the roar of the explosion roll like a giant clap of thunder down the valley and return a moment later. A million tiny incandescent fragments showered the mountainside, melting the snow where they fell, hissing and bubbling against the glass only a hand's width from his face. Then there was silence.

DeVore turned. Lehmann was standing in the doorway.

'What is it, Stefan?'

Lehmann looked past him a moment, as if recollecting what he had just seen. Then he came forward, handing DeVore a note. It was from Douglas. Handwritten. DeVore unfolded it and read.

Dear Howard,
I'm sorry it didn't work out. We tried. We really did try, didn't we? But life goes on. This is just to say that if ever you need anything – anything at all – just say.
With deepest regards,
John Douglas

DeVore stared at it a moment, then screwed it into a ball and threw it down. *Anything...* The words were meaningless. The man had given up. He and all the rest like him. Well, it was time now to go deeper, lower, to cultivate a different class of rebel. To shake the tree of State again. And shake and shake and shake. Until it fell.

*

The Officers' Club at Bremen was a spacious, opulently decorated place. Dark-suited Han servants, their shaven heads constantly bowed, moved silently between the huge, round-topped tables that lay like islands in an ocean of green-blue carpet. Tall pillars edged the great central hexagon, forming a walkway about the tables, like the cloisters of an ancient monastery, while, fifty ch'i overhead, the hexagonal panelling of the ceiling was a mosaic of famous battles, the Han victorious in all.

It was late afternoon and most of the tables were empty, but off to the right, halfway between the great double doorway and the bar, a group of eight officers was gathered about a table, talking loudly. Their speech, and the clutter of empty bottles on the table, betrayed that they were somewhat the worse for drink. However, as none of them was less than captain in rank, the duty officers smiled and turned away, allowing behaviour they would not have tolerated from lesser-ranking officers.

The focus of this group was the young major, Hans Ebert, the 'Hero of Hammerfest', who had been regaling them with stories about the reception he had attended that afternoon. Now, however, the conversation had moved on into other channels, and the low, appreciative laughter held a suggestion of dark enjoyments.

Auden, seeing how things were drifting, directed the conversation back to his superior. That was his role – to keep his master central at all times. Unlike the others, he had barely touched his drink all afternoon, yet it was not evident, for he seemed to lift his drink as often to his lips and refill his glass as often from the bottle. But his speech, unlike the others', was clear, precise.

'And you, Hans? How is that lady you were seeing?'

Ebert looked aside, smiling rakishly. 'Which of my ladies would that be, Will?'

Auden leaned forward to tap the end of his cigar against the tray, then sat back again in his chair. 'You know the one. The minister's wife.'

There was a gasp of surprise and admiration. A minister's wife! That smelled of danger. And danger was an aphrodisiac they all understood.

'Yes, tell us, Hans,' said Scott, his eyes bright with interest.

Ebert sipped at his glass relaxedly, then looked about the circle of eager, watching faces.

'She's my slave,' he said calmly. 'I can make her do anything I want. Anything at all. Take today, for instance. I had her two maids strip her and hold her down while I beat her with my cane. Then, while she watched, I had her maids. Afterwards, she was begging for it. But I shook my head. "You have to earn it," I said. "I want you to show me how much you love your maids."'

'No!' said Panshin, a rather portly colonel. 'And did she?'

Ebert sipped again. 'Didn't I say she was my slave?' He smiled. 'Right in front of me she got down on the floor with her maids and rolled about for more than twenty minutes, until all three of them were delirious, begging me to join them.'

Fest's eyes were bulging. 'And then you gave her one?'

Ebert set his glass down and slowly shook his head. 'Nothing so simple. You see, I have this ritual.'

'Ritual?' Scott swigged down his brandy with a quick tilt of his head, then set his glass down hard on the table. 'What kind of ritual?'

'I had all three of them kneel before me, naked, their heads bowed. Then I called them forward, one at a time, to kneel before the god and kiss the god's head. As each did so they had to repeat a few words. You know the sort of thing. "I promise to be faithful and obedient to the god and do whatever the god wishes." That sort of thing.'

'Kuan Yin!' said another of the captains, a man named Russ. 'Don't tell me, and then you had all three at once.',

Ebert laughed and finished his drink. 'I'm afraid not. The old girl was just about to take her turn when I noticed what time it was. "Sorry," I told her, "I didn't realize the time. I have to go. The T'ang awaits me."'

'Gods!' Scott spluttered, then shook his head. 'You're not kidding us, Hans. That really happened?'

'Less than six hours back.'

'And what did she say?'

Ebert laughed. 'What could she say? You don't keep a T'ang waiting.'

'And your promise?' said Russ. 'You promised you'd fuck her if she showed she loved her maids.'

Ebert reached out and tipped more wine into his glass. 'I'm a man of my word, Captain Russ. As you all know. When we've finished here I'll be returning to fulfil my promise.'

'And her husband?' Scott asked. 'Where was he while all of this was going on?'

'In his study. Reading the *Analects.*'

There was a great guffaw of laughter at that, which made heads turn at nearby tables.

'Power. That's what it's really all about,' said Ebert, his eyes half-closed, a faintly sybaritic smile on his lips. 'That's the key to sex. Power. It's something young Li Yuan will learn this very night. Master your sexuality and the world is yours. Succumb to it and...' He shrugged. 'Well... look at Fest here!'

The laughter rolled out again, dark, suggestive.

At that moment, on the threshold of the great doorway to the club, a rather dour-looking, almost ugly man, a Han, paused, looking in, his eyes drawn momentarily towards the laughter at the table to his right. He was different from the other Han inside the club in that he wore the powder-blue uniform of a Security officer, his chest patch showing him to be a captain. But he was a Han, all the same, and when he took a step across that threshold, a duty officer stepped forward, intercepting him.

'Excuse me, sir, but might I see your pass?'

Kao Chen stopped, then turned and faced the man, keeping his feelings in tight check. The man was within his rights, after all. He gave a terse bow and took his permit card from the top pocket of his tunic, then handed it to the officer. As the man studied the card intently, Chen was conscious how other, non-Han officers went through unhindered, even guests from other Security forces. But he had half expected this. The colour of his skin, the fold of his eyes – both were wrong here. The officer class of Security was almost totally made up of *Hung Mao*, descendants of the mercenary armies that had fought for the Seven against the tyrant Tsao Ch'un. Here Han were secondary; servants, not rulers. But he was an officer and he was thirsty. He had a right to sit and have a beer. And so he would.

The officer handed him back his pass, then gave a brief, almost slovenly salute. In terms of rank, Chen was his superior, but he was not *Hung Mao*, and so the rank meant little.

'Thank you, Lieutenant,' he said tightly, then made his way through, down the plushly carpeted steps and out into the main body of the club.

He was halfway across the floor before he realized who he was walking towards. He saw Ebert's eyes widen in recognition and decided to walk past quickly, but he was not to be so fortunate. Three paces past the table he was called back.

'Hey, you! Han! Come here!'

Chen turned slowly, then came back and stood in front of Ebert, his head bowed. 'Major Ebert.'

Ebert leaned back arrogantly in his chair, a sneering smile on his face. 'What in fuck's name do you think you're doing, Han?'

Chen felt himself go cold with anger, then remembered he was *kwai*. These were but words. And words could not hurt him. Only a knife could hurt a *kwai*. He answered Ebert calmly, civilly.

'I've just come off duty. I was hot and thirsty. I thought I would have a beer or two at the bar.'

'Then you can think again. There are rules in this place. No women and no Han.'

'No Han?'

He realized as soon as he said it that he had made a mistake. He should have bowed, then turned about and left. Now it was a question of face. His words, correct enough, innocuous enough in themselves, had challenged what Ebert had asserted. It did not matter that he, Kao Chen, had the right to use the club. That was no longer the issue.

Ebert leaned forward slightly, his voice hardening. 'Did you hear me, Han?'

Chen hesitated, then lowered his head slightly, afraid to let the anger in his eyes show. 'Excuse me, Major, but I am an officer in the service of the T'ang. Surely...'

Ebert leaned forward and threw his drink into Chen's face. 'Are you stupid? Don't you understand me?'

Chen was silent a moment, then bowed again. 'I apologize, Major. It was my fault. Might I buy you another drink before I leave?'

Ebert gave him a look of profound disgust. 'Just go, little Han. Now. Before I beat you senseless.'

Chen bowed low and backed away, mastering the pain, the fierce stinging in his eyes, his face perfectly controlled. Inside, however, he seethed, and at the doorway he looked back, hearing their laughter drift outward from the table, following him.

Laugh now, he thought. *Laugh good and long, Hans Ebert, for I'll not rest until my pride's restored and you lie humbled at my feet.*

At the table all eyes were once again on Ebert.

'The nerve of some of them,' he said, filling his glass again. 'Anyway. Where were we? Ah yes...' He stood up, then raised his glass. 'To Li Yuan and his bride! May this evening bring them clouds and rain!'

The answering roar was deafening. 'To Li Yuan!' they yelled. 'Clouds and rain!'

The ceremony was over; the last of the guests had departed; the doors of the inner palace were locked and guarded. Only the two of them remained.

Li Yuan turned from the doorway and looked across. Fei Yen sat in the tall-backed chair at the far side of the room, on the dais, as if enthroned. A *chi pao* of brilliant red was draped about her small and slender figure, while her dark hair was braided with fine strands of jewels. A thin cloth of red and gold veiled her features, an ancient *kai t'ou*, as worn by the brides of the Ching emperors for almost three centuries. Now that they were alone, she lifted the veil, letting him see her face.

She was beautiful. More beautiful than ever. His breath caught as he looked at her, knowing she was his. He knew now how his brother, Han Ch'in must have felt in his final moments, and grieved less for him. It would be fine to die now, knowing no more than this.

He walked across to her, hesitant, aware of her eyes upon him, watching him come.

He stopped at the foot of the steps, looking at her. The huge throne dwarfed her. She seemed like a child, sitting in her father's chair. Three steps led up to the dais, but standing there, his face was on the level of Fei Yen's. He studied her, conscious that in the years since he had first seen her she had grown to the fullness of womanhood.

His eyes narrowed with pain, looking at her, seeing how dark her eyes were. How deep and beautiful they were. How delicate the lashes. How finely drawn the curves of skin about the liquid centres. Eyes so dark, so vast he felt he could lose himself in their depths.

'Well?' Fei Yen leaned forward. She was smiling at him, her hand extended. 'What does my husband command?'

He felt a fresh thrill of delight course through his blood, at the same time hot and cold, both exquisite and painful. Her eyes held him, making him reach out and take her hand.

He looked down at her hand. So small and fine it was. Its warmth seemed to contradict its porcelain appearance, its strength oppose its apparent fragility. Her hand closed on his, drawing him up the steps to where she sat. He knelt, his head in her lap, her hands caressing his neck. For a moment it was enough. Then she lifted his head between her hands and made him move back, away from her.

They stood, facing each other.

Her hand went to the ruby-studded clasp at her right shoulder and released it. Slowly, with a faint silken rustle, the cloth unravelled, slipping from her body.

She stood there, naked but for the jewels in her hair, the bands of gold at her ankles and at her throat. Her skin was the white of swan's feathers, her breasts small, perfectly formed, their dark nipples protruding. Mesmerized, he looked at the curves of her flesh, the small, dark tangle of her sex, and felt desire wash over him so fiercely, so overpoweringly, he wanted to cry out.

Timidly he put out his hand, caressing her flank and then her breast, touching the dark brown nipple tenderly, as if it were the most fragile thing he had ever touched. She was watching him, her smile tender, almost painful now. Then, softly, she placed her hands upon his hips and pushed her face forward.

He moved closer, his eyes closed, his body melting. His hands caressed her shoulders, finding them so smooth, so warm they seemed unreal, while her lips against his were soft and wet and hot, like desire itself, their sweetness blinding him.

She reached down, releasing him, then drew him down on top of her. At once he was spilling his seed, even as he entered her. He cried out, feeling her shudder beneath him. And when he looked at her again he saw how changed her eyes were, how different her mouth – a simple gash of wanting now that he was inside her.

That look inflamed him, made him spasm again, then lie still on top of her.

They lay there a long while, then, as one, they stirred, noticing how awkwardly they lay, their bodies sprawled across the steps.

He stood and tucked himself in, aware of how incongruous the action seemed, then reached down to help her up, unable to take his eyes from her nakedness.

Saying nothing, she led him through into the bridal room. There she undressed him and led him to the bath and washed him, ignoring his arousal, putting him off until she was ready for him. Then, finally, they lay there on the low, wide bed, naked, facing each other, their lips meeting for tiny sips of kisses, their hands tenderly caressing each other's bodies.

'When did you know?' she asked, her eyes never leaving his.

'When I was eight,' he said and laughed softly, as if he knew it was madness. For more than half his young life he had loved her. And here she was, his wife, his lover. Eight, almost nine years his senior. Half a lifetime older than him.

For a time she was silent, her eyes narrowed, watching him. Then, at last, she spoke. 'How strange. Perhaps I should have known.' She smiled and moved closer, kissing him.

Yes, he thought, releasing her, then watching her again, seeing the small movements of her lashes, of the skin about her eyes, the line of her mouth. Cloud motion in the eyes, it seemed, the bones of her face moulded and remoulded constantly. He was fascinated by her. Mesmerized. He felt he could lie there for ever and never leave this room, this intimacy.

They made love again, slowly this time, Fei Yen leading him, guiding him, it seemed, bringing him to a climax more exquisite than the last, more painful in its intensity.

He lay there afterwards, watching the darkness in her face, the sudden colour in her cheeks and at her neck, and knew he would always want her. 'I love you,' he said finally, shaking his head slowly, as if he could not believe it. He had said the words so often in his head. Had imagined himself saying them to her. And now...

'I know,' she said, kissing him again. Then, relaxing, she settled down beside him, her head nestling into the fold of his arm, her cheek pressed soft and warm against his chest.

CHUNG KUO

Chapter 44

CONFLICTING VOICES

Li Yuan woke early and, loath to disturb her, went to his desk on the far side of the room. He sat there in the tight circle of the lamp's light, looking across at her, entranced by the vision of her sleeping form. Then, stirring himself, he took paper from the drawer and, after mixing water and ink from the ink block, began, writing the words in a neat, unhesitant hand down the page, right to left.

> Hot wings, perfumed like cinnamon,
> Beat about me, black as the moonless night.
> I heard your splendid cry in the silence,
> And knew the phoenix fed upon my heart.

He dipped the brush again, then looked across, realizing she was watching him.

'What are you doing, my love?'

He felt a tiny thrill, a shiver of pure delight, pass through him at her words. *My love...* How often he'd dreamed of her saying that. He smiled, then set the brush down.

'Nothing, my darling one. Sleep now. I'll wake you when it's time.'

He picked up the tiny, dragon-headed pot and shook sand over the paper to dry the ink, then lifted the sheet to blow it clean.

'Is it business?'

He looked up again, smiling. She had raised herself on one elbow and was looking across at him, her dark hair fallen loose across the silk of her shoulder.

Li Yuan folded the sheet in half and in half again, then put it in the pocket of his gown. He looked away a moment, towards the garden. It was dark outside; black, like a sea of ink pressed against the glass.

He looked back, smiling. 'No.'

'Then come to bed, my love. It's warm here.'

He laughed softly. 'Yes, but I must get ready.'

There was a meeting of the Council that afternoon and there was much to do beforehand. He ought to begin. Even so, he hesitated, seeing her thus. It was his first morning with her, after all. Surely his father would understand?

She was watching him silently, letting the darkness of her eyes, the silken perfection of her naked shoulder bring him to her. He stood, then went across, sitting beside her on the bed.

She leaned forward to greet him, her left hand moving between the folds of his gown to touch and caress his chest. As she did so, the covers slipped back, revealing her neck, the smooth perfection of her upper chest, the magnificence of her breasts. He looked down at them, then up into her face again.

'Fei Yen...'

Her lips parted slightly, her eyes widened, smiling. 'Husband?'

He laughed again, a brief sound of delight. 'Husband... It sounds so different from your lips.'

'Different?'

He shivered, then leaned forward to kiss her, gently, softly, holding her to him momentarily. Then he released her and sat back, looking at her again. Like something undeserved.

There was a small movement in her mouth, then she laughed. 'I have a present for you.'

'A present?'

'Yes. Wait there...'

Li Yuan reached out and took her arm gently, stopping her. 'Hold, my love. Look at you!' His eyes traced the form of her. 'What need have I for presents?'

'But this is different, Yuan. This is something I chose for you myself.'

'Ah...' he said, releasing her, then watched, his heart pounding in his chest as she turned from him, throwing the sheets aside, to reveal the slender curve of her back. She scrambled across the huge bed, then came back, a slim package in her hand.

'Here...'

He took it, but his eyes were elsewhere, drinking in the beauty of her.

'Well?' she said, enjoying the way he looked at her. 'Open it.'

He hesitated, then looked down, tugging at the bow to free the ribbon, then pulled the wrapping aside. It was a book. He opened the pages, then blushed and looked up.

'What is it?'

'It is a *chun hua*,' she said, coming alongside him, draping her warmth across his side and shoulder. 'A pillow book. Something to excite us when we're here, alone.'

He turned the pages slowly, reluctantly, pretending he had never seen its like, strangely appalled by the graphic nature of its sexual images. 'Fei Yen... we have no need for this. Why, I have only to look at you...'

'I know,' she said, turning his head gently with her fingers and kissing him softly on the cheek. 'But this will keep our love fresh and powerful; will raise us to new heights.'

He shuddered, closing his eyes, overwhelmed by the feeling of her warmth pressed up against him, the softness of her kisses against his flesh. He could smell the scent of their lovemaking on her skin. Could taste it on his tongue.

'I must get ready,' he said almost inaudibly. 'The Council...'

In answer she drew him down again, her kisses robbing him of his senses, enflaming him once more, making him surrender to her.

Prince Wang Sau-leyan stood on the balcony of his dead father's room, his hands resting lightly on the balustrade, his back to his brother's Chancellor. The broad sweep of the Nile lay below him, bisecting the empty landscape, its surface glittering in the morning light. He was dressed in a long silk sleeping robe of lavender decorated with butterflies, tied loosely at the waist. His feet were bare and his hair hung long, unbraided. He had been silent for some time, watching the slow, hovering flight of the birds high overhead, but now he lowered his head, finally acknowledging the waiting man.

'Greetings, Hung Mien-lo. And how is my brother this fine morning?'

Hung Mien-lo inclined his head. He was dressed formally, the three tiny pigtails of his beard braided tightly with silver thread, the dark silks he wore contrasting with the vermilion sash of office.

'The T'ang is poorly, Excellency. His nerves were bad and he did not sleep. He asks that you act as regent for him at today's Council. I have the authority here, signed and sealed.'

The Prince dipped his hand into a bowl on the balustrade at his side, scattering a handful of meat on to the desert floor, then watched the vultures swoop towards the subtly poisoned bait.

'Good. And our spies? What have they reported?'

Hung Mien-lo lifted his head, studying the Prince's back.

'That Li Shai Tung has a scheme. Something his son, Yuan, has proposed. I've sounded some of our friends.'

'And?'

The friends were a mixture of First Level businessmen and representatives, government officials and selected members of the Minor Families – all of them men of some influence outside the narrow circle of the Seven.

'They feel it would be best to oppose such a scheme.'

'I see.' He turned, looking at the Chancellor for the first time. 'This scheme... what does it involve?'

'They want to place a device in every citizen's head – a kind of tracking beam. They believe it would allow for a more effective policing of Chung Kuo.'

Wang Sau-leyan turned away. It was not a bad idea, but that was not the point. His purpose was to blunt Li Shai Tung's authority in Council, and what better way than to oppose his son? If, at the same time, he could win the support of certain influential members of the Above, then all the better. When his own plans came to fruition they would be reminded of his opposition to the scheme.

He turned, looking back fiercely at Hung Mien-lo. 'It is abominable. To put things in men's heads. Why, it would make them little more than machines!'

'Indeed, Excellency. And men should not be machines to be manipulated – should they?'

Both men laughed.

'You understand me well, Chancellor Hung. Too well, perhaps. But I can use you.'

Hung Mien-lo bowed low. 'As your Excellency desires.'

'Good.' Wang Sau-leyan smiled and turned, staring out across the delta towards the distant pinnacle of the lighthouse. 'Then you understand the last step we must take, you and I?'

Hung remained bowed, but his words came clear, unbowed, almost arrogant in their tone. 'I understand... *Chieh Hsia.*'

After the Chancellor had gone, Wang Sau-leyan stood there, watching the birds. At first they seemed unaffected by the poison, but then, first one and then another began to stagger unsteadily. One flapped its wings awkwardly, attempting to fly, lifting ten, maybe fifteen *ch'i* into the air before it fell back heavily to earth. He smiled. Six birds had taken the poison. He watched them stumble about for a time before they fell and lay still. More birds were gathering overhead, making slow circles in the cloudless sky. In a while they too would swoop. And then...

He turned away, tired of the game already – knowing the outcome – and went back inside.

'Sun!' he shouted impatiently. 'Sun! Where are you?'

Sun Li Hua, Master of the Inner Chamber, appeared in the doorway at once, his head bent low.

'Yes, Excellency?'

'Send the maids. At once! I wish to dress.'

Sun bowed and made to back away, but Wang Sau-leyan called him back.

'No... Send just the one. You know... Mi Feng.'

'As you wish, Excellency.'

He sniffed deeply, then went across to the full-length dragon mirror and stood there, looking at himself. So his brother was unwell. Good. He would feel much worse before the day was out.

Wang Sau-leyan smiled and combed his fingers through his hair, drawing it back from his forehead. Then, almost whimsically, he turned his head, exposing one ear to view. That mystery – the mystery of who had taken his father's ears – remained unsolved. He had had Hung Mien-lo make a thorough investigation of the matter, but it had been without result. They had vanished, as if they had never been.

The thought brought a smile to his lips. He turned, still smiling, and saw the girl.

Mi Feng was kneeling just inside the door, her head lowered almost to her lap, awaiting his pleasure.

'Come here,' he said brusquely, turning from her, moving across towards the great wardrobes that lined one side of the room. 'I want you to dress me, girl.'

She was his brother's maid, inherited from their father. In the wardrobe mirrors he saw her hesitate and glance up at his back.

'Well, girl? What are you waiting for? You heard me, didn't you?'

He noted her confusion; saw the way her face clouded momentarily before she bowed her head and began to move towards him.

He turned abruptly, making her start nervously.

'How is your sting, Little Bee? Did you serve my father well?'

Again he noted the movements in her face; the uncertainty, maybe even the suggestion of distaste. Well, who did she think she was? She was a servant, there to do his bidding, not the daughter of a T'ang.

She moistened her lips and spoke, her head kept low, her eyes averted. 'What do you wish to wear, my lord?'

White, he almost answered her. *White for mourning.*

'What do you suggest?' he asked, studying her more carefully, noting how delightfully she was formed, how petite her figure. 'What would my father have worn to Council?'

She looked up at him, then quickly away, clearly bewildered by what was happening. 'Forgive me, Prince Sau-leyan, but I am the T'ang's maid. Surely...'

He shouted at her, making her jump. 'Be quiet, girl! You'll do as you're told or you'll do nothing, understand me?'

She swallowed, then nodded her head.

'Good. Then answer me. What would my father have worn to Council?'

She bowed, then moved past him, keeping her head lowered. A moment later she turned back, a long robe held over one arm.

'Lay it out on the bed so that I can see it.'

He watched her move across to do as she was told, then smiled. Yes, the old man had chosen well with this one. He could imagine how the girl had wormed her way into the old boy's affections. She had kept his bed warm many a night, he was sure.

She had turned away from him, laying out the heavy, formal robe. He moved closer, coming up behind her, then bent down and lifted her gown up from the hem, exposing her buttocks and her lower back. She froze.

'You didn't answer me earlier,' he said. 'I asked you...'

'I heard you, Excellency.'

Her tone was sharper than it should have been. Impertinent. He felt a sudden flush of anger wash over him.

'Put your hands out,' he said, his voice suddenly cold. 'Lean forward and stretch them out in front of you.'

Slowly she did as she was told.

'Good,' he said. 'Now stay there.'

He went outside on to the balcony a moment, then returned, holding a cane he had broken from the bamboo plant. It was as long as his arm and as thick as his middle finger. He swished it through the air, once, then a second time, satisfied with the sound it made, then turned and looked across at her.

'I am not my father, Mi Feng. Or my brother, come to that. They were weak men. They held weak ideas. But I'm not like that. I'm stronger than them. Much stronger. And I'll have no impertinence from those beneath me.'

He moved closer, measuring the distance between himself and the girl, then brought the cane down hard across her buttocks.

She cried out involuntarily, her whole body tensing from the blow.

'Well?' he said, as if there were something she should say, some apology or word of mitigation. But she was silent, her body tensed against him, defiantly expectant. He shivered, angered by her silence, and lashed out, again and again, bringing the cane down wildly, impatiently, until, with a shudder, he threw it aside.

'Get up,' he said, tonelessly. 'Get up. I wish to be dressed.'

*

Fei Yen lay there, Yuan's head cradled between her breasts, her hands resting lightly on his back, her fingertips barely touching his flesh. He was sleeping, exhausted from their last bout of lovemaking, the soft exhalation of his breath warm against her skin. It was almost noon and the bedchamber was flooded with light from the garden. If she turned her head she could see the maple, by the pathway where they had walked so long ago.

She sighed and turned back, studying the neat shape of his head. It had been a sweet night, far sweeter than she had ever imagined. She thought of what they had done and her blood thrilled. She had fancied herself the famous concubine, Yang Kuei Fei, lying in the arms of the great T'ang Emperor, Ming Huang, and, at the moment of clouds and rain, had found herself transported. *A son*, she had prayed to Heaven; *let his seed grow in me and make a son!* And the joy of the possibility had filled her, making her cry out beneath him with the pleasure of it.

A son! A future T'ang! From these loins she would bring him forth. And he would be an emperor. A Son of Heaven.

She shivered, thrilled by the thought of it, then felt him stir against her.

'What is it?' he said sleepily.

Her hands smoothed his back, caressed his neck. 'I was thinking how hard it was before last night. How difficult to be alone.'

He lifted his head slightly, then lay back again.

'Yes,' he said, less drowsily than before. 'I can see that.'

He was silent for a time, his body at ease against her own, then he lifted himself up on his arms, looking down at her, his face serious. 'How was it? All those years before last night. How hard was that?'

She looked away. 'It was like death. As if not Han but I had died that day.' She looked up at him, fiercely, almost defiantly. 'I am a woman, Yuan, with a woman's appetites.' She swallowed. 'Oh, you just don't know...' For a moment longer her face was hard with past bitterness, then it softened and a smile settled on her lips and in her eyes. 'But now I am alive again. And it was you who brought me back to the living. My prince. My love...'

She made to draw him down again, but he moved back, kneeling there between her legs, his head bowed. 'Forgive me, my love, but I am spent. Truly I am.' He laughed apologetically, then met her eyes again. 'Tonight, I promise you, I will be a tiger again. But now I must dress. The Council...'

He turned to look at the timer beside the bed, then sat bolt upright.

'Gods! And you let me sleep!' He backed away from her, then stood there on the bare floor, naked, looking about him anxiously. 'I shall be late! Where is Nan Ho? Why did he not wake me?'

She laughed and stretched, then reached down and pulled the sheets up to her neck.

'I sent him away. They will excuse you this once if you are late. Besides, you needed to sleep.'

'But Fei Yen...' Then he laughed, unable to be angry with her. She was beautiful, and, yes, he had needed to sleep. What's more, they would forgive him this once. Even so...

He turned from her. 'All right. But now I must dress.'

He was halfway to the door when she called him back. 'Li Yuan! Please! You don't understand. I'll dress you.'

He turned. She had climbed from the bed and was coming towards him.

'You?' He shook his head. 'No, my love. Such a task is beneath you. Let me call the maids.'

She put her arms about his neck. 'You will do no such thing, my prince. I *want* to dress you. I *want* to serve you. As a wife should serve her master.'

He felt a small thrill go through him at the words. 'But I...'

Her kiss quietened him. He bowed his head slightly. 'As you wish.'

She smiled. 'Good. But first I must bathe you. After all, you cannot go to Council smelling like a singsong house.'

He laughed uneasily, then, seeing how she smiled at him, felt the unease fall from him. It was impossible to be angry with her, even when her words were ill-chosen, for that too was part of the charm – the sheer delight – of her. Like porcelain she looked, yet in the darkness she had been fire, black wings of fire, beating about him wildly.

When he was gone she looked about the room.

It was a strangely feminine room, unlike the rooms of her brothers. There were no saddles, no weapons of war on display. In their place were beautiful ceramic pots, filled with the most exquisite miniature trees and shrubs. And in place of heavy masculine colours were softer shades, delicately chosen to complement the colours of the garden outside. She looked about her, pleased by what she saw, then went across to the desk and sat.

She placed her left hand on the desk's broad surface, then lifted it, surprised. She licked at the tiny grains that had adhered to her palm, then understood. Of course. He had been writing.

She stood, then went back to the bed and picked up his sleeping robe. From whim, she tried it on, putting her arms into its sleeves and tying the slender sash about her waist. It was far too big for her, yet it felt somehow right to be wearing it. She laughed, then sat down on the bed, reaching into the pocket to take out the folded piece of paper.

She read it. Twice, and then a third time.

A poem. For her? It must have been. She shivered, then touched the tip of her tongue against her top teeth thoughtfully.

Yes. She could see it now: she would be everything to him. Indispensable. His wife. In all things his wife.

It was true what she had said. Or almost true. He *had* brought her back from death. From the death of all her hopes and dreams. Had given her back what she had always wanted.

And in return?

She smiled and drew his gown tighter about her. In return she would be his woman. That before all else. His helpmate and advisor. His champion and chief advocate. His lover and, when he needed it, a mother to him.

Yes, and that was the clue to Li Yuan. She had known it earlier, when he had rested his head between her breasts; had known then that it was a mother he wanted. Or at least someone to be the mother he had never had. Well, she would be that to him, amongst other things. And in time...

She shivered and slipped the poem back into the pocket of the gown.

In time she would have sons of her own. Seven sons. Each one of them a T'ang. She laughed and stood, letting the gown fall from her until she stood there, naked, lifting her arms defiantly. There! That was her dream. A dream she had shared with no one.

It seemed an impossibility, and yet she saw it clear. It *would* be so. Yes, but first she must be practical. First she must become all things to him. She would ask him this evening, after they had made love. She would bathe him and wash his hair, and then, when he was at his sweetest, would go down on her knees before him, pleading to be allowed always to serve him so.

He would agree. Of course he would. And then she would ask again. The maids, she would say; you must send them away. And he would do so. And then he would be hers. Completely, irrevocably hers.

Tender Willow and Sweet Rain were talking, laughing between them as they came into the room, but seeing Little Bee stretched out, face down on her bed, they fell silent.

'What is it?' Sweet Rain asked, moving closer. 'What's happened?'

Mi Feng looked up, her eyes red, her cheeks wet with tears, and shook her head.

'What did he do?' Tender Willow asked, coming alongside her sister.

Mi Feng swallowed, then let her head fall again, a great sob racking her body.

The two girls sat on the bed, either side of her, their arms about her, comforting her. But when Tender Willow leaned back, accidentally brushing against her buttocks, Mi Feng winced and gave a tiny moan.

The two girls exchanged looks, then nodded. Carefully, they lifted Mi Feng's robe, conscious of how she tensed.

'Kuan Yin...' Sweet Rain said softly, her voice pained. 'What did he do this with?'

'A cane,' came the whisper. 'A bamboo cane.'

Tender Willow stared at the cuts a moment longer, horrified, then shuddered. 'How *dare* he?' she said, outraged. 'Who does he think he is? You are the T'ang's maid, not his. He cannot be allowed to act like this.'

Mi Feng shook her head. A great shuddering sigh passed through her, then she spoke again; calmer, more clearly than before. 'You are wrong, sister. He may do as he wishes. He is a prince, after all. And what am I? Only a maid. A thing to be used or discarded. I learned that today, Tender Willow. I had it beaten into me. And the T'ang...' She laughed coldly, then swallowed, another shiver passing through her. 'The T'ang will do nothing.'

Tender Willow met her eyes momentarily, then looked away, feeling sick. Maybe it was true. The T'ang *would* do nothing. But this was too much. The Prince had gone too far this time. Maid or not, *thing* or not, she would not allow this to happen to her sister.

'I've creams,' she said gently, looking back, reaching out to touch and stroke her sister's brow. 'Ointments to soothe the cuts and help them heal.

Lie still, Little Bee, and I'll bring them. And don't worry. Everything will be all right.'

The servant bowed low and backed away, his message delivered. Tsu Ma allowed himself the slightest smile, then turned, greeting the newcomer.

'You're late, Li Yuan!' he said sternly, loud enough for the others to hear, then let the hard lines of his face melt into a broad grin. He put a hand on the young man's shoulder. 'Was it hard to get up this morning?'

'No...' Li Yuan began innocently, then blushed deeply as he saw the verbal trap and heard the great gust of laughter from the rest of the men on the great, broad balcony. He looked about and saw how each face – even his father's – was filled with a tolerant, good-natured humour. All but one. A young, moon-faced man stood alone by the ornamental rail, beyond the two small groups of men. He was staring back coldly at Li Yuan, as if irritated by his arrival. At first Li Yuan did not recognize him. Then he realized who it was. Wang Sau-leyan.

Tsu Ma squeezed his shoulder gently, then lowered his voice. 'Anyway, Yuan, come. The second session is not due to start for another half hour. There's time for talk and refreshments.'

He turned and drew Li Yuan out of the shadows into the warm, mid-afternoon sunlight, then began the formality of introducing him to the T'ang and those of their sons who were attending.

Li Yuan knew them all personally. All but the last.

'I'm surprised to find you here, Wang Sau-leyan,' he said, as he lifted his head.

'Surprised?' Wang Sau-leyan's eyes looked out past Li Yuan's shoulder, an expression of disdain on his pale, rounded face. 'Five years ago, perhaps. But as things are...' He laughed, no warmth in the laughter. 'My brother is unwell. His nerves...'

He glanced briefly at Li Yuan, then seemed to dismiss him, turning to concentrate his attention on Tsu Ma.

'Have you sounded the other T'ang about my proposal, Tsu Ma?'

Tsu Ma smiled pleasantly, concealing whatever he had been thinking. 'I have broached the matter.'

'And?'

Tsu Ma laughed kindly. 'Well, it's difficult, cousin. If you had given them more warning. If they had had just a little more time to consider all the possible ramifications of your suggestion...'

Wang Sau-leyan interrupted him curtly. 'What you mean is, no, they won't debate it.'

Tsu Ma gave the slightest suggestion of a shrug, the smile remaining on his lips. 'It was felt that it might be... how should I say?... *premature* to press the matter without consideration. But if the T'ang's regent would like to prepare something for the next meeting.'

Wang Sau-leyan leaned towards Tsu Ma angrily, the words hissing from him coldly. 'Four months from now! That's far too long! Why not today? Why are they so afraid to listen to new ideas?'

Heads had turned, but Tsu Ma seemed perfectly unflustered. He smiled, his whole manner calm and polite. 'I understand your impatience, Wang Sau...'

'*Impatience?* You insult me, Tsu Ma! For three hours I have listened patiently to the words of others. Have attended to their schemes. Yet now, when I beg my turn to speak, they deny me. Is that impatience?'

Li Yuan had seen the movements of the muscles in Tsu Ma's cheeks. Had known that, were he not a T'ang, Tsu Ma would have called the young Prince out and challenged him to a duel. Yet his control now in the face of such provocation was magnificent.

Tsu Ma smiled. 'Forgive me, Wang Sau-leyan. My words were ill chosen. Even so, it is neither the validity of your views nor the... *novelty* of your words that are at issue here. It is merely our way. All that we say here, all we decide upon, has a profound effect upon the lives of those we rule. It would not do to give less than the most serious consideration to such matters. Ill-considered change benefits no man.'

'You would lecture me, Tsu Ma?'

'Not at all. I wish merely to explain the position of my fellow T'ang. These things are matters of long standing. It is how we transact our business.'

'Then perhaps it ought to change.'

Tsu Ma laughed. 'Maybe so. Perhaps the Prince Regent would put the idea forward for the next Council to consider?'

Wang Sau-leyan lifted his chin slightly. 'Perhaps...' He let his eyes rest momentarily on Li Yuan, then looked back at Tsu Ma, giving the slightest inclination of his head. 'I thank you for your efforts, Tsu Ma. If my manner was terse, forgive me. That is *my* way. But do not mistake me. I too have the best interests of Chung Kuo at heart.'

Li Yuan watched as Wang Sau-leyan went across to greet the young T'ang of South America, Hou Tung-po, then turned back to Tsu Ma. 'Well! What *was* his proposal?'

Tsu Ma smiled. 'Not here,' he said quietly. Then, taking his shoulder again, he drew Li Yuan aside, his smile suddenly broader, more natural.

'So... tell me, cousin. How is that beautiful bride of yours?'

Helmstadt Armoury was a massive hexagonal block of three hundred levels, isolated from the stacks surrounding it by a space fifty *ch'i* in width. That two-li-deep chasm was spanned, at four separate levels, by three broad, connecting bridges, each bridge ending at a huge double gate, closed against intruders. To each side a whole battery of weapons – state-of-the-art equipment controlled from the guardroom within – covered these entry points to the complex.

Helmstadt was considered by its makers to be invulnerable: a fortress second only to the great nerve-centre of Bremen. But in less than thirty seconds, if everything went to plan, three of its gates would be open, the approaches unguarded.

DeVore crouched amongst his men in a side corridor on the City side of the bridge, looking down at his handset, watching through the complex's own Security cameras as his man approached the gate. The man was a lieutenant in the Armoury's back-up forces, called in on emergency standby after half the Armoury's regular garrison had been sent to help quell the riots in Braunschweig, thirty li away.

The lieutenant marched up to the gate, then came to attention, holding his pass up for inspection. Two of the overhead guns had swivelled about, covering him, but now, on the computer's recognition signal, they swung back, focusing once more on the mouth of the corridor beyond.

He moved forward, placing one eye to an indented pad set into the gate, then stepped back. Three seconds passed, then a panel irised back, chest high to him, revealing a keyboard. The lieutenant inserted his card, then tapped out the coded signal.

At once the gates began to open.

Elsewhere, at a gate on the far side of the stack and at another fifty levels down, the same thing was happening. Much now depended on timing. If just one of the gates remained unsecured then the odds would swing against them.

DeVore waited, tensed, counting. At thirty the screen of the handset went blank and he gave the signal. Immediately his men spilled out of the corridor and began to cross the bridge. If his inside man had failed they would be cut down instantly. But the guns remained silent. Beyond them, on the far side of the bridge, the great doors stayed open.

DeVore switched channels on the handset quickly, making sure. All three were blank, the transmission signals dead. He smiled, then, tucking the set inside his one-piece, followed his men out on to the bridge.

Inside, he found things well advanced. The level had been sealed off and all four of the big transit lifts secured. On the floor to one side a line of captives lay face down, bound at hand and foot. Most of the prisoners were only partly dressed, while two were completely naked. Only the five-man duty squad were fully dressed, but even they had been too surprised to put up any fight. Down below his men would be moving through the levels, securing all major entry points to the arsenal itself, isolating any remaining defenders scattered about these uppermost levels.

Much depended now on how the Ping Tiao fared, fifty levels down. If they could seal off the barracks and hold their gate all would be well. But even if they didn't, it would be more their loss than his. He needed the weapons, it was true, but there was something far more important here. Something he hadn't bothered to mention in the briefing.

He turned and called the lieutenant across.

'Which of these is the duty captain?'

The lieutenant went down the line, then stopped and bent down to touch the back of one of the half-dressed men.

'Good. Take him into the guardroom.'

While two of his men lifted the captain under the shoulders and dragged him away, DeVore turned to Lehmann. Of all of them he looked most at ease in the simple Ping Tiao clothes they were wearing.

'Stefan... Come here.'

Lehmann came across, then followed him into the guardroom.

The captain had been placed in a chair, his back to them. One of the men was busy binding him about the chest and legs.

'Who are you?' he was demanding as DeVore entered. 'You're not Ping Tiao. I can see that, despite your clothes and those fish symbols about your necks. You're too sharp, too well organized. Those scum wouldn't know how to break into a foodstore.'

'You're quite right, Captain,' DeVore said, coming round and sitting on the table edge, facing him.

The man's eyes widened. 'DeVore!'

DeVore laughed softly, then signalled for the two men to leave. When they were gone he looked past the man at Lehmann, who nodded and turned to lock the door.

'Good.' DeVore smiled. 'Now to business.'

The captain glared at him defiantly. 'What business? I have no business with you, DeVore.'

'No?' DeVore reached into the breast pocket of his one-piece and took out something small and flat and round, its white casing like a lady's compact. Looking across at the captain, he smiled. 'You have a nice family, Captain Sanders. A beautiful wife, two fine sons and the baby girl. Well, she's divine. A pretty little thing.'

Sanders watched, horrified, as DeVore opened the casing and activated the hologram within.

'You have them?' Sanders looked up at DeVore, swallowing drily, then looked back down at the tiny holo of his family, noting the look of anguish on his wife's face, the way the boys huddled against her.

DeVore smiled. 'As I said. To business.'

'What do you want?'

'Six numbers and five letters.'

Sanders understood at once. 'The lift...'

'Yes.'

It was a secret one-man shaft that went down from this level to the floor of the stack. He had seen it once, when he had been inspecting Helmstadt, eleven years ago; had travelled down and seen first-hand how it was defended. Now he would use what he knew.

Sanders hesitated, staring at the hologram. 'And if I do... they'll go free?'

'Of course.' DeVore snapped the case shut and slipped it back into the pocket of his one-piece. 'You might consider me a traitor, Captain Sanders, but I'm still a man of my word.'

Sanders studied DeVore a moment longer, doubt warring with fear in his eyes, then he nodded. 'All right. But it won't help you.'

'No?' DeVore leaned back slightly. 'Well, we'll see, neh? Just give me the code. I'll do the rest.'

Five thousand li to the east, in the magnificent palace at Astrakhan on the shore of the great inland sea, the Seven were in Council. As was their way, they sat not at a great table but in low, comfortable chairs drawn into a circle at one end of the room. Their manner seemed casual, as though they had met as friends to drink and talk of old times, yet here, on such occasions, all major policy decisions were made. Behind the T'ang, on simple stools, sat those sons who were attending – four in all, including Li Shai Tung's son, Li Yuan – while at a desk behind Tsu Ma sat two scribes. In this, the second session of the day, they had come at last to the central issue: the matter of the Confiscations. Tsu Ma was just coming to the end of his speech, leaning forward in his chair, his words a strong echo of Li Shai Tung's.

'...but that would be folly. There's no better way to put an end to all this bitterness and rivalry. At one stroke we can stabilize the market and placate those who, however mistakenly, might otherwise feel ill served by our generosity to those who sided with us.'

Tsu Ma paused and looked about the circle of his fellow T'ang, self-assured, his mouth and eyes forming a smile.

'Which is why I have no hesitation in seconding Li Shai Tung's proposal. The stewardship system will achieve the end we seek.'

There was a murmur of agreement from the older T'ang, but even as Tsu Ma sat back, Wang Sau-leyan leaned forward, his round face tensed with anger, his eyes hard. He spoke bitterly, staring about him angrily, challengingly.

'Can I believe what I hear? Have we not just fought a war? A war which, by the power of Heaven, we won. If that is so, why should we fear the bitterness of our enemies? Why should we seek to placate them? Would they have done the same? No! They would have destroyed us. And what then? What would they have offered us? Nothing! Not even the dignity of a decent burial. And yet you sit here worrying about your enemies and their feelings. Well, I say forget them! We must reward our friends! Publicly, so all can see. What better way to encourage support for the Seven?'

Wei Feng sat forward in his chair, his face grim, his hands spread in a gesture that suggested his despair at Wang's words.

'That's foolish talk, Wang Sau-leyan! Loyalty cannot be bought. It is like a tree. Long years go into its making. Your scheme would have us buy our friends.' He laughed scornfully. 'That would reduce our friendships to mere transactions, our dealings to the level of the marketplace.'

Wang Sau-leyan stared back at Wei Feng, his eyes narrowed.

'And what is wrong with the marketplace? Is it not that selfsame market that gives us our power? Be honest now – what's the truth of it? Does the love of our subjects sustain us, or is it the power we wield? Is there anyone here who does not fear the assassin's knife? Is there a single one of us who would walk the lowest levels unprotected?' Wang laughed scornfully and looked about him. 'Well, then, I ask again – what is so wrong with the marketplace? Wei Feng says I speak foolishly. With respect, cousin Wei, my thoughts are not idle ones. You are right when you talk of loyalty as a tree. So it was. But the War has felled the forests. And are we to wait a dozen, fifteen years for the new seed to grow?' He shook his head. 'We here are realists. We know how things stand. There is no time to grow such loyalty again. Times have changed. It is regrettable, but...'

He paused, spreading his hands.

'So. Let me ask again. What is wrong with rewarding our friends? If it achieves our end – if it breeds a kind of loyalty – why question what it is that keeps a man loyal? Love, fear, money... in the end it is only by force that we rule.'

There was a moment's silence after he had finished. Li Shai Tung had been looking down at his hands while Wang was speaking. Now he looked up and, with a glance at Tsu Ma and Wu Shih, addressed the Council.

'I hear what my cousin Wang says. Nevertheless, we must decide on this matter. We must formulate our policy here and now. I propose that this matter is put to the vote.'

Wang Sau-leyan stared at him a moment, then looked down. There was to be no delay, then? No further debate? They would have his vote now? Well, then, he would give them his vote.

Tsu Ma was leaning forward, taking a small cigar from the silver and ivory box on the arm of his chair. He glanced up casually. 'We are agreed, then, cousins?'

Wang Sau-leyan looked about him, watching his fellow T'ang raise their hands then let them fall again.

'Good,' said Tsu Ma, 'then let us move on quickly...'

Wang spoke up, interrupting Tsu Ma. 'Excuse me, cousin, but have you not forgotten something?'

Tsu Ma met his eyes, clearly puzzled. 'I'm sorry?'

'The vote. You did not ask who was against.'

Tsu Ma laughed awkwardly. 'I beg pardon...?'

'Six hands were raised. Yet there are seven here, are there not?'

Wang Sau-leyan looked about him, seeing the effect his words were having on his fellow T'ang. Like so much else, they had not expected this. In Council all decisions were unanimous. Or had been. For one hundred and twenty-six years it had been so. Until today.

It was Li Shai Tung who broke the silence. 'You mean you wish to vote against? After all we've said?'

Wei Feng, sat beside him, shook his head. 'It isn't done,' he said quietly. 'It just isn't our way...'

'Why not?' Wang asked, staring at him defiantly. 'We are Seven, not one, surely? Why must our voice be singular?'

'You misunderstand...' Tsu Ma began, but again Wang cut in.

'I misunderstand nothing. It is my right to vote against, is it not? To put on record my opposition to this item of policy?'

Tsu Ma hesitated, then gave a small nod of assent.

'Good. Then that is all I wish to do. To register my unease at our chosen course.'

At the desk behind Tsu Ma the secretary, Lung Mei Ho, had been taking down everything that was said for the official record, his ink brush moving quickly down the page. Beside him his assistant had been doing the same, the duplication ensuring that the report was accurate. Now both had stopped and were looking up, astonished.

'But that has been done already, cousin Wang. Every word spoken here is a matter of record. Your unease...' Tsu Ma frowned, trying to understand. 'You mean you really *do* wish to vote against?'

'Is it so hard to understand, Tsu Ma?' Wang looked past the T'ang at the scribe, his voice suddenly hard. 'Why aren't you writing, *Shih* Lung? Did anyone call these proceedings to a halt?'

Lung glanced at his master's back, then lowered his head hurriedly, setting down Wang's words. Beside him his assistant did the same.

Satisfied, Wang Sau-leyan sat back, noting how his fellow T'ang were glaring at him now or looking amongst themselves, uncertain how to act. His gesture, ineffective in itself, had nonetheless shocked them to the bone. As Wei Feng had said, it wasn't done. Not in the past. But the past was dead. This was a new world, with new rules. They had not learned that yet. Despite all, the War had taught them nothing. Well, he would change that. He would press their noses into the foul reality of it.

'One further thing,' he said quietly.

Tsu Ma looked up, meeting his eyes. 'What is it, cousin Wang?'

The sharpness in Tsu Ma's voice made him smile inside. He had rattled them – even the normally implacable Tsu Ma. Well, now he would shake them well and good.

'It's just a small thing. A point of procedure.'

'Go on...'

'Just this. The princes must leave. Now. Before we discuss any further business.'

He saw the look of consternation on Tsu Ma's face; saw it mirrored on every face in that loose circle. Then the room exploded in a riot of angry, conflicting voices.

DeVore braced himself as the lift fell rapidly, one hand gripping the brass and leather handle overhead, the other cradling the severed head against his hip. They had quick-frozen the neck to stop blood seeping against his uniform and peeled away the eyelids. In time the retinal pattern would decay, but for now it was good enough to fool the cameras.

As the lift slowed he prepared himself, lifting the head up in front of his face. When it stopped, he put the right eye against the indentation in the wall before him, then moved it away, tapping in the code. Three seconds, then the door would hiss open. He tucked the head beneath his arm and drew his gun.

'What's happening up top?'

The guard at the desk was turning towards him, smiling, expecting Sanders, but he had barely uttered the words when DeVore opened fire, blowing him from his seat. The second guard was coming out of a side room, balancing a tray with three bowls of *ch'a* between his hands. He thrust the tray away and went for his sidearm, but DeVore was too quick for him. He staggered back, then fell and lay still.

DeVore walked across to the desk and set the head down, then looked about him. Nothing had changed. It was all how he remembered it. In eleven years they had not even thought of changing their procedures. Creatures of habit, they were – men of tradition. DeVore laughed scornfully. It was their greatest weakness and the reason why he would win.

He went to the safe. It was a high-security design with a specially strengthened form of ice for its walls and a blank front that could be opened only by the correct sequence of light pulses on the appropriate light-sensitive panels. That too was unchanged. *It won't help you* – that's what Sanders had said. Well, Sanders and his like didn't think the way he thought. They approached things head on. But he...

DeVore laughed, then took the four tiny packets from the tunic and, taking out their contents, attached them to the ice on each side of the safe's rectangular front. They looked like tiny hoops, like snakes eating their own tails. Four similar hoops – much larger, their destructive capacity a thousand times that of these tiny, ring-like versions – had begun it all, ten years earlier, when they had ripped the Imperial Solarium apart, killing the T'ang's Minister Lwo Kang and his advisors. Now their smaller brothers would provide him with the means to continue that War.

He smiled, then went across to one of the side rooms and lay down on the floor. A moment later the explosion juddered the room about him. He waited a few seconds then got up and went back inside. The guardroom was a mess. Dust filled the air; machinery and bits of human flesh and bone littered the walls and floor. Where the safe had been the wall was ripped apart, while the safe itself, unharmed by the explosion, had tumbled forward and now lay there in the centre of the room, covered by debris.

He took off his tunic and wrapped it about the safe, then slowly dragged it across the floor and into the lift. He looked back into the room, then reached across and activated the lift. He had no need for the head this time

– there were no checks on who left the room, or on who used the lift to ascend. Again, that was a flaw in their thinking. He would have designed it otherwise: would have made it easier to break in, harder to get out. That way one trapped one's opponent – surrounded him. As in *wei chi*.

At the top Lehmann was waiting for him, a fresh one-piece over his arm.

'How are things?' DeVore asked, stripping off quickly and slipping into the dark green maintenance overalls.

Lehmann stared at the safe. 'The *Ping Tiao* have held their end. We've begun shipping the armaments out through the top east gate. Wiegand reports that the Security channels are buzzing with news of the attack. We should expect a counter-attack any time now.'

DeVore looked up sharply. 'Then we'd best get this out quick, neh?'

'I've four men waiting outside, and another two holding the west transit lift. I've told the *Ping Tiao* it's out of order.'

'Excellent. Anything else?'

'Good news. The rioting in Braunschweig has spilled over into neighbouring *hsien*. It seems our friends were right. It's a powder keg down there.'

'Maybe...' DeVore looked thoughtful for a moment, then nodded. 'Right. Get those men in here. I want this out of here before the *Ping Tiao* find out what we've done. Then we'll blow the bridges.'

Li Yuan went at once, not waiting for the T'ang to resolve their dispute. He went out on to the broad balcony and stood there at the balustrade, looking out across the blue expanse of the Caspian towards the distant shoreline. Wei Feng's son, Wei Chan Yin, joined him there a moment later, tense with anger.

For a time neither of them spoke, then Wei Chan Yin lifted his chin. His voice was cold and clear – the voice of reason itself.

'The trouble is, Wang Sau-leyan is right. We have not adapted to the times.'

Li Yuan turned his head, looking at the older man's profile. 'Maybe so. But there are ways of saying such things.'

Wei Chan Yin relaxed slightly, then gave a small laugh. 'His manners *are* appalling, aren't they? Perhaps it has something to do with his exile as a child.'

Their eyes met and they laughed.

Li Yuan turned, facing Wei Chan Yin. Wei Feng's eldest son was thirty-six, a tall, well-built man with a high forehead and handsome features. His eyes were smiling, yet at times they could be penetrating, almost frightening in their intensity. Li Yuan had known him since birth and had always looked up to him, but now they were equals in power. Differences in age meant nothing beside their roles as future T'ang.

'What does he want, do you think?'

Wei Chan Yin's features formed into a kind of facial shrug. He stared out past Li Yuan a moment, considering things, then looked back at him.

'My father thinks he's a troublemaker.'

'But you think otherwise.'

'I think he's a clever young man. Colder, far more controlled than he appears. That display back there – I think he was play-acting.'

Li Yuan smiled. It was what he himself had been thinking. Yet it was a superb act. He had seen the outrage on the faces of his father and the older T'ang. If Wang Sau-leyan's purpose had been merely to upset them, he had succeeded marvellously. But why? What could he gain by such tactics?

'I agree. But my question remains. What does he want?'

'Change.'

Li Yuan hesitated, waiting for Wei Chan Yin to say more. But Chan Yin had finished.

'Change?' Li Yuan's laughter was an expression of disbelief. Then, with a tiny shudder of revulsion, he saw what his cousin's words implied. 'You mean...'

It was left unstated, yet Wei Chan Yin nodded. They were talking of the murder of Wang Hsien. Chan Yin's voice sank to a whisper. 'It is common knowledge that he hated his father. It would make a kind of sense if his hatred extended to all that his father held dear.'

'The Seven?'

'And Chung Kuo itself.'

Li Yuan shook his head slowly. Was it possible? If so... He swallowed, then looked away, appalled. 'Then he must never become a T'ang.'

Wei Chan Yin laughed sourly. 'Would that it were so easy, cousin. But be careful what you say. The young Wang has ears in unexpected places. Between ourselves there are no secrets, but there are some, even amongst our own, who do not understand when to speak and when to remain silent.'

Again there was no need to say more. Li Yuan understood at once who Wei Chan Yin was talking of. Hou Tung-po, the young T'ang of South America, had spent much time recently with Wang Sau-leyan on his estates.

He shivered again, as if the sunlight suddenly had no strength to warm him, then reached out and laid his hand on Wei Chan Yin's arm.

'My father was right. These are evil times. Yet we are Seven. Even if some prove weak, if the greater part remain strong...'

Wei covered Li Yuan's hand with his own. 'As you say, good cousin. But I must go. There is much to be done.'

Li Yuan smiled. 'Your father's business?'

'Of course. We are our fathers' hands, neh?'

Li Yuan watched him go, then turned back and leaned across the balustrade, staring outward. But this time his thoughts went back to the day when his father had summoned him and introduced him to the sharp-faced official, Ssu Lu Shan. That afternoon had changed his life, for it had been then that he had learned of the Great Deception, and of the Ministry that had been set up to administer it.

History had it that Pan Chao's great fleet had landed here on the shores of Astrakhan in AD 98. He had trapped the Ta Ts'in garrison between his sea forces and a second great, land-based army and, after a battle lasting three days, had set up the yellow dragon banner of the Emperor above the old town's walls. But history lied. Pan Chao had, indeed, crossed the Caspian to meet representatives of the Ta Ts'in – consuls of Trajan's mighty Roman Empire. But no vast Han army had ever landed on this desolate shore, no Han had crossed the great range of the Urals and entered Europe as conquerors. Not until the great dictator, Tsao Ch'un, had come, little more than a century past.

Li Yuan shivered, then turned away, angry with himself. Lies or not, it was the world they had inherited; it did no good to dwell upon alternatives. He had done so for a time and it had almost destroyed him. Now he had come to terms with it: had made his peace with the world of appearances. And yet sometimes – as now – the veil would slip and he would find himself wishing it would fly apart, and that he could say, just once, *This is the truth of things*. But that was impossible. Heaven itself would fall before the words could leave his lips. He stared back at the doorway, his anger finding its focus once more in the upstart, Wang Sau-leyan.

Change... Was Prince Wei right? Was it Change Wang Sau-leyan wanted? Did he hunger to set the Great Wheel turning once again – whatever the cost? If so, they must act to stop him. Because Change was impossible. Inconceivable.

Or was it?

Li Yuan hesitated. *No*, he thought, *not inconceivable. Not now. Even so, it could not be. They could not let it be. His father was right: Change was the great destroyer. The turning Wheel crushed all beneath it, indiscriminately. It had always been so. If there was a single reason for the existence of the Seven it was this – to keep the Wheel from turning.*

He turned back, making his way through, his role in things suddenly clear to him. He would be the brake, the block that kept the Wheel from turning.

At the turn DeVore stopped and flattened himself against the wall of the corridor, listening. Behind him the four men rested, taking their breath, the safe nestled in the net between them. Ahead there were noises – footsteps, the muffled sound of voices. But whose? These levels were supposed to be empty, the path to the bridge clear.

DeVore turned and pointed to a doorway to their right. Without needing to be told they crossed the space and went inside. Satisfied, DeVore went to the left, moving down the corridor quickly, silently, conscious of the voices growing louder as he approached the junction. Before the turn he stopped and slipped into a side room, then waited, his ear pressed to the door. When they had gone by, he slipped out again, taking the right-hand turn, following them.

Ping Tiao. He was certain of it. But why were they here? And what were they doing?

Ten of them. Maybe more. Unless...

There was no reason for his hunch, yet he knew, even as he had it, that he was right. They were *Ping Tiao*. But not all of them. They had taken prisoners. High-ranking Security officers, perhaps. But why? For their ransom value? Or was there some other reason?

He frowned and ran on silently, knowing that he had to get closer to them, to make sure he was right, because if they *had* taken prisoners it was something he should know. Something he could use. He had agreed with Gesell beforehand that there would be no prisoners, but Gesell wasn't to be trusted.

The bridge was up ahead, the corridor on the far side of it cleared by his men earlier. But how had they found out about it? He had told Gesell nothing. Which meant they had a man inside his organization. Or had paid someone close to him for the information. Even so, they didn't know about the safe. Only he knew about that.

They were much closer now. He could hear them clearly. Three – no, four – voices. They had slowed down as they came near the bridge, cautious now, suspicious of some kind of trap. The next turn was only twenty *ch'i* ahead. From there he would be able to see them clearly. But it was risky. If they saw him...

DeVore slowed, then stopped just before the junction, hunched down, listening again. They had paused, perhaps to send one of their number ahead of them across the bridge. He waited, then, when he heard the call come back, put his head round the corner, keeping low, where they'd not expect to see anyone.

He took it all in at a glance, then moved back sharply. Five *Ping Tiao* and eight bound prisoners. As he'd thought. They weren't in uniform, but he could tell by their moustaches and the way they tied their hair that they were officers. Such things were a sign of rank as unmistakable as the patches on the chests of their dress uniforms.

So. Gesell was taking prisoners. He would find out why, then confront the man with the fact. It would be fun to hear what excuse he would give. Meanwhile, his man on the far side of the bridge could follow them, find out where they took their captives.

He smiled and was about to turn away when he heard footsteps coming back towards him.

'Go on across!' a voice called out, closer than before. 'Quick now! I'll meet up with you later.'

DeVore took a deep breath, then drew his gun. He looked at it a moment, then slipped it back into its holster. No. He would need to be quiet. Anyway, a knife was just as effective when it came to killing a man.

He looked about him quickly, wondering whether he should hide and let the man pass, then decided against it. He was almost certain he hadn't been seen, so he would have the element of surprise.

As the footsteps came on, he flattened himself against the wall. Then, as the man turned the corner, he reached out and pulled him close, whirling him about and pinning him against his chest, his right hand going to the man's throat, the knife's blade pressed tight against the skin.

'Cry out and you're dead,' he said softly in his ear.

'Turner!' It was a whisper of surprise.

'Shen Lu Chua,' he answered quietly, tightening his grip on the Han. 'What a surprise to meet you here.'

The Ping Tiao leader swallowed painfully, but he held his head proudly, showing no sign of fear. 'What are you doing here?'

DeVore laughed softly. 'You forget who holds the knife, Shen Lu Chua. Why is Gesell taking prisoners?'

'You saw... ? Of course.'

'Well?'

'You think I'd tell you?' Shen sniffed.

'It doesn't matter. I know what Gesell intends.'

Shen's mocking laughter confirmed it. This was his idea. And Gesell knew nothing of it. Which in itself was interesting. It meant there were splits in their ranks – divisions he could capitalize upon. But why be surprised? They were human, after all.

'You know nothing...'

But DeVore had stopped listening. Hugging Shen closer he thrust the tip of the knife up through the Han's neck, into the cavern of his mouth, then let him fall. For a moment he watched Shen lie there, struggling to remove the blade, small croaking noises coming from his ruined larynx, then he stepped forward and, kneeling over the man, tugged the head back sharply, breaking his neck.

Hung Mien-lo sat at his desk in his office, the small, desk-mounted screen at his side lit with figures. Standing before him, his head bowed, was the Master of the Inner Chamber, Sun Li Hua.

'You summoned me, Chancellor Hung?'

Hung Mien-lo glanced at Sun, then continued to tap in figures on the keyboard.

'You took your time, Master Sun.'

Sun kept his head lowered. 'I am a busy man. There was much to organize for my master.'

Hung sniffed. 'And which master is that, Sun?'

Sun smiled faintly. 'The same master we both serve.'

Hung Mien-lo raised his head and stared at Sun, then laughed and, reaching across, turned the screen about so that it faced the man.

'Do you recognize these figures, Master Sun?'

Sun raised his head for the first time, studying the screen. Then he looked back at Hung, his expression unchanged. 'Those look like the household accounts, Chancellor.'

'And so they are. But they're wrong. They've been tampered with. And not just once, but consistently, from what I can make out.' He touched the pad to clear the screen, then sat back, smiling. 'Someone has been milking them of quite considerable sums these last four years.'

Sun met his gaze openly. 'And?'

Hung nodded, admiring the man's coolness. 'And there are only three men who could have done it. I've questioned the other two, and it's clear that they are innocent. Which leaves you, Master Sun. Your family has prospered greatly these past four years.'

'Are you accusing me of embezzlement, Chancellor Hung?'

Hung Mien-lo smiled. 'I am.'

Sun stared back at him a while, then laughed. 'Is that all? Why, if every official who had massaged his accounts were to be arrested, the Seven would quickly find themselves short of servants.'

'Maybe so. But you have been caught, Master Sun. I've evidence enough to have you demoted to the Net.'

Sun looked back at him, untroubled, his smile intact. He recognized the big squeeze when he saw it. 'What do you want, Chancellor? What's the real reason for this meeting?'

'You think I have an ulterior motive, is that it, Master Sun?'

There was movement in Sun's squat face, then, uninvited, he sat down, his features set in a more serious expression. 'We are realists, you and I. We know how the wind blows.'

'What do you mean?'

Sun sat back, relaxing, his face filled with sudden calculation. 'We have been fortunate, you and I. Events have moved strongly in our favour this last year. We have risen while others have fallen away. Our families are strong, our kin powerful.'

'So?'

Sun's lips were smiling now, but his eyes were still cold and sharp. 'What I mean is this. We should be allies, Hung Mien-lo. Allies, not enemies.'

Hung Mien-lo leaned towards him, his expression suddenly hard, uncompromising. 'And if I say no?'

For the first time a flicker of uncertainty crossed Sun Li Hua's face. Then, reassuring himself, he laughed. 'You would not be talking to me if you had already decided. You would have had me arrested. But that's not your purpose, is it? You want something from me.'

But Hung was glaring at him, angry now. 'Have you no ears, man? No understanding of the situation you are in?' He shook his head, astonished. 'You have dared the ultimate, Sun Li Hua. You have killed a T'ang. And even the merest whisper in some ears of your involvement would bring about your certain death.'

'You have no proof...' Sun began, then saw that what Hung had said was true. Such a thing needed no proving: it was enough that suspicion existed. And then he understood what Hung Mien-lo had been getting at – why he had raised the matter of the embezzled funds. Demotion to the Net would make him vulnerable. Would place him beyond the protection of law and kin. He stared at his hands a moment, sobered. There was nothing he could do. Hung Mien-lo held *all* the cards.

He bowed his head. 'What do you want?'

Hung Mien-lo studied Sun Li Hua a moment, savouring his victory. For some time now he had wanted to humble the man, to pull him down from his high horse. Today, forced by the Prince to act, he had taken a gamble: had wagered that what he'd guessed about Sun and the old T'ang was true. And had won. But that was only the start. The next step raised the stakes considerably. This time he gambled with his life.

Thus far his hands had been clean. Thus far others had accomplished all he had wished for, as if on his behalf. But now...

He took a deep breath, studying the man, making certain in his own mind that this was what he wanted. Then, calmly, his voice controlled, he answered Sun.

'I'll tell you what I want. I want you to kill again. I want you to kill the new T'ang, Wang Ta-hung.'

Emily Ascher's face was dark with anger, her nostrils flared, her eyes wide, glaring at Gesell. She stood face on to him, her hands on her hips, her chin tilted back challengingly.

'Go on! Confront him with it! I bet the bastard denies it!'

Gesell's chest rose and fell violently. The news of Shen's death had shaken him badly. Things had been going so well...

'You're sure?'

She made a sharp, bitter sound of disgust. 'It was his knife. The blade with the pearled handle. The one we confiscated from him when he came to see us that time.'

'I see...'

She leaned closer, her voice lowered to a whisper. 'Then you'll kill him, neh? As you said you would if he double-crossed us?'

Gesell shuddered involuntarily, then nodded. 'If it's true,' he said softly. 'But he'll deny it.'

'Then you'll know it's true.'

'Yes...' He turned and looked across to where the albino was standing, watching their exchange. 'Where is he?' he demanded, his voice raised for the first time since they had come up in the lift.

'He'll be here,' Lehmann answered coldly.

'And if he's not?' Ascher asked.

'Then we die here,' Gesell said, not looking at her, returning the albino's cold stare.

In the distance there was the stutter of small arms fire, then a muffled explosion that made the floor shudder beneath their feet. The armaments had been shipped out more than fifteen minutes back. It was time to get out. But they couldn't. Not until Turner was here.

Gesell spat then turned away, pacing up and down slowly, looking about him at the men and women gathered in the corridors nearby. 'What's keeping him?' he muttered angrily. He could see how tense his people were, how quickly they had caught his mood. Under his breath he cursed Turner. Emily was right. They should never have got into this.

Then, as he turned back, he saw him.

'Well,' he said quietly, glancing at Ascher. 'Here he is now.'

DeVore spoke briefly to the albino, then came across. 'You're ready?'

Gesell shook his head. 'Not yet. I want some answers.'

'About Shen Lu Chua?'

Gesell laughed briefly, surprised by his audacity. 'You're a cool one, Turner. What happened?'

DeVore was staring back at him, his whole manner candid, open. 'I killed him. I had to. He attacked me.'

'Why?'

'I don't know. I tried to explain to him why I was there, but he gave me no chance.'

'No...' Gesell looked at Ascher, then back at DeVore. 'I knew Shen. He wouldn't do such a thing.'

'You knew him?' DeVore laughed. 'Then I guess you knew he was smuggling out eight prisoners? Senior Security officers.'

Gesell felt Ascher touch his elbow. 'He's lying...'

DeVore shook his head. 'No. Ask your man Mach to check on it. Shen's sidekick, Yun Ch'o, has taken them to an apartment in Ottersleben. Level Thirty-four. I think you know the place.'

Gesell tensed. Maybe Turner *was* bluffing, stalling for time. But that made no sense. As he said, it was easy for Mach to check. In any case, something else was bothering him. Something Turner hadn't yet explained.

'They tell me they found the body down at One-twenty. Even if it's as you say and Shen was double-crossing us, why were *you* down there?'

He stepped back sharply as DeVore reached into his uniform jacket. But it wasn't a weapon DeVore drew from his inner pocket. It was a map. Another map. DeVore handed it across to him.

'It was too good an opportunity to miss. I knew it was down there. I'd seen it, you see. Years ago.'

Gesell looked up at him again, his mouth open with surprise. 'Bremen... Gods! It's a Security diagram of Bremen.'

'A part of it. The rest I've sent on.'

'Sent on?' He was about to ask what Turner meant when one of his messengers pushed through the crowded corridor behind him and came up to him, almost breathless. He made the man repeat the message, then whirled about, facing Turner.

'There's a problem.'

'A problem?' DeVore raised his eyebrows.

'It seems we're trapped. The last of the bridges has been blown.'

'I know. I ordered it.'

'You *what?*'

'You heard. We're not going out that way. That's what they're waiting for, don't you see? They'll have worked out what we've done and they'll be sitting there, waiting to pick us off in the side corridors on the other side of the bridge. But I'm not going to give them the opportunity. I've a craft waiting for us on the roof.' DeVore glanced at the timer inset into his wrist. 'We've less than five minutes, however, so we'd best get moving.'

Gesell glanced at the map, then looked back at DeVore, astonished, the business with Shen forgotten. 'You've transporters?'

'That's what I said. But let's go. Before they work out what we're up to.'

'But where? Where are we going?'

DeVore smiled. 'South. To the mountains.'

CHUNG KUO

Chapter 45

CONNECTIONS

Wang Sau-leyan stood before the full-length dragon mirror in his dead father's room while his brother's maids dressed him, watching his own reflection.

'You should have seen them! You wouldn't believe how offended they were!' He laughed and bared his teeth. 'It was marvellous! They're such hypocrites! Such liars and schemers! And yet they fancy themselves so clean and pure.' He turned and glanced across at the Chancellor, his mouth formed into a sneer. 'Gods, but they make me sick!'

Hung Mien-lo stood there, his head lowered. He was unusually quiet, his manner subdued, but Wang Sau-leyan barely noticed him; he was too full of his triumph in Council that afternoon. Dismissing the maids, he crossed to the table and lifted his glass, toasting himself.

'I know how they think. They're like ghosts, they travel only in straight lines. But I'm not like them. They'll have prepared themselves next time, expecting me to be rude again – to trample on their precious etiquette. They'll meet beforehand to work out a strategy to deal with my "directness". You see if they don't. But I'll wrong-foot them again. I'll be so meek, so sweet-arsed and polite they'll wonder if I've sent a double.'

He laughed. 'Yes, and all the time I'll be playing their game. Undermining them. Suggesting small changes that will require further debate. Delaying and diverting. Querying and qualifying. Until they lose patience. And then...'

He stopped, for the first time noticing how Hung Mien-lo stood there.

'What is it, Chancellor Hung?'

Hung Mien-lo kept his head lowered. 'It is your brother, Excellency. He is dead.'

'Dead? How?'

'He... killed himself. This afternoon. An hour before you returned.'

Wang Sau-leyan set the glass down on the table and sat, his head resting almost indolently against the back of the tall chair.

'How very convenient of him.'

Hung Mien-lo glanced up then quickly looked down again. 'Not only that, but Li Shai Tung's armoury at Helmstadt was attacked this afternoon. By the Ping Tiao. They took a large amount of weaponry.'

Wang Sau-leyan studied the Chancellor's folded body, his eyes narrowed. 'Good. Then I want a meeting with them.'

The Chancellor looked up sharply. 'With the Ping Tiao? But that's impossible, Chieh Hsia...'

Wang Sau-leyan stared at him coldly. 'Impossible?'

Hung's voice when it came again was smaller, more subdued than before. 'It will be... difficult. But I shall try, Chieh Hsia.'

Wang Sau-leyan leaned forward, lifting his glass again. 'Make sure you do, Hung Mien-lo, for there are others just as hungry for power as you. Not as talented perhaps but, then, what's talent when a man is dead?'

Hung Mien-lo looked up, his eyes meeting the new T'ang's momentarily, seeing the hard, cold gleam of satisfaction there, then bowed low and backed away.

Kao Chen stood in the corridor outside the temporary mortuary, his forehead pressed to the wall, his left hand supporting him. He had not thought he could be affected any longer – had thought himself inured to the worst Man could do to his fellow creatures – yet he had found the sight of the mutilated corpses deeply upsetting. The younger ones especially.

'The bastards...' he said softly. There had been no need. They could have tied them up and left them. Surely they'd got what they wanted? But to kill all their prisoners. He shuddered. It was like that other business with the hostages – Captain Sanders's young family. There had been no need to kill them, either.

He felt a second wave of nausea sweep up from the darkness inside him and clenched his teeth against the pain and anger he felt.

'Are you all right, sir?'

His sergeant, a *Hung Mao* ten years Chen's senior, stood a few paces distant, his head lowered slightly, concerned but also embarrassed by his officer's behaviour. He had been assigned to Kao Chen only ten days before and this was the first time they had been out on operations together.

'Have you seen them?'

The sergeant frowned. 'Sir?'

'The dead. Cadets, most of them. Barely out of their teens. I kept thinking of my son.'

The man nodded. 'The *Ping Tiao* are shit, sir. Scum.'

'Yes...' Chen took a breath then straightened up. 'Well... let's move on. I want to look at their dead before I report back.'

'Sir.'

Chen let his sergeant lead on, but he had seen the doubt in the man's eyes.

All of this looking at the dead was quite alien to him – no doubt his previous officers hadn't bothered with such things – but Chen knew the value of looking for oneself. It was why Tolonen had recruited Karr and himself: because they took such pains. They noticed what others overlooked. Karr particularly. And he had learned from Karr. Had been taught to see the small betraying detail – the one tiny clue that changed the whole picture of events.

'Here it is, sir.'

The sergeant came to attention outside the door, his head bowed. Chen went inside. Here things were different, more orderly, the bodies laid out in four neat rows on trestle tables. And, unlike the other place, here the bodies were whole. These men had died in action: they had not been tied up and butchered.

He went down the first of the rows, pausing here and there to pull back the covering sheets and look at a face, a hand, frowning to himself now, his sense of 'wrongness' growing with every moment. Finally, at the head of the row, he stopped beside one of the corpses, staring down at it. There was something odd – something he couldn't quite place – about the dead man.

He shook his head. No, he was imagining it. But then, as he made to move on, he realized what it was. The hair. He went closer and lifted the head between his hands, studying it. Yes, there was no doubt about it, the dead man's hair was cut like a soldier's. Quickly he went down the row, checking the other corpses. Most of them had normal short hair – styles typical of the lower levels – but there were five with the same military-style cut, the hair trimmed back almost brutally behind the ear and at the line of the nape.

'Sergeant!'

The man appeared at the doorway at once.

'Bring me a comset. A unit with a visual connection.'

'Sir!'

While he waited he went down the line again, studying the men he had picked out. Now that he looked he saw other differences. Their nails were manicured, their hands smooth, uncalloused. They were all *Hung Mao*, of course, but of a certain kind. They all had those grey-blue eyes and chiselled features that were so typical of the men recruited by Security. Yes, the more he looked at them, the more he could imagine them in uniform. But was he right? And, if so, what did it mean? Had the *Ping Tiao* begun recruiting such types, or was it something more ominous than that?

The sergeant returned, handing him the comset, then stood there, watching, as Chen drew back the eyelid of the corpse with his thumb and held the machine's lens over the eye, relaying an ID query through to Central Records.

He had his answer almost immediately. There were six 'likelies' that approximated to the retinal print, but only one of the full body descriptions fitted the dead man. It was as Chen had thought: he was ex-Security.

Chen went down the line, making queries on the others he had picked out. The story was the same: all five had served in the Security forces at some point. And not one of them had been seen for several years. Which meant that either they had been down in the Net or they had been outside. But what did it signify? Chen pressed to store the individual file numbers, then put the comset down and leaned against one of the trestles, thinking.

'What is it, sir?'

Chen looked up. 'Oh, it's nothing, after all. I thought I recognized the man, but I was mistaken. Anyway, we're done here. Have the men finish up then report to me by four. The General will want a full report before the day's out.'

'Sir!'

Alone again, Chen walked slowly down the rows, taking one last look at each of the five men. Like the other dead, they wore the Ping Tiao symbol – a stylized fish – about their necks and were dressed in simple Ping Tiao clothes. But these were no common terrorists.

Which was why he had lied to the sergeant. Because if this was what he thought it was he could trust no one.

No. He would keep it strictly to himself for the time being, and in the meantime he would find out all he could about the dead men: discover where they had been stationed and who they had served under.

As if he didn't already know. As if he couldn't guess which name would surface when he looked at their files.

Nan Ho, Li Yuan's Master of the Inner Chamber, climbed down from the sedan and, returning the bow of the Grand Master of the Palace, mounted the ancient stone steps that led up to the entrance of the summer palace.

At the top he paused and turned, looking back across the ruins of the old town of Ch'ing Tao. Beyond it the bay of Chiao Chou was a deep cobalt blue, the grey-green misted shape of Lao Shan rising spectacularly from the sea, climbing three li into the heavens. A thousand li to the east was Korea and beyond it the uninhabitable islands of Japan.

It was a year since he had last visited this place – a year and two days, to be precise – but from where he stood, nothing had changed. For his girls, however, that year had been long and difficult: a year of exile from Tongjiang and the Prince they loved.

He sighed and turned back, following the Grand Master through. This was the smallest of the T'ang's summer palaces and had lain unused since his great-grandfather's days. It was kept on now only out of long habit, the staff of fifty-six servants undisturbed by the needs of their masters.

Such a shame, he thought as he made his way through the pleasantly shaded corridors into the interior. Yet he understood why. There was danger here. It was too open; too hard to defend from attack. Whereas Tongjiang...

He laughed. The very idea of attacking Tongjiang!

The Grand Master slowed and turned, bowing low. 'Is anything the matter, Master Nan?'

'Nothing,' Nan Ho answered, returning the bow. 'I was merely thinking of the last time I was here. Of the crickets in the garden.'

'Ah...' The Grand Master's eyes glazed over, the lids closed momentarily, then he turned back, shuffling slowly on.

The two girls were waiting in the Great Conservatory, kneeling on the tiles beside the pool, their heads bowed.

He dismissed the Grand Master, waiting until he had left before he hurried across and pulled the two girls up, holding one in each arm, hugging them tightly to him, forgetting the gulf in rank that lay between them.

'My darlings!' he said breathlessly, his heart full. 'My pretty ones! How have you been?'

Pearl Heart answered for them both.

'Oh, Master Nan... it's so good to see you! We've been so lonely here!'

He sighed deeply. 'Hush, my kittens. Hush now, stop your crying. I've news for you. Good news. You're leaving this place. Two weeks from now.'

They looked up at him, joy in their faces, then quickly averted their eyes again. Yes, they had changed, he could see that at once. What had the Grand Master done to them to make them thus? Had he been cruel? Had there been worse things that that? He would find out. And if the old man had misbehaved he would have his skin for it.

Sweet Rose looked up at him hopefully. 'Li Yuan has asked for our return?'

He felt his heart wrenched from him that he had to disappoint her.

'No, my little one,' he said, stroking her arm. 'But he wishes to see you.' *One last time*, he thought, completing the sentence in his head. 'And he has a gift for you both. A special gift...' He shivered. 'But he must tell you that. I come only as a messenger, to help prepare you.'

Pearl Heart was looking down again. 'Then she will not have us,' she said quietly.

He squeezed her to him. 'It would not be right. You know that. It was what we spoke of last time we were here together.'

He remembered the occasion only too well. How he had brought them here in the dark of night, and how they had wept when he had explained to them why they must not see their beloved Prince again. He swallowed, thinking of that time. It had been hard for Li Yuan, too. And admirable in a strange way. For there had been no need, no custom to fulfil. He recalled arguing with Li Yuan – querying his word to the point where the Prince had grown angry with him. Then he had shrugged and gone off to do as he was bid. But it was not normal. He still felt that deeply. A man – a prince, especially – needed the company of women. And to deny oneself for a whole year, merely because of an impending wedding! He shook his head. Well, it was like marrying one's dead brother's wife: it was unheard of.

And yet Li Yuan had insisted. He would be 'pure' for Fei Yen. As if a year's abstinence could make a man pure! Didn't the blood still flow, the sap still rise? He loved his master dearly, but he could not lie to himself and say Li Yuan was right.

He looked down into the girls' faces, seeing the disappointment there. A year had not cured *them* of their love. No, and neither would a lifetime, if it were truly known. Only a fool thought otherwise. Yet Li Yuan was Prince and his word was final. And though he was foolish in this regard, at least he was not cruel. The gift he planned to give them – the gift Nan Ho had said he could not speak of – was to be their freedom. More than that, the two sisters were to be given a dowry, a handsome sum – enough to see them well married, assured the luxuries of First Level.

No, it wasn't cruel. But, then, neither was it kind.

Nan Ho shook his head and smiled. 'Still... let us go through. We'll have some wine and make ourselves more comfortable,' he said, holding them tighter against him momentarily. 'And then you can tell me all about the wicked Grand Master and how he tried to have his way with you.'

Chuang Lian, wife of Minister Chuang, lay amongst the silken pillows of her bed, fanning herself indolently, watching the young officer out of half-lidded eyes as he walked about her room, stopping to lift and study a tiny statue, or to gaze out at the garden. The pale cream sleeping robe she wore had fallen open, revealing her tiny breasts, yet she acted as if she were unaware, enjoying the way his eyes kept returning to her.

She was forty-five – forty-six in little over a month – and was proud of her breasts. She had heard how other women's breasts sagged, either from neglect or from the odious task of child-bearing, but she had been lucky. Her husband was a rich man – a powerful man – and had hired wet-nurses to raise his offspring. And she had kept her health and her figure. Each morning, after exercising, she would study herself in the mirror and thank Kuan Yin for blessing her with the one thing that, in this world of Men, gave a woman power over them.

She had been beautiful. In her own eyes she was beautiful still. But her husband was an old man now and she was still a woman, with a woman's needs. Who, then, could blame her if she took a lover to fill the idle days with a little joy? So it was for a woman in her position, married to a man thirty years her senior; yet there was still the need to be discreet – to find the right man for her bed. A young and virile man, certainly, but also a man of breeding, of quality. And what better than this young officer?

He turned, looking directly at her, and smiled. 'Where is the Minister today?'

Chuang Lian averted her eyes, her fan pausing in its slow rhythm, then starting up again, its measure suddenly erratic, as if indicative of some inner disturbance. It was an old game, and she enjoyed the pretence; yet there was no mistaking the way her pulse quickened when he looked at her like that. Such a predatory look it was. And his eyes – so blue they were. When he looked at her it was as if the sky itself gazed down at her through those eyes. She shivered. He was so different from her husband. So alive. So strong. Not the smallest sign of weakness in him.

She glanced up at him again. 'Chuang Ming is at his office. Where else would he be at this hour?'

'I thought perhaps he would be here. If I were him...'

His eyes finished the sentence for him. She saw how he looked at her breasts, the pale flesh of her thighs, showing between the folds of silk, and felt a tiny shiver down her spine. He wanted her. She knew that now. But it would not do to let him have her straight away. The game must be played out – that was half its delight.

She eased up on to her elbows, putting her fan aside, then reached up to touch the single orchid in her hair. 'Chuang Ming is a proper *Lao Kuan*, a "Great Official". But in bed...' She laughed softly, and turned her eyes on him again. 'Well, let us say he is *hsiao jen*, neh? A little man.'

When he laughed he showed his teeth. Such strong, white, perfect teeth. But her eyes had been drawn lower than his face, wondering.

He came closer, then sat on the foot of the bed, his hand resting gently on her ankle. 'And you are tired of little men?'

For a moment she stared at his hand where it rested against her flesh, transfixed by his touch, then looked up at him again, her breath catching unexpectedly in her throat. This was not how she had planned it.

'I...'

But his warm laughter, the small movements of his fingers against her foot, distracted her. After a moment she let herself laugh, then leaned forward, covering his hand with her own. So small and delicate it seemed against his, the dark olive of her flesh a stark contrast to his whiteness.

She laced her fingers through his, meeting his eyes. 'I have a present for you.'

'A present?'

'A first-meeting gift.'

He laughed. 'But we have met often, *Fu Jen* Chuang.'

'Lian...' she said softly, hating the formality of his 'Madam', even if his eyes revealed he was teasing her. 'You must call me Lian here.'

Unexpectedly he drew her closer, his right hand curled gently but firmly about her neck, then leaned forward, kissing her brow, her nose. 'As you wish, my little lotus...'

Her eyes looked up at him, wide, for one brief moment afraid of him – of the power in him – then she looked away, laughing, covering her momentary slip; hoping he had not seen through, into her.

'Sweet Flute!' she called lightly, looking past him, then looking back at him, smiling again. 'Bring the *ch'un tzu's* present.'

She placed her hand lightly against his chest, then stood up, moving past him but letting her hand brush against his hair then rest upon his shoulder, maintaining the contact between them, feeling a tiny inner thrill when he placed his hand against the small of her back.

Sweet Flute was her *mui tsai*, a pretty young thing of fifteen her husband had bought Chuang Lian for her last birthday. She approached them now demurely, her head lowered, the gift held out before her.

She felt the young officer shift on the bed behind her, clearly interested in what she had bought him, then, dismissing the girl, she turned and faced him, kneeling to offer him the gift, her head bowed.

His smile revealed his pleasure at her subservient attitude. Then, with the smallest bow of his head, he began to unwrap the present. He let the bright red wrapping fall, then looked up at her. 'What is it?'

'Well, it's not one of the Five Classics...'

She sat beside him on the bed and opened the first page, then looked up into his face, seeing at once how pleased he was.

'Gods...' he said quietly, then laughed. A soft, yet wicked laugh. 'What is this?'

She leaned into him, kissing his neck softly, then whispered in his ear. 'It's the Chin P'ing Mei, the Golden Lotus. I thought you might like it.'

She saw how his finger traced the outlines of the ancient illustration, pausing where the two bodies met in that most intimate of embraces. Then he turned his head slowly and looked at her.

'And I brought you nothing...'

'No,' she said, closing the book, then drawing him down beside her, her gown falling open. 'You're wrong, Hans Ebert. You brought me yourself.'

The eighth bell was sounding as they gathered in Nocenzi's office at the top of Bremen fortress. Besides Nocenzi, there were thirteen members of the General Staff, every man ranking captain or above. Ebert had been among the first to arrive, tipped off by his captain, Auden, that something was afoot.

Nocenzi was grim-faced. The meeting convened, he came swiftly to the point.

'Ch'un tzu, I have brought you here at short notice because this evening, at or around six, a number of senior Company Heads – twenty-six in all – were assassinated, for no apparent reason that we can yet make out.'

There was a low murmur of surprise. Nocenzi nodded sombrely, then continued.

'I've placed a strict media embargo on the news for forty-eight hours, to try to give us a little time, but we all know how impossible it is to check the passage of rumour, and the violent death of so many prominent and respected members of the trading community will be noticed. Moreover, coming so closely upon the attack on Helmstadt Armoury, we are concerned that the news should not further destabilize an already potentially explosive situation. I don't have to tell you, therefore, how urgent it is that we discover both the reason for these murders and the identity of those who perpetrated them.'

One of the men seated at the front of the room, nearest Nocenzi, raised his hand.

'Yes, Captain Scott?'

'Forgive me, sir, but how do we know these murders are connected?'

'We don't. In fact, one of the mysteries is that they're all so very different – their victims seemingly unconnected in any way whatsoever. But the very fact that twenty-six separate assassinations took place within the space of ten minutes on or around the hour points very clearly to a very tight orchestration of events.'

Another hand went up. Nocenzi turned, facing the questioner. 'Yes, Major Hoffmann?'

'Could this be a Triad operation? There have been rumours for some time that some of the big bosses have been wanting to expand their operations into the higher levels.'

'That's so. But no. At least, I don't think so. Immediate word has it that the big gang bosses are as surprised as we are by this. Two of the incidents involved small Triad-like gangs – splinter elements, possibly trying to make a name for themselves – but we've yet to discover whether they were working on their own or in the pay of others.'

Ebert raised his hand, interested despite himself in this new development. He would much rather have still been between the legs of the Minister's wife, but if duty called, what better than this?

'Yes, Major Ebert?'

'Is there any discernible pattern in these killings? I mean, were they all *Hung Mao*, for instance, or were the killings perhaps limited to a particular part of the City?'

Nocenzi smiled tightly. 'That's the most disturbing thing about this affair. You see, the victims are mixed. Han and *Hung Mao*. Young and old. And the locations, as you see...' he indicated the map that had come up on the screen behind him '...are scattered almost randomly. It makes one think that the choice of victims may have been random. Designed, perhaps, to create the maximum impact on the Above. Simply to create an atmosphere of fear.'

'*Ping Tiao*?' Ebert asked, expressing what they had all been thinking. Before the attack on Helmstadt it would have been unthinkable – a laughable conclusion – but now...

'No.'

Nocenzi's certainty surprised them all.

'At least, if it is *Ping Tiao*, then they're slow at claiming it. And in all previous *Ping Tiao* attacks, they've always left their calling cards.'

That was true. The *Ping Tiao* were fairly scrupulous about leaving their mark – the sign of the fish – on all their victims.

'There are a number of possibilities here,' Nocenzi continued, 'and I want to assign each of you to investigate some aspect of this matter. Is this Triad infiltration? Is it the beginning of some kind of violent trade war? Is it, in any respect, a continuation of Dispersionist activity? Is it pure terrorist activity? Or is it – however unlikely – pure coincidence?'

Captain Russ laughed, but Nocenzi shook his head. 'No, it's not entirely impossible. Unlikely, yes, even improbable, but not impossible. A large number of the murders had possible motives. Gambling debts, company feuds, adultery. And however unlikely it seems, we've got to investigate the possibility.'

Ebert raised his hand again. 'Who'll be co-ordinating this, sir?'

'You want the job, Hans?'

There was a ripple of good-humoured laughter, Ebert's own amongst it. Nocenzi smiled. 'Then it's yours.'

Ebert bowed his head, pleased to be given the chance to take on something as big as this at last. 'Thank you, sir.'

Nocenzi was about to speak again when the doors at the far end of the room swung open and Marshal Tolonen strode into the room. As one the officers stood and came to sharp attention, their heads bowed.

'*Ch'un tzu!*' Tolonen said, throwing his uniform cap down on to the desk and turning to face them, peeling off his gloves as he did so. 'Please, be seated.'

Nocenzi moved to one side as the Marshal stepped forward.

'I've just come from the T'ang. He has been apprised of the situation and has given orders that we are to make this matter our first priority over the coming days.' He tapped his wrist, indicating the tiny screen set into his flesh. 'I have been listening in to your meeting and am pleased to see that you understand the seriousness of the situation. However, if we're to crack this one we've got to act quickly. That's why I've decided to overrule General Nocenzi and assign each of you two of the murder victims.'

Hoffmann raised his hand. 'Why the change, sir?'

'Because if there's any pattern behind things, it ought to be discernible by looking at the facts of two very different murders. And with thirteen of you looking at the matter, we ought to come up with *something* pretty quickly, don't you think?'

Hoffmann bowed his head.

'Good. And, Hans... I appreciate your keenness. It's no less than I'd expect from you. But I'm afraid I'll have to tie your hands somewhat on this one. That's not to say you won't be Co-ordinator, but I want you to work closely with me on this. The T'ang wants answers and I've promised him that he'll have them before the week's out. So don't let me down.'

Ebert met the Marshal's eyes and bowed his head, accepting the old man's decision, but inside he was deeply disappointed. So he was to be tied to the old man's apron strings yet again! He took a deep breath, calming himself, then smiled, remembering suddenly how Chuang Lian had taken his penis between her tiny, delicate toes and caressed it, as if she were holding it in her hands. Such a neat little trick. And then there was her *mui tsai*... what was her name...? Sweet Flute. Ah, yes, how he'd like to play that one!

He raised his eyes and looked across at Tolonen as General Nocenzi began to allocate the case files. Maybe the Marshal would be 'in command' nominally, but that was not to say he would be running things. Russ, Scott, Fest, Auden – these were *his* men. He had only to say to them...

The thought made him smile. And Tolonen, glancing across at him at that moment, saw his smile and returned it strongly.

It was well after ten when Chen arrived back at the apartment. Wang Ti and the children were in bed, asleep. He looked in on them, smiling broadly as he saw how all four of them were crowded into the same bed, the two-year-old, Ch'iang Hsin, cuddled against Wang Ti's chest, her hair covering her plump little face, the two boys to her right, young Wu pressed close against his elder brother's back.

He stood there a moment, moved, as he always was, by the sight of them, then went back through to the kitchen and made himself a small *chung* of *ch'a*.

It had been a long day, but there was still much to do before he could rest. He carried the porcelain *chung* through to the living-room and set it down on the table, then moved the lamp close, adjusting its glow so that it illuminated only a tight circle about the steaming bowl. He looked about him a moment, frowning, then went across to the shelves, searching until he found the old lacquered box he kept his brushes and ink block in.

He set the box down beside the *chung*, then went out into the hall and retrieved the files from the narrow table by the door, beneath his tunic.

He paused, then went back and hung his tunic on the peg, smiling, knowing Wang Ti would only scold him in the morning if he forgot.

Switching off the main light, he went back to the table and pulled up a chair. Setting the files down to his right, he sat back a moment, yawning, stretching his arms out to the sides, feeling weary. He gave a soft laugh then leaned forward again, reaching for the *chung*. Lifting the lid, he took a long sip of the hot *ch'a*.

'Hmm... that's good,' he said quietly, nodding to himself. It was one of Karr's. A gift he had brought with him last time he had come to dinner. *Well, my friend*, he thought; *now I've a gift for you.*

He reached across and drew the box closer, unfastening the two tiny catches, then flipped the lid back.

'Damn it...' he said, making to get up, realizing he had forgotten water to mix the ink, then reached for the *chung* again and dipped his finger, using the hot *ch'a* as a substitute. He had heard tell that the great poet, Li Po, had used wine to mix his ink, so why not *ch'a*? Particularly one as fine as this.

He smiled, then, wiping his finger on his sleeve, reached across and drew the first of the files closer.

Today he had called in all the favours owed him; had pestered friend and acquaintance alike until he'd got what he wanted. And here they were. Personnel files. Income statements. Training records. Complete files on each of the six men who had died at Helmstadt. The so-called *Ping Tiao* he had checked up on. Their files and two others.

He had gone down to Central Records, the nerve-centre of Security Personnel at Bremen. There, in Personnel Queries, he had called upon Wolfgang Lautner. Lautner, one of the four senior officers in charge of the department, was an old friend. They had been in officer training together and had been promoted to captain within a month of each other. Several times in the past Chen had helped Lautner out, mainly in the matter of gambling debts.

Lautner had been only too happy to help Chen, giving him full access to whatever files he wanted – even to several that were, strictly speaking, 'off limits'. All had gone smoothly until Chen, checking up on a person-nel number that had appeared on several of the files, came up against a computer block.

He could see it even now, the words pulsing red against the black of the screen.

INFORMATION DENIED. LEVEL-A CODE REQUIRED.

Not knowing what else to do, he had taken his query direct to Lautner. Had sat there beside him in his office as he keyed in the Level-A code. He remembered how Lautner had looked at him, smiling, his eyebrows raised inquisitively, before he had turned to face the screen.

'Shit...' Lautner had jerked forward, clearing the screen, then had turned abruptly, looking at Chen angrily, his whole manner changed completely. 'What in fuck's name are you doing, Kao Chen?'

'I didn't know...' Chen had begun, as surprised as his friend by the face that had come up on the screen, but Lautner had cut him off sharply.

'Didn't know? You expect me to believe that? Kuan Yin preserve us! He's the last bastard I want to find out I've been tapping into his file. He'd have our balls!'

Chen swallowed, remembering. Yes, he could still feel Ebert's spittle on his cheek, burning there like a badge of shame. And there, suddenly, he was, a face on a screen, a personnel coding on the files of three dead ex-Security men. It was too much of a coincidence.

Chen drew the *chung* closer, comforted by its warmth against his hands. He could still recall what Ebert had said to him, that time when they had raided the Overseer's House – the time young Pavel had died. Could remem-ber vividly how Ebert had stood there, looking towards the west where Lodz Garrison was burning in the darkness, and said how much he admired DeVore.

Yes, it all made sense now. But the knowledge had cost him Lautner's friendship.

He lifted the lid from the *chung* and drank deeply, as if to wash away the bitter taste that had risen to his mouth.

If he was right, then Ebert was DeVore's inside man. It would certainly explain how the Ping Tiao had got into Helmstadt Armoury and stripped it of a billion yuan's worth of equipment. But he had to prove that, and prove it conclusively. As yet it was mere coincidence.

He began working through the files again, checking the details exhaustively, page by page, looking for something – anything – that might point him in the right direction.

He had almost finished when he heard a movement on the far side of the room. He looked up and saw young Wu in the darkness of the doorway. Smiling, he got up and went across, lifting the five-year-old and hugging him to his chest.

'Can't you sleep, Kao Wu?'

Wu snuggled into his father's shoulder. 'I want a drink,' he said sleepily, his eyes already closed.

'Come... I'll make you one.'

He carried him through, dimming the kitchen light. Then, one-handed, he took a mug from the rack and squeezed a bulb of juice into it.

'Here...' he said, holding it to the child's lips.

Wu took two sips, then snuggled down again. In a moment he was asleep again, his breathing regular, relaxed.

Chen set the mug down, smiling. The warm weight of his son against his shoulder was a pleasant, deeply reassuring sensation. He went back out, into the hallway, and looked across to where he had been working. The files lay at the edge of the circle of light, face down beside the empty chung.

It was no good; he would have to go back. He had hoped to avoid it, but it was the only way. He would have to risk making direct enquiries on Ebert's file.

He looked down, beginning to understand the danger he was in. And not just himself. If Ebert were DeVore's man, then none of them was safe. Not here, nor anywhere. Not if Ebert discovered what he was doing. And yet, what choice was there? To do nothing? To forget his humiliation and his silent vow of vengeance? No. Even so, it made him heavy of heart to think, even for a moment, of losing all of this. He shivered, holding Kao Wu closer, his hand gently stroking the sleeping boy's neck.

And what if Lautner had taken steps to cover himself? What if he had already gone to Ebert?

No. Knowing Lautner he would do nothing. And he would assume that Chen would do nothing, too. Would gamble on him not taking any further risks.

Achh, thought Chen bitterly; *you really didn't know me, did you?*

He took Wu through to his bed and tucked him in, then he went through to the other bedroom. Wang Ti was awake, looking back at him, Ch'iang Hsin's tiny figure cuddled in against her side.

'It's late, Chen,' she said softly. 'You should get some sleep.'

He smiled. 'I should, but there's something I have to do.'

'At this hour?'

He nodded. 'Trust me. I'll be all right.'

Something about the way he said it made her get up on to one elbow. 'What is it, Chen? What are you up to?'

He hesitated, then shook his head. 'It's nothing. Really, Wang Ti. Now go to sleep. I'll be back before morning.'

She narrowed her eyes, then, yawning, settled down again. 'All right, my husband. But take care, neh?'

He smiled, watching her a moment longer, filled with the warmth of his love for her, then turned away, suddenly determined.

It was time to make connections. To find out whether Ebert really was in DeVore's pay.

Outside it was dark, the evening chill, but in the stables at Tongjiang it was warm in the glow of the lanterns. The scents of hay and animal sweat were strong in the long, high-ceilinged barn, the soft snorting of the animals in their stalls the only sound to disturb the evening's silence. Li Yuan stood in the end stall, feeding the Arab from his hand.

'Excellency...'

Li Yuan turned, smiling, at ease here with his beloved horses. 'Ah... Master Nan. How did it go? Are my girls well?'

Nan Ho had pulled a cloak about his shoulders before venturing outdoors. Even so, he was hunched into himself, shivering from the cold.

'They are well, my lord. I have arranged everything as you requested.'

Li Yuan studied him a moment, conscious of the hesitation. 'Good.' He looked back at the horse, smiling, reaching up to smooth its broad, black face, his fingers combing the fine dark hair. 'It would be best, perhaps, if we kept this discreet, Master Nan. I would not like the Lady Fei to be troubled. You understand?'

He looked back at Nan Ho. 'Perhaps when she's out riding, neh?'

'Of course, my lord.'

'And, Nan Ho...'

'Yes, my lord?'

'I know what you think. You find me unfeeling in this matter. Unnatural, even. But it isn't so. I love Fei Yen. You understand that?' Li Yuan bent and took another handful of barley from the sack beside him, then offered it to the Arab, who nibbled contentedly at it. 'And if that's unnatural, then this too is unnatural...'

He looked down at his hand, the horse's muzzle pressed close to his palm, warm and moist, then laughed. 'You know, my father has always argued that good horsemanship is like good government. And good government like a good marriage. What do you think, Nan Ho?'

Master Nan laughed. 'What would I know of that, my lord? I am but a tiny part of the great harness of State. A mere stirrup.'

'So much?' Li Yuan wiped his hand on his trouser leg, then laughed heartily. 'No, I jest with you, Master Nan. You are a whole saddle in yourself. And do not forget I said it.' He grew quieter. 'I am not ungrateful. Never think that, Master Nan. The day will come...'

Nan Ho bowed low. 'My lord...'

When he had gone, Li Yuan went outside, into the chill evening air, and stood there, staring up into the blackness overhead. The moon was low and bright and cold. A pale crescent, like an eyelid on the darkness.

And then?

The two words came to him, strong and clear, like two flares in the darkness. Nonsense words. And yet, somehow, significant. But what did they mean? Unaccountably, he found himself filled with sudden doubts. He thought of what he had said to Nan Ho of horsemanship and wondered if it were really so. Could one master one's emotions as one controlled a horse? Was it that easy? He loved Fei Yen – he was certain of it – but he also loved Pearl Heart and her sister, Sweet Rose. *Could* he simply shut out what he felt for them as if it had never been?

He walked to the bridge and stood there, holding the rail tightly, suddenly, absurdly obsessed with the words that had come unbidden to him. *And then?*

He shivered. *And then what?* He gritted his teeth against the pain he suddenly felt. 'No!' he said sharply, his breath pluming out from him. No. He would not succumb. He would ride out the pain he felt. Would deny that part of him. For Fei Yen. Because he loved her. Because...

The moon was an eyelid on the darkness. And if he closed his eyes he could see it, dark against the brightness inside his head.

But the pain remained. And then he knew. He missed them. Missed them terribly. He had never admitted it before, but now he knew. It was as if he had killed part of himself to have Fei Yen.

He shuddered, then pushed back, away from the rail, angry with himself. 'You are a prince. A *prince!*'

But it made no difference. The pain remained. Sharp, bitter, like the image of the moon against his inner lid, dark against the brightness there.

Chen sat there, hunched over the screen, his pulse racing as he waited to see whether the access code would take.

Thus far it had been easy. He had simply logged that he was investigating illicit Triad connections. A junior officer had shown him to the screen then left him there, unsupervised. After all, it was late, and hardly anyone used the facilities of Personnel Enquiries at that hour. Chen was almost the only figure in the great wheel of desks that stretched out from the central podium.

The screen filled. Ebert's face stared out at him a moment, life-size, then shrank to a quarter-size, relocating at the top right of the screen. Chen gave a small sigh of relief. It worked!

The file began: page after page of detailed service records.

Chen scrolled through, surprised to find how highly Ebert was rated by his superiors. Did he know what they thought of him? Had he had access to this file? Knowing Ebert, it was likely. Even so, there was nothing sinister here. Nothing to link him to DeVore. No, if anything, it was exemplary. Maybe it was simple coincidence, then, that Ebert had served with three of the dead men. But Chen's instinct ruled that out. He scrolled to the end of the file, then keyed for access to Ebert's accounts.

A few minutes later he sat back, shaking his head. Nothing. Sighing, he keyed to look at the last of the sub-files: Ebert's expenses. He flicked through quickly, noting nothing unusual, then stopped.

Of course! It was an *expenses* account. Which meant that all the payments on it ought to be irregular. So what was this monthly payment doing on it? The amount differed, but the date was the same each month. The fifteenth. It wasn't a bar invoice, for those were met from Ebert's other account. And there was a number noted against each payment. A Security Forces service number, unless he was mistaken.

Chen scrolled back, checking he'd not been mistaken, then jotted the number down. Yes, here it was, the link. He closed the file and sat back, looking across at the central desk. It was quiet over there. Good. Then he would make this one last query.

He keyed the service number, then tapped in the access code. For a moment the screen was blank and Chen wondered if it would come up as before – INFORMATION DENIED. LEVEL-A CODE REQUIRED. But then a face appeared.

Chen stared at it a moment, then frowned. For some reason he had expected to recognize it, but it was just a face, like any other young officer's face; smooth-shaven and handsome in its strange, *Hung Mao* fashion.

For a time he looked through the file, but there was nothing there. Only that Ebert had worked with the man some years before – in Tolonen's office, when they were both cadets. Then why the payments? Again he almost missed it: was slow to recognize what was staring him in the face, there on the very first page of the file. It was a number. The reference coding of the senior officer the young cadet had reported to while he had been stationed in Bremen ten years earlier. Chen drew in his breath sharply.

DeVore!

He shut the screen down and stood, feeling almost light-headed now that he had made the connection. *I've got you now, Hans Ebert, he thought. Yes, and I'll make you pay for your insult.*

Chen picked up his papers and returned them to his pocket, then looked across at the central desk again, remembering how his friend Lautner had reacted – the sourness of that moment tainting his triumph. Then, swallowing his bitterness, he shook his head. So it was in this world. It was no use expecting otherwise.

He smiled grimly, unconsciously wiping at his cheek, then turned and began to make his way back through the web of gangways to the exit.

Yes, he thought. *I've got you now, you bastard. I'll pin your balls to the fucking floor for what you've done. But first you, Axel Haavikko. First you.*

Chapter 46

THICK FACE, BLACK HEART

DeVore stood there on the mountainside, the lifeless bodies of the two alpine foxes dangling from leather thongs at his back, their fur smeared with blood. In his left hand he held the crossbow he had killed them with, in his right the two blood-caked bolts he had pulled from their flesh.

It was an hour after dawn and the mountains below him were wreathed in mist. He was high up where he stood, well above the snow-line. To his left, below him, the mountainside was densely wooded, the tall pines covering most of the lower slopes, stretching down into the mist. He laughed, enjoying the freshness of the morning, his breath pluming away from him. Surely there was no better sight in the world than the alps in high summer? He looked about him, then, slipping the bolts into the deep pocket of his furs, began to make his way down, heading for the ruins of the castle.

He was halfway down when he stopped, suddenly alert. There had been movement down below, among the ruins. He moved quickly to his right, his hand reaching for one of the bolts, hurriedly placing it into the stock and winding the handle.

He scrambled behind some low rocks and knelt, the crossbow aimed at the slopes below. His heart was beating fast. No one was meant to be out here at this hour. Even his own patrols...

He tensed. A figure had come out and now stood there, one hand up to its eyes, searching the mountainside. A tall, thin figure, its angular frame strangely familiar. Then it turned, looking up the slope, its predatory gaze coming to rest on the rocks behind which DeVore was crouching.

Lehmann... DeVore lowered the crossbow and stood, then went down the slope, stopping some ten, fifteen *ch'i* from the albino, the crossbow held loosely in his left hand.

'Stefan! What in the gods' names are you doing here?'

Lehmann looked past him a moment, then looked back, meeting his eyes. 'Our friends are getting restless. They wondered where you were.'

DeVore laughed. 'They're up already?' He moved closer, handing the foxes over to the albino. 'Here... hold these for me.'

Lehmann took them, barely glancing at the dead animals. 'I wondered where you went to in the mornings. It's beautiful, neh?'

DeVore turned, surprised, but if he hoped to find some expression of wonder in the albino's face, he was disappointed. Those pale pink eyes stared out coldly at the slopes, the distant peaks, as if beauty were merely a form of words, as meaningless as the rest.

'Yes,' he answered. 'It is. And never more so than at this hour. Sometimes it makes me feel like I'm the last man. The very last. It's a good feeling, that. A pure, clean feeling.'

Lehmann nodded. 'We'd best get back.'

DeVore laughed coldly. 'Let them wait a little longer. It'll do that bastard Gesell good.'

Lehmann was silent a moment, his cold eyes watching the slow, sweeping movements of a circling eagle, high up above one of the nearer peaks. For a while he seemed lost in the sight, then he turned his head and stared at DeVore penetratingly. 'I thought he was going to kill you over that Shen Lu Chua business.'

DeVore looked back at him, surprised. 'Did you?' He seemed to consider it a moment then shook his head. 'No. Gesell's far too cautious. You know the Han saying, *p'eng che luan tzu kuo ch'iao?*'

Lehmann shook his head.

DeVore laughed. 'Well, let's just say he's the kind of man who holds on to his testicles when crossing a bridge.'

'Ah...'

DeVore studied the albino a moment, wondering what it would take to penetrate that cold exterior and force a smile, a grimace of anger, a tear.

He looked down. Perhaps nothing. Perhaps he *was* as empty of emotions as he seemed. But that could not be. He was human, after all. There had to be something he wanted. Something that kept him from simply throwing himself from the cliff on to the rocks below.

But what?

DeVore smiled faintly, detaching himself from the problem, and looked up to find Lehmann still staring at him. He let his smile broaden, as if to make connection with something behind – far back from – the unsmiling surface of that unnaturally pallid face.

Then, shaking his head, he turned, making his way across to the tower and the tunnels beneath.

The *Ping Tiao* leaders were waiting in the conference room, the great window wall giving a clear view of the slopes. Outside the light was crisp and clear, but a layer of mist covered the upper slopes. Even so, the view was impressive. One had a sense of great walls of rock climbing the sky.

DeVore stood in the doorway a moment, looking in. Six of them were gathered in the far left corner of the room, seated about the end of the great table, as far from the window as they could. He smiled, then turned, looking across. Only one of them was standing by the window, looking out. It was the woman – Gesell's lover – Emily Ascher.

He went in.

Noticing him, two of the men made to stand, but Gesell reached out to either side, touching their arms. They sat back, looking warily between Gesell and DeVore.

'Turner...' Gesell greeted DeVore bluntly, his whole manner suddenly alert, businesslike.

'Gesell...' He gave the slightest nod of acknowledgment, then went to the window, staring outward, as if unconscious of the woman standing at his side. Then he turned back, smiling. 'So?'

While he'd been gone, his lieutenant, Wiegand, had shown them around the base, letting them see the mask – the surface installation – while giving no hint of the labyrinth of tunnels that lay beneath.

Gesell glanced at Mach, then looked back, a faint sneer on his lips. 'You want me to say I'm impressed – is that it, *Shih* Turner?'

'Did I say that?'

Gesell leaned forward, lacing his fingers together. 'No. But you're very much a product of your level. And your level likes to impress all those beneath it with the grandeur of their works.'

'That's true enough. And are you impressed? Are my works grand enough for you?'

DeVore kept his words light yet challenging, concealing his distaste for the man. Arrogant little bastard. He thought he knew everything. He was useful just now, admittedly – a key to things. But once he'd unlocked a few doors he could be discarded.

He waited for Gesell to respond, but it was Mach who answered him.

'It's very pretty, Shih Turner, but what's it all for? The enemy is in there, in the City, not out here in the Wilds. I don't see the point of building something like this.'

DeVore stared back at Mach, then nodded. *How astute of you*, he thought. *How clever to penetrate so far with just one look. But you haven't seen it all. You haven't seen the great hangars, the missile silos, the training halls. And because you haven't you've no idea what this really is. To you this seems a mere shadow of Bremen – a great fortress designed with only one thought in mind: to protect itself against attack. But this is different. My aim is not to defend my position here but to attack my opponents. To cut their lines and penetrate their territory.*

'So you think all this a waste of time?'

He saw how Mach looked at Gesell, then lowered his head slightly, letting Gesell take charge again. That concession was further confirmation of what he already suspected. The ideas, the very words the *Ping Tiao* used – these belonged to Mach. But it was Gesell who held the power. Gesell to whom Mach deferred when his words had to be turned into actions.

Gesell leaned forward. 'Wasteful, yes. But not a total waste. You seem beyond the reach of the Seven here, and that's good. And I've seen how your men fight. They're well trained, well disciplined. In that respect we could learn from you.'

DeVore hid his surprise at Gesell's candidness. 'But?'

Gesell laughed and looked about him. 'Well, look at this place! It's so cut off from the realities of what's going on. So *isolated*. I mean, how can you know what's happening – what's *really* happening in the levels – when you're so far from it all?'

DeVore was smiling. 'Is that what you think?'

He clicked his fingers. At once a panel slid back overhead and a bank of screens lowered itself into the room: screens that showed scenes from a dozen different levels of the City. Turning back, DeVore saw how impressed they were despite themselves.

'What do you want to see?' he asked. 'Where would you like to go in the City? My cameras are everywhere. My eyes and ears. Watching and listening and reporting back. Taking the pulse of things.'

As he spoke the images changed, moving from location to location, until, when he clicked his fingers a second time, they froze, all twelve screens showing the same image.

'But that's Shen Lu Chua's man, Yun Ch'o...' Gesell began, recognizing the figure below the camera.

'It's Ottersleben,' said Mach quietly. 'Level Thirty-Four. He must have taken this earlier.'

DeVore studied them; saw how Mach looked down, as if considering what this meant, then looked back up again, watching as a dozen images of himself led a dozen *Ping Tiao* assault squads in the raid on their comrade Yun Ch'o's apartment. Beside him, Gesell was leaning right forward, fascinated by the unfolding action. He saw the brief fight; saw Yun Ch'o fall, mortally wounded, then watched as the eight hostages – the eight Security officers DeVore had told them would be there – were led out into the corridor. When it was over Gesell looked back at DeVore, smiling tightly.

'That was clever of you, Turner. A nice trick. But it doesn't mean much *really*, does it?'

'Like the T'ang's ear, you mean, or the map of Helmstadt?' DeVore laughed, then moved closer. 'You're a hard man to convince, *Shih* Gesell. What must I do to satisfy you?'

Gesell's features hardened. 'Show me the other maps. The maps of Bremen.'

'And in return?'

But before Gesell could answer, the woman, Ascher, interrupted him.

'You're talking deals here, but it's still a mystery to me, *Shih* Turner. If you're so powerful, if you can do so much, then why do you need us? This base you've had built, the raid on Helmstadt, the killing of Wang Hsien – any one of these things is far beyond anything we could do. So why us?'

Gesell was glaring at her angrily. DeVore studied the *Ping Tiao* leader a moment, then half turned, looking back at the woman.

'Because what I can do is limited.'

She laughed coldly, staring back at him, her dislike unconcealed. 'Limited by what?'

'By funding. By opportunity.'

'And we have those?'

'No. But you have something much more valuable. Your organization has potential. Vast potential. All this – everything I've patiently built over the last eight years – is, as *Shih* Mach so rightly identified, inflexible. Your organization is different. It's a kind of organism, capable of vast growth. But to achieve that you need to create the best climate for that growth. What we did yesterday was a beginning. It raised your public profile while giving you considerable firepower. Both things strengthened you considerably. Without me, however, you would have had neither.'

Gesell interrupted. 'You're wrong. You needed us.'

DeVore turned back. 'Not at all. I could have taken Helmstadt on my own. You've seen my men, *Shih* Gesell. You've even remarked on how good their training and discipline is. Well, I've a thousand more where they came from. And a thousand beyond them. No, I asked you to join me yesterday because such a relationship as we must forge has to be reciprocal. There has to be give and take. I gave you Helmstadt. As, in time, I'll give you Bremen. But you must give me something back. Not a great thing. I'd not ask that of you yet. But some small thing to cement our partnership. Some favour I might find it difficult to undertake myself.'

'A small thing?' Gesell was staring at him suspiciously.

'Yes. I want you to kill someone for me. A child.'

'A child?'

DeVore clicked his fingers. The images on the screens changed; showed a dozen separate portraits of an adolescent girl, her ash-blonde, shoulder-length hair loose in some shots, tied in plaits in others. Her straight-boned, slender figure was caught in a dozen different poses: dressed casually as if at home; or elegantly in the latest First Level fashions.

'But that's...'

'Yes,' DeVore said, looking up at the screens. 'It's Jelka Tolonen. Marshal Tolonen's daughter.'

Jelka had just finished her exercises when her father entered the exercise hall. Her instructor, Siang Che, seeing him, bowed then backed away, busying himself at the far end of the gym.

She turned, hearing a different tread, then laughed, her young face breaking into a great beam of a smile. 'Daddy! You're back early!' She ran across, reaching up to hug him to her. 'What's up? I didn't expect you until the weekend.'

'No,' he said, smiling down at her, lowering his head to kiss her brow. 'I'd almost forgotten...'

'Forgotten?'

Tolonen put one hand on her shoulder. 'Not here. Let's go through. I'll talk to you once you've changed, neh?'

He stood there, looking about her room while she showered. It was not a typical young girl's room. Not by any means. In a box in one corner were flails and batons, practice swords, chucks and staffs, while to its side, high up on the wall, was a brightly coloured painting of Mu-Lan, the famous warrior heroine, dressed in full military armour, her expression fierce as she took up a defensive pose. Old maps and charts covered the front of the built-in wardrobes to the left, while to the right most of the wall space was filled with Jelka's own hand-drawn designs – machines and weaponry, their ugly purpose disguised somehow by the sleek elegance of her pen.

An old armchair to one side displayed a touch of luxury, heaped as it was with colourful silk cushions, but her bed was spartan, a simple dark blue sheet covering it. Beside it, beneath a half-length mirror, was her study desk, a *wei chi* board set up to the right, books and papers stacked neatly on the left at the back. He went across and looked, interested to see what she was reading.

At the very front of the table, face down beside her comset, was a copy of Sun Tzu's *The Art Of War*, the *Ping Fa*. He picked it up and read the passage she had underlined:

If not in the interests of the state, do not act. If you cannot succeed, do not use troops. If you are not in danger, do not fight.

He smiled. Ten thousand books had been written on the subject since Sun Tzu first wrote his treatise two thousand five hundred years before and not one had come as close to capturing the essence of armed struggle as the *Ping Fa*. He set the book down again, then studied the *wei chi* board a moment, noting how a great spur of black stones cut between two areas of white territory, separating them. There were other books piled up on the desk – the *San Kuo Yan Yi*, the *Romance Of The Three Kingdoms*, Tseng Kung-liang's *Wu Ching Tsung Yao*, his *Essentials of the Martial Classics*, and the *Meng Ke* amongst them – but what took the Marshal's interest was a small, floppy, orange-covered volume tucked away at the back of the desk. He reached across and pulled it from the pile.

It was an ancient thing, the cover curling at the edges, the paper within yellowed badly. But that was not what had caught his eye. It was the words on the cover. Or, rather, one word in particular. *China.*

He stared at the cover for a time, frowning. He had not heard that term – not seen it in print – in more than forty years. China. The name Chung Kuo, the Middle Kingdom, had had before Tsao Ch'un. Or at least the name it had been called in the West. He leafed through it, reading at random, then closed it, his pulse racing. Islam and Communism. America and Russia. Soviets and Imperialists. These were lost terms. Terms from another age. A forgotten, forbidden age. He stared at the cover a moment longer, then nodded to himself, knowing what he must do.

He turned, hearing her in the next room, singing softly to herself as she dressed, then forced himself to relax, letting the anger, the tension drain from him. It was a mistake, almost certainly. Even so, he would find out who had given this to her and make them pay.

'Well?' she asked, standing in the doorway, smiling across at him. 'Tell me, then. What is it?'

She saw how he looked down at the book in his hands.

'In a moment. First, where did you get this?'

'That? It was on your shelves. Why, shouldn't I have borrowed it?'

'My shelves?'

'Yes. It was in that box of things you had delivered here three weeks ago. My *amah*, Lu Cao, unpacked it and put it all away. Didn't you notice?'

'She shouldn't have,' he began irritably. 'They were things General Nocenzi had sent on to me. Things we'd unearthed during the Confiscations. Special things...'

'I'm sorry, Father. I'll tell her. But she wasn't to know.'

'No...' He softened, then laughed, relieved that it was only that. 'Did you read any of it?'

'Some.' She smiled, looking inside herself a moment. 'But it was odd. It presented itself as a factual account, but it read more like a fiction. The facts were all wrong. Almost all of it. And that map at the front...'

'Yes...' He weighed the book in his hand a moment, then looked up at her again. 'Well, I guess no harm's done. But listen. This is a forbidden book. If anyone were to find you had read even the smallest part of it...' He shook his head. 'Well, you understand?'

She bowed her head. 'As you wish, Father.'

'Good. Then this other matter...' He hesitated, then gave a short laugh. 'Well, you know how long Klaus Ebert and I have been friends. How close our families have always been.'

She laughed. '*Shih* Ebert has been like an uncle to me.'

Her father's smile broadened momentarily. 'Yes. But I've long wished for something more than that. Some stronger, more intimate bond between our families.'

'More intimate...' She stared at him, not understanding.

'Yes,' he said, looking back at her fondly. 'It has long been my dream that you would one day wed my old friend's son.'

'Hans? Hans Ebert?' Her eyes were narrowed now, watching him.

'Yes.' He looked away, smiling. 'But it's more than a dream. You see, Klaus Ebert and I came to an arrangement.'

She felt herself go cold. 'An arrangement?'

'Yes. Klaus was very generous. Your dowry is considerable.'

She laughed nervously. 'I don't understand. Dowry? What dowry?'

He smiled. 'I'm sorry. I should have spoken to you about all this before, but I've not had time. Things were so busy, and then, suddenly, the day was upon me.'

The coldness melted away as a wave of anger washed over her. She shook her head defiantly. 'But you can't...'

'I can,' he said. 'In fact, there's no question about it, Jelka. It was all arranged, ten years back.'

'Ten years?' She shook her head, astonished. 'But I was four...'

'I know. But these things must be done. It is our way. And they must be done early. Hans is heir to a vast financial empire, after all. It would not do to have uncertainty over such matters. The markets...'

She looked down, his words washing over her unheard, her breath catching in her throat. Her father had sold her – sold her to his best friend's son. Oh, she'd heard of it. Indeed, several of her schoolfriends had been engaged in this manner. But this was herself.

She looked up at him again, searching his eyes for some sign that he understood how she felt, but there was nothing, only his determination to fulfil his dream of linking the two families.

Her voice was soft, reproachful. 'Daddy... how could you?'

He laughed, but his laughter now was hard, and his words, when they came, held a slight trace of annoyance.

'How could I what?'

Sell me, she thought, but could not bring herself to say the words. She swallowed and bowed her head. 'You should have told me.'

'I know. But I thought... well, I thought you would be pleased. After all, Hans is a handsome young man. More than half the girls in the Above are in love with him. And you... well, you alone will be his wife. The wife of a general. The wife of a Company head. And not just any Company, but GenSyn.'

It was true. She ought to be pleased. Her friends at school would be jealous of her. Green with envy. But somehow the thought of that palled in comparison with the enormity of what her father had done. He had not asked her. In this, the most important thing she would ever do, he had not taken her feelings into consideration. Would he have done that if her mother had been alive?

She shivered, then looked up at him again.

'So I *must* marry him?'

He nodded tersely, his face stern. 'It is arranged.'

She stared back at him a moment, surprised by the hard edge to his voice, then bowed her head. 'Very well. Then I shall do as you ask.'

'Good.' He smiled tightly, then glanced down at the timer at his wrist. 'You'd best call your *amah*, then, and have her dress you. It's after eleven now and I said we'd be there by one.'

She stared at him, astonished. 'This afternoon?'

He looked back at her, frowning, as if surprised by her question. 'Of course. Now hurry, my love. Hurry, or we'll be late.'

Jelka hesitated, watching him a moment longer – seeing how he looked down at the book in his hand as if it were a mystery he needed to resolve

– then she turned and went through into the other room, looking for Lu Cao.

'Well, what is it?'

Auden took Ebert to one side, out of earshot of the two guards. 'I think we may have stumbled on to something.'

Ebert smiled. 'What kind of thing?'

'A link. A possible explanation for what happened the other night?'

Ebert's smile broadened. 'How good a link? Good enough to make me late for an appointment with the Minister's wife?'

Auden returned the smile. 'I think so.'

They went inside. The prisoner was a Han. A young man in his late twenties. He was well dressed and neatly groomed, but sweating profusely.

'Who is this?' Ebert asked, as if the man had no existence, no identity other than that which he or Auden gave him.

'He's a close relative of one of the murdered men. The victim was a merchant, Lu Tung. This is his third cousin, Lu Wang-pei. It seems he depended on Lu Tung for funds. To repay gambling debts and the like.'

Lu Wang-pei had bowed his head at the mention of his name, but neither of the officers paid him the slightest attention. His eyes followed them as they moved about the room, but otherwise he was perfectly still. In this he had no choice, for he was bound tightly to the chair.

Ebert looked about him at the sparsely furnished room. 'So what have you found?'

'Forensic evidence shows that the bomb was hidden inside a package – a present delivered to Lu Tung's apartments only minutes before the explosion. It seems that our man here delivered that package.'

'I see. So in this case we have our murderer?'

'Yes and no. Wang-Pei had no idea what it was he was delivering. That's not to say he wasn't culpable in some small degree, because he did agree to deliver it.'

'For someone else?'

Auden smiled. 'That's right. For three men. Business rivals of Lu Tung's, so they claimed. It seems they bought up our friend's gambling debts, then offered to wipe the slate clean if he'd do a little favour for them.'

'The package.'

'Exactly. They told him they wanted to frighten his uncle. To shake him up a little.'

Ebert laughed. 'Well... And so they did!'

'Yes,' Auden looked down momentarily. 'And there it would end, were it not for the fact that Wang-Pei here didn't trust his new friends. He secreted a camera on him when he went to make his collection. Here...'

He handed the flat 3-D image to Ebert, then watched as his initial puzzlement changed into a smile of enlightenment. 'DeVore...'

Auden nodded. 'Yes. But it was the two at the front Wang-Pei dealt with. They did all the talking.'

'And who are they?'

'One's an ex-Security man. Max Wiegand. A good man, it seems. He had an excellent service record.'

'And the other?'

'We couldn't get a trace on him. But look at the pallor of his skin. He looks albinic. If so he might be wearing contact lenses to disguise the colour of his eyes.'

'Hmm...' Ebert handed back the flat. 'And what does our man here know?'

'Nothing much. I think he's telling the truth. I've checked on the gambling debts. I'd guess it happened exactly as he told us.'

Ebert nodded, then turned, looking directly at the Han for the first time since he'd entered the room. 'All right. Leave him with me a moment. I'll see whether we can find out anything more.'

When Auden had gone, he went across and stood there directly in front of the Han, looking down at him contemptuously.

'As far as I'm concerned, *Shih Lu*, I couldn't care a shit if you Han butchered one another until the corridors ran red. If that was all that was at stake here I'd let you go. But it's not. You made a mistake. A fortunate mistake for me. But for you...'

He lashed out viciously, catching the Han across the nose. Wang-Pei drew his head back, groaning, his eyes wide with shock. Blood ran freely from his nose.

'Tell me the truth. What's your connection to these men? When did you first start working for them?'

Wang-Pei made to shake his head, but Ebert hit him again: a stinging blow across the ear that made him cry out, his face distorted with pain.

'I never saw them before...' he began. 'It's as I said...'

The third blow knocked him backwards, the chair tilting out from under him. Ebert followed through at once, kicking him once, twice, in the stomach. Hard, vicious kicks that made the Han double up, gasping.

'You know nothing, neh? Nothing! You fuck-head! You pissing fuck-head chink! Of course you know nothing!'

He kicked again, lower this time. The Han began to vomit. Ebert turned away, disgusted. Of course he knew nothing. DeVore was not that stupid. But he *had* slipped up this time. He should have kept out of it. Should have let his two henchmen do all the front work.

The door beside him opened.

'Are you all right... ?'

He looked across at Auden, smiling. 'I'm fine. But this one's dead.'

Auden stared back at him a moment, then nodded. 'And the guards?'

Ebert looked back at the Han, his smile broadening. 'They saw nothing. Okay? You deal with them, Will. I'll recompense you.'

The Han lay there, wheezing for breath, his frightened eyes staring up at them imploringly.

Auden nodded. 'All right. But why? After all, we have the link.'

'Yes. And we're going to keep it, understand me? I *want* DeVore. I want to nail him. But I want it to be me. *Me.* Understand? Not some other bastard.'

Auden looked down, his expression thoughtful. 'I see.'

'Good. Then I'll leave you to tidy things up. I've kept the Minister's wife waiting far too long already.'

Chen was waiting for Haavikko when he came out of the Officers' Mess. He hung back, careful not to let the young *Hung Mao* see him even though he could see that he was the worse for drink. He smiled bitterly. Yes, that was in the file, too, along with all the brawling, the whoring, the gambling and all the other derelictions of duty. But that was as nothing beside the fact of his treason. Chen felt a shiver of anger ripple through him and let his hand rest momentarily on the handle of his knife. Well, he would cut a confession from him if he had to, piece by tiny piece. Because if Haavikko was behind the butchery at Helmstadt...

He stopped, moving in to the side. Up ahead of him Haavikko had paused, leaning against the wall unsteadily, as if about to be sick. But when a fellow officer approached him, he turned quickly, his movements exaggerated by drunkenness, letting out a string of obscenities. The officer put his hands out before him in apology, backing away, then turned and walked off, shaking his head.

Chen felt the bile rise again. Haavikko was a disgrace. To think what he might have become. He shook his head, then began to move again, keeping the man in sight.

Twenty levels down he watched as Haavikko fumbled with the combination to his door, then slumped against the wall, making three attempts at it before he matched his eye to the indented pad. Then Chen was moving quickly, running the last few *ch'i* as the door began to iris closed.

Haavikko swung round, his bleary eyes half-lidded, his jacket already discarded, as Chen came through into the room.

'What the fuck... ?'

Chen had drawn his knife. A big knife with a wickedly curved blade that glinted razor-sharp in the overhead lights. 'Haavikko? Axel Haavikko?'

He saw the flicker of fear in the young man's eyes as he staggered back and almost fell against the bed.

'Wha... what d'you want?' The words were slurred, almost incoherent.

'I think you know...' Chen began, moving closer. But suddenly Haavikko was no longer awkward, his movements no longer slow and clumsy. Chen found himself thrown backward by the man's charge, the knife knocked from his hand by a stinging blow. But before Haavikko could follow up, Chen had rolled aside and jumped to his feet again, his body crouched in a defensive posture.

Haavikko was facing him, crouched, his eyes wide, watching Chen's every movement, all pretence at drunkenness peeled from him. He swayed gently, as if about to attack, but it was clear to Chen that that was not Haavikko's intention. He was waiting for Chen to go for his knife, which lay just behind him by the door. It was what he himself would have done. Chen gave the slightest nod, suddenly respectful of the man's abilities. No one, not even Karr, had ever been fast enough to knock his knife from his hand.

'Well?' Haavikko said, clearly this time, the word formed like a drop of acid. 'What do you want?'

Chen lifted his chin in challenge. 'I'll tell you what I want. I want answers.'

Haavikko laughed bitterly. 'Answers? What do you mean?' But there was a slight hesitation in his eyes, the slightest trace of fear.

'I think you know more than you're letting on. I think you've done one or two things you're ashamed of. Things that aren't even on your file.'

Chen saw how he blanched at that, how the skin about his eyes tightened.

'Who sent you? Was it Liu Chang?'

'Liu Chang? Who's that?'

Haavikko snorted in disgust. 'You know damned well who I mean. Liu Chang, the brothel keeper. From the Western Isle. Did he send you? Or was it someone else?'

Chen shook his head. 'You've got me wrong, Lieutenant. I'm a soldier, not a pimp's runner. You forget where we are. This is Bremen. How would a pimp's runner get in here?'

Haavikko shook his head. 'I'd credit him with anything. He's devious enough, don't you think?'

Who? he wondered, but said, 'It's Chen... Captain Kao Chen.'

Haavikko laughed sourly, then shook his head. 'Since when did they make a Han captain?'

Slowly Chen's hand went to his jacket.

'Try anything and I'll break your neck.'

Chen looked back at him, meeting his eyes coldly, his fingers continuing to search his pocket, emerging a moment later with his pass. He threw it across to Haavikko, who caught it deftly, his eyes never leaving Chen's face.

'Back off... Two paces.'

Chen moved back, glancing about him at the room. It was bare, undecorated. A bed, a wardrobe, a single chair. A picture of a girl in a frame on the tiny bedside table. Haavikko's uniform tunic hung loosely on the door of the wardrobe where he had thrown it.

Haavikko looked at the pass, turned it in his hand, then threw it back at Chen, a new look – puzzlement, maybe curiosity – in his eyes.

Chen pocketed the pass. 'You're in trouble, aren't you, Haavikko? Out of your depth.'

'I don't know what you mean.'

'Oh, I think you do. Your friends have dumped you in it this time. Left you to carry the can.'

Haavikko laughed scathingly. 'Friends? I've no friends, Captain Kao. If you've read my file, you'll know that much about me.'

'Maybe. And maybe that's just another pose – like the pretence of drunkenness you put on for me earlier.'

Haavikko breathed deeply, unevenly. 'I saw you earlier, when I went into the mess. When you were still there when I came out, I knew you were following me.'

'Who were you meeting?

'I wasn't meeting anyone. I went in there to find something out.'

Chen narrowed his eyes. 'You weren't meeting Fest, then? I note he entered the mess just before you. You used to serve with him, didn't you?'

Haavikko was silent a moment, then he shook his head. 'I wasn't meeting Fest. But, yes, I served with him. Under General Tolonen.'

'And under Major DeVore, too.'

'I was ensign to DeVore for a month, yes.'

'At the time of Minister Lwo's assassination.'

'That's so.'

Chen shook his head. 'Am I to believe this crap?'

Haavikko's lips formed a sneer. 'Believe what you like, but I wasn't meeting Fest. If you must know, I went in there to try to overhear what he was saying.'

'Are you blackmailing him?'

Haavikko bristled. 'Look, what *do* you want? Who are you working for, Captain Kao?'

Chen met the challenge in his eyes momentarily, then looked about the room again. Something had been nagging at him. Something he didn't realize until he noticed the lieutenant's patch on the tunic hanging from the cupboard door. Of course! Haavikko had been the same rank these last eight years. But why? After all, if he *was* working for Ebert...

Chen looked back at Haavikko, shaking his head, then laughed quietly.

Haavikko had tensed, his eyes narrowed, suspicious. 'What is it?'

But Chen was laughing strongly now, his whole manner suddenly different. He sat down on the bed, looking up at Haavikko. 'It's just that I got you wrong. Completely wrong.' He shook his head. 'I thought you were working for Ebert.'

'Ebert! That bastard!' Then realisation dawned on Haavikko. 'Then...' He gave a short laugh. 'Gods! And I thought...'

The two men stared at each other a moment, their relief – their sudden understanding – clouded by the shadow of Ebert.

'What did he do?' Chen asked, getting up, his face serious, his eyes filled with sympathy. 'What did he do to you, Axel Haavikko, to make you destroy yourself so thoroughly?'

Haavikko looked down, then met Chen's eyes again. 'It's not in the file, then?'

Chen shook his head.

'No. I guess it wouldn't be. He'd see to that, wouldn't he?' He was quiet a moment, staring at Chen sympathetically. 'And you, Kao Chen? What did he do to make you hate him so?'

Chen smiled tightly. 'Oh, it was a small thing. A matter of face.' But he was thinking of his friend, Pavel, and of his death in the attack on the Overseer's House. That too he set down against Hans Ebert.

'Well... What now, Kao Chen? Do we go our own ways, or is our hatred of him strong enough to bind us?'

Chen hesitated, then smiled and nodded. 'Let it be so.'

The rest of the Ping Tiao leaders had gone straight to the cruiser, clearly unnerved at being out in the open, but the woman, Ascher, held back, stopping at the rail to look out across the open mountainside. DeVore studied her a moment, then joined her at the rail.

'The mountains. They're so different...'

He turned his head, looking at her. She had such finely chiselled features, all excess pared from them. He smiled, liking what he saw. There was nothing gross, nothing soft about her: the austere, almost sculpted beauty of her was accentuated by the neat cut of her fine, jet-black hair, the trimness of her small, well-muscled body. Such a strong, lithe creature she was, and so sharp of mind. It was a pity. She was wasted on Gesell.

'In what way different?'

She continued staring outward, as if unaware of his gaze. 'I don't know.

Harder, I suppose. Cruder. Much more powerful and untamed than they seem on the screen. They're like living things...'

'They're real, that's why.'

'Yes...' She turned her head slightly, her breath curling up in the cold air.

He inclined his head towards the cruiser. 'And you... you're different, too. You're real. Not like them. This, for instance. Something in you responds to it. You're like me in that. It touches you.'

Her eyes hardened marginally, then she looked away again. 'You're wrong. We've nothing in common, *Shih* Turner. Not even this. We see it through different eyes. We want different things. Even from this.' She shivered, then looked back at him. 'You're a different kind of creature from me. You served *them*, remember? I could never do that. Could never compromise myself like that, whatever the end.'

'You think so?'

'I know.'

He smiled. 'Have it your way. But remember this when you go away from here, Emily Ascher. I know you. I can see through you, like ice.'

She held his gaze a moment longer, proudly, defiantly, then looked back at the mountains, a faint smile on her lips. 'You see only mirrors. Reflections of yourself in everything. But that's how your kind think. You can't help it. You think the world's shaped as you see it. But there's a whole dimension you're blind to.'

'Love, you mean? Human understanding? Goodness?' He laughed, then shook his head. 'Those things don't exist. Not really. They're illusions. Masks over the reality. And the reality is like these peaks – it's beautiful, but it's also hard, uncompromising and cold, like the airless spaces between the stars.'

She was silent a moment, as if thinking about what he had said. Then she turned back to him. 'I must go. But thank you for letting me see this.'

DeVore smiled. 'Come again. Any time you want. I'll send my cruiser for you.'

She studied him a moment, then turned away, the smallest sign of amusement in her face. He watched her climb the steps and go inside. Moments later he heard the big engines of the cruiser start up.

He turned and looked across towards the snow-buried blister of the dome. Lehmann was standing by the entrance, bare-headed, a tall, gaunt figure even in his bulky furs. DeVore made his way across, while behind him the big craft lifted from the hangar and turned slowly, facing the north.

'What is it?'

'Success,' Lehmann answered tonelessly. 'We've found the combination.'

He let his hand rest on Lehmann's arm momentarily, turning to watch the cruiser rise slowly into the blue, then turned back, smiling, nodding to himself. 'Good. Then let's go and see what we've got.'

Minutes later he stood before the open safe, staring down at the contents spread out on the floor at his feet. There had been three compartments to the safe. The top one had held more than two hundred bearer credits – small 'chips' of ice worth between fifty and two hundred thousand *yuan* apiece. A second, smaller compartment in the centre had contained several items of jewellery. The last – making up the bulk of the safe's volume – had held a small collection of art treasures: scrolls and seals and ancient pottery.

DeVore bent down and picked up one of the pieces, studying it a moment. Then he turned and handed it to Lehmann. It was a tiny, exquisitely sculpted figure of a horse. A white horse with a cobalt-blue saddle and trappings, and a light brown mane and tail.

'Why this?' Lehmann asked, looking back at him.

DeVore took the piece back, examining it again, then looked up at Lehmann. 'How old would you say this is?'

Lehmann stared back at him. 'I know *what* it is. It's T'ang dynasty – fifteen hundred years old. But that isn't what I meant. Why was it there, in the safe? What were they doing with it? I thought only the Families had things like this these days.'

DeVore smiled. 'Security has to deal with all sorts. What's currency in the Above isn't always so below. Certain Triad bosses prefer something more... *substantial*, shall we say, than money.'

Lehmann shook his head. 'Again, that's not what I meant. The bearer credits – they were payroll, right? Unofficial expenses for the eight garrisons surrounding the Wilds.'

DeVore's smile slowly faded. Then he gave a short laugh. 'How did you know?'

'It makes sense. Security has to undertake any number of things which they'd rather weren't public knowledge. Such things are costly precisely because they're so secretive. What better way of financing them than by allocating funds for non-existent weaponry, then switching those funds into bearer credits?'

DeVore nodded. That was exactly how it worked.

'The jewellery likewise. It was probably taken during the Confiscations. I should imagine it was set aside by the order of someone fairly high up – Nocenzi, say – so it wouldn't appear on the official listings. Officially it never existed, so no one has to account for it. Even so, it's real and can be sold. Again, that would finance a great deal of secret activity. But the horse...'

DeVore smiled, for once surprised by the young man's sharpness. The bearer credits and jewellery: those were worth, at best, two billion *yuan* on the black market. That was sufficient to keep things going for a year at present levels. In the long term, however, it was woefully inadequate. He needed four, maybe five times as much simply to complete the network of fortresses. In this respect the horse and the two other figures – the tiny moon-faced buddha and the white jade carving of Kuan Yin – were like gifts from the gods. Each one was worth as much as – and potentially a great deal more than – the rest of the contents of the safe combined.

But Lehmann was right. What *were* they doing there? What had made Li Shai Tung give up three such priceless treasures? What deals was he planning to make that required so lavish a payment?

He met the albino's eyes and smiled. 'I don't know, Stefan. Not yet.'

He set the horse down and picked up the delicate jade-skinned goddess, turning it in his hands. It was perfect. The gentle flow of her robes, the serene expression of her face, the gentle way she held the child to her breast: each tiny element was masterful in itself.

'What will you do with them?'

'I'll sell them. Two of them, anyway.'

Yes, he thought, *Old Man Lever will find me a buyer. Someone who cares more for this than for the wealth it represents.*

'And the other?'

DeVore looked down at the tiny, sculpted goddess. 'This one I'll keep. For now, anyway. Until I find a better use for her.'

He set it down again, beside the horse, then smiled. Both figures were so realistic, so perfect in every detail, that it seemed momentarily as if it needed only a word of his to bring them both to life. He breathed deeply, then nodded to himself. It was no accident that he had come upon these things; neither was it instinct alone that made him hold on to the goddess now. No, there was a force behind it all, giving shape to events, pushing like a dark wind at the back of everything. *As in his dreams...*

He looked up at Lehmann and saw how he was watching him.

And what would you make of that, my ultra-rational friend? Or you, Emily Ascher, with your one-dimensional view of me? Would you think I'd grown soft? Would you think it a weakness in me? If so, you would be wrong. For that's my strength: that sense of being driven by the darkness.

At its purest – in those few, rare moments when the veil was lifted and he saw things clearly – he felt all human things fall from him; all feeling, all sense of self erased momentarily by that dark and silent pressure at the back of him. At such moments he was like a stone – a pure white stone – set down upon the board, a mere counter, played by some being greater than himself in a game the scale of which his tiny, human mind could scarcely comprehend.

A game of dark and light. Of suns and moons. Of space and time itself. A game so vast, so complicated...

He looked down, moved deeply by the thought: by the cold, crystalline-pure abstraction of such a vast and universal game.

'Are you all right?'

Lehmann's voice lacked all sympathy; it was the voice of mechanical response.

DeVore smiled, conscious of how far his thoughts had drifted from this room, this one specific place and time. 'Forgive me, Stefan. I was thinking...'

'Yes?'

He looked up. 'I want you to track the woman for me. To find out what you can about her. Find out if it's true what they say about her and Gesell.'

'And?'

He looked down at the jade-skinned goddess once again. 'And nothing. Just do it for me.'

She kept her silence until they were back in Gesell's apartment. There, alone with him at last, she turned on him angrily, all of her pent-up frustration spilling out.

'What in the gods' names are we doing working with that bastard?'

He laughed uncomfortably, taken aback by her outburst. 'It makes good sense,' he began, trying to be reasonable, but she cut him off angrily.

'*Sense?* It's insane, that's what it is! The surest way possible of cutting our own throats! All that shit he was feeding us about his inflexibility and our potential for growth. That's nonsense! He's *using* us! Can't you see that?'

He glared back at her, stiff-faced. 'You think I don't know what he is? Sure, he's trying to use us, but we can benefit from that. And what he said is far from nonsense. It's the truth, Em. You saw his set-up. He *needs* us.'

She shook her head slowly, as if disappointed in him. 'For a time, maybe. But as soon as he's wrung every advantage he can get from us, he'll discard us. He'll crunch us up in one hand and throw us aside. As for his "weakness" – his "inflexibility" – we saw only what he wanted us to see. I'd stake my life that there's more to that base than meets the eye. Much more. All that "openness" he fed us was just so much crap. A mask, like everything else about our friend.'

Gesell took a long breath. 'I'm not so sure. But even if it is, we can still benefit from an alliance with him. All the better, perhaps, for knowing what he is. We'll be on our guard.'

She laughed sourly. 'You're naive, Bent Gesell, that's what you are. You think you can ride the tiger.'

He bridled and made to snap back at her, then checked himself, shaking his head. 'No, Em. I'm a *realist*. Realist enough to know that we can't keep on the way we've been going these last few years. You talk of cutting our own throats... well, there's no more certain way of doing that than by ignoring the opportunity to work with someone like Turner. Take the raid on Helmstadt, for instance. Dammit, Emily, but he was *right*! When would we *ever* have got the opportunity to attack a place like Helmstadt?'

'We'd have done it. Given time.'

He laughed dismissively. 'Given time...'

'No, Bent, you're wrong. Worse than that, you're impatient, and your impatience clouds your judgment. There's more at issue here than whether we grow as a movement or not. There's the question of what *kind* of movement we are. You can lie to yourself all you want, but working with someone like Turner makes us no better than him. No better than the Seven.'

He snorted. 'That's nonsense and you know it! What compromises have we had to make? None! Nor will we. You forget – if there's something we don't want to do, we simply won't do it.'

'Like killing Jelka Tolonen, for instance?'

He shook his head irritably. 'That makes good sense and you know it.'

'*Why?* I thought it was our stated policy only to target those who are guilty of corruption or gross injustice?'

'And so it is. What is Tolonen if not the very symbol of the system we're fighting against.'

'But his *daughter*...?'

He waved her objection aside. 'It's a war, Emily. Us or them. And if working with Turner gives us a bit more muscle, then I'm all for it. That's not to say we have to go along with everything he wants. Far from it. But as long as it serves our cause, what harm is there in that?'

'What *harm*...?'

'Besides, if you felt so strongly about this, why didn't you raise the matter in council when you had the chance. Why have it out with me? The decision was unanimous, after all.'

She laughed sourly. '*Was* it? As I recall, we didn't even have a vote. That aside, I could see what the rest of you were thinking – even Mach. I could see the way all of your eyes lit up at the thought of attacking Helmstadt. At the thought of getting your hands on all those armaments.'

'And now we have them. Surely that speaks for itself? And Turner was right about the publicity, too. Recruitment will be no problem after this. They'll flock to us in droves.'

'You miss my point...'

She would have said more, would have pursued the matter, but at that moment there was an urgent knocking on the door. A moment later Mach came into the room. He stopped, looking from one to the other, sensing the tension in the air, then turned to face Gesell, his voice low and urgent.

'I have to speak to you, Bent. Something's come up. Something strange. It's...' He glanced at Emily. 'Well, come. I'll show you.'

She saw the way they excluded her and felt her stomach tighten with anger. The *Ping Tiao* was supposedly a brotherhood – a *brotherhood!* she laughed inwardly at the word – of equals, yet for all their fine words about sexual equality, when it came to the crunch their breeding took over; and they had been bred into this fuck-awful system where men were like gods and women nothing.

She watched them go, then turned away, her anger turned to bitterness. Maybe it was already too late. Maybe Turner had done his work already as far as Bent Gesell was concerned; the germ of his thought already in Gesell's bloodstream, corrupting his thinking, silting up the once-strong current of his idealism, the disease spreading through the fabric of his moral being, transforming him, until he became little more than a pale shadow of Turner. She hoped not. She hoped against hope that it would turn out otherwise, but in her heart of hearts she knew it had begun. And nothing – nothing she or any of them could do – could prevent it. Nothing but to say no right now, to refuse to take one more step down this suicidal path. But even then it was probably too late. The damage was already done. To say no to Turner now would merely set the man against them.

She went through into the washroom and filled the bowl. While she washed she ran things through her mind, trying to see how she had arrived at this point.

For her it had begun with her father. Mikhail Ascher had been a System man: a Junior Credit Agent, Second Grade, in the T'ang's Finance Ministry, the Hu Pu. Born in the Lowers, he had worked hard, passing the Exams, slowly making his way up the levels, until, in his mid-thirties, he had settled in the Upper Mids, taking a Mid-Level bride. It was there that Emily had been born, into a world of order and stability. Whenever she thought of her father, she could see him as he had been before it all happened, dressed in his powder-blue silks, the big, square badge of office prominent on his chest, his face clean-shaven, his dark hair braided in the Han fashion. A distant, cautious, conservative man, he had seemed to her the paradigm of what their world was about; the very archetype of order. A strict New Confucian, he had instilled into her values that she still, to this day, held to be true. Values that – had he but known it – the world he believed in had abandoned long before he came into it.

She leaned back from the sink, remembering. She had been nine years old.

Back then, before the War, trade had been regular and credit rates relatively stable, but there were always minor fluctuations – tenths, even hundredths of a percentage point. It was one of those tiny fluctuations

– a fluctuation of less than 0.05 of a per cent – that her father was supposed to have 'overlooked'. It had seemed such a small thing to her when he had tried to explain it to her. Only much later, when she had found out the capital sum involved and worked out just how much it had cost the Hu Pu, did she understand the fuss that had been made. The Senior Credit Agent responsible for her father's section had neglected to pass on the rate change and, to save his own position, had pointed the finger at her father, producing a spurious handwritten note to back up his claim. Her father had demanded a tribunal hearing, but the Senior Agent – a Han with important family connections – had pulled strings and the hearing had found in his favour. Her father had come home in a state of shock. He had been dismissed from the Hu Pu.

She could remember that day well; could recall how distraught her mother was, how bemused her father. That day his world fell apart about him. Friends abandoned him, refusing to take his calls. At the bank their credit was cancelled. The next day the lease to their apartment was called in for 'Potential Default'.

They fell.

Her father never recovered from the blow. Six months later he was dead, a mere shell of his former self. And between times they had found themselves demoted down the levels. Down and down, their fall seemingly unstoppable, until one day she woke and found herself in a shared apartment in Fifty-Eight, a child bawling on the other side of the thin curtain, the stench of the previous night's overcooked soypork making her want to retch.

Not their fault. Yes, but that wasn't what she had thought back then. She could still recall the sense of repugnance with which she had faced her new surroundings, her marked distaste for the people she found herself among. So coarse they were. So dirty in their habits.

No, she had never really recovered from that. It had shaped her in every single way. And even when her aversion had turned to pity and her pity into a fiery indignation, still she felt, burning within her chest, the dark brand of that fall.

Her mother had been a genteel woman, in many ways a weak woman, wholly unsuited to the bustle of the Lows, but she had done her best, and in the years that followed had tried in every way to keep the standards that her husband had once set. Unused to earning a living, she had broken with a lifetime's habits and gone looking for work. Eventually she had found it, running a trader's stall in the busy Main where they lived. The job had bruised her tender Mid-Level sensibilities sorely, but she had coped.

Emily shuddered, remembering. *Why do you do it?* she had asked her mother whenever she returned, tearful and exhausted, from a day working the stall, and the answer was always the same: *For you. To get you out of this living hell.* It was her hard work that had put Emily through college, her determination, in the face of seemingly overwhelming odds, that had given Emily her chance. But for what? To climb the levels again? To take part in the same charade that had destroyed her father? No. She was set against that path. Secretly – for she knew that even to mention it would hurt her mother badly – she had harboured other dreams.

She had joined the *Ping Tiao* eight years back, in its infancy, before the War. Back then there had been a lot of talk about ultimate goals and of keeping the vision pure. But eight years was a long time to keep the flame of idealism burning brightly, especially when they had had to face more than their fill of disappointments. And all that time she had been Bent's woman; his alone, fired by his enthusiasm, his vision of how things might be. But things had changed. It was hard to say now whether those ideals still fired them or whether, in some small way, they had become the very thing they once professed to hate.

She stared at her reflection in the mirror, trying, as she so often tried, to get beyond the surface of each eye and see herself whole and clear. So hard to do, it was. She looked down again, shaking her head. There was no doubting it. Her fall had opened her eyes to the evil of the world, a world in which good men and women could be left to fester in the shit-heap of the lower levels while the corrupt and the unscrupulous wallowed in undeserved luxury high above. A world unfit for decent beings. No, and she would never feel at ease in the world while such moral discrepancies existed.

She sighed and turned from the bowl, drying her face and upper arms. So maybe Bent was right. Maybe she was just being silly about the Tolonen girl. Maybe it *would* help bring this rotten pile come crashing down. And yet it didn't feel right. Because it wasn't Jelka Tolonen's fault that she had been born into this world of levels. And so long as she had no proof that the girl was anything other than a pawn of circumstance, she would not feel happy undertaking such a task.

Not for herself, let alone for a bastard like Turner.

Besides, what *was* his motive? Why did he want the General's daughter dead? Was it as he said, to weaken the General and thus undermine the T'ang's Security forces? Or was it something personal? Some slight he'd suffered at the General's hands?

She shivered again, remembering the moment on the mountainside beside Turner. To think that he thought they had something – *anything* – in common! She laughed and felt the laugh turn sour, recalling his words.

'Love, you mean? Human understanding? Goodness? Those things don't exist. Not really. They're illusions. Masks over the reality. And the reality is like these peaks – it's beautiful, but it's also hard, uncompromising and cold, like the airless spaces between the stars.'

Well, maybe that was how he saw it, but the truth was otherwise. It was as she had said: he was lacking a dimension; lacking, essentially, any trace of basic human feeling. The Han had a saying for the behaviour of such men, *Hou lian, hei hsin*, 'Thick face, black heart', and it was never more true than of Turner. Only in his case thick face, black heart had reached its ultimate, where the face is so thick it is formless, the heart so black it is colourless. His nihilism was pure, untempered by any trace of pity. And that was why they should not be working with him, for while their paths might coincide for a time, their aims were diametrically opposed.

In time they would have to fight the man. That was, if he had not, between times, robbed them of the will to fight.

The *mui tsai* bowed deeply, then backed away two paces.

'Major Ebert. Please, come in. My mistress offers her apologies. She is afraid she will be late.'

The girl kept her head lowered, as if from politeness, but a faint flush at her neck and cheeks betrayed her embarrassment at being left alone with the young major.

'Oh? Not ill news, I hope.'

'I believe not, Excellency, but she was summoned urgently. She knew you would understand.'

Ebert moved past her slowly, turning to keep his eyes on her. Yes, she was a pretty young thing. Sixteen, seventeen at most. He could see the shape of her breasts beneath the thin silk of the dress she wore, the fullness of her hips. She was a peach. An absolute peach, ripe for the picking.

He moved closer. 'How long will your mistress be?'

She turned to face him, her eyes averted. 'She said she would not be long, Excellency. Fifteen minutes, perhaps. Twenty at the most. Her husband...'

She fell silent, looking up at him, surprised. Ebert had moved closer, taking her left hand in his own, while with his other hand he held her breast.

'Good,' he said, smiling. 'Then come. There's time for other things, neh?'

The linen cupboard was in the next room; a tiny chamber in itself, wide drawers and rows of silk chi pao, the full-length elegant formal dresses arrayed in a rainbow of stunning colours to either side. He had noticed it on his previous visit, had seen the cushioned floor and thought how nice it might be...

He pushed the girl down, on to the cushions, laughing softly, enjoying the way she looked back at him, a strange wantonness in her dark eyes.

Afterwards they lay there, the soft hiss of their breathing the only sound in the silence. The scent of their lovemaking was mixed deliciously with the faded perfumes of the dresses ranged on either side above them: a sweet, musky smell that, with the warm presence of her naked body beneath him, made him stir again.

She laughed softly, then turned her head to look at him. 'That was nice...'

'Yes...' He let out a small, shuddering breath. Maybe he'd offer to buy her from Chuang Lian...

He felt her stiffen, then draw back from him, and opened his eyes. Then he heard the sound. It came from the other room. The sound of rustling silks.

'Gods...' the girl whispered anxiously, searching for her dress. But Ebert was smiling. Had they been at it that long, then? Or had the Minister's wife come back earlier than expected? He pulled his trousers up over his knees, then climbed to his feet, beginning to button himself up.

The girl had pulled the dress over her head and was fumbling at the fastenings. Ebert turned to her and put his finger against his lips, then, reaching past her for his belt, pushed her back into the linen cupboard and closed the door.

Fastening the last button, his belt in his hand, he went out into the other room.

'Lian, my love...'

She turned, clearly not expecting him, momentarily embarrassed by her state of half undress. Then, with a laugh, she let the garment fall from her and, her breasts exposed, put out her arms to welcome him.

'Quickly,' she said, drawing him down on to the bed, her hands fumbling with the buttons of his trousers. 'Gods, I've missed you...' She looked up at him, her eyes filled with an unnatural agitation.

'Slowly...' he said, pushing her down, amused by the strange urgency of her actions. 'What's up, my darling? Why so tense?'

She paused, then looked away, shuddering with disgust. 'Of all the times...' She looked back up at him, uncertain whether to say, then she looked down again, sniffing, her hands reaching out to take his. 'It was my husband. He doesn't ask for me often, but when he does...'

Ebert laughed. 'So the old man still fucks you, eh?'

He saw the brief flare of anger in her eyes. Then she relented and laughed. 'He tries. But it's like trying to fuck a goldfish...'

'Hmm...' He thought of the girl, crouched still in the linen cupboard, and felt a little shudder of desire wash through him. 'And you wanted a pike... ?'

Her eyes met his, all pretence gone from them suddenly. But all he could see was how lined she was, how old; how her breasts sagged, her flesh folded upon itself at neck and stomach. He shivered, thinking of the mui tsai, of the taut silken surfaces of her young flesh, then leaned closer, kissing the woman's cheek and neck, closing his eyes, trying to imagine that it was Sweet Flute he was kissing. But the scent of her was different – was old and faded like her flesh, her powder sickly sweet, like the scent of a corpse.

He moved back, shuddering, all desire suddenly dead in him. She had just come from her husband, was unwashed from the old man's feeble groping. The thought of it made his stomach churn. He could see her under him, the old man's wrinkled, emaciated buttocks tightening as he came.

And was he to take his place now? To be the man her husband clearly couldn't be?

'What is it?' she said, her eyes narrowed, her whole body suddenly tensed.

'I...' He shook his head. 'I'm tired, that's all. I...' He fished for an excuse, then remembered the Han he'd beaten earlier. 'I've been on duty thirty hours. Something urgent came up and I had to see to it. A number of senior Company men were murdered...'

She swallowed and looked down. 'I heard...'

He looked at her, suddenly disgusted, not only by her but by his involvement with her. And when she reached out to touch and hold him, he drew back sharply from her.

He saw her draw her hand back, then, her face wrinkling, lift it to her nose. Her mouth fell open, then she jerked her head up, glaring at him, her eyes black with anger. 'What's this? Is this what you mean by *duty*?' She nodded her head exaggeratedly. 'Oh, I understand it now. You've been screwing my *mui tsai*, haven't you? You've been having fun here while I've been on my knees before my husband...'

He laughed, delighted by the image that came to mind. 'On your knees, Madam Chuang?'

There was a dark flash of fury behind her eyes, then she swung her hand at him, trying to slap his face, but he caught her hand easily and threw her back down on to the bed. Oh, he could fuck her now. Could do it to her in anger. To humiliate her. But from desire?

'What if I have?' he taunted her. 'What if I tell you that your *mui tsai* fucks like a dream? That she's ten times the woman you are, neh?'

She had bared her teeth. 'You're a liar. She's only a girl...'

He sneered at her. 'You think you were hot, eh? Is that it? You think you could make me come just thinking about what you did to me, eh? Well, let me tell you, Madam Chuang... you weren't so good. I've had much better below the Net. Clapped out old singsong girls who'd do it for a single *yuan*!' He saw how she made to answer him and put his hand brutally over her mouth. 'No... it was simply the thought of fucking a Minister's wife. Of shitting in his nest. It *amused* me. But now I'm bored. I've had enough of you, old woman. Your haggard old frame bores me.'

He stood, fastening himself, pulling his belt about him, watching her all the while, contempt burning in his eyes. He could see now how weak she was, how frail under that brittle carapace of hers. She thought herself so hard, so sophisticated, but she was just a spoilt little girl grown old. Tediously old.

'I'll bury you...' she said quietly, almost hissing the words through her teeth. 'You can smile now, but I'll destroy you, Hans Ebert. Your name will be shit by the time I'm finished with you.'

He laughed dismissively. 'And yours? What will your name be worth, Madam Chuang, if the truth came out? How would you hold your head up in company if it were known what appetites you harboured inside that ancient, wizened skull of yours?'

'You bastard...' She shivered and drew the blanket up about her breasts. 'I'll have you, Ebert. See if I don't.'

He went to the door, then turned, looking back in at her, crouched there on the bed. 'You'll have me?' He looked down, laughing, then looked back at her, his face suddenly hard, uncompromising. 'You'll have *me*?' He shook his head, then laughed: a cruel, dismissive laugh. 'Go suck on your husband's prick!'

Two hours later, Klaus Stefan Ebert, Head of GenSyn, stood on the front steps of his family's mansion, his broad hand extended to his old friend Tolonen. The Marshal had become a grey-haired, stiff-mannered old man in the fifty-odd years Ebert had known him, the uniform a second skin, but he remembered a simpler, less daunting fellow – the gay companion of his adolescence.

The two men embraced, the warmth of their greeting overriding the formality of the occasion. This was more than politics. They grinned at one another and slapped each other's backs.

'I'm glad,' said Tolonen, tears brimming in his eyes.

'And I,' responded Ebert, holding him at arm's length and smiling fiercely into his face. 'This is a day to remember, Knut. Truly a day to remember!'

Jelka stood there at the bottom of the steps, a tall, willowy girl of four-teen with long, straight, ash-blonde hair and beautiful blue eyes. She was no longer the child Ebert remembered so vividly. Now she was not far from womanhood.

Ebert smiled and nodded. She would make his son a perfect bride.

His son, Hans, stood behind him at the top of the steps, a tall twen-ty-eight-year-old, broad-shouldered yet lithe of build. He was considered extremely handsome by those who dictated taste in the Above, and, as heir to the mighty GenSyn Empire, he was rated the most attractive unattached male in City Europe.

Hans barely looked at his bride-to-be. There was time enough for that. He stood there, at ease, his dress uniform immaculate, his short blond hair styled fashionably with a double pigtail. He watched the two men embrace and recognized the significance of all this, his role in it. The Marshal was like a second father to him, his commanding officer.

It was a perfect match. Strategically, logically, it was the obvious thing to do, and when his father had suggested it, ten years back, he had agreed at once.

As he stood there he imagined the power he would one day wield, not merely as his father's son but as commander of the forces of the T'ang. He had dreams. Dreams he could not share. And they began here.

He looked at his intended – the child. She was studying him, looking at him with a critical eye, as if to sum up and dismiss him. He glared at her, then relented, remembering, letting his face form into a smile, as if the first were only mischief.

He looked her up and down. She possessed the unformed figure of a girl. Pretty enough, but not a woman. Not a patch on the women he knew, anyway.

He smiled and looked away. Still, he would arrange things. Make life pleasant for himself. A wife was not a gaoler, after all.

They went inside, Jelka bowing her head, her cheeks flushed, as the contracts were presented and endorsed by all parties.

He signed, then straightened, looking across the table at her. In three years he would be her husband. Three years. But who knew how things would be in three years' time? And the girl? In three years she would be seventeen. Again he smiled, remembering the *mui tsai*. *And you, my little one?* he wondered, looking across at the Marshal's daughter. *What will you be like on our wedding night? Are you the frigid, nervous type, or is there fire in your loins?* His smile broadened, seeing how she looked away, the colour deepening at her neck. *Yes, well, we'll see. And even if you prove a disappointment, there will be others – plenty of others – to sweeten my nights.*

And in the meantime maybe he would buy the *mui tsai*. After all, it wasn't every woman who could make love like that. Gifted, she'd been. He turned, taking the Marshal's offered hand, smiling back fiercely at the two old men.

Yes, he would buy the *mui tsai*. And later, when her temper had cooled, he would go and see Madam Chuang again, and make it up with her.

Jelka sat at her father's side, sipping at her bowl of *ch'a*, conscious of the stifling opulence of the room. She looked about her, feeling an unease that had nothing to do with her personal situation.

She shuddered and looked down. The Eberts flaunted their wealth, displaying it with an ostentation she found quite tasteless. Ornate Ming vases rested on hideous plinths: heavy, brutal things in garish colours. In recesses of the curiously shaped room, huge canvases hung in heavy gilt frames, the pictures dark, suggestive of blood.

Across from her, Hans's two sisters were staring at her with an unconcealed hostility, the younger a year or so older than Jelka, the elder in her early twenties. She tried not to look at them, knowing they saw her only as a rival. More disconcerting was the creature serving them: a goat-like being, grown in GenSyn's vats. She shivered when its pink-eyed stare met her own and, in a deep but toneless voice, it asked if she would like more *ch'a*. She looked at its pinched, three-toed hand and shook her head, noting the fine silk of its cuffs, the stylish cut of its trousers.

She had the oddest feeling of being in a dream, unreality piled upon unreality. Yet this was real. Was the reality of power. She looked at her future husband and saw him with a clarity that almost overwhelmed her. He was a tall young man, taller than her father, and handsome. Yet there was a cruelty, an arrogance in his handsomeness that made her shudder. She could see his pride, his intense sense of self-importance; saw it in how he held his head, in the cold indifference of his eyes.

Even so, it didn't reach her yet; didn't touch or move her. Three years was a long time. She could not imagine how she would feel three years from now. This much – this ritual of contracts, of pledges and vague promises – seemed a small thing to do to satisfy her father.

She smiled, looking at her father, sensing his pride in her. It pleased her, as always, and she reached out to hold and touch his arm. She saw how Old Man Ebert smiled at that: a tender, understanding smile. He was cut from a different cloth to the rest of his family. Beside him his wife, Berta, looked away, distanced from everything about her, her face a mask of total indifference to the whole proceeding. A tall, elegant woman, hers was a cold, austere beauty: the beauty of pine forests under snow. A rarefied, inhuman beauty.

With that same clarity with which she had seen the son, Jelka saw how Berta Ebert had shaped her children in their father's absence. Saw how their cold self-interest was a reflection of their mother's.

She held her father's arm, feeling its warmth, its strength and solidity, and drew comfort from that. He loved her. Surely he would allow nothing that would harm her?

On the way over he had talked to her of the reasons behind this marriage. Of the need to build strong links between the Seven and the most powerful of the new, commercial Families. It was the way forward, and her union with Hans would cement the peace they had struggled hard to win. GenSyn had remained staunchly loyal to the Seven in the recent War and Li Shai Tung had rewarded them for that loyalty. Klaus Ebert had taken over mining contracts on Mars and the Uranus moons as well as large holdings in three of the smaller communications companies. Her marriage would make this abstract, commercial treaty a personal thing. Would make it a thing of flesh and blood.

She understood this. Even so, it seemed a long way off. Before then she had to finish her schooling, the rest of her childhood. She looked at Hans Ebert dispassionately, as if studying a stranger.

She turned in her seat, her cup empty, to summon the servant. It came to her without a word, as if it had anticipated her wish, bowing to her as it filled her cup. Yet before it moved back into the shadows of the room it looked up at her, meeting her eyes a second time, holding them a moment with its dark, intimate knowledge of things she did not know.

Jelka turned her head away, looking past her father, meeting the eyes of her future husband. Blue eyes, not pink. Startlingly blue. Colder, harder eyes. Different...

She shuddered and looked down. *And yet the same. Somehow, curiously, the same.*

Wang Sau-leyan raised the silk handkerchief to his face and wiped his eyes. For a moment he stood there, his well-fleshed body shaking gently, the laughter still spilling from his lips, then he straightened up and sniffed loudly, looking about him.

Behind him the tomb was being sealed again, the rosewood litter carried away. Servants busied themselves, sweeping the dirt path with brushes of twigs, while, to one side, the six New Confucian officials stood in a tight circle, talking quietly amongst themselves.

'That was rich, Hung, don't you think?' Wang said, turning to face his Chancellor, ignoring the looks of displeasure of his fellow T'ang. 'I had visions of my brother getting up out of the casket to chastise the poor buggers!'

'My lord...' Hung's face was a picture of dismay. He glanced about him at the gathered T'ang, then lowered his head. 'It was unfortunate...'

'Unfortunate!' Wang's laughter rang out again. 'Why, it could only have happened to Ta-hung! Who else but my brother would find himself thrown into his own tomb!' With the last few words Wang Sau-leyan made a mime of the casket sliding into the tomb.

It had been an accident. At the top of the steps, one of the bearers had tripped and, the balance of the casket momentarily lost, the remaining bearers had lost their grip. The whole thing had tumbled down the steps, almost throwing out its occupant. Wang Sau-leyan, following close behind, had stood there at the tomb's mouth, doubled up with laughter. He had not stopped laughing since. Throughout the ceremony, he had giggled, oblivious of the astonished looks of the officials.

Now, however, his fellow T'ang were looking amongst themselves, appalled by his behaviour. After a moment the oldest of them, Wei Feng, stepped forward.

'What is this, Wang Sau-leyan? Have you no feelings for your dead brother? We came to honour him today – to pay our respects to his souls as they journey on. This laughter is not fitting. Have you forgotten the rites, Wang Sau-leyan? It is your duty...'

'Hell's teeth, Wei Feng, I know my duty. But it was funny. Genuinely funny. If he had not been dead already, that last fall would have killed him!' Wang Sau-leyan stared back at his fellow T'ang momentarily, then looked away. 'However... forgive me, cousins. It seems that I alone saw the humour in the moment.'

Wei Feng looked down, his anger barely contained. Never in all his years had he seen anything like it.

'There are times for humour...'

Wang's huff of disgust was clearly disrespectful. He moved past Wei Feng as if the older man wasn't there, confronting the other T'ang.

'If my brother had been a man to respect I would have shown him some respect, but my brother was a fool and a weakling. He would never have been T'ang but for the death of my elder brothers.' Wang looked about him, nodding his head. 'Yes, and I know that goes for me, too, but understand me, cousins. I'll not play hollow tongue to any man. I'll speak as I feel. As I am, not as you'd have me seem. So you'll understand me if I say that I disliked my brother. I'm not glad he's dead. No, I'd not go that far, for even a fool deserves breath. But I'll not be a hypocrite. I'll shed no false tears for him. I'll save them for men who deserve them. For men I truly love. Likewise I'll keep my respect for those who deserve respect.'

Tsu Ma had been staring past Wang while he spoke. Now he looked back at him, his face inexpressive, his eyes looking up and down the length of Wang Sau-leyan, as if to measure him.

'And yet your brother was T'ang, Wang Sau leyan. Surely a T'ang deserves respect?'

'Had the man filled the clothes...'

'And he did not?'

Wang Sau-leyan paused, realizing suddenly what dangerous seas he had embarked upon. Then he laughed, relaxing, and looked back at Tsu Ma.

'Don't mistake me, Tsu Ma. I speak only of my brother. I knew him well. In all the long history of the Seven there was never one like him. He was not worthy to wear the imperial yellow. Look in your hearts, all of you, and tell me that I'm wrong. In all honesty, was there one of you who, knowing my father was dead, rejoiced that Ta-hung was T'ang?'

He looked about them, seeing the grudging confirmation in every face.

'Well, let us keep our respect for those that deserve it, neh? For myself I'd gladly bow to any of my cousins here. You are men who have proved your worth. You, indeed, are T'ang.'

He saw how that mollified them and laughed inwardly. They were all so vain, so title-proud. And hypocrites, too, for if the truth were known they cared as little for Ta-hung as he. No, they had taken offence not at his denigration of his brother but at the implied mockery of his brother's title, for by inference it mocked them also.

He moved through, between their ranks, bowing to each of them as he passed, then led them on along the pathway and up the broad marble steps into the ancient palace.

As for himself he cared not a jot for the trappings of his title. He had seen enough of men and their ways to know how hollow a mere title could be. No, what he valued was not the title 'T'ang' but the reality of the power it gave him, the ability to say and do what he had always dreamed of saying and doing. The power to offend, if offence was what he wished. To be a T'ang and not have that was to be nothing – was to be an actor in a tiresome play, mouthing another's words, constrained by bonds of ritual and tradition.

And he would not be that.

As the servants made their way amongst his guests, offering wine and sweetmeats, he looked about him again, a faint smile coming to his lips as he remembered that moment at the entrance to the tomb.

Yes, he thought, *it was not your fate to be T'ang, Ta-hung. You were designed for other things than kingship. And yet T'ang you became.*

Wang smiled and took a cup of wine from the servant, then turned away, looking out through the window at the walled garden and the great marbled tablet of the tomb at its centre.

It was unfortunate. He had not disliked his brother. Despised him, maybe – though even that was too strong a word for the mild feeling of irritation he had felt – but not hated him as he had his father and his two eldest brothers. However, Ta-hung had had the misfortune of being born before him. As a younger brother he would have been no threat, but as T'ang he had been an obstacle – a thing to be removed.

He sipped at his wine and turned his head, looking across at his Chancellor. Hung Mien-lo was talking to Tsu Ma, his head lowered in deference. Smoothing things over, no doubt. Wang looked down, smiling, pleased by his morning's work.

It was true, he *had* found the accident genuinely amusing, but he had grasped at once that it was the perfect pretext for annoying his fellow T'ang – the perfect irritant – and he had exaggerated his response. He had seen how they bridled at his irreverence. And afterwards it had given him the opportunity to play the bluff, honest man. To put his heart upon his sleeve and flaunt it before them. He took a deep breath, then looked up again, noting how their eyes went to him constantly. Yes, he thought. *They hate me now, but they also admire me in a grudging way. They think me crass but honest. Well, let them be mistaken on both counts. Let them take the surface show for the substance, for it will make things easier in the days to come.*

He turned again, looking back at the tomb. They were dead – every one of them who had been in the room that day he had been exiled. Father and mother, brothers and uncles all. Dead. And he had had them killed, every last one.

And now *I'm T'ang and sleep in my father's bed with my father's wives and my father's maids.*

He drained his glass, a small ripple of pleasure passing through him. *Yes. He had stopped their mouths and closed their eyes. And no one would ever again tell him what he could or couldn't do.*

No one.

Two hours later, Wang Sau-leyan sat in his father's room, in the big, tall-backed chair, side-on to the mirror, his back to the door.

He heard the door open, soft footsteps pad across the tiles.

'Is that you, Sweet Rain?'

He heard the footsteps pause and imagined the girl bending low as she bowed. A pretty young thing, perhaps the prettiest of his father's maids.

'*Chieh Hsia?*'

He half turned, languid from the wine he'd drunk, and put his hand out. 'Have you brought the lavender bowl?'

There was the slightest hesitation, then, 'I have, *Chieh Hsia.*'

'Good. Well, come then. I want you to see to me as you used to see to my father.'

Again there was the slightest hesitation before she acted. Then she came round, bowing low, and knelt before him, the bowl held delicately in the long, slender fingers of her left hand.

He had seen the film of his father's final evening, had seen how Sweet Rain had ministered to him, milking the old man into the lavender bowl. Well, now she would do the same for him. But no one would be watching this time. He had turned off the cameras. No one but he would know what he did within the privacy of his bedroom walls.

He drew the gown back from his lap, exposing his nakedness. His penis was still quite flaccid.

'Well, girl? What are you waiting for?'

He let his head fall back and closed his eyes, waiting. There was the faint rustle of silks as she moved closer, then he felt her fingers brush against his flesh. He shivered, then nodded to himself, feeling his penis stir between her fingers. Such a delicate touch she had – like silk itself – her fingers caressing the length of him slowly, tantalizingly, making his breath catch in his throat.

He opened his eyes, looking down at her. Her head was lowered, intent on what she was doing, the darkness of her hair held up with a single white jade pin.

'Is this how you touched my father?'

She glanced up. 'No, *Chieh Hsia*. But I thought...'

And still her fingers worked on him, gathering the whole of him up into that tiny nexus of pleasure, there between his legs.

'Thought what?' he asked after a moment, the words barely audible.

She hesitated, then looked up at him again; candidly this time. 'Every man is different, *Chieh Hsia*. Likewise their needs...'

He nodded slowly. *Gods, but it was delightful. He would never have dreamed that a woman's hands could be so potent an instrument of pleasure.*

Her eyes met his again. 'If the T'ang would prefer, I could... kiss him there.'

He shuddered. The word 'kiss' promised delights beyond imagining. He gave a tiny nod. 'Yes. I'd like that.'

He heard her set the bowl down and let his head fall back, his eyes close, then felt her lift him to her lips. Again he shivered, drawn up out of himself by the sheer delight of what she was doing. For a while, then, he seemed to lapse out of himself, becoming but a single thread of perfect pleasure, linked to the warm wetness of her mouth; a pleasure that grew and grew...

He didn't hear the door open. Neither did he hear the second set of foot-steps pad almost silently across the tiles towards him, but a movement in the girl in front of him – the slightest tensing of her left hand where it rested on his knee – made him open his eyes suddenly and look up, his gaze going to the mirror.

Tender Willow was almost upon him, the knife already raised in her right hand. At once he kicked out with his right leg, pushing Sweet Rain away from him, and lurched forward, out of the seat.

It was not a moment too soon. Tender Willow's knife missed his shoulder by a fraction, tearing into the silken cushioning of the chair, gashing the wooden beading. Wang turned quickly, facing her, twice her weight and a full *ch'i* taller – but still the girl came on, her face filled with hatred and disgust.

As she thrust the knife at him a second time, he moved forward, knocking her arm away, then, grabbing her neck brutally, he smashed her head down into the arm of the chair, once, then a second time. She fell and lay still.

He stood there a moment, his breath hissing sharply from him, then turned and kicked out at Sweet Rain again, catching her in the stomach, so that she wheezed, her breath taken from her. His face was dark now, twisted with rage.

'You foxes…' he said quietly, his voice trembling. 'You foul little bitches…'

He kicked again, catching the fallen maid fully on the side of the head, then turned back and spat on the other girl.

'You're dead. Both of you.'

He looked about him, noting the broken bowl and, beside it, a single white jade pin, then bent down and recovered the knife from the floor. He straightened up, then, with a slight shudder, walked to the door and threw it open, calling the guards.

PART ELEVEN SHELLS

AUTUMN 2206

Between the retina and the higher centres of the cortex the innocence of vision is irretrievably lost – it has succumbed to the suggestion of a whole series of hidden persuaders.
—Arthur Koestler, *The Act Of Creation*

That which we experience in dreams, if we experience it often, is in the end just as much a part of the total economy of our soul as is anything we 'really' experience: we are by virtue of it richer or poorer.
—Friedrich Nietzsche, *Beyond Good And Evil*

Chapter 47

THE INNOCENCE OF VISION

Ben came upon the cottage from the bay path, climbing the steep slope. At the lower gate he turned, looking back across the bay. New growth crowded the distant foreshore, masking where the fire had raged five years earlier. Only at the hill's crest, where the old house had stood, did the new vegetation end. There the land was fused a glassy black.

The tall seventeen-year-old shook his head, then turned to face the cottage. Landscott was a long, low shape against the hill, its old stone walls freshly whitewashed, its roof thatched. A flower garden stretched up to it, its blooms a brilliant splash of colour beside the smooth greenness of the lawn. Behind and beside it other cottages dotted the hillside, untenanted yet perfectly maintained. Shells, they were. Part of the great illusion. His eyes passed over them quickly, used to the sight.

He looked down at his left hand where it rested on the gatepost, conscious of a deep, unsatisfied itch at the join between the wrist and the new hand. The kind of itch you couldn't scratch, because it was inside, beneath the flesh. The join was no longer sore, the hand no longer an unaccustomed weight at the end of his arm, as it had been for the first year. Even so, something of his initial sense of awkwardness remained.

The scar had healed, leaving what looked like a machined ridge between what was his and what had been given. The hand itself looked natural enough, but that was only illusion. He had seen what lay beneath the fibrous dermal layer. It was much stronger than his right hand and, in subtle ways, much better – far quicker in its responses. He turned it, moving it like the machine it was rather than the hand it pretended to be, then smiled to himself. If he wished he could have it strengthened and augmented: could transform it into any kind of tool he needed.

He let it fall, then began to climb again, crossing the gradual slope of the upper garden. Halfway across the lawn he slowed then stopped, surprised, hearing music from inside the cottage. Piano music. He tilted his head, listening, wondering who it was. The phrase was faltering at first, the chords uncertain. Then, a moment later, the same chords were repeated, confidently this time, all sense of hesitation gone.

Curious, he crossed the lawn and went inside. The music was coming from the living-room. He went to the doorway and looked in. At the far side of the room his mother was sitting at a piano, her back to him, her hands resting lightly on the keys.

'Mother?' Ben frowned, not understanding. The repetition of the phrase had been assured, almost professional, and his mother did not play.

She turned, surprised to see him there, a slight colour at her cheeks. 'I...' Then she laughed and shook her head. 'Yes, it was me. Come. I'll show you.'

He went across and sat beside her on the long, bench-like piano seat. 'This is new,' he said, looking down at the piano. Then, matter-of-factly, he added, 'Besides, you don't play.'

'No,' she said, but began anyway: a long, introductory passage, more complex than the phrase she had been playing – a fast, passionate piece played with a confidence and skill the earlier attempt had lacked. He watched her hands moving over the keys, surprised and delighted.

'That's beautiful,' he said when she had finished. 'What was it?'

'Chopin. From the Preludes.' She laughed, then turned and glanced at him, her eyes bright with enjoyment.

'I still don't understand. That was excellent.'

'Oh, I wouldn't say that.' She leaned back, staring down at the keyboard. 'I'm rather rusty. It's a long while since I played.'

'Why didn't you play before now?'

'Because it's an obsession.'

She had said it without looking at him, as if it explained everything. He looked down at her hands again, saw how they formed shapes above the keys.

'I had to think of you and Meg. I couldn't do both, you understand.

Couldn't play and look after you. And I wanted to bring you up. I didn't trust anyone else to do the job.'

'So you gave up this?'

If anything, he understood it less. To have such a gift and not use it... it was not possible.

'Oh, there were plenty of times when I felt like playing. I ached to do it. It was like coming off a drug. A strong, addictive drug. And in denying that part of me I genuinely felt less human. But there was no choice. I wanted to be a mother to you, not simply a presence flitting through your lives.'

He frowned, not following her. It made him realize how little he knew about her. She had always been too close, too familiar. He had never thought to ask her about herself, about her life before she had met his father.

'My own mother and father were never there, you see.' Her hands formed a major chord, then two quick minors. It sounded familiar, yet, like the Chopin, he couldn't place it.

'I was determined not to do to you what they did to me. I remember how isolated I felt. How unloved.' She smiled, reaching across to take his right hand – his human hand – and squeeze it.

'I see.'

It awed him to think she had done that for them. He ran the piece she had played through his memory, seeing where she placed emphasis, where she slowed. He could almost feel the music. Almost.

'How does it *feel* to be able to do that?'

She drew in a long breath, looking through him, suddenly distant, her eyes and mouth lit with the vaguest of smiles, then shook her head. 'No. I can't say. There aren't the words for it. Raised up, I guess. Changed. *Different* somehow. But I can't say what, exactly.'

For the first time in his life Ben felt something like envy, watching her face. Not a jealous, denying envy, but a strong desire to emulate.

'But why now?'

'Haven't you guessed?' She laughed and placed his right hand on the keyboard. 'You're usually so quick.'

'You're going to teach me.'

'Both of you,' she answered, getting up and coming behind him so that she could move his arms and manipulate his hands. 'Meg asked me to. And she wouldn't learn unless you could too.'

He thought about it a moment, then nodded.

'What was that piece you were playing when I came in? It sounded as if you were learning it for the first time, yet at the same time knew it perfectly.'

She leaned closer, her warmth pressed against his shoulder, her long, dark hair brushing against his cheek. 'It wasn't originally a piece for piano, that's why. It was scored for the string and woodwind sections of an orchestra. It's by Grieg. "Wedding Day at Troldhaugen".' She placed her hands either side of his own and repeated the phrase he had heard, then played a second, similar one.

'That's nice,' he said. Its simplicity appealed to him.

'You came back early,' she said. 'What's up? Didn't you want to go into town?'

He turned, meeting her eyes. 'Father called. The T'ang has asked him to stay on a few days.'

There was a brief movement of disappointment in her face. It had been three months since she had seen Hal.

'A few more days,' she said quietly. 'Ah, well, it'll soon pass.' Then, smiling, she put her hand on his arm. 'Perhaps we'll have a picnic. You, me and Meg. Like old times. What do you think?'

Ben looked back at her, seeing her anew, the faintest smile playing on his lips and in his eyes. 'It would be nice,' he said. But already his thoughts were moving on, his mind toying with the possibilities of the keyboard. Pushing things further. 'Yes,' he said, getting up and going over to her. 'Like old times.'

The next morning found Ben in the shadowed living-room, crouched on his haunches, staring intently at the screen that filled half the facing wall. He was watching one of the special Security reports that had been prepared for his father some months before, after the T'ang of Africa's assassination. It was an interesting document, not least because it showed things that were thought too controversial – too inflammatory – for general screening.

The Seven had acted swiftly after Wang Hsien's death, arresting the last few remnants of opposition at First Level – thus preventing a further outbreak of the War between the factions in the Above – but even they had been surprised by the extent of the rioting lower down the City. There had been riots before, of course, but never on such a widespread scale, nor with such appalling consequences. Officials of the Seven, Deck Magistrates amongst them, had been beaten and killed. Security posts had been destroyed and Security troops forced to pull out of some stacks in fear of their lives. Slowly, very slowly, things had settled, the fires burning themselves out, and in some parts of the City – in East Asia and North America, particularly – Security had moved back within days to quell the last few pockets of resistance. Order had been restored. But for how long?

He knew it was a warning. A sign of things to come. But would the Seven heed it? Or would they continue to ignore the problems that beset those who lived in the lowest levels of the City, blaming the unrest on groups like the Ping Tiao?

Ben rubbed at his chin thoughtfully. To the respectable Mid-Level citizenry, the Ping Tiao were bogeymen – the very type and symbol of those destructive forces the War had unleashed – and MidText, their media channel, played heavily upon their fears. But the truth was otherwise.

The Ping Tiao had first come into the news eighteen months back, when three members of their faction had kidnapped and murdered a Mid-Level Administrator. They had issued pamphlets claiming that the Administrator was a corrupt and brutal man who had abused his position and deserved his fate. It was the truth, but the authorities had countered at once, depicting the dead official as a well-respected family man who had been the victim of a group of madmen. Madmen who wanted only one thing – to level the City and destroy Chung Kuo itself.

As the weeks passed and further Ping Tiao 'outrages' occurred, the media had launched a no-holds-barred campaign against the group, linking their name with any outbreak of violence or civil unrest. There was a degree of truth behind official claims, for the tactics of the Ping Tiao were certainly of the crudest kind, the seemingly random nature of their targets aiming at maximum disruption. However, the extent of Ping Tiao activities was greatly exaggerated, creating the impression that if only the Ping Tiao could be destroyed, the problems they represented would vanish with them.

The campaign had worked. Or at least in the Mid-Levels it had worked. Further down, however, in the cramped and crowded levels at the bottom of the City, the Ping Tiao were thought of differently. There they were seen as heroes, their cause as a powerful and genuine expression of long-standing grievances. Support for the terrorists grew and grew. And would have continued growing but for a tragic accident in a Mid-Level creche.

Confidential high-level sources later made it quite clear that the Ping Tiao had had nothing to do with what was termed 'The Lyon's Canton Massacre', but the media had a field day, attacking the Ping Tiao for what they called its 'cowardly barbarism and inhumanity'.

The effect was immediate. The tide of opinion turned against the Ping Tiao overnight, and a subsequent Security operation against the terrorists resulted in the capture and execution of over eight hundred members of the faction – most of them identified by previously sympathetic friends and neighbours.

For the Ping Tiao those few weeks had been disastrous. They had sunk into obscurity. Yet in the past few days they seemed to have put that behind them. Fish emblems – the symbol of the Ping Tiao – had been seen everywhere throughout the levels, painted on walls or drawn in blood on the faces of their victims.

But the authorities had hit back hard. MidText, for instance, had played heavily on old fears. The present troubles, they asserted, were mainly the result of a conspiracy between the Ping Tiao and a small faction in the Above who financed their atrocities.

Ben froze the tape momentarily, thinking back to what Li Shai Tung had said – on that evening five years earlier – about knowing his enemy. It was on this level, accepting at face value the self-deluding half-truths of the MidText images, that Li Shai Tung had been speaking then. But these men – terrorist and Company men alike – were merely cyphers: the scum on the surface of the well. And the well was deep. Far deeper than the Seven dared imagine.

He let the tape run. At once the babble began again, the screen filling once more with images of riot and despoliation.

Vast crowds surged through the lower levels, destroying guard posts and barriers, wrecking storefronts and carrying off whatever they could lay their hands on. Unfortunate officials were beaten to death before the camera, or bound and doused in petrochemicals before being set on fire. Ben saw how the crowd pressed in tightly about one such victim, roaring their approval as a frail, grey-bearded magistrate was hacked to death. He noted the ugly brutality in every face, and nodded to himself. Then the image changed, switching to another crowd, this one more orderly. Hastily made banners were raised on every side, demanding increased food rations, a resumption of state aid to the jobless and an end to travel restrictions. 'Pien hua!' they chanted in their hundred thousands, 'Pien hua!'

Change!

There was a burning indignation in many of the faces; in others a fierce, unbridled need that had no outlet. Some waved long knives or clubs in the air and bared their teeth in ferocious animal smiles, a gleam of sheer delight in their eyes at having thrown off all restraints. For many this was their first taste of such freedom and they danced frenziedly in time with the great chant, intoxicated by the madness that raged on every side.

'PIEN HUA! PIEN HUA! PIEN HUA! PIEN HUA!'

Ben watched the images flash up one after another, conscious of the tremendous power, the dark potency that emanated from them. It was primordial. Like some vast movement of the earth itself. And yet it was all so loosely reined, so undirected. Change, they demanded. But to what?

No one knew. No one seemed capable of imagining what Change might bring. In time, perhaps, someone would find an answer to that question – would draw the masses to him and channel that dark tide of discontent. But until then, the Seven had been right to let the storm rage, the flood waters rise unchecked; for they knew the waters would recede, the storm blow itself out. To have attempted to control that vast upsurge of feeling or repress it could only have made things worse.

Ben blanked the screen, then stood, considering what he had seen. Wang Hsien's death may have been the catalyst, but the real causes of the mass violence were rooted much deeper. Were, in fact, as old as Man himself. For this was how Man really was beneath his fragile shell of culture. And not just those he had seen on the screen, the madness dancing in their eyes, but all of Mankind. For a long time they had tried to fool themselves, pretending they were something else – something more refined and spiritual, something more god-like and less animal than they really were. But now the lid was off the well, the darkness bubbling to the surface once again.

'Ben?'

He turned. Meg was watching him from the doorway, the morning sunlight behind her throwing her face and figure into shadow, making her look so like his mother that, momentarily, he mistook her. Then, realizing his error, he laughed.

'What is it?' she asked, her voice rich and low.

'Nothing,' he answered. 'Is it ready?'

She nodded, then came into the room. 'What were you watching?'

He glanced at the empty screen, then back at her. 'I was looking at Father's tapes. About the riots.'

She looked past him. 'I thought you weren't interested.'

'I'm not. At least, not in the events themselves. But the underlying meaning of it all... *that* fascinates me. The faces – they're like windows to their souls. All their fears and aspirations show nakedly. But it takes something like this to do it. Something big and frightening. And then the mask slips and the animal stares out through the eyes.'

And the *Ping Tiao*, he thought. I'm interested in them, too. Because they're something new. Something the City has been missing until now. A carp to fill an empty pool.

'Well... shall we go out?'

She smiled. 'Okay. You first.'

On the lawn beside the flower-beds, their mother had spread out a picnic on a big red and white checked tablecloth. As Ben came out into the open she looked across at him and smiled. In the sunlight she seemed much younger than she really was, more Meg's older sister than her mother. He went across and sat beside her, conscious of the drowsy hum of bees, the rich scent of the blooms masking the sharp salt tang of the bay. It was a perfect day, the blue above them broken here and there by big, slow-drifting cumuli.

Ben looked down at the picnic spread before them. It all looked newly created. A wide basket filled with apples lay at the centre of the feast, their perfect, rounded greenness suggesting the crispness of the inner fruit. To the left the eye was drawn to the bright yellow of the butter in its circular, white china dish and, beside it, the richer, almost honeyed yellow of the big wedge of cheddar. There was a big plate of thick-cut ham, the meat a soft pink, the rind a perfect snowy white, and next to that a fresh-baked loaf, three slices cut from it and folded forward, exposing the fluffy whiteness of the bread. Bright red tomatoes beaded with moisture shared a bowl with the softer green of a freshly washed lettuce, while other, smaller bowls held tiny radishes and onions, peeled carrots, grapes and celery, redcurrants and watercress.

'It's nice,' he said, looking to his mother.

Pleased, she handed him a plate. A moment later Meg reappeared, carrying a tray on which were three tall glasses and a jug of freshly made iced lemonade. He laughed.

'What is it?' Meg asked, setting the tray down.

'This,' he said, indicating the spread laid out before them.

Meg's smile faded slowly. 'What's wrong? Don't you like it?'

'No,' he said softly, reassuringly. 'It's marvellous.' He smiled, then leaned forward, beginning to transfer things to his plate.

Meg hesitated, then poured from the jug, handing him the cold, beaded glass. 'Here.'

He set his plate down, then took the glass and sipped. 'Hmm,' he said, his eyes smiling back at her. 'Perfect.'

Beside him his mother was busy, filling a plate for Meg. She spoke without looking at him.

'Meg tells me you've been reading Nietzsche.'

He glanced across at Meg. She was looking down, a faint colour in her cheeks.

'That's right.' He sipped again, then stared at the side of his glass intently.

His mother turned her head, looking at him. 'I thought you'd read Nietzsche.'

'I did. When I was eight.'

'Then I don't understand. I thought you said you could never read a thing twice.'

He met her eyes. 'So I thought. But it seems I was wrong.'

She was silent a while, considering, then looked back at him again. 'Then you *can* forget things, after all?'

He shook his head. 'It's not a question of forgetting. It's just that things get embedded.'

'Embedded?'

He paused, then set his glass down, realizing he would have to explain.

'I realized it months ago, when Father quoted something from Nietzsche to me. Two lines from *Ecce Homo*. The memory should have come back clearly, but it didn't. Oh, it was clear enough in one sense – I could remember the words plain enough. I could even see them on the page and recall where I was when I read them. But that was it, you see. That's what I mean by things getting embedded. When Father triggered that specific memory, it came back to me in *context*, surrounded by all the other ragbag preoccupations of my eight-year-old self.'

Ben reached out and took a tomato from the bowl and polished it on his sleeve, then looked up at his mother again, his face earnest, almost frowning.

'You see, those lines of Nietzsche were interlaced with all kinds of other things. With snatches of music – Mahler and Schoenberg and Shostakovich – with the abstract paintings of Kandinsky and Klee, the poetry of Rilke and Donne and Basho, and god knows what else. A thousand intricate strands. Too many to grasp at a single go. But it wasn't just a case of association by juxtaposition – I found that my reading, my very understanding of Nietzsche, was coloured by those things. And try as I might, I couldn't shake those impressions loose and see his words fresh. I had to separate it physically.'

'What do you mean?' Beth asked, leaning forward to take a grape from the bunch.

'I mean that I had to return to the text. To read the words fresh from the page again. Free from all those old associations.'

'And?' It was Meg who asked the question. She was leaning forward, watching him, fascinated.

He looked down, then bit into the tomato. He chewed for a moment, then swallowed and looked up again. 'And it worked. I liberated the words from their old context.'

He popped the rest of the tomato into his mouth and for a while was silent, thoughtful. The two women watched him, indulging him, as always placing him at the very centre of things. The tomato finished, he took a long sip of his lemonade. Only then did he begin again.

'It's as if my mind is made up of different strata. It's all there – fossilized, if you like, and available if I want to chip away at it – but my memory, while perfect, is nonetheless selective.'

Ben laughed and looked at his sister again. 'Do you remember that

Borges story, Meg? "Funes The Memorious" about the boy with perfect recall, confined to his bed, entrapped by the perfection – the overwhelming detail – of past moments. Well, it isn't like that. It could never be like that, amusing as the concept is. You see, the mind accords certain things far greater significance than others. And there's a good reason for that. The undermind recognizes what the conscious intelligence too often overlooks – that there is a hierarchy of experience. Some things matter more to our deeper self than others. And the mind returns them to us strongly. It thrusts them at us, you might say – in dreams, and at quiet moments when we least suspect their presence.'

'Why should it do that?'

Ben gave a tiny shrug. He took an apple from the basket and lifted it to his mouth. 'Maybe it has to do with something programmed into us at the genetic level. A code. A key to why we're here, like the cyphers in Augustus's journal.'

As Ben bit deeply into the apple, Meg looked across at her mother and saw how she had looked away at the mention of Augustus and the journal.

'But why Nietzsche?' Meg asked, after a moment. She could not understand his fascination with the nineteenth-century German philosopher. To her the man was simply an extremist, a fanatic. He understood nothing of those purely human things that held a society together – nothing of love, desire or sacrifice. To her mind his thinking was fatally flawed. It was the thinking of a hermit, a misanthrope. But Man was a social animal; he did not exist in separation from his fellows, nor could he for longer than one human lifetime. And any human culture was the product of countless generations. In secret she had struggled with the man's difficult, spiky prose, trying to understand what it was Ben saw in him, but it had served only to confirm her own distaste.

Ben chewed the piece of apple, then smiled. 'There's an almost hallucinatory clarity about his thinking that I like. And there's a fearlessness, too. He's not afraid to offend. There's nothing he's afraid to look at and investigate at depth, and that's rare in our culture. Very rare.'

'So?' Meg prompted, noting how her mother was watching Ben again, a fierce curiosity in her eyes.

He looked at the apple, then shrugged and bit again.

Beth broke her long silence. 'Are you working on something new?'

Ben looked away. Then it was true. He had begun something new. Yes, she should have known. He was always like this when he began something new – fervent, secretive, subject to great swings of mood.

The two women sat there, watching him as he finished the apple, core and all, leaving nothing.

He wiped his fingers on the edge of the cloth, then looked up again, meeting Meg's eyes. 'I was thinking we might go along to the cove later on and look for shells.'

She looked away, concealing her surprise. It had been some while since they had been down to the cove, so why had he suggested it just now? Perhaps it was simply to indulge her love of shells, but she thought not. There was always more to it than that with Ben. It would be fun, and Ben would make the occasion into a kind of game, but he would have a reason for the game. He always had a reason.

Ben laughed and reached out to take one of the tiny radishes from the bowl. 'And then, tomorrow, I'll show you what I've been up to.'

Warfleet Cove was a small bay near the mouth of the river. A road led towards it from the old town, ending abruptly in a jumble of rocks, the shadow of the Wall throwing a sharp but jagged line over the rocks and the hill beyond. To the left the land fell away to the river, bathed in brilliant sunlight. A path led down through the thick overgrowth – blackberry and bramble, wildflowers and tall grasses – and came out at the head of the cove.

Ben stepped out on to the flattened ledge of rock, easing the strap of his shoulder bag. Below him the land fell away steeply to either side, forming a tiny, ragged flint-head of a bay. A shallow spill of shingle edged the sandy cove. At present the tide was out, though a number of small rockpools reflected back the sun's brilliance. Low rocks lay to either side of the cove's mouth, narrowing the channel. It was an ancient, primitive place, unchanged throughout the centuries, and it was easy to imagine Henry Plantagenet's tiny fleet anchored here in 1147, waiting to sail to Jerusalem to fight the Infidel in the Second Crusade. Further round the headland stood the castle, built by Henry Tudor, Henry VII, whose son had broken with the papacy. Ben breathed deeply and smiled to himself. This was a place of history. From the town itself the Pilgrim Fathers had sailed in August 1620 to the new lands of America, and in June 1944 part of the great invasion fleet had sailed from here – five hundred ships, bound for Normandy and the liberation of Europe from Hitler and the Nazis.

All gone, he thought wryly, turning to look at his sister. *All of that rich past gone, forgotten – buried beneath the ice of the Han City.*

'Come on,' he said. 'The tide's low. We'll go by the rocks on the north lip. We should find something there.'

Meg nodded and followed him, taking his hand where the path was steepest, letting him help her down.

At the far edge of the shingle they stopped and took off their shoes, setting them down on the stones. Halfway across the sand, Ben stopped and turned, pointing down and back, tracing a line. 'Look!'

She looked. The sun had warmed the sand, but where they had stepped, their feet had left wet imprints, dark against the almost white, compacted sand. They faded even as she watched, the most distant first, the nearest last.

'Like history,' he said, turning away from her and walking on towards the water's edge.

Or memory, Meg thought, looking down at her feet. She took a step then stopped, watching how the sharp clarity of the imprint slowly decayed, like an image sent over some vast distance, first at the edges, then – in a sudden rush -at the very centre, breaking into two tiny, separate circles before it vanished. It was as if the whole had sunk down into the depths beneath the sand and was now stored in the rock itself.

'Here!' he called triumphantly. She hurried over to where he was crouched near the water's edge and bent down at his side.

The shell was two-thirds embedded in the sand. Even so, its shape and colouring were unmistakable. It was a pink-mouthed murex. She clapped her hands, delighted, and looked at him.

'Careful when you dig it out, Ben. You mustn't damage the spines.'

He knew, of course, but said nothing, merely nodded and pulled his bag round to the front, opening up the flap.

She watched him remove the sand in a circle about the shell, then set the tiny trowel down and begin to remove the wet, hard-packed sand with his fingers. When he had freed it, he lifted it carefully between his fingers and took it across to one of the rockpools to clean.

She waited. When he came back, he knelt in front of her and, opening out the fingers of her right palm, set the pale, white-pink shell down on her palm. Cleaned, it looked even more beautiful. A perfect specimen, curved and elegant, like some strange, fossil fish.

'The hedgehog of the seas,' he said, staring at the shell. 'How many points can you count?'

It was an old game. She lifted the shell and, staring at its tip – its 'nose' – began to count the tiny little nodes that marked each new stage on the spiral of growth.

'Sixteen,' she said, handing the shell back.

He studied it. 'More like thirty-four,' he said, looking up at her. He touched the tip of the shell gently. 'There are at least eighteen in that first quarter of an inch.'

'But they don't count!' she protested. 'They're too small!'

'Small they may be, but they do count. Each marks a stage in the mollusc's growth, from the infinitesimally tiny up. If you X-rayed this you'd see it. The same form repeated and repeated, larger and larger each time, each section sealed off behind the shellfish – outgrown, if you like. Still growing even at the creature's death. Never finished. The spiral uncompleted.'

'As spirals are.'

He laughed and handed her back the shell. 'Yes. I suppose by its nature it's incomplete. Unless twinned.'

Meg stared at him a moment. 'Ben? What *are* we doing here?'

His dark green eyes twinkled mischievously. 'Collecting shells. That's all.'

He stood and walked past her, scanning the sand for new specimens. Meg turned, watching him intently, knowing it was far more complex than he claimed, then got up and joined him in the search.

Two hours later they took a break. The sun had moved behind them and the far end of the cove was now in shadow. The tide had turned an hour back and the sea had already encroached upon the sands between the rocks at the cove's mouth. Ben had brought sandwiches in his bag and they shared them now, stretched out on the low rocks, enjoying the late afternoon sunlight, the shells spread out on a cloth to one side.

There were more than a dozen different specimens on the bright green cloth – batswing and turitella, orchid spider and flamingo tongue, goldmouth helmet and striped bonnet, pelican's foot, mother of pearl, snakeshead cowrie and several others – all washed and gleaming in the sun. A whole variety of shapes and sizes and colours, and not one of them native to the cold grey waters of the English south coast.

But Meg knew nothing of that.

It had begun when Meg was only four. There had been a glass display case on the wall in the hallway, and, noting what pleasure Meg derived from the form and colour of the shells, Hal Shepherd had bought new specimens in the City and brought them back to the Domain. He had scattered them by hand in the cove at low tide and taken Meg back the next day to 'find' them. Ben, seven at the time, had understood at once, but had gone along with the deception, not wishing to spoil Meg's obvious enjoyment of the game. And when his father had suggested he rewrite his great-grandfather's book on shells to serve the deception, Ben had leaped at the opportunity. That volume now rested on the shelves in place of the original, a clever, subtle parody. Now he, in his turn, carried on his father's game. These shells that now lay on the cloth he had scattered only two days ago.

Seagulls called lazily, high overhead. He looked up, shielding his eyes, then looked back at Meg. Her eyes were closed, her body sprawled out on the rock, like a young lioness. Her limbs and face were heavily tanned, almost brown against the pure white of her shorts and vest. Her dark hair lay in thick long curls against the sun-bleached rock. His eyes, however, were drawn continually to the fullness of her breasts beneath the cloth, to the suggestive curve of leg and hip and groin, the rounded perfection of her shoulders, the silken smoothness of her neck, the strange nakedness of her toes. He shivered and looked away, disturbed by the sudden turn of his thoughts.

So familiar she was, and yet, suddenly, so strange.

'What are you thinking?' she asked, softly, almost somnolently.

The wind blew gently, mild, warm against his cheek and arm, then subsided. For a while he listened to the gentle slosh of the waves as they broke on the far side of the great mound of rock.

Meg pulled herself up on to one elbow and looked across at him. As ever, she was smiling. 'Well? Cat got your tongue?'

He returned her smile. 'You forget. There are no cats.'

She shook her head. 'You're wrong. Daddy promised me he'd bring one back this time.'

'Ah.' He nodded, but said nothing of what he was thinking. Another game. Extending the illusion. If their father brought a cat back with him, it too would be a copy – GenSyn, most like – because the Han had killed all the real cats long ago.

'What are you going to call him?'

She met his eyes teasingly. 'Zarathustra, I thought.'

He did not rise to her bait. Zarathustra had been Nietzsche's poet-philosopher, the scathingly bitter loner who had come down from his mountain hermitage to tell the world that God was dead.

'A good name. Especially for a cat. They're said to be highly independent.'

She was watching him expectantly. Seeing it, he laughed. 'You'll have to wait, Meg. Tomorrow, I promise you. I'll reveal everything then.'

Even the tiny pout she made – so much a part of the young girl he had known all his life – was somehow different today. Transformed and strangely, surprisingly erotic.

'Shells…' he said, trying to take his mind from her. 'Have you ever thought how like memory they are?'

'Never,' she said, laughing, making him think for a moment she had noticed something in his face.

He met her eyes challengingly. 'No. Think about it, Meg. Don't most people seal off their pasts behind them stage by stage, just as a mollusc outgrows its shell, sealing the old compartment off behind it?'

She smiled at him, then lay down again, closing her eyes. 'Not you. You've said it yourself. It's all still there. Accessible. All you have to do is chip away the rock and there it is, preserved.'

'Yes, but there's a likeness even so. That sense of things being embedded that I was talking of. You see, parts of my past *are* compartmentalized. I can remember what's in them, but I can't somehow return to them. I can't feel what it was like to be myself back then.'

She opened one eye lazily. 'And you want to?'

He stared back at her fiercely. 'More than anything. I want to capture what it felt like. To save it, somehow.'

'Hmm… ' Her eye was closed again.

'That's it, you see. I want to get *inside* the shell. To feel what it was like to be there before it was all sealed off to me. Do you understand that?'

'It sounds like pure nostalgia.'

He laughed, only his laughter was just a little too sharp. 'Maybe... but I don't think so.'

She seemed wholly relaxed now, as if asleep, her breasts rising and falling slowly. He watched her for a while, disturbed once more by the strength of what he felt. Then he lay down and, following her example, closed his eyes, dozing in the warm sun.

When he woke the sun had moved further down the sky. The shadow of the Wall had stretched to the foot of the rocks beneath them and the tide had almost filled the tiny cove, cutting them off. They would have to wade back. The heavy crash of a wave against the rocks behind him made him twist about sharply. As he turned a seagull cried out harshly close by, startling him. Then he realized. Meg was gone.

He got to his feet anxiously. 'Meg! Where are you?'

She answered him at once, her voice coming from beyond the huge tumble of rock, contesting with the crash of another wave. 'I'm here!'

He climbed the rocks until he was at their summit. Meg was below him, to his left, crouched on a rock only a foot or so above the water, leaning forward, doing something.

'Meg! Come away! It's dangerous!'

He began to climb down. As he did so she turned and stood up straight. 'It's okay. I was just...'

He saw her foot slip beneath her on the wet rock. Saw her reach out and steady herself, recovering her footing. And then the wave struck.

It was bigger than all the waves that had preceded it and broke much higher up the rocks, foaming and boiling, sending up a fine spray, like glass splintering before some mighty hammer. It hit the big, tooth-shaped rock to his right first, then surged along the line, roaring, buffeting the rocks in a frenzy of white water.

One moment Meg was there, the next she was gone. Ben saw her thrust against the rocks by the huge wave, then disappear beneath the surface. As the water surged back there was no sign of her.

'Meg!!!'

Ben pressed the emergency stud at his neck, then scrambled down the rocks and stood there at the edge, ignoring the lesser wave that broke about his feet, peering down into the water, his face a mask of anguish, looking for some sign of her.

At first nothing. Nothing at all. Then... *there!* He threw himself forward into the water, thrusting his body down through the chill darkness towards her. Then he was kicking for the surface, one arm gripping her tightly.

Gasping, Ben broke surface some twenty feet out from the rocks and turned on to his back, cradling Meg against him, face up, her head against his neck.

At first the waves helped him, carrying him in towards the rocks, but then he realized what danger he was in. He turned his head and looked. As the wave ebbed, it revealed a sharp, uneven shelf of rock. If he let the waves carry them in, they might be dashed against that shelf. But what other option was there? If he tried to swim around the rocks and into the cove he would be swimming against the current and it would take too long. And he had little time if he was to save Meg. He would have to risk it.

He slowed himself in the water, trying to judge the rise and fall of the waves, then kicked out. The first wave took him halfway to the rocks. The second lifted them violently and carried them almost there.

Almost. The wave was beginning to ebb as he reached out with his left hand and gripped the ledge. As the water surged back a spear of pain jolted through his arm, making him cry out. Then he was falling, his body twisting round, his side banging painfully against the rock.

For a moment it felt as if his hand were being torn from his arm, but he held on, waiting for the water to return, his artificial fingers biting into the rock, Meg gripped tightly against him. And when it came he kicked out fiercely, forcing himself up on to the land, then scrambled backwards, pushing desperately with his feet against the rock, away from the water, Meg a dead weight against him.

Ignoring the pain in his hand, he carried Meg up on to a ledge above the water and set her down, fear making his movements urgent. Her lips and the lobes of her ears were tinged with blue.

He tilted her head back, forcing her chin up, then pinched her nose shut with the finger and thumb of his left hand. Leaning over her, he sealed his lips about her open mouth and gave four quick, full breaths.

Ben moved his head back and checked the pulse at her neck. Her heart was still beating. He watched her chest fall, then, leaning forward again, breathed into her mouth, then, three seconds later, once more.

Meg shuddered then began to gag. Quickly he turned her head to the side, allowing her to bring up seawater and the part-digested sandwich she had eaten only an hour before. Clearing her mouth with his fingers, he tilted her head back again and blew another breath into her, then turned her head again as she gagged a second time. But she was breathing now. Her chest rose and fell, then rose again. Her eyelids fluttered.

Carefully, he turned her over, on to her front, bending her arm and leg to support the lower body, then tilted her chin back to keep the airway open. Her breathing was more normal now, the colour returning to her lips.

Ben sat back on his heels, taking a deep breath. She had almost died. His darling Meg had almost died. He shuddered, then felt a faint tremor pass through him like an aftershock. Gods! For a moment he closed his eyes, feeling a strange giddiness, then opened them again and put his hand down to steady himself.

Below him another wave broke heavily against the rocks, throwing up a fine spray. The tide was still rising. Soon they would be cut off completely. Ben looked about him, noting from the length of the shadows how late it was. They had slept too long. He would have to carry her across, and he would have to do it now.

He took a deep breath, preparing himself, then put his arms beneath her and picked her up, turning her over and cradling her, tilting her head back against his upper arm. Then he began to climb, picking his way carefully across the mound of rocks and down, into shadow.

The water was almost waist deep and, for the first twenty or thirty feet he lifted Meg up above it, afraid to let the chill get at her again. Then he was carrying her through horseheads of spume little more than knee deep and up on to the shingle.

He set her down on the shingle close to where they had left their sandals. She was still unconscious, but there was colour in her cheeks now and a reassuring regularity to her breathing. He looked about him but there was nothing warm to lay over her, nothing to give her to help her body counter the shock it would be feeling.

He hesitated a moment, then, knowing there was nothing else to be done before help arrived, he lay down beside her on the shingle and held her close to him, letting the warmth of his body comfort her.

★

Meg woke before the dawn, her whole body tensed, shivering, remember-ing what had happened. She lay there, breathing deeply, calming herself, staring through the darkness at the far wall where her collection of shells lay in its glass case. She could see nothing, but she knew it was there, conch and cowrie, murex and auger, chambered nautilus and spotted babylon, red mitre and giant chiragra – each treasured and familiar, yet different now; no longer so important to her. She recalled what Ben had said of shells and memory, of sealed chambers and growth, and knew she had missed something. He had been trying to say something to her, to seed an idea in her mind. But what?

She reached up, touching the lump on the side of her head gingerly, examining it with her fingers. It was still tender, but it no longer ached. The cut had been superficial and the wound had already dried. She had been lucky. Very lucky.

She sat up, yawning, then went still. There was a vague rustling, then the noise of a window being raised in Ben's room. For a moment she sat there, listening. Then she got up, pulled on her robe and went softly down the passage to his room. Ben was standing at the window, naked, leaning across the sill, staring out into the darkness.

Meg went to him and stood at his side, her hand on the small of his back, looking with him, trying to see what he was seeing. But to her it was only darkness. Her vision was undirected, uninformed.

She felt him shiver and turned her head to look into his face. He was smiling, his eyes bright with some knowledge she had been denied.

'It has something to do with this,' he said softly, looking back at her. 'With dark and light and their simple interaction. With the sunlight and its absence. So simple that we've nearly always overlooked it. It's there in the Tao, of course, but it's more than a philosophy – more than simply a way of looking at things – it's the very fabric of reality.'

He shivered, then smiled at her. 'Anyway... how are you?'

'I'm fine,' she answered in a whisper.

She had a sudden sense of him. Not of his words, of the all-too-sim-ple thing he'd said, but of his presence there beside her. Her hand still lay there on the firm, warm flesh of his back, pressing softly, almost unnoticed against his skin. She could feel his living pulse.

He was still looking at her, his eyes puzzling at something in her face.

She looked down at the place where her hand rested against his back, feeling a strange connective flow, stronger than touch, aware of him standing there, watching her; of the tautness, the lean muscularity of his body.

She had never felt this before. Never felt so strange, so conscious of her own physical being, there, in proximity to his own. His nakedness disturbed her and fascinated her, making her take a long, slow breath, as if breathing were suddenly hard.

As he turned towards her, her hand slipped across the flesh of his back until it rested against his hip. She shivered, watching his face, his eyes, surprised by the need she found in them.

She closed her eyes, feeling his fingers on her neck, moving down to gently stroke her shoulders. For a moment she felt consciousness slipping, then caught herself, steadying herself against him. Her fingers rested against the smooth channels of his groin, the coarse pubic hair tickling the knuckles of her thumbs.

She looked down at him and saw how fierce and proud he stood for her. Without thinking, she let her right hand move down and brush against his sex.

'Meg...' It was a low, desirous sound. His hands moved down her body, lifting her nightgown at the waist until his hands held her naked hips, his fingers gently caressing the soft smoothness of her flesh. She closed her eyes again, wanting him to go further, to push down and touch her, there where she ached for him.

'Meg...?'

She opened her eyes, seeing at once the strange mixture of fear and hurt, confusion and desire in his eyes.

'It's all right... ' she whispered, drawing him to her, reassuring him. She led him to the bed and lay there, letting him take the gown from her.

It hurt. For all his gentleness, his care, it hurt to take him inside her. And then the pain eased and she found she was crying, saying his name over and over, softly, breathlessly, as he moved against her. She responded eagerly, pressing up against him again and again until his movements told her he was coming. Trembling, she held him tighter, pulling him down into her, her hands gripping his buttocks, wanting him to spill his seed inside her. Then, as his whole body convulsed, she gasped, a wave of pure, almost painful pleasure washing over her. For a time she lapsed from consciousness, then, with a tiny shudder, she opened her eyes again.

They lay there, brother and sister, naked on the bloodied bed, their arms about each other. Ben slept, his chest rising and falling slowly while she watched its movement closely. She looked at his face, at his long dark lashes, his fine, straight nose and firm, full lips. A face the mirror of her own. Narcissistically, she traced the shape of his lips with her fingers, then let her hand rest on his neck, feeling the pulse there.

The look of him reminded her of something in Nietzsche, from the section in the *Zarathustra* called 'The Dance Song'. She said the words softly, tenderly, her voice almost a whisper.

'"To be sure, I am a forest and a night of dark trees: but he who is not afraid of my darkness will find rosebowers too under my cypresses.

'"And he will surely find too the little god whom girls love best: he lies beside the fountain, still, with his eyes closed."'

She shivered and looked down the length of their bodies, studying the differences that gender made between them. The fullness of her breasts and hips, the slenderness of his. The strangeness of his penis, so very different in rest; so sweet and harmless now, all the brutality, the lovely strength of it dissipated.

She felt a warmth, an achingly sweet tenderness rise up in her, looking at him, seeing how vulnerable he was in sleep. Unguarded and open. A different creature from his waking self. She wanted to kiss him there and wake that tiny bud, making it flower splendidly once more.

Meg closed her eyes and shivered. She knew what they had done. But there was no shame in her, no regret.

She loved him. It was quite simple. Sisters should love their brothers. But her love for him was different in kind. She loved him with more than a simple, sisterly devotion. For a long time she had loved him like this: wholly, without barriers.

And now he knew.

She got up, careful not to disturb him, and put on her gown. For a moment longer she stood there, looking down at his sleeping, perfect form, then left him, returning to her room.

And as she lay there, her eyes closed, drifting into sleep, her left hand pressed softly against her sex, as if it were his.

★

'How's my invalid?'

Beth Shepherd set the tray down on the floor, then went to the window and pulled back the curtains, letting the summer sunlight spill into the room.

Meg opened her eyes slowly, smiling. 'I'm fine. Really I am.'

Beth sat on the bed beside her daughter and parted her hair, examining the wound. 'Hmm. It looks all right. A nice clean cut, anyway.' For a moment she held her hand to Meg's brow, then, satisfied that she wasn't feverish, smiled and began to stroke her daughter's hair.

'I'm sorry...' Meg began, but her mother shook her head.

'Ben's told me what happened. It was an accident, that's all. You'll know better in future, won't you?'

'If it wasn't for Ben...'

Beth's fingers hesitated, then continued to comb Meg's thick, dark hair. 'I'd say that made you even, wouldn't you? A life for a life.'

Meg looked up at her. 'No. It was different. Totally different. He risked himself. He could have died.'

'Maybe. But would you have done less?'

Meg hesitated, then answered quietly, 'I guess not.' She shivered and looked across at the glass case that held her shells. 'You know, I can't imagine what it would be like here without Ben.'

'Nor I. But have your breakfast. That's if you feel like eating.'

Meg laughed. 'I'm ravenous, and it smells delicious.'

Beth helped Meg sit up, plumping pillows behind her, then took the tray from the floor and set it down on Meg's lap. There was grapefruit and pancakes, fresh orange and coffee, two thick slices of buttered toast and a small pot of honey.

Meg tucked in heartily, watched by her mother. When she was done, Beth clapped her hands and laughed. 'Goodness, Meg! You should fall in the water more often if it gives you an appetite like that!'

Meg sighed and lay back against the pillows, letting her mother take the tray from her and set it aside.

Beth turned back to her, smiling. 'Well? Are you staying in bed, or do you want to get up?'

Meg looked down, embarrassed. 'I want to talk.'

'What about?'

'About you, and Father. About how you met and fell in love.'

Beth laughed, surprised. 'Goodness! What brings this on?'

Meg coloured slightly. 'Nothing. It's just that I realized I didn't know.'

'Well... all right. I'll tell you.' She took a deep breath, then began. 'It was like this. When I was eighteen I was a pianist. I played all the great halls of the world, performing before the very highest of First Level society – the *Supernal*, as they call themselves. And then, one day, I was asked to play before the T'ang and his court.'

'That must have been exciting.'

'Very.' She took her daughter's hand and squeezed it gently. 'Anyway, that night, after the performance, everyone was telling me how well I'd played, but I was angry with myself. I had played badly. Not poorly, but by my own standards I had let myself down. And before the T'ang of all people. It seemed that only your father sensed something was wrong. It was he, I later found out, who had arranged the whole affair. He had seen me perform before and knew what I was capable of.

'Well. After the reception he took me aside and asked me if I'd been nervous. I had, of course. It's not every day that an eighteen-year-old is called to perform before one of the Seven. But that wasn't an excuse. I told him how ashamed I was at having let the T'ang down, and – to my surprise and chagrin – he agreed with me. Right there and then he took me into the T'ang's own quarters and, craving Li Shai Tung's forgiveness for intruding, made me sit at the piano again and play. "Your best this time, Elizabeth," he said. "Show the T'ang why I boasted of you." And I did, and this time, with just your father and the T'ang listening, I played better than I'd ever played in my life.'

'What did you play? Can you remember?'

Her mother smiled, looking off into the distance. 'Yes. It was Beethoven's Sonata in F Minor, the *Appassionata*. It was only when I had finished that I realized I had just committed a capital offence.'

Meg's mouth fell open. 'Gods! Of course! It's a prohibited piece, isn't it? Like all of Beethoven's work! But what did the T'ang do?'

Beth looked down at her daughter and ruffled her hair. 'He clapped. He stood up and applauded me. Then he turned to your father and said, "I don't know what that was, Hal, and I don't want to know, but you were right to bring the girl back. She's in a class of her own."'

'And?'

'And for a year nothing. I thought your father had forgotten me, though I often thought of him and of what he had done for me that evening. But then, out of the blue, I received an invitation from him, asking me to come and visit the Domain.'

Meg sat forward eagerly. 'And that's when it all happened?'

Beth shook her head. 'No. Not at all. I was flattered, naturally, but such a request was impossible to comply with. I was only nineteen. It was six years before I would come of age, and my mother and father would have forbidden me to go even if I had asked them.'

'So what did you do?'

Beth laughed. 'I did the only thing I could. I sent him an invitation to my next concert.'

'And he came?'

'No. What happened next was strange. My father called on me. I hadn't seen him in over six months, and then, the day after I'd sent the note to Hal, there was my father, larger than life, telling me that he'd arranged a husband for me.'

Meg's mouth fell open a second time. 'A husband?'

'Yes. The son of an old friend of his. A rich young buck with no talent and as little intelligence.'

Meg clutched her mother's hands tightly. 'And you said no. You told your father you were in love with Hal Shepherd and wanted to marry him. Is that right?'

Beth laughed. 'Gods, no. I had no say in it. Anyway, I wasn't in love with your father then. I quite liked him. He was handsome and intelligent, and I felt a kind of... affinity with him. But beyond that nothing. Not then, anyway. What I didn't realize, however, was that your father had fallen in love with me. It seems he had spent that whole year trying to forget me, but then, when he heard about my engagement, he went mad and challenged my intended to a duel.'

Meg blinked. 'He did *what*?'

'Yes.' Beth laughed delightedly. 'An old-fashioned duel, with swords.'

'*And*?' Meg's eyes were big and round.

'Well... My father was horrified, naturally. My fiancé wanted to fight, but Hal had something of a reputation as a swordsman and my father was certain he would kill my future husband. He asked Hal to call on him to try to sort things out.'

'And they came to an arrangement?'

Beth leaned forward. 'Not straight away. Though that's not the story my father told. You see, I listened secretly from the next room when they met. My father was angry at first. "You can't have her," he said. "If you kill this man, I'll arrange a marriage with another." "Then I'll kill him, too!" Hal said. My father was taken aback. "And I'll find another suitor. You can't kill them all." But Hal was determined. His voice rang out defiantly. "If I have to, I'll kill every last man in Chung Kuo! Don't you see? I *want* your daughter."'

Beth laughed, then sat back, her face suddenly more thoughtful, her eyes gazing back in time. Then, more quietly, 'Gods, Meg. You don't know how thrilling it is to be wanted like that.'

Meg watched her mother a moment longer, then looked down, giving a small shudder. 'Yes... And your father gave in to Hal?'

'Gods, no. He was a stubborn man. And a mercenary one. You see, he'd found out how much Hal was worth by then. All this was a kind of play-acting, you understand, to put up the price.'

Meg frowned, not understanding.

'He wanted a dowry. Payment for me.'

Meg made a small noise of astonishment.

'Yes. And he got it, too. He threatened to stop Hal from marrying me until I was twenty-five unless he paid what he asked.'

'And did he?'

'Yes. Twice what my father asked, in fact.'

'Why?'

Beth's smile widened. 'Because, Hal said, my father didn't know the half of what he had given life to.'

Meg was silent for a while, considering. Then she looked up at her mother again. 'Did you hate your father?'

Beth hesitated, a sadness in her face. 'I didn't know him well enough to hate him, Meg. But what I knew of him I didn't like. He was a little man, for all his talent. Not like Hal.' She shook her head gently, a faint smile returning to the corners of her mouth. 'No, not like your father at all.'

'Where's Ben?' Meg asked, interrupting her reverie.

'Downstairs. He's been up hours, working. He brought a lot of equipment up from the basement and set it up in the living-room.'

Meg frowned. 'What's he up to?'

Beth shook her head. 'I don't know. Fulfilling a promise, he said. He said you'd understand.'

'Ah...' *Shells,* she thought. *It has to do with shells.*

And memory.

Ben sat in a harness at the piano, the dummy cage behind him, its morph mimicking his stance. A single thin cord of conduit linked him to the morph. Across the room, a trivee spider crouched, its programme searching for discrepancies of movement between Ben and the morph. Meg sat down beside the spider, silent, watching.

A transparent casing covered the back of Ben's head, attached to the narrow, horseshoe collar about his neck. Within the casing a web of fine cilia made it seem that Ben's blond hair was streaked with silver. These were direct implants, more than sixty in all, monitoring brain activity.

Two further cords, finer than the link, led down from the ends of the collar to Ben's hands, taped to his arms every few inches. Further hair-fine wires covered Ben's semi-naked body, but the eye was drawn to the hands.

Fine, flexible links of ice formed crystalline gloves that fitted like a second skin about his hands. Sensors on their inner surfaces registered muscular movement and temperature changes.

Tiny pads were placed all over Ben's body, measuring his responses and feeding the information back into the collar.

As he turned to face Meg, the morph turned, faceless and yet familiar in its gestures, its left hand, like Ben's, upon its thigh, the fingers splayed slightly.

Meg found the duplication frightening – deeply threatening – but said nothing. The piano keyboard, she noted, was normal except in one respect. Every key was black.

'Call Mother in, Meg. She'd like to hear this.'

The morph was faceless, dumb, but in a transparent box at its feet was a separate facial unit – no more than the unfleshed suggestion of a face, the musculature replaced by fine wiring. As Ben spoke, so the half-formed face made the ghost-movements of speech, its lips and eyes a perfect copy of Ben's own.

Meg did as she was told, bringing her mother from the sunlight of the kitchen into the shadows of the living-room. Beth Shepherd sat beside her daughter, wiping her hands on her apron, attentive to her son.

He began.

His hands flashed over the keys, his fingers living jewels, coaxing a strange, wistful, complex music from the ancient instrument. A new sound from the old keys.

When he had done, there was a moment's intense silence, then his mother stood and went across to him. 'What *was* that, Ben? I've never heard its like. It was…' She laughed, incredulous, delighted. 'And I presumed to think that I could teach *you* something!'

'I wrote it,' he said simply. 'Last night, while you were all asleep.'

Ben closed his eyes, letting the dissonances form again in his memory. Long chordal structures of complex dissonances, overlapping and repeating, twisting about each other like the intricate threads of life, the long chains of deoxyribonucleic acid. It was how he saw it. Not A and C and G Minor, but Adenine and Cytosine and Guanine. A complex, living structure.

A perfect mimicry of life.

The morph sat back, relaxing after its efforts, its chest rising and falling, its hands resting on its knees. In the box by its feet the eyes in the face were closed, the lips barely parted, only a slight flaring of the nostrils indicating life.

Meg shuddered. She had never heard anything so beautiful, or seen anything so horrible. It was as if Ben were being played. The morph, at its dummy keyboard, seemed far from being the passive recipient of instructions. A strange power emanated from the lifeless thing, making Ben's control of things seem suddenly illusory: the game of some greater, more powerful being, standing unseen behind the painted props.

So this was what Ben had been working on. A shiver of revulsion passed through her. And yet the beauty – the strange, overwhelming beauty of it. She shook her head, not understanding, then stood and went out into the kitchen, afraid for him.

★

Ben found her in the rose garden, her back to him, staring out across the bay. He went across and stood there, close by her, conscious more than ever of the naked form of her beneath the soft gauze dress she wore. Her legs were bare, her hair unbraided. The faintest scent of lavender hung about her.

'What's up?' he asked softly. 'Didn't you like it?'

She turned her head and gave a tight smile, then looked back. It was answer enough. It had offended her somehow.

He walked past her slowly, then stopped, his back to her, his left hand on his hip, his head tilted slightly to the left, his right hand at his neck, his whole body mimicking her stance. 'What didn't you like?'

Normally she would have laughed, knowing he was ragging her, but this time it was different. He heard her sigh and turn away, and wondered, for a moment, if it was to do with what had happened in the night.

She took a step away, then turned back. He had turned to follow her. Now they stood there, face to face, a body's length separating them.

'It was...'

She dropped her eyes, as if embarrassed.

He caught his breath, moved by the sight of her. She might have died. And then he would never have known. He spoke softly, coaxingly; the way she so often spoke to him, drawing him out. 'It was what?'

She met his eyes. 'It was frightening.' He saw her shiver. 'I felt...' She hesitated, as if brought up against the edge of what she could freely say to him. This reticence was something new in her and unexpected, a result of the change in their relationship. Like something physical in the air between them.

'Shall we walk? Along the shore?'

She hesitated, then smiled faintly. 'Okay.'

He looked up. The sky was clouding over. 'Come. Let's get our boots and coats. It looks like it might rain.'

An hour later they were down at the high-water level, their heavy boots sinking into the mud, the sky overcast above them, the creek and the distant water meadows to their left. It was low tide and the mud stretched out to a central channel that meandered like an open vein cut into a dark cheek, glistening like oil whenever the sun broke through the clouds.

For a time they walked in silence, hand in hand, conscious of their new relationship. It felt strange, almost like waking to self-conscious-ness. Before there had been an intimacy, almost a singularity about them – a seamless continuity of shared experience. They had been a single cell, unbreached. But now? Now it was different. It was as if this new, purely physical intimacy had split that cell, beginning some ancient, inexorable process of division.

Perhaps it was unavoidable. Perhaps, being who they were, they had been fated to come to this. And yet...

It remained unstated, yet both felt an acute sense of loss. It was there, implicit in the silence, in the sighs each gave as they walked the shoreline.

Where the beach narrowed, they stopped and sat on a low, gently sloping table of grey rock, side by side, facing back towards the cottage. The flat expanse of mud lay to their right now, while to their left, no more than ten paces away, the steep, packed earth bank was almost twice their height, the thickly interwoven branches of the overhanging trees throwing the foot of the bank into an intense shade. It could not be seen from where they sat, but this stretch of the bank was partly bricked, the rotting timbers of an old construction poking here and there from the weathered surface. Here, four centuries before, French prisoners from the Napoleonic Wars had ended their days, some in moored hulks, some in the makeshift gaols that had lined this side of the creek.

Ben thought of those men now. Tried to imagine their suffering, the feel-ing of homesickness they must have felt, abandoned in a foreign land. But there was something missing in him – some lack of pure experience – that made it hard for him to put himself in their place. He did not know how it felt to be away from home. Here was home and he had always been here. And there, in that lack of knowledge, lay the weakness in his art.

It had begun long before last night. Long before Meg had come to him. And yet last night had been a catalyst – a clarification of all he had been feeling.

He thought of the words his father had quoted back at him and knew they were right.

Ultimately, no one can extract from things, books included, more than he already knows. What one has no access to through experience one has no ear for.

It was so. For him, at least, what Nietzsche had said was true. And he had no access. Not here.

He was restless. He had been restless for the past twelve months. He realized that now. It had needed something like this to bring it into focus for him. But now he knew. He had to get out.

Even before last night he had been thinking of going to college in the City. To Oxford, maybe, or the Technical School at Strasburg Canton. But he had been thinking of it only as the natural path for such as he; as a mere furthering of his education. Now, however, he knew there was more to it than that. He needed to see life. To experience life fully, at all its levels. Here he had come so far, but the valley had grown too small for him, too confined. He needed something more – something *other* – than what was here in the Domain.

'If I were to...' he began, turning to face Meg, then fell silent, for at the same time she had turned her head and begun to speak to him.

They laughed, embarrassed. It had never happened before. They had always known instinctively when the other was about to speak. But this... it was like being strangers.

Meg shivered, then bowed her head slightly, signalling he should speak, afraid to repeat that moment of awkwardness.

Ben watched her a moment. Abruptly, he stood and took three paces from her, then turned and looked back at her. She was looking up at him from beneath the dark fall of her hair.

'I've got to leave here, Meg.'

He saw at once how surprised she was. There was a widening of her eyes, the slightest parting of her lips, then she lowered her head. 'Ah...'

He was silent, watching her. But as he made to speak again, she looked up suddenly, the hurt and anger in her eyes unexpected.

'Is it because of last night?'

He sighed. 'It has nothing to do with us. It's me. I feel constrained here. Boxed in. It feels like I've outgrown this place. Used it up.'

As he spoke he stared away from her at the creek, the surrounding hills, the small, white-painted cottages scattered amongst the trees. Overhead, the sky was a lid of ashen grey.

'And I *have to* grow. It's how I am.' He looked at her fiercely, defiantly. 'I'll die if I stay here much longer, Meg. Can't you see that?'

She shook her head, her voice passionate with disagreement. 'It's not so, Ben. You've said it yourself. It's a smaller world in there. You talk of feeling boxed in, here, in the Domain. But you're wrong. That's where it's really boxed in. Not here. We're outside all of that. Free of it.'

He laughed strangely, then turned aside. 'Maybe. But I have to find that out. For myself.' He looked back at her. 'It's like that business with memory. I thought I knew it all, but I didn't. I was wrong, Meg. I'd assumed too much. So now I've got to find out. Now. While I still can.'

Her eyes had followed every movement in his face, noting the intense restlessness there. Now they looked down, away from his. 'Then I don't understand you, Ben. Surely there's no hurry?'

'Ah, but there is.'

She looked up in time to see him shrug and turn away, looking out across the mud towards the City.

The City. It was a constant in their lives. Wherever they looked, unless it was to sea, that flat, unfeatured whiteness defined the limits of their world, like a frame about a picture, or the edge of some huge, encroaching glacier. They had schooled themselves not to see it. But today, with the sky pressed low and featureless above them, it was difficult not to see it as Ben saw it – as a box, containing them.

'Maybe... ' she said, below her breath. But the very thought of him leaving chilled her to the bone.

He turned, looking back at her. 'What were you looking for?'

She frowned. 'I don't follow you.'

'Before the wave struck. You were about to tell me something. You'd seen something.'

She felt a sudden coldness on the back of her hand and looked. It was a spot of rain. She brushed at it, then looked back at her brother.

'It was a shell. One I'd never seen before. It was attached to the rock but I couldn't free it with my fingers. It was like it was glued there. A strange, ugly-looking shell, hard and ridged, shaped like a nomad's tent.'

More spots of rain fell, distinct and heavy. Ben looked up at the sky, then back at her. 'We'd best get back. It's going to chuck down.'

She went across to him and took his hand.

'Go,' she said. 'But not yet. Not just yet.'

He leaned forward, kissing her brow, then moved back, looking at her, his dark green eyes seeing nothing but her for that brief moment. 'I love you, Megs. Understand that. But I can't help what I am. I have to go. If I don't...'

She gave the smallest nod. 'I know. Really. I understand.'

'Good.' This time his lips touched hers gently, then drew away.

She shivered and leaned forward, wanting to kiss him once again, but just then the clouds burst overhead and the rain began to come down heavily, pocking the mud about their feet, soaking their hair and faces in seconds.

'Christ!' he said, raising his voice against the hard, drumming sound of the rain. For a moment neither of them moved, then Meg turned and, pointing to the bank, yelled back at him.

'There! Under the trees!'

Ben shook his head. 'No. Come on! There's half a day of rain up there. Let's get back!' He took her hands, tugging at her, then turned and, letting her hands fall from his, began to run back along the shore towards the cottage. She caught up with him and ran beside him, laughing now, sharing his enjoyment of the downpour, knowing – suddenly knowing without doubt – that just as he had to go, so he would be compelled to return. In time. When he had found what he was looking for.

Suddenly he stopped and, laughing, throwing his hands up towards the sky, turned his eyes on her again. 'It's beautiful!' he shouted. 'It's bloody beautiful!'

'I know!' she answered, looking past him at the bay, the tree-covered hillsides misted by the downpour, the dour-looking cottages on the slope before them.

Yes, she thought. You'll miss this in the City. There it never rains. Never in ten thousand years.

Chapter 48

COMPULSIONS

That night he dreamed.

He was floating above a desert, high up, the jet-black, lavatic sands stretching off to the horizon on every side. Tall spirals of dust moved slowly across the giant plain, like fluted pillars linking Heaven and Earth. A cold wind blew. Over all, a black sun sat like a sunken eye in a sky of bloodied red.

He had come here from dead lands, deserted lands, where temples to forgotten gods lay in ruins, open to the sky; had drifted over vast mountain ranges, their peaks a uniform black, the purest black he'd ever seen, untouched by snow or ice; had glided over plains of dark, fused glass, where the image of his small, compacted self flew like a doppelganger under him, soaring to meet him when he fell, falling as he rose. And now he was here, in this empty land, where colour ended and silence was a wall within the skull.

Time passed. Then, with a huge, almost animal shudder that shook the air about him, the sands beneath him parted, the great dunes rolling back, revealing the perfect smoothness of a lake, its red-tinged waters like a mirror.

He fell. Turning in the air, he made an arrow of himself, splitting the dark, oily surface cleanly. Down he went, the coal black liquid smooth, unresistant, flowing about his body like cold fire.

Deep he went, so deep that his ears popped and bled. His lungs, like flowers, blossomed in the white cage of his chest, bursting, flooding his insides with a fiery hotness. For a moment the blackness was within, seeping into him through every pore; a barrier through which he must pass. Then he was through; freed from his normal, human self. And still he sank, like a spear of iron, down through the blackness, until there, ten miles beneath the surface, the depths were seared with brightness.

The lake's bed was white, like bone; clean and polished and flat, like something made by men. It glowed softly from beneath, as if another land – miraculous and filled, as bright as this was dark – lay on the far side of its hard, unyielding barrier.

He turned his eyes, drawn to something to his left. He swam towards it.

It was a stone. A dark, perfect circle of stone, larger than his palm. It had a soft, almost dusted surface. He touched it, finding it cool and hard. Then, as he watched, it seemed to melt and flow, the upper surface flattening, the thin edge crinkling. Now it was a shell, an oyster, its circumference split by a thin, uneven line of darkness.

His hand went to his waist and took the scalpel from its tiny sheath, then slipped its edge between the plates. Slowly, reluctantly, they parted, like a moth's wings opening to the sun.

Inside was a pearl of darkness – a tiny egg so dark, so intensely black, that it seemed to draw all light into itself. He reached out to take it, but even as he closed his left hand about the pearl, he felt its coldness burn into his flesh then fall, like a drop of Heaven's fire, on to the bed below.

Astonished, he held the hand up before his face and saw the perfect hole the pearl had made. He turned the hand. Right through. The pearl had passed right through.

He shivered. And then the pain came back, like nothing he had ever experienced.

Ben woke and sat upright, beaded in sweat, his left hand held tightly in his right, the pain from it quite real. He stared at it, expecting to see a tiny hole burned through from front to back, but there was no outward sign of what was wrong. It spasmed again, making him cry out, the pain unbelievable – worse than the worst cramp he had ever had.

'Shit!' he said beneath his breath, annoyed at himself for his weakness. *Control the pain*, he thought. *Learn from it.* He gritted his teeth and looked at the timer on the wall beside his bed. It was just after five.

He must have damaged the hand, getting Meg out of the water.

When the pain subsided he got up, cradling the hand against his chest, and began to dress. It was more difficult than he had imagined, for the slightest awkward movement of the hand would put it into spasm again, taking his breath. But eventually it was done and, quietly, he made his way out and down the passageway.

The door to Meg's room was open. Careful not to wake her, he looked inside. Her bed was to the left against the far wall, the window just above her head. She lay on her front, her hair covering her face, her shoulders naked in the shadow, her right arm bent above the covers. The curtains were drawn, the room in partial darkness, but a small gap high up let in a fragment of the early morning sun, a narrow bar of golden light. It traced a contoured line across the covers and up the wall, revealing part of her upper arm. He stared at it a moment, oblivious of the dull pain in his hand, seeing how soft her flesh seemed in this light.

For a moment he hesitated, wondering if he should wake her.

And if he did?

He shivered, remembering how she had come to him in the night, and felt that same strong stirring of desire. Though it disturbed him, he could not lie to himself. He wanted her. More now than before. Wanted to kiss the softness of her neck and see her turn, warm and smiling, and take him in her arms.

The shiver that ran up his spine was like the feeling he had when listening to an exquisite piece of music, or on first viewing a perfect work of art. But how so? he wondered. Or was all art grounded in desire?

The fingers of his damaged hand clenched again. He took a sharp intake of breath against the pain and leaned his shoulder against the doorpost. It was the worst yet and left him feeling cold and weak, his brow beaded with sweat. He would have to have it seen to today. This morning, if possible. But first there was something he must do.

He went down and unlatched the door that led into the garden. Outside the air was sharp, fresh, the sky clear after the rain. Long shadows lay across the glittering, dew-soaked grass, exaggerating every hump and hollow, making the ground seem rutted and uneven. The roses were beaded with dew, the trestle table dark and wet.

He was still a moment, listening to the call of birds in the eaves above him and in the trees down by the water. It was strange how that sound seemed always not to breach but to emphasize the underlying silence.

The pain came again, more bearable this time. He braced himself against it, then, when it was fading, lifted the injured hand to his face. There was the faintest scent of burning. A sweet, quite pleasant scent. He pressed it against his cheek. It was warm. Unnaturally warm.

Cradling the hand against his chest, he stared out across the lawn towards the shadowed bay. The tide was high. Sunlight lay in the trees on the far side of the water, creeping slowly towards the waterline.

He smiled. This much never changed: each day created anew; light flying out from everything, three hundred metres in a millionth of a second, off on its journey to infinity.

He went down, across the lawn and on to the narrow gravel path that led, by way of an old, rickety gate, into the meadows. The grass here was knee high, uncut since his father had left, three months past, the tall stems richly green and tufted. He waded out into that sea of grass, ignoring the path that cut down to the meandering creek, making for the Wall.

There, at the foot of the Wall, he stopped, balanced at the end of a long rib of rock that protruded above the surrounding marshland. The Wall was an overpowering presence here, the featureless whiteness of its two-li height making a perfect geometric turn of one hundred and twenty degrees towards the southeast. It was like being in the corner of a giant's playbox, the shadow of the Wall so deep it seemed almost night. Even so, he could make out the great circle of the Seal quite clearly, there, at the bottom of the Wall, no more than thirty paces distant.

Ben squatted and looked about him. Here memory was dense. Images clustered about him like restless ghosts. He had only to close his eyes to summon them back. There, off to his left, he could see the dead rabbit from five years before, sunk into the grass. And there, just beyond it, his father, less than a year ago, looking back towards him but pointing at the Seal, explaining the new policy the Seven had drawn up for dealing with incursions from the Clay. He turned his head. To his right he could see Meg, a hundred, no, a thousand times, smiling or thoughtful, standing and sitting, facing towards him or away, running through the grass or simply standing by the creek, looking outward at the distant hills. Meg as a child, a girl, a woman. Countless images of her. All stored, hoarded in his mind. And for what? Why such endless duplication of events?

He shuddered, then turned, looking back at the cottage, thinking how ageless it seemed in this early morning light. He looked down, then rubbed the back of his left hand with his right, massaging it. It felt better now, more relaxed, which made him think it was some form of cramp. But did machines get cramp?

He breathed deeply, then laughed. *And what if we're all machines? What if we're merely programmed to think otherwise?*

Then the answer would be, yes, machines get cramp.

It was strange, that feeling of compulsion he had had to come here. Overpowering, like his desire for Meg. It frightened him. And even when it was purged it left him feeling less in control of himself than he had ever been. Part of that, of course, was the drugs – or the absence of them. It was over a week now since he had last taken them. But it was more than that. He was changing. He could feel it in himself. But into what? And for what purpose?

He stared at the Seal a moment longer, then looked away, disturbed. It was like in his dream. The bottom of the lake: that had been the Wall. He had sunk through the darkness to confront the Wall.

And?

He shivered. No, he didn't understand it yet. Perhaps, being what he was – schizophrenic – he *couldn't* understand it. Not from where he was, anyway. Not from the inside. But if he passed through?

He stared at the Wall intently, then looked down. And if his father said no? If his father said he couldn't go to college?

Ben got to his feet, turning his back upon the Wall. If Hal said no he would defy him. He would do it anyway.

'Again, Meg. And this time try to relax a bit. Your fingers are too tense. Stretch them gently. Let them *feel* for the notes. Accuracy is less important than feeling at this stage. Accuracy will come, but the feeling has to be there from the start.'

Meg was sitting beside her mother at the piano. It was just after nine and they had been practising for more than an hour already, but she was determined to master the phrase – to have something to show Ben when he returned.

She began again. This time it seemed to flow better. She missed two notes and one of the chords was badly shaped, yet, for all its flaws, it sounded much more like the phrase her mother had played than before. She turned and saw Beth was smiling.

'Good, Meg. Much better. Try it again. This time a little slower.'

She did as she was bid, leaning forward over the keys. This time it was note perfect and she sat back, pleased with herself, feeling a genuine sense of achievement. It was only a small thing, of course – nothing like Ben's playing – yet it was a start: the first step in her attempt to keep up with him.

She looked round again. Her mother was watching her strangely.

'What is it?'

Beth took her hand. 'You're a good child, Meg. You know that? Nothing comes easy to you. Not like Ben. But you work at it. You work hard. And you never get disheartened. I've watched you labour at something for weeks, then seen Ben come along and master it in a few moments. And always – without fail – you've been delighted for him. Not envious, as some might be. Or bitter. And that's...' She laughed. 'Well, it's remarkable. And I love you for it.'

Meg looked down. 'He needs someone.'

'He does, doesn't he?'

'I mean...' Meg placed her free hand gently on the keys, making no sound. 'It must be difficult being as he is. Being so alone.'

'Alone? I don't follow you, Meg.'

'Like Zarathustra, up in his cave on the mountainside. Up where the air is rarefied, and few venture. Only with Ben the mountain, the cave are in his head.'

Beth nodded thoughtfully. 'He's certainly different.'

'That's what I mean. It's his difference that makes him alone. Even if there were a hundred thousand people here, in the Domain, he would be separate from them all. Cut off by what he is. That's why I have to make the effort. To try to reach him where he is. To try to understand what he is and what he needs.'

Beth looked at her daughter, surprised. 'Why?'

'Because he's Ben. And because I love him.'

She reached out and gently brushed Meg's cheek with her knuckles. 'That's nice. But you don't have to worry. Give him time. He'll find someone.'

Meg looked away. Her mother didn't understand. There *was* no one else for Ben. No one who would ever understand him a tenth as well. Not one in the whole of Chung Kuo.

'Do you want to play some more?'

Meg shook her head. 'Not now. This afternoon, perhaps?'

'All right. Some breakfast, then?'

Meg smiled. 'Why not?'

They were in the kitchen, at the big, scrubbed pine table, their meal finished, when there were footsteps on the flagstones outside. The latch creaked, then the door swung outward. Ben stood in the doorway, looking in, his left arm held strangely at his side.

'That smells good.'

His mother got up. 'Sit down. I'll cook you something.'

'Thanks. But not now.' He looked at Meg. 'Are you free, Megs? I need to talk.'

Meg looked across at her mother. She had been about to help her with the washing. 'Can I?'

Beth smiled and nodded. 'Go on. I'll be all right.'

Meg got up, taking her plate to the sink, then turned back, facing him. 'Where have you been... ?' She stopped, noticing how he was holding his left arm. 'Ben? What have you done?'

He stared at her a moment, then looked towards his mother. 'I've damaged the hand. I must have done it on the rocks.' He held it out to her. 'I can barely use it. If I try to it goes into spasm.'

Beth wiped her hands, then went to him. She took the hand carefully and studied it, Meg at her side, her face filled with concern.

'Well, there's no outward sign of damage. And it was working perfectly well yesterday.'

Ben nodded. 'Yes. But that stint at the piano probably didn't help it any.'

'Does it hurt?' Meg asked.

'It did. When I woke up. But I've learned how not to set it off. I pretend the problem's higher up. Here.' He tapped his left shoulder with his right hand. 'I pretend the whole arm's dead. That way I'm not tempted to try to use the hand.'

Beth placed his arm back against his side, then turned away, looking for something in the cupboards. 'Have you notified anyone?'

He nodded. 'Two hours back. When I came in from the meadows. They're sending a man this afternoon.'

She turned back, a triangle of white cloth between her hands. 'Good. Well, for now I'll make a sling for you. That'll ease the strain of carrying it about.'

He sat, letting his mother attend to him. Meg, meanwhile, stood beside him, her hand resting gently on his shoulder.

'Why was the keyboard black? I mean, totally black?'

He looked up at her. 'Why?'

Meg shrugged. 'It's been playing on my mind, that's all. It just seemed... strange. Unnecessary.'

Beth, kneeling before him, fastening the sling at his shoulder, looked up, interested in what he would say.

'It's just that I find the old-style keyboard distracting. It preconditions thought; sets the mind into old patterns. But that all-black keyboard is only a transitional stage. A way of shaking free old associations. Ultimately I want to develop a brand-new keyboard – one better suited to what I'm doing.'

'There!' Beth tightened the knot then stood up. 'And what *are* you doing?'

Ben met her eyes candidly. 'I don't know yet. Not the all of it, anyway.' He stood, moving his shoulder slightly. 'Thanks. That's much easier.' Then he looked across at Meg. 'Are you ready?'

She hesitated, wondering for a moment if she might persuade him to listen to the piano phrase she had learned that morning, then smiled and answered him softly. 'Okay. Let's go.'

It was late morning, the sun high overhead, the air clear and fresh. They sat beneath the trees on the slope overlooking the bay, sunlight through the branches dappling the grass about them, sparkling on the water below. Above them, near the top of the hillside, obscured by a small copse of trees, was the ruined barn, preserved as it had been when their great-great-great-grandfather, Amos, had been a boy.

For two hours they had rehearsed the reasons why Ben should leave or stay. Until now it had been a reasonably amicable discussion, a clearing of the air, but things had changed. Now Meg sat there, her head turned away from her brother, angry with him.

'You're just pig stubborn! Did you know that, Ben? Stubborn as in stupid. It's not the time. *Not now.*'

He answered her quietly, knowing he had hurt her. 'Then when is the time? I have to do this. I *feel* I have to. And all the rest… that's just me rationalizing that feeling. It's the feeling – the instinct – that I trust.'

She turned on him, her eyes flashing. 'Instinct! Wasn't it you who said that instinct was just a straitjacket – the Great Creator's way of showing us whose fingers are really on the control buttons?'

He laughed, but she turned away from him. For once this was about something other than what *he* wanted. This was to do with Meg, with *her* needs.

'Don't make it hard, Megs. Please don't.'

She shivered and stared outward, across the water, her eyes burning, her chin jutting defiantly. 'Why ask me? You'll do what you want to anyway. Why torment me like this when you know you've decided already what you're going to do?'

He watched her, admiring her, wanting to lean forward and kiss her neck, her shoulder. She was wearing a long, nut-brown cotton dress that was drawn in below the breasts and buttoned above. The hem of it was gathered about her knees, exposing the tanned flesh of her naked calves. He looked down, studying her feet, noting the delicacy of the toes, the finely rounded nails. She was beautiful. Even her feet were beautiful. But she could not keep him here. Nothing could keep him. He must find himself. Maybe then he could return.

'Don't chain me, Meg. Help me become myself. That's all I'm asking.'

She turned angrily, as if to say something, then looked down sharply, her hurt confusion written starkly on her face.

'I want to help you, Ben. I really do. It's just…'

He hardened himself against her, against the pity he instinctively felt. She was his sister. His lover. There was no one in the world he was closer to and it was hard to hurt her like this, but hurt her he must, or lose sight of what he must become. In time she would understand this, but for now the ties of love blinded her to what was best. And not just for him, but for the two of them.

'Keep me here, Meg and it'll die in me. It'll turn inward and fester. You know it will. And I'll blame you for that. Deep down I'll come to hate you for keeping me here. And I never want to hate you. *Never.*'

She met his eyes, her own moist with unshed tears. Then she turned and came to him, holding him, careful not to hurt his damaged arm, her head laid warmly, softly, on his right shoulder.

'Well?' he said after a while. 'Will you support me against Father?'

He noticed the slight change in her breathing. Then she moved back away from him, looking at him intently, as if reading something in his face.

'You think he'll try to stop you?'

Ben nodded. 'He'll make excuses. The uncertainty of the times. My age.'

'But what if he's right, Ben? What if it is too dangerous? What if you *are* too young?'

'Too young? I'm seventeen, Meg. Seventeen! And, apart from that one visit to Tongjiang, I've never seen anything other than this, never been anywhere but here.'

'Is that so bad?'

'Yes. Because there's more to life than this. Much more. There's a whole new world in there. One I've no real knowledge of. And I need to experience it. Not at second hand, through a screen, but close up.'

She looked down. 'What you were saying, Ben, about me chaining you. I'd never do that. You know I wouldn't. And I *can* free you. But not in there. Not in the City.' She raised her eyes. 'This is our place. Right here. It's what we've been made for. Like the missing pieces of a puzzle.' She paused, then, more earnestly, she went on, 'We're not like them, Ben. We're different. Different *in kind*. Like aliens. You'll find that out.'

'All part of Amos's great experiment, eh?'

'Maybe...' But it wasn't what she had meant. She was thinking less of genetic charts than of something deeper in their natures – some sense of connection with the earth that they had, and that others – cut off by the walls and levels of the City – lacked. It was as if they were at the same time both more and less advanced as human beings, more primitive and yet more exalted spiritually. They were the bridge between Heaven and Earth – the link between the distant past and the far future. For them, therefore, the City was an irrelevancy – a wrong direction Man had taken – and for Ben to embrace it was simply foolish, a waste of his precious time and talents.

Besides which, she needed him. Needed him as much – though he did not see it yet – as he needed her. It would break her heart to see him go.

'Is that all?' he asked, sensing she had more to say.

She answered him quietly, looking away past him as she spoke. 'No. It's more than that. I worry about you. All this business with morphs and mimicry. I fear where it will take you.'

'Ah...' He smiled and looked down, plucking a tall stem of grass and putting it to his mouth. 'You know, Meg, in the past there was a school of thought that associated the artist with Satan. They argued that all art was blasphemy – an abrogation of the role of the Creator. They claimed that all artists set themselves up in place of God, making their tiny satanic palaces – their pandemoniums – in mimicry of God's eternal City. They were wrong, of course, but in a sense it's true. All art is a kind of mimicry, an attempt to get closer to the meaning of things.

'Some so-called artists are less interested in understanding why things are as they are than in providing a showcase for their own egotism, but in general true art – art of the kind that *sears* you – is created from a desire to understand, not to replace. Mimicry, at that level, is a form of worship.'

She laughed softly. 'I thought you didn't believe in God.'

'I don't. But I believe in the reality of all this that surrounds us. I believe in natural processes. In the death of stars and the cycle of the seasons. In the firing of the synapses and the inexorable decay of the flesh. In the dark and the light.'

'And in the City, too?'

He smiled. 'That too is a process, part of the natural flow of things, however "unnatural" it might seem. The City is an expression of human intelligence, which, after all, is a natural thing. It's too easy to dismiss its artificiality as an antithesis to nature, when all it really is is an attempt to simplify and thus begin to understand the complexity of natural processes.'

'And to control those processes.'

'Yes, but there are levels of control. For instance, what controls us that makes us want to control other things? Is it all just genetics? And even if it is, what reason is there for that? We've been asking ourselves that question since DNA was first isolated, and we're still no closer to an answer.'

She looked away sharply, as if suddenly tired of the conversation. 'I don't know, Ben. It all seems suddenly so bleak. So dark.'

Again he misread her comment, mistook its surface content for its deeper meaning. 'Yes,' he said, staring out across the water. 'But what is darkness? Is it only a space waiting to be filled? Or has it a purpose? Something other than simple contrast?'

'Ben...'

He looked back at her, surprised by the brittle tone she had used. She was looking at him strangely.

'Yes?'

'What about us? How do we fit in with all these processes?'

'We're a focus, a filter...'

But she was shaking her head. 'No. I didn't mean that. I meant us. You and me. Is that just process? Just a function of the universe? Is what I feel for you just another fact to be slotted into the great picture? Or is there more to it than that? Are there parts of it that just don't fit?'

Again the bitterness in her voice surprised him. He had thought it resolved between them, but now he understood: it would never be finally resolved until he was gone from here.

'Three years,' he said. 'That's all I'll need. You'll be, what... seventeen – my age now – when I come back. It's not long, Meg. Really it isn't.'

She rose, moving away, then stood at the edge of the trees above him, her back turned.

'You talk of dying if you stay. But I'll die if you go. Don't you understand that, Ben? Without you here it'll be like I'm dead.' She turned to him, her eyes wide with hurt and anger. 'You're my eyes, my ears, the animating force behind each moment of my day. Without you... I don't exist!'

He gave a short laugh, surprised by her intensity. 'But that's silly, Meg. Of course you exist. Besides, there's Mother...'

'Gods! You really don't understand, do you?'

There was that same, strange, unreadable movement in her face, then, abruptly, she turned away, beginning to climb the slope.

Ben got up awkwardly and made to follow her, making his way between the trees, careful not to knock his useless arm, but she had begun to run now, her whole body leaning into the slope as she struggled to get away from him.

At the edge of the trees he stopped, wincing from the sudden pain in his hand, then called out to her. 'Meg! Stop! Please stop!'

She slowed then stood there, just below the barn, her back to him, her head lowered, waiting.

Coming to her, he moved round her, then lifted her face with his good hand. She was crying.

'Meg...' he said softly, torn by what he saw. 'Please don't cry. There's no reason to cry. Really there isn't.'

She swallowed, then looked aside, for a moment like a hurt four-year-old. Then, more defiantly, she met his eyes again, bringing up a hand to wipe the tears away.

'I love you,' he said gently. 'You know that.'

'Then make love to me again.'

He laughed, but his eyes were serious. 'What, here?'

She stared back at him challengingly. 'Why not?'

He turned her slightly. From where they stood they could see the cottage clearly down below.

She turned back, her eyes watching him closely, studying his face. 'All right. Up there, then. In the barn.'

He turned and looked, then nodded, a shiver passing down his spine.

She reached down, taking his good hand, then led him up the slope. At the barn door she turned, drawing him close, her arms about his neck. It was a long, passionate kiss, and when she pulled away from him her eyes were different. Older than he remembered them, more knowing.

She turned and led him through. Inside, the barn was filled with shadows. Bars of sunlight, some broad, some narrow, slanted down from gaps between the planks that formed the sides of the barn, creating broken veils of light from left to right.

'Quick,' she said, leading him further in. 'Before Mother calls us in for lunch.'

He smiled and let himself be led, thrilled by the simple pressure of her hand against his own.

'Here,' she said, looking about her. A barrier of wooden slats formed a stall in the far left-hand corner; a space the size of a small box-room, filled waist-high with old hay. The warm, musty smell of the hay was strong but pleasant. Light, intruding from two knot-holes higher up, laced the shadows with twin threads of gold. Meg turned and smiled at him. 'Lie down. I'll lie on top of you.'

He sat, easing himself down on to the hay, feeling it yield beneath him, then let his head fall back, taking care not to jolt his hand. Lying there, looking up at her, his left arm still cradled in its sling, he felt like laughing.

'Are you sure this is such a good idea?'

Her smile, strange, enigmatic at first, widened as she slowly undid the buttons at the front of her dress, then pulled it up over her shoulders. Beneath the dress she was naked.

Ben felt his breath catch in his throat. 'Meg...'

She bent over him and eased the sling from his arm, then straddled him, the soft, warm weight of her pressed down against him, as she began to unbutton his shirt.

Meg's face lay but a short space from his face, her lips slightly parted, the tip of her tongue peeping through, her eyes concentrating on her busy fingers. But Ben's eyes were drawn to her breasts, to the hard, provocative shapes of her nipples.

He reached up and cupped her left breast in his hand, feeling its smooth warmness, then eased forward until his lips brushed against the budlike nipple.

Meg shuddered, her fingers faltering a moment. Ben drew back slightly, looking up into her face once more. Her eyes were closed, her lips parted more fully, reminding him fleetingly of one of those ancient paintings of religious ecstasy. He shivered then leaned forward again, drawing the breast back to his mouth, his tongue wetly tracing the stiff brown berry of the nipple, teasing it with his teeth and lips and tongue, conscious of Meg pressing herself down into him with each small motion.

He lay back again, ignoring the dull pain of the reawakened pulse in his hand, watching as her eyes slowly opened, smiling back at him.

For a while he lay there, letting her undress him. Then, his clothes set aside, she climbed above him again, the smooth warmth of her flesh against his own making him shiver with anticipation.

'Close your eyes...'

He lay there, letting her make love to him, slowly at first, then, as the ancient rhythm took her, wildly, urgently, her hands gripping his shoulders tightly, her face changed, unrecognisable, her teeth clenched fiercely, her eyes staring wildly down at him. In it he saw a reflection of the agony he was suffering from his damaged hand. That lay beside him, quivering, the fingers clenched tight, trapped in a prolonged spasm that was as pain-ful as her lovemaking was delightful. Faster and more furious she moved, until, with a shudder that brought on his own orgasm, she arched her back and cried out, forcing herself against him as if to breach him, as if to press through the flesh that separated them and *become* him.

Afterwards he lay still, the pain in his hand ebbing slowly. Meg lay across him, sleeping, her dark hair fanned across his chest. Two small bands of light lay across their shadowed bodies, like golden ribbons joining their flesh, striping them at chest and hip, tracing the contours of their expired lust.

Ben looked down the length of their bodies, studying the play of shadow within shadow, noting where flesh seemed to merge with flesh. The scent of their lovemaking filled the tiny space, mingling with the smell of old hay. It seemed part of the shadows, the dust-specked bands of light.

He closed his eyes, thinking. What had she meant by this? To show her love for him? Her need? Perhaps. But needs were of different kinds. She had been wrong earlier. Though she thought so now, she would not die for missing him. She would wait, as she always waited, knowing he would be back. But he – he *had* to go. He would go mad – literally, mad – if he did not leave this place. Each day now it grew worse. Each day the feeling grew in him, feeding his restlessness, stoking the fire of dissatisfaction that raged in his belly.

Out. He had to get out. Or 'in' as she preferred to call it. Whichever, he had to get away. Far away from here. Even from those he loved.

'Ben...! Meg...!'

The calls were muted, distant, from the slope below the barn. Meg stirred and lifted her head slowly, turning to face him.

'What's that?'

He smiled and leaned forward, kissing her nose. 'It's all right. It's only Mother calling us in. It must be lunchtime.'

'Ah...' She went to relax back, then pushed herself up abruptly, suddenly awake. 'Only Mother!'

'Mind...' he said, wincing at the pain that shot up his arm where she had knocked his hand.

Her face was all concern. 'Oh, Ben, I'm sorry...'

Then they were laughing, clutching each other, Ben's hand held out to one side as he embraced her. And outside, more distantly, moving away from them now, the call came again.

'Ben...! Meg...!'

Beth stood in the gateway at the bottom of the lower garden, relaxed, her apron tied loosely about her dress, waiting for them. She had let her hair down and she was smiling.

'Where were you?' she said as they came up to her. 'I was looking everywhere. Didn't you hear me calling?'

Meg looked away, but Ben went straight to his mother. 'We were in the barn,' he said casually. 'It was warm in there and musty. We were talking, then we fell asleep. We must have missed you calling.'

'I see,' she said, smiling, ruffling his hair.

'I'm sorry,' he said, falling in beside her while Meg walked on ahead. 'Lunch isn't spoiled, I hope.'

Beth smiled and shook her head. 'I wasn't calling you for lunch. It's your father. He's home.'

Meg turned. 'Daddy...' Then, without a further word, she raced up the slope and disappeared inside the house.

Ben walked beside his mother, taking her arm. 'Is he okay?'

'What do you mean?'

Ben stopped, looking at her. Her voice had seemed strange, her answer too defensive. His query had been politeness, but she had taken it for something more meaningful.

'What's wrong with him?'

Beth looked away. 'I don't know. He seems much older, somehow. Tired.'

'Perhaps it's overwork. Things have been bad in there.'

'Yes... Maybe that's it.'

They walked on. Up ahead, from inside the cottage, they could hear Meg's squeals of delight. Then she appeared, cradling what looked like a tiny, animated fur hat. She thrust the bundle at Ben.

'Isn't he just adorable?'

Ben held the kitten up to his face, meeting its strange, alien eyes. 'Hello, there, Mog. I'm Ben.'

Meg took the kitten back at once. 'Don't hurt him. And it's not Mog. It's Zarathustra.'

'Of course.' Ben reached out and rubbed the kitten between the ears, then moved past Meg into the doorway.

His father was sitting just inside, in the intense shadow of the hallway. Seeing Ben, his face creased into a smile.

'Ben! How are you, lad?'

'I'm fine,' he answered, moving inside, feeling his mother's hand on his shoulder. 'And you, Father?'

'I've been busy. Run ragged, you might say. I feel like I've put the whole world to rights these last few days.'

Hal Shepherd sat back in the tall-backed, armless chair, his arms stretched wide in a gesture of expansiveness. The old fire still burned in his eyes, but Ben could see at once that he was ill. He saw the lines of tiredness and strain, the redness at the corners of his eyes, the way his muscles stood out at his neck when he spoke, and knew it was more than simple fatigue.

'The kitten's beautiful. What is it? GenSyn?'

Hal shook his head. 'No, Ben. It's a real kitten. We confiscated its parents from Madam Moore the day the warrant was signed for her husband's arrest. It seems there are a few cats left in the Wilds. Moore must have smuggled it in through quarantine for her.'

'Or bribed his way.'

'More likely...' Hal took a deep breath – awkwardly, Ben thought – then smiled again. 'I brought something back for you, too.'

'A dog?'

Hal laughed, for a moment almost his old, vital self. 'Now that *would* be something, wouldn't it? But, no, I'm afraid not. Although I've a feeling that, as far as you're concerned, you might find it a lot more interesting than a dog.'

'What is it?'

Hal's smile remained while he studied his son, as if this was a sight he had not expected to see again. Then, with a brief glance past him, at Beth, he said, 'It's downstairs. In the cellar workrooms. I've rigged one of them up ready for you to try.'

Ben frowned, trying to work out what his father meant, then he understood. 'It's a *pai pi*! You've brought back a *pai pi*!'

'Not one, Ben. Eight of them.'

'Eight!' Ben laughed, astonished. 'Christ! Where did you get them? I thought they'd all been destroyed years ago. They've been banned more than sixty years, haven't they?'

'That's right. But there are collectors amongst the Above. Men who secretly hold on to banned technology. These were found in the collection of a First Level Executive.'

Ben understood at once. 'The Confiscations...'

'Exactly. The man was a Dispersionist. We were going to destroy them, but when I told Li Shai Tung of your interest, he signed a special order permitting me to take them out of the City. Here in the Domain, you see, the Edict has no power. We Shepherds can do as we wish.'

'Can I try one now?'

Beth, her hand still on Ben's shoulder, answered for her husband. 'Of course. Meg and I will get dinner ready while you're downstairs.'

Meg, coming in from outside, protested. 'That's unfair! Why can't I join them?'

Hal laughed. 'Well... Ben might be a bit embarrassed.'

'What do you mean?' Meg asked, cuddling the struggling kitten under her chin.

'Just that it's a full-body experience. Ben has to be naked in the harness.'

Meg laughed. 'Is that all?' She turned away slightly, a faint colour in her cheeks. 'He was practically naked when he was working with the morph.'

Hal looked at his son, narrowing his eyes. 'You've been using the morph, Ben? What for?'

'I'll tell you,' Ben said, watching Meg a moment, surprised by her sudden rebelliousness. 'But later. After I've tried the *pai pi*.'

The cellars beneath the cottage had been added in his great-great-grandfather's time, but it was only in the last decade that his father had set up a studio in one of the large, low-ceilinged rooms. Beneath stark, artificial lighting, electronic equipment filled two-thirds of the floor space, a narrow corridor between the free-standing racks leading to a cluttered desk by the far wall. To the left of the desk a curtain had been drawn across, concealing the open space beyond.

Ben went through. The eight *pai pi* lay on the desk, the small, dark, rectangular cases small enough to fit into the palm of his hand. He picked them up, one at a time, surprised by the weight of them. They looked like lozenges or like the 'chops' executives used to seal official documents, each one imprinted with the logo of the manufacturing company. *Pai pi* – the name meant, literally, 'a hundred pens' – provided full-body experiences, a medium that had blossomed briefly in the earliest days of the City as an entertainment for the very rich. The 'cassettes' themselves were only the software, the operational instructions; the hardware stood off to one side.

Hal pulled back a curtain. 'There! What do you think?'

The couch was a work of art in itself, its curved, boat-like sides inlaid in pearl and ivory, the dark, see-through hood shaped like the lid of an ancient sarcophagus. At present the hood was pulled back, like a giant insect's wing, exposing the padded interior. Dark blue silks – the colour that same blue-black the sky takes on before the dark – masked the internal workings of the machine, while depressed into the padded silk was a crude human shape. Like the instruments of some delicious mechanism of torture, fine filaments extended from all parts of the depression, the thread-like wires clustered particularly thickly about the head. These – the 'hundred pens' from which the art form derived its name, though only eighty-one in actu-ality – were the input points which, when the machine was operational, fed information to all the major loci of nerves in the recipient's body.

'It's beautiful,' said Ben, going close and examining the couch with his fingers. He bent and sniffed at the slightly musty innards. 'I wonder if he used it much?'

It was a deceptively simple device. A tiny, one-man dream palace. You lay down and were connected up; then, when the hood was lowered, you began to dream. Dreams that were supposed to be as real as waking.

'Have you tried it out?'

'One of the technicians did. With permission, of course.'

'And?'

Hal smiled. 'Why don't you get in? Try it for yourself.'

He hesitated, then began to strip off, barely conscious of his father watching – the fascination of the machine casting a spell over him. Naked, he turned, facing his father. 'What now?'

Hal came up beside him, his movements slower, heavier than Ben remem-bered, then bent down beside the machine and unfolded a set of steps.

'Climb inside, Ben. I'll wire you up.'

Fifteen minutes later he was ready, the filaments attached, the hood lowered. With an unexpected abruptness it began.

He was walking in a park, the solid shapes of trees and buildings surrounding him on every side. Overhead the sky seemed odd. Then he realized – he was inside the City and the sky was a ceiling fifty ch'i above him. He was aware of the ghostly sense of movement in his arms and legs, of the nebulous presence of other people about him, but nothing clear. Everything seemed schematic, imprecise. Even so, the overall illusion of walking in a park was very strong.

A figure approached him, growing clearer as it came closer, as if forming ghost-like from a mist of nothingness. A surly-looking youth, holding a knife.

The youth's mouth moved. Words came to Ben, echoing across the space between them.

'Hand over your money or I'll cut you!'

He felt his body tense, his mouth move and form words. They drifted out from him, unconnected to anything he was thinking.

'Try and get it, scumbag!'

Time seemed to slow. He felt himself move backward as the youth lunged with the knife. Turning, he grabbed the youth's arm and twisted, making the knife fall from his hand. He felt a tingle of excitement pass through him. The moment had seemed so real, the arm so solid and actual. Then the youth was falling away from him, stumbling on the ground, and he was following up, his leg kicking out, straight and hard, catching the youth in the side.

He felt the two ribs break under the impact of his kick, the sound – exaggerated for effect – seeming to fill the park. He moved away – back to normal time now – hearing the youth moan, then hawk up blood – the gobbet richly, garishly red.

He felt the urge to kick again, but his body was moving back, turning away, a wash of artificial satisfaction passing through him.

Then, as abruptly as it had begun, it ended.

Through the darkened glass of the hood he saw the dark shape of his father lean across and take the cassette from the slot. A moment later the catches that held down the hood were released with a hiss of air and the canopy began to lift.

'Well? What do you think?'

'I don't know,' Ben answered thoughtfully. 'In some ways it's quite powerful. For a moment or two the illusion really had me in its grasp. But it was only for a moment.'

'What's wrong with it, then?'

Ben tried to sit up but found himself restrained.

'Here, let me do that.'

He lay back, relaxing as his father freed the tiny suction pads from the flesh at the back of his scalp and neck.

'Well...' Ben began, then laughed. 'For a start it's much too crude.'

Hal laughed with him. 'What did you expect, Ben? Perfection? It was a complex medium. Think of the disciplines involved.'

'I have been. And that's what I mean. It lacks all subtlety. What's more, it ends at the flesh.'

'How do you mean?'

'These...' He pulled one of the tiny suckers from his arm. 'They provide only the vaguest sensation of movement. Only the shadow of the actuality. If they were somehow connected directly to the nerves, the muscles, then the illusion would be more complete. Likewise the connections at the head. Why not input them direct into the brain?'

'It was tried, Ben. They found that it caused all kind of problems.'

'What kind of problems?'

'Muscular atrophy. Seizures. Catalepsy.'

Ben frowned. 'I don't see why. You're hardly in there longer than three minutes.'

'In that case, yes. But there were longer tapes. Some as long as half an hour. Continual use of them brought on the symptoms.'

'I still don't see why. It's only the sensation of movement, after all.'

'One of the reasons they were banned was because they were so addictive. Especially the more garish productions – the sex and violence stims, for instance. After a while, you see, the body begins to respond to the illusion: the lips to form the words; the muscles to make the movements. It's that unconscious mimicry that did the damage. It led to loss of control over motor activity and, in a few cases, to death.'

Ben peeled the remaining filaments from his body and climbed out.

'Why were the tapes so short?'

'Again, that's due to the complexity of the medium. Think of it, Ben. It's not just a question of creating the visual backdrop – the environment – but of synchronizing muscular movement to fit into that backdrop.'

'Nothing a good computer couldn't do, surely?'

'Maybe. But only if someone were skilled enough to programme it to do the job in the first place.'

Ben began to pull his shirt on, then paused, shaking his head. 'There were other things wrong with it, too. The hood, for instance. That's wrong. I had a sense all the while of the world beyond the machine. Not only that, but there was a faint humming noise – a vibration – underlying everything. Both things served to distance me from the illusion. They reminded me – if only at some deep, subconscious level – that I *was* inside a machine. That it *was* a fiction.'

Hal went over to the desk and sat, the strain of standing for so long showing in his face. 'Is that so bad, Ben? Surely you have the same in any art form? You know that the book in your hands is just paper and ink, the film you're watching an effect of light on celluloid, a painting the result of spreading oils on a two-dimensional canvas. The medium is always there, surely?'

'Yes. But it doesn't have to be. Not in this case. That's what's so exciting about it. For the first time ever you can dispense with the sense of "medium" and have the experience direct, unfiltered.'

'I don't follow you, Ben. Surely you'll always be aware that you're lying inside a machine, no matter how good the fiction?'

'Why?' Ben buttoned the shirt, pulled on his pants and trousers, and went over to his father, standing over him, his eyes burning. 'What if you could get rid of all the distractions? Wouldn't that change the very nature of the fiction you were creating? Imagine it! It would seem as real as this now – as me talking to you here, now, you sitting there, me standing, the warm smell of oil and machinery surrounding us, the light just so, the temperature just so. Everything as it is. Real. As real as real, anyway.'

'Impossible,' Hal said softly, looking away. 'You could never make something that good.'

'Why not?' Ben turned away a moment, his whole body fired by a sudden enthusiasm. 'What's preventing me from doing it? Nothing. Nothing but my own will.'

Hal shrugged, then looked back at his son, a faint smile of admiration lighting his tired features momentarily. 'Perhaps. But it's not as easy as that, Ben. That little clip you experienced. How long do you think it was?'

Ben considered. 'Two minutes. Maybe slightly longer.'

Hal laughed, then grew more serious. 'It was two minutes fourteen seconds, and yet it took a team of eight men more than three weeks to make. It's a complex form, Ben. I keep telling you that. To do what you're talking about, well, it would take a huge team of men years to achieve.'

Ben turned, facing his father, his face suddenly very still. 'Or a single man a lifetime?'

Hal narrowed his eyes. 'What do you mean?'

'I mean myself. My calling. For months now I've been experimenting with the morph. Trying to capture certain things. To mimic them, then reproduce them on a tape. But this... these *pai pi*... they're the same kind of thing. Stores of experience. Shells, filled with the very yoke of being. Or, at least, they could be.'

'Shells... I like that. It's a good name for them.'

Strangely, Ben smiled. 'It is, isn't it? Shells.'

Hal studied his son a moment then looked down. 'I had another reason for showing these to you. Something more selfish.'

'Selfish?'

'Yes. Something I want you to help me with.'

'Ah...'

The hesitation in Ben's face surprised him.

'There's something I have to ask you first,' Ben said quickly. 'Something I need from you.'

Hal sat back slightly. So Beth was right. Ben *was* restless here. Yes, he could see it now. 'You want to leave here. Right?'

Ben nodded.

'And so you can. But not now. Not just yet.'

'Then when?'

Again, the hardness in Ben's voice was unexpected. He had changed a great deal in the last few months. Had grown, become his own man.

'Three months. Is that so long to wait?'

Ben was still a moment, considering, then shook his head. 'No. I guess not. You'll get me into Oxford?'

'Wherever you want. I've already spoken to the T'ang.'

Ben's eyes widened with surprise.

Hal leaned forward, concealing his amusement, and met his son's eyes defiantly. 'You think I don't know how it feels?' He laughed. 'You forget. I was born here, too. And I too was seventeen once, believe it or not. I know what it's like, that feeling of missing out on life. I know it all too well. But I want something from you in return. I want you to help me.'

Ben took a breath, then nodded. 'All right. But how?'

Hal hesitated, then looked away. 'I want to make a *pai pi*... a Shell. For your mother. Something she can keep.'

Ben frowned. 'I don't understand. Why? And what kind of Shell?'

Hal looked up slowly. He seemed suddenly embarrassed. 'Of myself. But it's to be a surprise. A present. For her birthday.'

Ben watched his father a moment, then turned and looked back at the ornate casing of the machine. 'Then we should make a few changes to that, don't you think? It looks like a coffin.'

Hal shuddered. 'I know...'

'We should get workmen in...' Ben began, turning back, then stopped as he saw how his father was staring down at his hands. Hands that were trembling like the hands of a very old man.

Ben's voice was almost a whisper. 'What's wrong?'

He saw how his father folded his hands together, then looked up, a forced smile shutting out the fear that had momentarily taken hold of his features.

'It's nothing. I...'

He stopped and turned. Meg was standing just behind him. She had entered silently.

'The man's come,' she said hesitantly.

'The man?'

Meg looked from one to the other, disturbed by the strange tension in the room; aware that she had interrupted something. 'The man from Pros-Tek. He's come to see to Ben's hand.'

'Ben's hand?' Hal turned, looking across at Ben, then he laughed. A brief, colourless laugh. 'Of course. Your mother said.'

Ben's eyes didn't leave his father for a moment. 'Thanks. Tell Mother I'll be up.'

She hesitated, wanting to ask him what was wrong, but she could see from the look of him that she was excluded from this.

'Ben?'

Still he didn't look at her. 'Go on. I told you. I'll be up.'

She stood there a moment longer, surprised and hurt by the sudden curtness in his voice. Then, angered, she turned and ran back down the space between the racks and up the steps.

At the top of the steps she stopped, calming herself. Hal had said no. That was it! And now Ben was angry with her, because she didn't want him to go either. Meg shivered, her anger suddenly washed from her; then, giving a soft laugh, she pushed the door open and went through.

The hand lay on the table, filaments trailing from the precisely severed wrist like fine strands of hair. It was not like the other hand. This one shone silver in the light, its surfaces soft and fluid like mercury. Yet its form suggested heaviness and strength. Meg, staring at it from across the room, could imagine the being from which it had been cut: a tall, faceless creature with limbs on which the sunlight danced like liquid fire. She could see him striding through the grass below the cottage. See the wood of the door splinter like matchwood before his fist.

She shuddered and turned, looking back at the man kneeling at Ben's side. As she looked he glanced up at her and smiled, a polite, pleasant smile. He was a Han. Lin Hou Ying, his name was. A tiny, delicate man in his sixties, with hands that were so small they seemed like a child's. Hands so doll-like and delicate, in fact, that she had asked him if they were real.

'These?' He held them up to her, as if for her appraisal. Then he had laughed. 'These hands are mine. I was born with them. But as to what is real...'

He had almost finished removing the damaged hand by now. As she watched he leaned close, easing the pressure on the vice that held the hand, then bent down and selected one of the tiny instruments from the case on the floor beside his knee. For a moment longer he was busy, leaning over the hand, making the final few adjustments that would disconnect it.

'There,' he said, finally, leaning back and looking up into Ben's face. 'How does that feel?'

Ben lifted his left arm up towards his face, then turned it, studying the clean line of the stump. 'It's strange,' he said, after a moment. 'The pain's gone. And yet it feels as if the hand's still there. I can flex my fingers now and they don't hurt.'

Lin Hou Ying smiled. 'Good. That's a sure sign it was only the unit that was damaged. If you had twisted it badly or damaged the nerve connections it might have been more difficult. As it is, I can fit you with a temporary unit until the old one is repaired.'

'That thing there?'

Lin glanced across. 'Yes. I'm sorry it's so ugly.'

'No. Not at all. I think it's quite beautiful.'

Meg laughed uncomfortably. 'No. Shih Lin's right. It's ugly. Brutal.'

'It's only a machine,' Ben answered, surprised by the vehemence, the bitterness in her voice. 'It has no life other than that which we give it.'

'It's horrible,' she insisted. 'Like the morph.'

Ben shrugged and looked back at Lin Hou Ying. 'Does it function like the other one?'

The small man had been studying the hand in the vice, probing it with one of the tiny scalpels. He looked up, smiling.

'In certain ways, yes, but in others it's a vast improvement on this model here. Things have changed greatly in the last five years. Prosthetics among them. The response time's much enhanced. It's stronger, too. And in that particular model...' he indicated the hand on the table with a delicate motion of his head '...there's a remote override.'

Ben stared at it a moment, then looked back at Lin Hou Ying. 'Why's that?'

Lin stood and went across to the carrying case that stood on the floor beside the table. Earlier he had taken the hand from it. 'Look,' he said, taking something from inside. 'Here's the rest of the unit.'

It was an arm. A silver arm. Ben laughed. 'How much more of him have you?'

Lin laughed, then brought the arm across. In his other hand he held a control box. 'Some of our customers have lost far more than you, Shih Shepherd. The arm is a simple mechanism. It is easy to construct one. But a hand. Well, a hand is a complex thing. Think of the diversity of movements it's possible to make with a hand. Rather than waste our efforts making a single unit of hand and arm together, we decided long ago to specialize

– to concentrate on the hands. And this...' he handed Ben the control box '...controls the hand.'

'Can I?'

Lin lowered his head slightly. 'As you wish, *Shih* Shepherd.'

For a while Ben experimented, making the fingers bend and stretch, the hand flex and clench. Then he turned it and made it scuttle, slowly, awkwardly, like a damaged crab, on the table's surface.

Ben set the box down. 'Can I keep this?'

Lin bowed his head. 'Of course. And the arm?'

Ben laughed, then looked across at Meg and saw how she was watching him. He looked down. 'No. Take the arm.'

Just then the door at the far end of the room opened and his mother came in, carrying a small tray. Behind her came the kitten, Zarathustra.

'Refreshments, *Shih* Lin?'

The small man bowed low. 'You honour me, *nu shi*.'

Beth made to set the tray down on the table beside the silver hand, but as she did so, the kitten jumped up on the chair beside her and climbed up on to the table.

'Hey...'

Meg made to move forward, but Ben reached out, holding her arm with his right hand. 'No. Leave him. He's only playing.'

His mother turned, looking at him.

'There,' he said, indicating a small table to one side of the room.

He watched her go across and set the tray down, then looked back at the kitten. It was sniffing at the fingers of the hand then lifting its head inquisitively.

'Don't...' Meg said quietly.

He half turned, looking at her. 'I won't hurt it.'

'No,' she said, brushing his hand aside and moving across to lift the kitten and cradle it. 'He's real. Understand? Don't toy with him.'

He watched her a moment, then looked down at the control box in his lap. *Real*, he thought. *But how real is real? For if all I am is a machine of blood and bone, of nerve and flesh, then to what end do I function? How real am I?*

Machines of flesh. The phrase echoed in his head. And then he laughed. A cold, distant laughter.

'What is it, Ben?'

He looked up, meeting his mother's eyes. 'Nothing.'

He was quiet a moment, then he turned, looking across at the Han. 'Relax a while, *Shih* Lin. I must find my father. There's something I need to ask him.'

He found Hal in the dining room, the curtains drawn, the door to the kitchen pulled to. In the left-hand corner of the room there was a low table on which was set the miniature apple trees the T'ang had given the Shepherds five years before. The joined trees were a symbol of conjugal happiness, the apple an omen of peace, but also of illness.

His father was kneeling there in the darkened room, his back to Ben, his forearms stretched out across the low table's surface, resting either side of the tree, his head bent forward. He was very still, as if asleep, or meditating, but Ben, who had come silently to the doorway, knew at once that his father had been crying.

'What is it?' he said softly.

Hal's shoulders tensed; slowly his head came up. He stood and turned, facing his son, wiping the tears away brusquely, his eyes fierce, proud.

'Shut the door. I don't want your mother to hear. Or Meg.'

Ben closed the door behind him, then turned back, noting how intently his father was watching him, as if to preserve it all. He smiled faintly. *Yes,* he thought, *there's far more of me in you than I ever realized. Brothers, we are. I know it now for certain.*

'Well?' he asked again, his voice strangely gentle. He had often questioned his own capacity for love, wondering whether what he felt was merely some further form of self-delusion, yet now, seeing his father there, his head bowed, defeated, beside the tiny tree, he knew beyond all doubt that he loved him.

Hal's chest rose and fell in a heavy, shuddering movement. 'I'm dying, Ben. I've got cancer.'

'Cancer?' Ben laughed in disbelief. 'But that's impossible. They can cure cancers, can't they?'

Hal smiled grimly. 'Usually, yes. But this is a new kind, an artificial carcinoma, tailored specifically for me, it seems. Designed to take my immune system apart piece by piece. It was *Shih* Berdichev's parting gift.'

Ben swallowed. Dying. No. It wasn't possible. Slowly he shook his head.

'I'm sorry, Ben, but it's true. I've known it these last two months. They can delay its effects, but not for long. The T'ang's doctors give me two years. Maybe less. So, you see, I've not much time to set things right. To do all the things I should have done before.'

'What things?'

'Things like the Shell.'

For a moment Ben's mind missed its footing. Shells... He thought of Meg and the beach and saw the huge wave splinter along the tooth-like rocks until it crashed against her, dragging her back, away beneath the foaming surface, then heard himself screaming – *Meg!!!* – while he stood there on the higher rocks, impotent to help.

He shivered and looked away, suddenly, violently displaced. Shells... Like the stone in the dream – the dark pearl that passed like a tiny, burning star of nothingness through his palm. For a moment he stared at where his hand ought to have been in disbelief, then understood.

'What is it, Ben?'

He looked up. 'I don't know. I've never...'

He stopped. It was like a wave of pure darkness hitting him. A sheer black cliff of nothingness erasing all thought, all being from him. He staggered and almost fell, then he was himself again, his father's hands holding his upper arms tightly, his heavily lined face thrust close to Ben's own, the dark green eyes filled with concern and fear.

'Ben? What is it?'

'Darkness,' he whispered. 'It was like...'

Like what? He shuddered violently. And then the earlier thing came back to him. Shells... *Pai pi.* That was what his father meant. And that was why they had to make one. Because he was dying. Yes. It all made sense.

'Like what?' his father asked, fleshing the thought.

'Nothing,' he answered, calmer now. 'The Shell. I understand it now.'

'Good. Then you'll help me sketch things out for the team?'

Ben frowned. 'Team? What team?'

The pressure of Hal's hands on Ben's arms had eased, but he made no move to take them away. 'I've arranged for a team of technicians to come here and work with us on the Shell. I thought we could originate material for them.'

Ben looked down. For a long time he was silent, thoughtful. Then he looked up again. 'But why do that? Why can't we do the whole thing?'

Hal laughed. 'Don't be daft, Ben.'

'No. I'm serious. Why can't we do the whole thing?'

'Didn't you hear me, earlier? It would take ages. And I haven't got ages. Besides, I thought you wanted to get away from here. To Oxford.'

'I do. But this...' He breathed deeply, then smiled and reached up to touch his father's face with his one good hand. 'I love you. So trust me. Three months. It's long enough, I promise you.'

He saw the movement in his father's face; the movements of control; of pride and love and a fierce anger that it should need such a thing to bring them to this point of openness. Then he nodded, tears in his eyes. 'You're mad, Ben, but yes. Why not? The T'ang can spare me.'

'Mad...' Ben was still a moment, then he laughed and held his father to him tightly. 'Yes. But where would I be without my madness?'

Ben turned from the open kitchen window. Behind him the moon blazed down from a clear black sky, speckled with stars. His eyes were dark and wide, like pools, reflecting the immensity he had turned from.

'What makes it all real?'

His mother paused, the ladle held above the casserole, the smell of the steaming rabbit stew filling the kitchen. She looked across at her son, then moved ladle to plate, spilling its contents beside the potatoes and string beans. She laughed and handed it to him. 'Here.'

She was a clever woman. Clever enough to recognize that she had given birth to something quite other than she had expected. A strange, almost alien creature. She studied her son as he took the plate from her, seeing how his eyes took in everything, as if to store it all away. His eyes devoured the world. She smiled and looked down. There was a real intensity to him – such an intellectual hunger as would power a dozen others.

Ben put his plate down, then sat, bringing his chair in closer to the table. 'I'm not being rhetorical. It's a question. An honest-to-goodness question.'

She laughed. 'I don't know. It seems almost impertinent to ask.'

'Why?'

She shrugged. It was scarcely the easiest of questions to raise at the dinner table. *Who made the universe?* he might as well have asked. Or *Why is life?* Who knew what the answer was?

Rabbit stew, maybe. She laughed.

Ben had gone very quiet, very watchful. A living microscope, quivering with expectancy.

'Two things come to mind,' she said, letting the ladle rest in the pot. 'And they seem to conflict with each other. The first is the sense that it'll all turn out exactly as we expect it. What would you call that? – a sense of continuity, perhaps. But not just that. There's also a sense we have that it will all continue, just as it ever did, and not just stop dead suddenly.'

'And the second?' It was Meg. She was standing in the doorway, watching them.

Beth smiled and began ladling stew into a plate for her.

'The second's the complete opposite of the first. It's our ability to be shocked, surprised, or horrified by things we ought to have seen coming. Like death...' Her voice tailed off.

'A paradox,' said Ben, looking down. He took a spoon from the table and began to ladle up the stock from his plate, as if it were a soup. Then he paused and nodded. 'Yes. But how can I use that knowledge?'

There he had her. She in a lifetime had never fathomed that.

She turned to Meg, offering her the plate. 'Where's Father?'

'He'll be down. He said there was something he had to do.'

She watched Meg take her place, then began to pour stew into another plate. It was unlike Hal to be late to table. But Hal had changed. Something had happened. Something he couldn't bring himself to tell her just yet.

'I'm sorry to keep you, Beth.' Hal was standing in the doorway, something small hidden behind his back. He smiled, then came forward, offering something to her.

'What is it?' She wiped her hands on her apron, then took the tiny present from him.

He sat, then leaned back, his arms stretched wide in a gesture of expansiveness. The old fire still burned in his eyes, but she could see that he was unwell.

She shivered and looked down at the tiny parcel, then, with a brief smile at him, began unwrapping it.

It was a case. A tiny jewel case. She opened it, then looked up, surprised.

'Hal... It's beautiful!'

She held it up. It was a silver ring. And set into the ring was a tiny drop-shaped pearl. A pearl the colour of the night.

Meg leaned forward excitedly. 'It is beautiful! But I thought all pearls were white...'

'Most are. Normally they're selected for the purity of their colour and lustre – all discoloured pearls being discarded. But in this instance the pearl was so discoloured it attained a kind of purity of its own.'

Beth studied the pearl a moment, delighted, then looked up again. Only then did she notice Ben, sitting there, his spoon set down, his mouth fallen open.

'Ben?'

She saw him shiver, then reach out to cover the cold, silvered form of his left hand with the fleshed warmth of his right. It was a strangely disturbing gesture.

'I had a dream,' he said, his eyes never leaving the ring. 'The pearl was in it.'

Meg laughed. 'Don't listen to him. He's teasing you.'

'No.' He had turned the silvered hand and was rubbing at its palm, as if at some irritation there. 'It was in the dream. A pearl as dark as nothingness itself. I picked it up and it burned its way through my palm. That's when I woke. That's when I knew I'd damaged the hand.'

Hal was looking at his son, concerned. 'How odd. I mean, it wasn't until this morning, just as I was leaving, that Tolonen brought it to me. He knew I was looking for something special. Something unusual. So your dream preceded it.' He laughed strangely. 'Perhaps you willed it here.'

Ben hesitated, then shook his head. 'No. It's serendipity, that's all. Coincidence. The odds are high, but...'

'But real,' Meg said. 'Coincidence. It's how things are, isn't it? Part of the real.'

Beth saw how Ben's eyes lit at that. He had been trying to fit it into things. But now Meg had placed it for him. Had *allowed* it. But it was strange. Very strange. A hint that there was more to life than what they experienced through their senses. Another level, hidden from them, revealed only in dreams.

She slipped the ring on, then went across to Hal and knelt beside him to kiss him. 'Thank you, my love. It's beautiful.'

'Like you,' he said, his eyes lighting momentarily.

She laughed and stood. 'Well. Let's have some supper, eh? Before it all goes cold.'

Hal nodded and drew his chair in to the table. 'Oh, by the way, Ben, I've some news.'

Ben looked across and picked up his spoon again. 'About the team?'

'No. About the other thing. I've arranged it.'

'Ah...' Ben glanced at Meg, then bent his head slightly, spooning stew into his mouth.

'What other thing?' Meg asked, looking at Ben, a sudden hardness in her face.

Ben stared down at his plate. 'You know. Oxford. Father's said I can go.'

There was a moment's silence, then, abruptly, Meg pushed her plate away and stood. 'Then you *are* going?'

'Yes.'

She stood there a moment, then turned away, storming out down the steps. They could hear her feet pounding on the stairs. A moment later a door slammed. Then there was silence.

Ben looked across and met his mother's eyes. 'She's bound to take it hard.'

Beth looked at her son, then away to the open window. 'Well...' She sighed. 'I suppose you can't stay here for ever.' She looked down, beginning to fill her own plate. 'When do you plan to go?'

'Three months,' Hal answered for him. 'Ben's going to work on something with me before then. Something new.'

She turned, looking at Hal, surprised. 'So you'll be here?'

But before he could answer, Ben pushed back his chair and stood. 'I'd best go to her. See she's all right.'

'There's no need...' she began. But Ben had already gone. Down the steps and away through the dining room, leaving her alone with Hal.

'You're ill,' she said, letting her concern for him show at last.

'Yes,' he said. 'I'm ill.'

The door was partly open, the room beyond in shadow. Through the window on the far side of the room the moon shone, cold and white and distant. Meg sat on her bed, her head and shoulder turned from him, the moonlight glistening in her long, dark hair.

He shivered, struck by the beauty of her, then stepped inside.

'Meg...' he whispered. 'Meg, I've got to talk to you.'

She didn't move; didn't answer him. He moved past her, looking out across the bay, conscious of how the meadows, the water, the trees of the far bank – all were silvered by the clear, unnatural light. Barren, reflected light, no strength or life in it. Nothing grew in that light.

He looked down. There, on the bedside table, beside the dull silver of his hand, lay a book. He lifted it and looked. It was Nietzsche's *Zarathustra*, the Hans Old etching on the cover. From the ancient paper cover Nietzsche stared out at the world, fierce-eyed and bushy-browed, uncompromising in the ferocity of his gaze. So he himself would be. So he would stare back at the world, with an honest contempt for the falseness of its values. He opened the book where the leather bookmark was and read the words she had underlined. *To be sure, I am a forest and a night of dark trees...* Beside it, in the margin, she had written 'Ben'. He felt a small shiver pass down his spine, then set the book down, turning to look at her again.

'Are you angry with me?'

She made a small noise of disgust. He hesitated, then reached out and lifted her chin gently with his good hand, turning her face into the light. Her cheeks were wet, her eyes liquid with tears, but her eyes were angry.

'You want it all, don't you?'

'Why not? If it's there to be had?'

'And never mind who you hurt?'

'You can't breathe fresh air without hurting someone. People bind each other with obligation. Tie each other down. Make one another suffocate in old, used-up air. I thought you understood that, Meg. I thought we'd agreed?'

'Oh, yes,' she said bitterly. 'We agreed all right. You told me how it would be and what my choices were. Take it or leave it. I had no say.'

'And you wanted a say?'

She hesitated, then drew her face back, looking down, away from him. 'I don't know... I just feel... hurt by it all. It feels like you're rejecting me. Pushing me away.'

He reached out again, this time with his other hand, not thinking. She pushed it from her, shuddering. And when she looked up, he could see the aversion in her eyes.

'There's a part of you that's like that, Ben. Cold. Brutal. Mechanical. It's not all of you. Not yet. But what you're doing – what you plan… I've said it before, but it's true. I fear for you. Fear that, *that*…' she pointed to the hand '…will take you over, cell by cell, like some awful, insidious disease, changing you to its own kind of thing. It won't show on the surface, of course, but I'll know. I'll see it in your eyes, and know it from the coldness of your touch. That's what I fear. That's what hurts. Not you going, but your reasons for going.'

He was silent for a moment, then he sat down next to her. 'I see.'

She was watching him, the bitterness purged from her eyes. She had said it now. Had brought to the surface what was eating at her. She reached out and took his hand – his human hand – and held it loosely.

'What do you want, Ben? What, more than anything, do you want?'

He said it without hesitation, almost, it seemed, without thought.

'Perfection. Some pure and perfect form.'

She shivered and looked away. Perfection. Like the hand. Or like the moonlight. Something dead.

'Do you love me?'

She heard him sigh, sensed the impatience in him. 'You know I do.'

She turned slightly, looking at him, her smile sad, resigned now. Letting his hand fall from hers, she stood and lifted her dress up over her head, then lay down on the bed beside him, naked, pulling him down towards her.

'Then make love to me.'

As he slipped from his clothes she watched him, knowing that, for all his words, this much was genuine – this need of his for her.

You asked what's real, she thought. This… this alone is real. This thing between us. This unworded darkness in which we meet and merge. This and this only. Until we die.

'I love you,' he said softly, looking down at her. 'You know that.'

'Yes,' she said, closing her eyes, shuddering as he pressed down into her. 'I know…'

And yet it wasn't enough. For him it would never be enough.

CHUNG KUO

IN TIMES TO COME...

C hung Kuo: The Art of War is the fifth volume of a vast dynastic saga that covers more than half a century of this vividly realized future world. In the fifteen volumes that follow, the Great Wheel of fate turns through a full historical cycle, transforming the social climate of Chung Kuo utterly. Chung Kuo is the portrait of these turbulent – and often apocalyptic – times and the people who lived through them.

In Chung Kuo: An Inch of Ashes, as the population continues to grow, the Seven find they must make further concessions. The great Edict of Technological Control – the means by which the Seven have kept Change at bay for more than a century – is to be relaxed, the House at Weimar re-opened, in return for guarantees of population controls. For the first time, the Seven are forced to tackle the problems of their world, facing up to the necessity for limited change. But is it too late? Are the great tides of unrest unleashed by earlier wars about to overwhelm them?

It certainly seems to, and when DeVore manages to persuade Li Yuan's newly appointed general, Hans Ebert, to secretly ally with him, the writing seems to be on the wall. Handsome, strong and intelligent, Ebert is heir to genetics and pharmaceuticals company GenSyn, Chung Kuo's largest manufacturing concern. He's also a vain, amoral young man, a cold-blooded 'hero' with the secret ambition of deposing the Seven and becoming 'King of the World'.

Having married his brother's wife, the beautiful Fei Yen ('Flying Swallow'), Prince Li Yuan has settled to his new role as his father's helper. He loves the work, only the task requires long hours, and Fei Yen feels neglected by her husband. Consumed by passion, she has a brief, clandestine affair with his cousin, the handsome young T'ang of East Asia, Tsu Ma; one which, if disclosed, would destroy the Seven. Tsu Ma ends the affair, but has the damage been done?

Kim Ward, rescued as a child from the Clay – that dark and hostile land beneath the City's foundations – has fulfilled his early promise and proved something of a scientific genius. Scouts from the great Companies look to buy his services. Even the great T'ang, Li Shai Tung, is interested in the boy's talent. But there are others who seek to destroy him, so no one else can use him. As for Ben Shepherd, he has gone to college, in 'Oxford'. Or at least the place that calls itself that these days. His failure to fit in drives him home again, but not before he falls in love for the first time, with his future wife, Christine, and gets his first glimpse – in the Oven Man's ash-painted picture of the Feast of the Dead – of where his own art ought to be heading.

CHARACTER LISTING

MAJOR CHARACTERS

Ascher, Emily
: Trained as an economist, she joined the *Ping Tiao* revolutionary party at the turn of the century, becoming one of its policy-formulating 'Council of Five'. A passionate fighter for social justice, she was also once the lover of the *Ping Tiao*'s unofficial leader, Bent Gesell.

DeVore, Howard
: A one-time major in the T'ang's Security forces, he has become the leading figure in the struggle against the Seven. A highly intelligent and coldly logical man, he is the puppetmaster behind the scenes as the great 'War of the Two Directions' takes a new turn.

Ebert, Hans
: Son of Klaus Ebert and heir to the vast GenSyn Corporation, he is a captain in the Security forces, admired and trusted by his superiors. Ebert is a complex young man: a brave and intelligent officer, he also has a selfish, dissolute and rather cruel streak.

Fei Yen
: Daughter of Yin Tsu, one of the heads of the 'Twenty-Nine', the minor aristocratic families of Chung Kuo. The classically beautiful 'Flying Swallow', her marriage to the murdered Prince Li Han Ch'in nullified, is set to marry Han's brother, the young Prince Li Yuan. Fragile in appearance, she is surprisingly strong-willed and fiery.

Haavikko, Axel

Smeared by the false accusations of his fellow officers, Lieutenant Haavikko has spent the best part of a decade in debauchery and self-negation. At core, however, he is a good, honest man, and circumstances will raise him from the pit into which he has fallen.

Kao Chen

Once an assassin from the Net, the lowest levels of the great City, Chen has raised himself from his humble beginnings to become an officer in the T'ang's Security forces. As friend and helper to Karr, he is one of the foot-soldiers in the War against DeVore.

Karr, Gregor

A major in the Security forces, he was recruited by Marshal Tolonen from the Net. In his youth he was an athlete and, later, a 'blood' – a to-the-death combat fighter. A giant of a man, he is to become the 'hawk' Li Shai Tung flies against his adversary, DeVore.

Lehmann, Stefan

Albino son of the former Dispersionist leader, Pietr Lehmann, he has become a lieutenant to DeVore. A cold, unnaturally dispassionate man, he seems to be the very archetype of nihilism, his only aim to bring down the Seven and their great City.

Li Shai Tung

T'ang of City Europe and one of the Seven, the ruling Council of Chung Kuo, Li Shai Tung is now entering his eighties. For many years he was the fulcrum of the Council and unofficial spokesman for the Seven, but the murder of his heir, Han Ch'in, has weakened him, undermining his once strong determination to prevent Change at all costs.

Li Yuan

Second son of Li Shai Tung, he becomes heir to City Europe after the murder of his elder brother. Thought old before his time, his cold, thoughtful manner conceals a passionate nature, expressed in his wooing of his dead brother's wife, Fei Yen.

Shepherd, Ben

Son of Hal Shepherd, the T'ang's chief advisor, and great-great-grandson of City Earth's Architect. Shepherd is born and brought up in the Domain, an idyllic valley in the south-west of England where, deciding not to follow in his father's footsteps and become advisor to Li Yuan, he pursues instead his calling as an artist, developing a whole new art form, the Shell, which will eventually have a cataclysmic effect on Chung Kuo's society.

Tolonen, Jelka	Daughter of Marshal Tolonen, Jelka has been brought up in a very masculine environment, lacking a mother's influence. However, her genuine interest in martial arts and in weaponry and strategy mask a very different side to her nature, a side brought out by violent circumstances.
Tolonen, Knut	Marshal of the Council of Generals and one-time General to Li Shai Tung, Tolonen is a big, granite-jawed man and the staunchest supporter of the values and ideals of the Seven. Possessed of a fiery, fearless nature, he will stop at nothing to protect his masters, yet after long years of war even his belief in the necessity of stasis has been shaken.
Tsu Ma	T'ang of West Asia and one of the Seven, the ruling Council of Chung Kuo, Tsu Ma has thrown off his former dissolute ways as a result of his father's death and become one of Li Shai Tung's greatest supporters in Council. A strong, handsome man, he has still, however, a weakness in his nature: one that is almost his undoing.
Wang Sau-leyan	Fourth and youngest son of Wang Hsien, T'ang of Africa, the murder of his two eldest brothers has placed him closer to the centre of political events. Thought of as a wastrel, he is, in fact, a shrewd and highly capable political being who is set – through circumstances of his own devising – to become the harbinger of Change inside the Council of the Seven.
Ward, Kim	Born in the Clay, that dark wasteland beneath the great City's foundations, Kim has a quick and unusual bent of mind. His vision of a giant web, formulated in the darkness, has driven him up into the light of the Above. However, after a traumatic fight and a long period of personality reconstruction, he has returned to things not quite the person he was. Or so it seems, for Kim has lost none of the sharpness that has made him the most promising young scientist in the whole of Chung Kuo.

THE SEVEN AND THE FAMILIES

An Liang-chou	Minor Family prince
An Sheng	head of the An family (one of the 'Twenty-Nine' Minor Families)

Chi Hsing	T'ang of the Australias
Chun Wu-chi	head of the Chun family (one of the 'Twenty-Nine' Minor Families)
Fu Ti Chang	Minor Family princess
Hou Tung-po	T'ang of South America
Hsiang K'ai Fan	Minor Family prince
Hsiang Shao-erh	head of the Hsiang family (one of the 'Twenty-Nine' Minor Families) and father of Hsiang K'ai Fan and Hsiang Wang
Hsiang Wang	Minor Family prince
Lai Shi	Minor Family princess
Li Ch'i Chan	brother and advisor to Li Shai Tung
Li Feng Chiang	brother and advisor to Li Shai Tung
Li Shai Tung	T'ang of Europe
Li Yuan	second son of Li Shai Tung and heir to City Europe
Li Yun Ti	brother and advisor to Li Shai Tung
Mien Shan	Minor Family princess
Pei Chao Yang	son and heir of Pei Ro-hen
Pei Ro-hen	head of the Pei family (one of the 'Twenty-Nine' Minor Families)
Tsu Ma	T'ang of West Asia
Tsu Tao Chu	third son of Tsuchang, deceased first son of Tsu Tiao
Wang Hsien	T'ang of Africa
Wang Sau-leyan	fourth son of Wang Hsien
Wang Ta-hung	third son of Wang Hsien and heir to City Africa
Wei Chan Yin	eldest son of Wei Feng and heir to City East Asia
Wei Feng	T'ang of East Asia
Wu Shih	T'ang of North America
Yi Shan-ch'i	Minor Family prince
Yin Chang	Minor Family prince; son of Yin Tsu and elder brother to Fei Yen
Yin Fei Yen	'Flying Swallow', Minor Family princess; daughter of Yin Tsu; widow of Li Han Ch'in
Yin Sung	Minor Family prince; elder brother of Fei Yen and son and heir of Yin Tsu
Yin Tsu	head of Yin family (one of the 'Twenty-Nine' Minor Families)
Yin Wei	younger brother of Fei Yen
Yin Wu Tsai	Minor Family princess and cousin of Fei Yen

FRIENDS AND RETAINERS OF THE SEVEN

Auden, William	captain in Security
Chai	servant to Wang Hsien
Chang Li	Chief Surgeon to Li Shai Tung
Chang Shih-sen	personal secretary to Li Yuan
Ch'in Tao Fan	Chancellor of East Asia
Chu Ta Yun	Minister of Education for City Europe
Chuang Ming	Minister to Li Shai Tung
Chung Hu-Yan	Chancellor to Li Shai Tung
Ebert, Berta	wife of Klaus Ebert
Ebert, Hans	major in Security and heir to GenSyn
Ebert, Klaus Stefan	head of GenSyn (Genetic Synthetics) and advisor to Li Shai Tung
Erkki	guard to Jelka Tolonen
Fan Liang-wei	painter to the court of Li Shai Tung
Fest, Edgar	captain in Security
Fischer, Otto	head of Personal Security at Wang Hsien's palace in Alexandria
Fu	servant to Wang Hsien
Haavikko, Axel	lieutenant in Security
Haavikko, Vesa	sister of Axel Haavikko
Helm	general in Security, City South America
Heng Yu	Son of Heng Fan and nephew of Heng Chi-Po
Hoffmann	major in Security
Hua	personal surgeon to Li Shai Tung
Hung Feng-chan	Chief Groom at Tongjiang
Hung Mien-lo	advisor to Wang Ta-hung; Chancellor of City Africa
Kao Chen	captain in Security
Karr, Gregor	'blood', and, later, major in Security
Lautner, Wolfgang	captain in Security Personnel at Bremen
Little Bee	Maid to Wang Hsien
Lung Mei Ho	secretary to Tsu Ma
Mi Feng	see 'Little Bee'
Nan Ho	Li Yuan's Master of the Inner Chambers
Nocenzi, Vittorio	General of Security, City Europe
Panshin, Anton	colonel in Security
Pearl Heart	maid to Li Yuan
Rahn, Wolf	lieutenant in Security, City Africa
Russ	captain in Security
Sanders	captain of Security at Helmstadt Armoury

Scott	captain of Security
Shepherd, Ben	son of Hal Shepherd
Shepherd, Beth	wife of Hal Shepherd
Shepherd, Hal	advisor to Li Shai Tung and head of the Shepherd family
Shepherd, Meg	daughter of Hal Shepherd
Stifel	alias of Otto Fischer
Sun Li Hua	Wang Hsien's Master of the Inner Chambers
Sweet Rain	maid to Wang Hsien
Sweet Rose	maid to Li Yuan
Tender Willow	maid to Wang Hsien
Tolonen, Helga	aunt of Jelka Tolonen
Tolonen, Jelka	daughter of Knut Tolonen
Tolonen, Jon	brother of Knut Tolonen
Tolonen, Knut	Marshal of the Council of Generals and father of Jelka Tolonen
Wang Ta Chuan	Li Shai Tung's Master of the Inner Palace at Tongjiang
Wen	captain of Security on Mars
Wu Ming	servant to Wang Ta-hung
Ying Chai	assistant to Sun Li Hua
Ying Fu	assistant to Sun Li Hua
Yu	surgeon to Li Yuan

DISPERSIONISTS

Barrow, Chao	Representative of the House in Weimar
Berdichev, Soren	head of SimFic (Simulated Fictions) and leader of the Dispersionists
Berdichev, Ylva	wife of Soren Berdichev
Blake, Peter	head of personnel for Berdichev's SimFic Corporation
Cherkassky, Stefan	ex-Security assassin and friend of DeVore
DeVore, Howard	former major in Li Shai Tung's Security forces
Douglas, John	Company head
Duchek, Albert	Administrator of Lodz
Ecker, Michael	company head
Kubinyi	lieutenant to DeVore
Lehmann, Stefan	albino son of former Dispersionist leader, Pietr Lehmann and lieutenant to DeVore
Moore, John	company head

Moore, Paul   Senior Executive of Berdichev's SimFic Corporation
Parr, Charles   company head
Reid, Thomas   lieutenant to DeVore
Ross, Alexander   company head
Schwarz   lieutenant to DeVore
Scott   alias of DeVore
Turner   alias of DeVore
Wiegand, Max   lieutenant to DeVore
Weiss, Anton   banker

PING TIAO

Ascher, Emily   economist and member of the 'Council of Five'
Gesell, Bent   unofficial leader of the Ping Tiao and member of the
                       'Council of Five'
Mach, Jan   maintenance official for the Ministry of Waste
                       Recycling and member of the 'Council of Five'
Mao Liang   Minor Family princess and member of the 'Council
                       of Five'
Shen Lu Chua   computer expert and member of the 'Council of Five'
Yun Ch'o   lieutenant to Shen Lu Chua

OTHER CHARACTERS

Anton   friend of Kim Ward on the Recruitment Project
The Architect   one of the psych team on the Recruitment Project
Barycz, Jiri   scientist on the Wiring Project
Baxi   chief of the tribe in the Clay
Beattie, Douglas   alias of DeVore
Bergson   Overseer on the plantation; alias for DeVore
Boden, Mikhail   alias of DeVore
The Builder   part of the psych team on the Recruitment Project
Chan Wen-fu   friend of Heng Chian-ye
Chan Shui   young worker in the Casting Shop
Chuang Lian   wife of Minister Chuang
Crimson Lotus   sing-song girl in Mu Chua's
Ebert, Lutz   half-brother of Klaus Ebert
Ellis, Michael   assistant to Director Spatz
Endfors, Pietr   best friend of Knut Tolonen
Enge, Marie   serving woman at the Dragon Cloud teahouse
Fang Hui   guard on the plantation

Ganz, Joseph	alias of DeVore
Golden Heart	young prostitute bought by Hans Ebert for his household
Hammond, Joel	Senior Technician on the Wiring Project
Heng Chian-ye	son of Heng Chi-po and nephew of Heng Yu
Herrick	an illegal implant specialist
Hong	'Hsien' or District Judge
Janko	bully in the Casting Shop
Josef	friend of Kim Ward's on the Recruitment Project
Kao Ch'iang Hsin	infant daughter of Kao Chen
Kao Wu	infant son of Kao Chen
Kung Wen-fa	Senior Advocate from Mars
Ling Hen	henchman for Herrick
Lin Hou Ying	maintenance engineer for ProsTek
Liu Chang	brothel keeper/pimp
Loehr	alias of DeVore
Lotte	student at Oxford; sister of Wolf
Lo Wen	personal servant to Hans Ebert
Lo Ying	'Panchang' or 'Supervisor'; friend of Kao Chen
Lo Yu-Hsiang	Senior Representative in the House at Weimar
Lu Cao	amah (maidservant) to Jelka Tolonen
Lu Ming Shao	'Whiskers Lu', Triad boss
Lu Nan Jen	the 'Oven Man'
Lu Wang-pei	murder suspect
Maitland, Idris	mother of Stefan Lehmann
Matyas	Clayborn boy in the Recruitment Project
Mu Chua	'Madam' of the House of the Ninth Ecstasy, a sing-song house, or brothel
Novacek, Lubos	merchant; father of Sergey Novacek
Novacek, Sergey	student at Oxford and sculptor
Nung	Supervisor of the Casting Shop
Peng Yu-wei	tutor to the Shepherd children
Peskova	lieutenant of the guards on the plantation
Reynolds	alias of DeVore
Schenck, Hung-li	Governor of the Mars Colony
Shang Li-Yen	tutor on the Recruitment Project
Siang Che	martial arts instructor to Jelka Tolonen
Spatz, Gustav	Director of the Wiring Project
Sung	Supervisor on the plantation
Sweet Flute	mui tsai to Madam Chuang Lian
Sweet Honey	sing-song girl in Mu Chua's

T'ai Cho	tutor and 'guardian' to Kim Ward
Tarrant	Company head
Tissan, Catherine	student at Oxford
Tolonen, Hannah	aunt to Knut Tolonen
Tom	'Greaser', part of Matyas's gang
Tong Chou	alias of Kao Chen
Tsang Yi	friend of Heng Chian-ye
Tung Liang	boy in the Casting Shop
Tung T'an	Senior Consultant at the Melfi Clinic
Turner	alias of DeVore
Wang Ti	wife of Kao Chen
Ward, Kim	Lagasek, or 'Starer'; 'Clayborn', orphan and scientist
White Orchid	sing-song girl in Mu Chua's
Wolf	student at Oxford and brother of Lotte
Wolfe	Security soldier
Yu, Madam	First Level socialite
Yung Pi-chi	Head of the Yung family
Zhakar	Speaker of the House of Representatives

THE DEAD

Aaltonen	Marshal and Head of Security for City Europe
Anders	a mercenary
Anderson	Director of The Project
Ascher, Mikhail	junior credit agent in the Finance Ministry, the Hu Pu, and father of Emily Ascher
Bakke	Marshal in Security
Barrow, Chao	member of the House of Representatives; Dispersionist
Beatrice	daughter of Cathy Hubbard, granddaughter of Mary Reed
Big Wen	a 'landowner'
Boss Yang	an exploiter of the people
Buck, John	Head of Development at the Ministry of Contracts
Ch'eng I	Minor Family prince and son of Ch'eng So Yuan
Ch'eng So Yuan	Minor Family head
Chang Hsuan	Han painter from the 8th century
Chang Lai-hsun	nephew of Chang Yi Wei
Chang Li Chen	Junior Dragon, in charge of drafting the Edit of Technological Control
Chang Lui	woman who adopted Pavel

Chang Yan	Guard on the Plantations
Chang Yi Wei	senior brother of the Chang clan owners of MicroData
Chang Yu	Tsao Ch'un's appointment as First Dragon
Chao Ni Tsu	Grand Master of wei chi and computer genius. Servant of Tsao Ch'un
Chen So I	Head of the Ministry of Contracts
Chen Yu	steward to Tsao Ch'un in Pei Ch'ing
Cheng Yu	one of the original Seven, advisor to Tsao Ch'un
Chi Fei Yu	an usurer
Chi Lin Lin	legal assistant to Yang Hong Yu
Ching Su	friend of Jiang Lei
Chiu Fa	media commentator on the Mids news channel
Cho Hsiang	subordinate to Hong Cao and middleman for Pietr Lehmann
Cho Yi Yi	Master of the Bedchamber at Tongjiang
Chu Heng	'kwai' or hired knife; a hireling of DeVore
Chun Hua	wife of Jiang Lei
Chung Hsin	'Loyalty'; a bond-servant to Li Shai Tung
Croft, Rebecca	'Becky', daughter of Leopold, with the lazy eye
Curtis, Tim	Head of Human Resources GenSyn
Dag	a mercenary
Dick, Philip Kindred	American science fiction writer
Duchek, Albert	Administrator of Lodz and Dispersionist
Ebert, Gustav	genetics genius and co-founder of GenSyn, Genetic Synthetics
Ebert, Ludovic	son of Gustav Ebert and a GenSyn director
Ebert, Wolfgang	financial genius and co-founder of GenSyn, Genetic Synthetics
Einar	a mercenary
Endfors, Jenny	wife of Knut Tolonen and mother of Jelka
Fan Chang	one of the original Seven, advisor to Tsao Ch'un
Fan Cho	son of Fan Chang
Fan Lin	son of Fan Chang
Fan Peng	eldest wife of Fan Chang
Fan Si-pin	Master of wei chi from the 18th century
Fan Ti Yu	son of Fan Chang
Feng I	Colonel in charge of Tsao Ch'un's elite force
Gosse	elite guard at the Domain
Grant, Thomas	captain in security
Griffin, James B.	Sixtieth President of the United States of America

Haavikko, Knut	major in security
Heng Chi-Po	Minister of Transportation for City Europe
Henrik	a mercenary
Ho	steward to Jiang Lei
Hong Cao	middle man for Pietr Lehmann
Hou Hsin-Fa	one of the original Seven, advisor to Tsao Ch'un
Hsu Jung	friend of Jiang Lei
Hubbard, Beth	daughter of Tom and Mary Hubbard
Hubbard, Cathy	daughter of Tom and Mary Hubbard
Hubbard, Mary	wife of Tom Hubbard and mother of Cathy. Second wife of Jake Reed
Hubbard, Meg	daughter of Tom and Mary Hubbard
Hubbard, Tom	farmer, resident in Church Knowle. Huband of Mary Hubbard and father of Beth, Meg and Cathy. Best friend to Jake Reed
Hui	receptionist for GenSyn
Hui Chang Ye	senior legal advocate for the Chang family
Hung	Tsao Ch'uns spy in Jiang Lei's camp
Hwa	'Blood', or fighter, beneath the Net
Jiang Ch'iao-chieh	eldest daughter of Jiang Lei
Jiang Lei	general of Tsao Ch'un's Eighteenth Banner Army, also known as Nai Liu
Jiang Lei	general of Tsao Ch'un's Eighteenth Banner Army, also known as Nai Lu
Jiang Lo Wen	granddaughter of Jiang Lei
Jiang San-chieh	youngest daughter of Jiang Lei
Jung	steward to Tobias Lahm
Kao Jyan	assassin
Karl	a mercenary
Kirov, Alexander	Marshal to the Seven, Head of the Council of Generals
Krenek, Henryk	Senior Representative of the Martian Colonies
Krenek, Irina	wife of Henryk Krenek
Krenek, Josef	company head
Krenek, Maria	wife of Josef Krenek
Ku	Marshal of the Fourth Banner Army
Kurt	Chief Technician for GenSyn
Lahm, Tobias	Eighth Dragon at the Ministry
Lao Jen	Junior Minister to Li Shai Tung
Lehmann, Pietr	Under Secretary of the House of Representatives and father of Stefan Lehmann and leader of Dispersionists

Li Chang So	sixth son of Li Chao Ch'in
Li Chao Ch'in	one of the original Seven, advisor to Tsao Ch'un
Li Fu Jen	third son of Li Chao Ch'in
Li Han Ch'in	first son of Li Shai Tung and heir to City Europe
Li Kuang	fifth son of Li Chao Ch'in
Li Peng	eldest son of Li Chao Ch'in
Li Po	T'ang dynasty poet
Li Shen	second son of Li Chao Ch'in
Li Weng	fourth son of Li Chao Ch'in
Lin Yua	first wife of Li Shai Tung
Ling	steward at the Black Tower
Ludd, Drew	biggest grossing actor in Hollywood and star of Ubik
Lung Ti	secretary to Edmund Wyatt
Lwo Kang	son of Lwo Chun-yi and Li Shai Tung's Minster of the Edit of Technological Control
Ma Shao Tu	senior servant to Li Chao Ch'in
Maitland (Fu Jen)	Stefan Lehmann's mother
Mao Tse T'ung	first Ko Ming emperor of China (ruled 1948–1976 AD)
Melfi, Charles	father of Alexandra Shepherd
Ming Hsin-far	senior advocate for GenSyn
Nai Liu	'Enduring Willow'; pen name of Jiang Lei and the most popular Han poet of his time
P'eng Chuan	Sixth Dragon at the Ministry ('The Thousand Eyes')
P'eng K'ai-chi	Nephew of P'eng Chuan
Palmer, Joshua	'Old Josh', record collector
Pan Chao	the great hero of Chung Kuo, who conquered Asia in the 1st century AD
Pan Tsung-yen	friend of Jiang Lei
Pavel	Young worker on the Plantations
Pei Ko	one of the original Seven, advisor to Tsao Ch'un
Pei Lin-Yi	eldest son of Pei Ko
Ragnar	a mercenary
Raikkonen	Marshal in Security
Reed, Anne	first wife of Jake Reed; mother of Peter Reed and sister of Mary Hubbard (Jake's second wife)
Reed, Jake	'Login' or 'Webdancer' for Hinton Industries. Father of Peter and Tom Reed
Reed, Mary	sister of Jake Reed
Reed, Peter	son of Jake and Anne Reed. GenSyn Executive
Reed, Tom	son of Jane and Mary Reed

Rheinhardt	Media Liaison Officer for GenSyn
Schwartz	Aide to Marshal Aaltonen
Shao Shu	First Steward at Chun Hua's mansion
Shao Yen	major in Security, friend of Meng Hsin-far
Shen Chen	son of Shen Fu
Shen Fu	The First Dragon, Head of the Ministry ('The Thousand Eyes')
Shepherd, Alexandra	wife of Amos Shepherd and daughter of Charles Melfi
Shepherd, Amos	Great-great grandfather of Hal Shepherd. Chief advisor to Tsao Ch'un and architect of City Earth
Shepherd, Augustus	Son of Amos Shepherd
Shepherd, Augustus Raedwald	Great-great uncle to Ben Shepherd
Shepherd, Beth	daughter of Amos Shepherd
Shu Liang	Senior Legal Advocate
Shu San	Junior Minister to Lwo Kang
Si Wu Ya	'Silk Raven'; wife Supervisor Sung
Ssu Lu Shan	official of the Ministry, the 'Thousand Eyes'
Su Ting-an	Master of wei chi from the 18th century
Su Tung-p'o	Han official and poet of the 11th century
Svensson	Marshal in Security
Tai Yu	Moonflower', maid to Gustav Ebert; a GenSyn clone
Teng	common citizen of Chung Kuo
Teng Fu	Guard on the Plantation
Teng Liang	Minor Family princess betrothed to Prince Ch'eng I
Trish	Artificial Intelligence 'filter avatar' for Jake Reed's penthouse apartment
Ts'ao Pi	Number Three' steward at Tsao Ch'un's court in Pei Ch'ing
Tsao Ch'l Yuan	youngest son of Tsao Ch'un
Tsao Ch'un	ex-member of the Chinese politburo and architect of 'the Collapse'. Mass murderer and tyrant; 'creator' of Chung Kuo
Tsao Heng	second son of Tsao Ch'un
Tsao Hsiao	Tsao Ch'un's elder brother
Tsao Wang-po	eldest son of Tsao Ch'un
Tsu Chen	one of the original Seven, advisor to Tsao Ch'un
Tsu Lin	eldest son of Tsu Chen
Tsu Shi	steward to Gustav Ebert, a GenSyn clone
Tsu Tiao	T'ang of West Asia
Tu Mu	assistant to Alison Winter at GenSyn

Wang An-Shih	Han official and poet of the 11th century
Wang Chang Ye	eldest son of Wang Hsien
Wang Hui So	one of the original Seven, advisor to Tsao Ch'un
Wang Lieh Tsu	second son of Wang Hsien
Wang Lung	eldest son of Wang Hui So
Wang Yu-lai	'Cadre', servant of the Ministry, 'The Thousand Eyes', instructed to report back on Jiang Lei
Wei	a judge
Weis, Anton	banker and Dispersionist
Wen P'ing	Tsao Ch'un's man. A bully
Weo Shao	chancellor to Tsao Ch'un
Winter, Alison	Jake Reed's girlfriend at New College and evaluation executive at GenSyn
Winter, Jake	son of Alison Winter
Wolfe	elite guard in the Domain
Wu Chi	AI (Artificial Intelligence) to Tobias Lahm
Wu Hsien	one of the original Seven, advisor to Tsao Ch'un
Wyatt, Edmund	company head, Dispersionist, and (unknown to him) father of Kim Ward
Wyatt, Edmund	businessman and (unknown to him) father of Kim Ward
Yang Hong Yu	legal advocate
Yang Lai	Minister under Li Shai Tung
Yo Jou Hsi	a judge
Yu Ch'o	family retainer to Wang Hui So

GLOSSARY OF MANDARIN TERMS

It is not intended to belabour the reader with a whole mass of arcane Han expressions here. Some – usually the more specific – are explained in context. However, as a number of Mandarin terms are used naturally in the text, I've thought it best to provide a brief explanation of those terms.

aiya!	a common expression of surprise or dismay
amah	a domestic maidservant
Amo Li Jia	The Chinese gave this name to North America when they first arrived in the 1840s. Its literal meaning is 'The Land Without Ghosts'.
an	A saddle. This has the same sound as the word for peace, and thus is associated in the Chinese mind with peace.
catty	the colloquial term for a unit of measure formally called a *jin*. One catty – as used here – equals roughly 1.1. pounds (avoirdupois), or (exactly) 500 gm. Before 1949 and the standardization of Chinese measures to a metric standard, this measure varied district by district, but was generally regarded as equalling about 1.33 pounds (avoirdupois).
ch'a	Tea. It might be noted that *ch'a shu*, the Chinese art of tea, is an ancient forebear of the Japanese tea ceremony *chanoyu*. *Hsiang p'ien* are flower teas, *Ch'ing ch'a* are green, unfermented teas.
ch'a hao t'ai	literally, a 'directory'
ch'a shu	The art of tea, adopted later by the Japanese in their tea ceremony. The *ch'a* god is Lu Yu and his

	image can be seen on banners outside teahouses throughout Chung Kuo.
chan shih	a 'fighter', here denoting a *tong* soldier
chang	ten *ch'i*, thus about 12 feet (Western)
Chang-e	The goddess of the Moon, and younger sister of the Spirit of the Waters. The moon represents the very essence of the female principal, *Yin*, in opposition to the Sun, which is *Yang*. Legend has it that Chang-e stole the elixir of immortality from her husband, the great archer Shen I, then fled to the Moon for safety, where she was transformed into a toad, which, so it is said, can still be seen against the whiteness of the moon's surface.
chang shan	Literally 'long dress', which fastens to the right. Worn by both sexes. The woman's version is a fitted, calf-length dress similar to the *chi pao*. A south China fashion, it is also known as a *cheung sam*.
chao tai hui	an 'entertainment', usually, within *Chung Kuo*, of an expensive and sophisticated kind
chen yen	true words; the Chinese equivalent of a mantra
ch'eng	The word means both 'City' and 'Wall'.
Ch'eng Ou Chou	City Europe
Ch'eng Hsiang	'Chancellor', a post first established in the Ch'in court more than two thousand years ago
ch'i	a Chinese 'foot'; approximately 14.4 inches
ch'i	'Inner strength'; one of the two fundamental 'entities' from which everything is composed. Li is the 'form' or 'law', or (to cite Joseph Needham) the 'principal of organization' behind things, whereas *ch'i* is the 'matter-energy' or 'spirit' within material things, equating loosely to the *Pneuma* of the Greeks and the *prana* of the ancient Hindus. As the sage Chu Hsi (AD 1130–1200) said, 'The li is the *Tao* that pertains to "what is above shapes" and is the source from which all things are produced. The *ch'i* is the material [literally instrument] that pertains to "what is within shapes", and is the means whereby things are produced... Throughout the universe there is no *ch'i* without li. Or li without *ch'i*.'
chi ch'i	common workers, but used here mainly to denote the ant-like employees of the Ministry of Distribution
Chia Ch'eng	Honorary Assistant to the Royal Household

chi'an	a general term for money
chiao tzu	a traditional North Chinese meal of meat-filled dumplings eaten with a hot spicy sauce
Chieh Hsia	Term meaning 'Your Majesty', derived from the expression 'Below the Steps'. It was the formal way of addressing the Emperor, through his Ministers, who stood 'below the steps'.
chi pao	literally 'banner gown', a one-piece gown of Manchu origin, usually sleeveless, worn by women
chih chu	a spider
ch'in	A long (120 cm), narrow, lacquered zither with a smooth top surface and sound holes beneath, seven silk strings and thirteen studs marking the harmonic positions on the strings. Early examples have been unearthed from fifth century BC tombs, but it probably evolved in the fourteenth or thirteenth century BC. It is the most honoured of Chinese instruments and has a lovely mellow tone.
Chin P'ing Mei	The Golden Lotus, an erotic novel, written by an unknown scholar – possibly anonymously by the writer Wang Shih-chen – at the beginning of the seventeenth century as a continuation of the Shui Hui Chuan, or 'Warriors of the Marsh', expanding chapters 23 to 25 of the Shan Hui, which relate the story of how Wu Sung became a bandit. Extending the story beyond this point, the Golden Lotus has been accused of being China's great licentious (even, perhaps, pornographic) novel. But as C.P. Fitzgerald says, 'If this book is indecent in parts, it is only because, telling a story of domestic life, it leaves out nothing.' It is available in a three volume English-language translation.
ch'ing	pure
ching	Literally 'mirror', here used also to denote a perfect GenSyn copy of a man. Under the Edict of Technological Control, these are limited to copies of the ruling T'ang and their closest relatives. However, mirrors were also popularly believed to have certain strange properties, one of which was to make spirits visible. Buddhist priests used special 'magic mirrors' to show believers the form into which they would be reborn. Moreover, if a man looks into one of these mirrors and fails to recognize his own face, it is a

	sign that his own death is not far off. [See also *hu hsin chung*.]
ch'ing ch'a	green, unfermented teas
Ch'ing Ming	The Festival of Brightness and Purity, when the graves are swept and offerings made to the deceased. Also known as the Festival of Tombs, it occurs at the end of the second moon and is used for the purpose of celebrating the spring, a time for rekindling the cooking fires after a three-day period in which the fires were extinguished and only cold food eaten.
Chou	Literally, 'State', but here used as the name of a card game based on the politics of Chung Kuo. See Book Four, 'The Feast Of The Dead'.
chow mein	This, like chop suey, is neither a Chinese nor a Western dish, but a special meal created by the Chinese in North America for the Western palate. A transliteration of *chao mian* (fried noodles), it is a distant relation of the *liang mian huang* served in Suchow.
ch'u	the west
chun hua	Literally, 'Spring Pictures'. These are, in fact, pornographic 'pillow books', meant for the instruction of newly-weds.
ch'un tzu	An ancient Chinese term from the Warring States period, describing a certain class of noblemen, controlled by a code of chivalry and morality known as the *li*, or rites. Here the term is roughly, and sometimes ironically, translated as 'gentlemen', The *ch'un tzu* is as much an ideal state of behaviour – as specified by Confucius in the *Analects* – as an actual class in Chung Kuo, though a degree of financial independence and a high standard of education are assumed a prerequisite.
chung	a lidded ceramic serving bowl for *ch'a*
chung hsin	loyalty
E hsing hsun huan	A saying: 'Bad nature follows a cycle.'
er	two
erh tzu	son
erhu	a traditional Chinese instrument
fa	punishment

fen	A unit of currency; see *yuan*. It has another meaning, that of a 'minute' of clock time, but that usage is avoided here to prevent any confusion.
feng yu	A 'phoenix chair', canopied and decorated with silver birds. Coloured scarlet and gold, this is the traditional carriage for a bride as she is carried to her wedding ceremony.
fu jen	'Madam', used here as opposed to *t'ai t'ai*, 'Mrs'
fu sang	The hollow mulberry tree; according to ancient Chinese cosmology this tree stands where the sun rises and is the dwelling place of rulers. *Sang* (mulberry) however has the same sound as *sang* (sorrow) in Chinese.
Han	Term used by the Chinese to describe their own race, the 'black-haired people', dating back to the Han dynasty (210 BC–AD 220). It is estimated that some ninety-four per cent of modern China's population are *Han* racially.
Hei	Literally 'black'. The Chinese pictogram for this represents a man wearing war paint and tattoos. Here it refers specifically to the genetically manufactured half-men, made by GenSyn and used as riot police to quell uprisings in the lower levels of the City.
ho yeh	*Nelumbo Nucifera*, or lotus, the seeds of which are used in Chinese medicine to cure insomnia
Hoi Po	the corrupt officials who dealt with the European traders in the nineteenth century, more commonly known as 'hoppos'
Hsia	a crab
hsiang p'en	flower *ch'a*
hsiao	Filial piety. The character for *hsiao* is comprised of two parts, the upper part meaning 'old', the lower meaning 'son' or 'child'. This dutiful submission of the young to the old is at the heart of Confucianism and Chinese culture generally.
Hsiao chieh	'Miss', or an unmarried woman. An alternative to *nu shi*.
hsiao jen	'Little man/men'. In the *Analects*, Book XIV, Confucius writes, 'The gentleman gets through to what is up above; the small man gets through to what is down below.' This distinction between 'gentlemen'

(ch'un tzu) and 'little men' (hsiao jen), false even in Confucius's time, is no less a matter of social perspective in Chung Kuo.

hsien — Historically an administrative district of variable size. Here the term is used to denote a very specific administrative area, one of ten stacks – each stack composed of 30 decks. Each deck is a hexagonal living unit of ten levels, two li, or approximately one kilometre, in diameter. A stack can be imagined as one honeycomb in the great hive that is the City. Each hsien of the city elects one Representative to sit in the House at Weimar.

Hsien Ling — Chief Magistrate, in charge of a Hsien. In Chung Kuo these officials are the T'ang's representatives and law enforcers for the individual hsien. In times of peace each hsien would also elect one Representative to sit in the House at Weimar.

hsueh pai — 'snow white', a derogatory term here for Hung Mao women

Hu pu — the T'ang's Finance Ministry

hu hsin chung — See ching, re Buddhist magic mirrors, for which this was the name. The power of such mirrors was said to protect the owner from evil. It was also said that one might see the secrets of futurity in such a mirror. See the chapter 'Mirrors' in The White Mountain for further information.

hu t'ieh — A butterfly. Anyone wishing to follow up on this tale of Chuang Tzu's might look to the sage's writings and specifically the chapter 'Discussion on Making All Things Equal'.

hua pen — Literally 'story roots', these were précis guidebooks used by the street-corner storytellers in China for the past two thousand years. The main events of the story were written down in the hua pen for the benefit of those storytellers who had not yet mastered their art. During the Yuan or Mongol dynasty (AD 1280–1368) these hua pen developed into plays, and, later on – during the Ming dynasty (AD 1368–1644) – into the form of popular novels, of which the Shui Hu Chuan, or 'Outlaws of the Marsh' remains one of the most popular. Any reader interested in following this up might purchase Pearl Buck's translation, rendered as 'All Men Are Brothers' and first published in 1933.

Huang Ti	Originally Huang Ti was the last of the 'Three Sovereigns' and the first of the 'Five Emperors' of ancient Chinese tradition. Huang Ti, the Yellow Emperor, was the earliest ruler recognized by the historian Ssu-ma Ch'ien (136–85 BC) in his great historical work, the *Shih Chi*. Traditionally, all subsequent rulers (and would-be rulers) of China have claimed descent from the Yellow Emperor, the 'Son of Heaven' himself, who first brought civilization to the black-haired people. His name is now synonymous with the term 'emperor'.
hun	The higher soul or 'spirit soul', which, the Chinese believe, ascends to Heaven at death, joins Shang Ti, the Supreme Ancestor, and lives in his court for ever more. The *hun* is believed to come into existence at the moment of conception (see also *p'o*).
hun tun	'The Chou believed that Heaven and Earth were once inextricably mixed together in a state of undifferentiated chaos, like a chicken's egg. Hun Tun they called that state' (*The Broken Wheel*, Chapter 37). It is also the name of a meal of tiny sack-like dumplings.
Hung Lou Meng	*The Dream of Red Mansions*, also known as *The Story Of The Stone*, a lengthy novel written in the middle of the 18th century. Like the *Chin Ping Mei*, it deals with the affairs of a single Chinese family. According to experts the first eighty chapters are the work of Ts'ao Hsueh-ch'in, and the last forty belong to Kao Ou. It is, without doubt, the masterpiece of Chinese literature, and is available from Penguin in the UK in a five-volume edition.
Hung Mao	Literally 'redheads', the name the Chinese gave to the Dutch (and later English) seafarers who attempted to trade with China in the seventeenth century. Because of the piratical nature of their endeavours (which often meant plundering Chinese shipping and ports) the name continues to retain connotations of piracy.
Hung Mun	the Secret Societies or, more specifically, the Triads
huo jen	literally, 'fire men'
I Lung	The 'First Dragon', Senior Minister and Great Lord of the 'Ministry', also known as 'The Thousand Eyes'
jou tung wu	literally 'meat animal': 'It was a huge mountain of flesh, a hundred ch'i to a side and almost twenty ch'i

in height. Along one side of it, like the teats of a giant pig, three dozen heads jutted from the flesh, long, eyeless snouts with shovel jaws that snuffled and gobbled in the conveyor-belt trough...'

kai t'ou	A thin cloth of red and gold that veils a new bride's face. Worn by the Ch'ing empresses for almost three centuries.
kan pei!	'good health!' or 'cheers!' – a drinking toast
kang	the Chinese hearth, serving also as oven and, in the cold of winter, as a sleeping platform
k'ang hsi	A Ch'ing (or Manchu) emperor whose long reign (AD 1662–1722) is considered a golden age for the art of porcelain-making. The lavender-glazed bowl in 'The Sound Of Jade' is, however, not kang-hsi but Chun chou ware from the Sung period (960-1127) and considered amongst the most beautiful (and rare) wares in Chinese pottery.
kao liang	a strong Chinese liquor
Ko Ming	'Revolutionary'. The Tien Ming is the Mandate of Heaven, supposedly handed down from Shang Ti, the Supreme Ancestor, to his earthly counterpart, the Emperor (Huang Ti). This Mandate could be enjoyed only so long as the Emperor was worthy of it, and rebellion against a tyrant – who broke the Mandate through his lack of justice, benevolence and sincerity – was deemed not criminal but a rightful expression of Heaven's anger.
k'ou t'ou	The fifth stage of respect, according to the 'Book of Ceremonies', involves kneeling and striking the head against the floor. This ritual has become more commonly known in the West as kowtow.
ku li	'Bitter strength'. These two words, used to describe the condition of farm labourers who, after severe droughts or catastrophic floods, moved off their land and into the towns to look for work of any kind – however hard and onerous – spawned the word 'coolie' by which the West more commonly knows the Chinese labourer. Such men were described as 'men of bitter strength', or simply 'ku li'.
Kuan Hua	Mandarin, the language spoken in mainland China. Also known as kuo yu and pai hua.
Kuan Yin	The Goddess of Mercy. Originally the Buddhist male bodhisattva, Avalokitsevara (translated into Han as

'He who listens to the sounds of the world', or 'Kuan Yin'), the Han mistook the well-developed breasts of the saint for a woman's and, since the ninth century, have worshipped Kuan Yin as such. Effigies of Kuan Yin will show her usually as the Eastern Madonna, cradling a child in her arms. She is also sometimes seen as the wife of *Kuan Kung*, the Chinese God of War.

Kuei Chuan	'Running Dog', here the name of a Triad
kuo yu	Mandarin, the language spoken in most of Mainland China. Also rendered here as *kuan hua* and *pai hua*.
kwai	An abbreviation of *kwai tao*, a 'sharp knife' or 'fast knife'. It can also mean to be sharp or fast (as a knife). An associated meaning is that of a 'clod' or 'lump of earth'. Here it is used to denote a class of fighters from below the Net, whose ability and self-discipline separate them from the usual run of hired knives.
Lan Tian	'Blue Sky'
Lang	a covered walkway
lao chu	sing-song girls, slightly more respectable than the common *men hu*
lao jen	'old man' (also *weng*); used normally as a term of respect
lao kuan	a 'Great Official', often used ironically
lao shih	term that denotes a genuine and straightforward man – bluff and honest
lao wai	an outsider
li	A Chinese 'mile', approximating to half a kilometre or one third of a mile. Until 1949, when metric measures were adopted in China, the li could vary from place to place.
Li	'Propriety'. See the Li *Ching* or 'Book Of Rites' for the fullest definition.
Li Ching	'The Book Of Rites', one of the five ancient classics
liang	A Chinese ounce of roughly 32gm. Sixteen liang form a *catty*.
liu k'ou	The seventh stage of respect, according to the 'Book of Ceremonies'. Two stages above the more familiarly known 'k'ou t'ou' (kowtow) it involves kneeling and striking the forehead three times against the floor, rising to one's feet again, then

kneeling and repeating the prostration with three touches of the forehead to the ground. Only the *san kuei chiu k'ou* – involving three prostrations – was more elaborate and was reserved for Heaven and its son, the Emperor (see also *san k'ou*).

liumang	punks
lu nan jen	literally 'Oven Man', title of the official who is responsible for cremating all of the dead bodies
lueh	'that invaluable quality of producing a piece of art casually, almost uncaringly'
lung t'ing	'dragon pavilions', small sedan chairs carried by servants and containing a pile of dowry gifts.
Luoshu	The Chinese legend relates that in ancient times a turtle crawled from a river in Luoshu province, the patterns on its shell forming a three by three grid of numeric pictograms, the numbers of which – both down and across – equalled the same total of fifteen. Since the time of the Shang (three thousand-plus years ago) tortoise shells were used in divination, and the Luoshu diagram is considered magic and is often used as a charm for easing childbirth.
ma kua	a waist-length ceremonial jacket
mah jong	Whilst, in its modern form, the 'game of the four winds' was introduced towards the end of the 19th century to Westerners trading in the thriving city of Shanghai, it was developed from a card game that existed as long ago as AD 960. Using 144 tiles, it is generally played by four players. The tiles have numbers and also suits – winds, dragons, bamboos and circles.
mao	A unit of currency. See *yuan*.
mao tai	a strong, sorghum-based liquor
mei fa tzu	common saying, 'It is fate!'
mei hua	'plum blossom'
mei mei	sister
mei yu jen wen	'Subhumans'. Used in *Chung Kuo* by those in the City's uppermost levels to denote anyone living in the lower hundred.
men hu	Literally, 'the one standing in the door'. The most common (and cheapest) of prostitutes.

min	literally 'the people'; used (as here) by the Minor Families in a pejorative sense, as an equivalent to 'plebeian'
Ming	The Dynasty that ruled China from 1368 to 1644. Literally, the name means 'Bright' or 'Clear' or 'Brilliant'. It carries connotations of cleansing.
mou	A Chinese 'acre' of approximately 7,260 square feet. There are roughly six mou to a Western acre, and a 10,000-mou field would approximate to 1666 acres, or just over two and a half square miles.
Mu Ch'in	'Mother', a general term commonly addressed to any older woman
mui tsai	Rendered in Cantonese as 'mooi-jai'. Colloquially it means either 'little sister' or 'slave girl', though generally, as here, the latter. Other Mandarin terms used for the same status are pei-nu and yatou. Technically, guardianship of the girl involved is legally signed over in return for money.
nan jen	common term for 'Man'
Ni Hao?	'How are you?'
niao	literally 'bird', but here, as often, it is used euphemistically as a term for the penis, often as an expletive
nu er	daughter
nu shi	an unmarried woman, a term equating to 'Miss'
Pa shi yi	literally 'Eighty-One', here referring specifically to the Central Council of the New Confucian officialdom
pai nan jen	literally 'white man'
pai pi	'hundred pens', term used for the artificial reality experiments renamed 'Shells' by Ben Shepherd
pan chang	supervisor
pao yun	a 'jewelled cloud' ch'a
pau	a simple long garment worn by men
pau shuai ch'i	the technical scientific term for 'half-life'
p'i p'a	a four-stringed lute used in traditional Chinese music
Pien Hua!	Change!
p'ing	an apple, symbol of peace
ping	the east

Ping Fa	Sun Tzu's *The Art Of War*, written over two thousand years ago. The best English translation is probably Samuel B. Griffith's 1963 edition. It was a book Chairman Mao frequently referred to.
Ping Tiao	Levelling. To bring down or make flat. Here, in Chung Kuo, it is also a terrorist organization.
p'o	The 'animal soul' which, at death, remains in the tomb with the corpse and takes its nourishment from the grave offerings. The p'o decays with the corpse, sinking down into the underworld (beneath the Yellow Springs) where – as a shadow – it continues an existence of a kind. The p'o is believed to come into existence at the moment of birth (see also *hun*).
sam fu	An upper garment (part shirt, part jacket) worn originally by both males and females, in imitation of Manchu styles; later on a wide-sleeved, calf-length version was worn by women alone.
san	three
San chang	the three palaces
san kuei chiu k'ou	The eighth and final stage of respect, according to the 'Book Of Ceremonies', it involves kneeling three times, each time striking the forehead three times against the ground before rising from one's knees (in *k'ou t'ou* one strikes the forehead but once). This most elaborate form of ritual was reserved for Heaven and its son, the Emperor. See also *liu k'ou*.
san k'ou	abbreviated form of *san kuei chiu k'ou*
San Kuo Yan Yi	*The Romance of The Three Kingdoms*, also known as the *San Kuo Chih Yen I*. China's great historical novel, running to 120 chapters, it covers the period from AD 168 to 265. Written by Lo Kuan-chung in the early Ming dynasty, its heroes, Liu Pei, Kuan Chung and Chang Fei, together with its villain, Ts'ao Ts'ao, are all historical personages. It is still one of the most popular stories in modern China.
sao mu	the 'Feast of the Dead'
shang	the south
shan shui	The literal meaning is 'mountains and water', but the term is normally associated with a style of landscape painting that depicts rugged mountain scenery with river valleys in the foreground. It is a highly popular

	form, first established in the T'ang Dynasty, back in the seventh to ninth centuries AD.
shao lin	specially trained assassins, named after the monks of the *shao lin* monastery
shao nai nai	Literally, 'little grandmother'. A young girl who has been given the responsibility of looking after her siblings.
she t'ou	a 'tongue' or taster, whose task is to safeguard his master from poisoning
shen chung	'caution'
shen mu	'she who stands in the door': a common prostitute
shen nu	'god girls': superior prostitutes
shen t'se	special elite force, named after the 'palace armies' of the late T'ang dynasty
Shih	'Master'. Here used as a term of respect somewhat equivalent to our use of 'Mister'. The term was originally used for the lowest level of civil servants, to distinguish them socially from the run-of-the-mill 'Misters' (*hsian sheng*) below them and the gentlemen (*ch'un tzu*) above.
shou hsing	a peach brandy
Shui Hu Chuan	*Outlaws of the Marsh*, a long historical novel attributed to Lo Kuan-chung but re-cast in the early 16th century by 'Shih Nai-an', a scholar. Set in the eleventh century, it is a saga of bandits, warlords and heroes. Written in pure *pai hua* – colloquial Chinese – it is the tale of how its heroes became bandits. Its revolutionary nature made it deeply unpopular with both the Ming and Manchu dynasties, but it remains one of the most popular adventures among the Chinese populus.
siang chi	Chinese chess, a very different game from its Western counterpart
Ta	'Beat', here a heavily amplified form of Chinese folk music, popular amongst the young
ta lien	an elaborate girdle pouch
Ta Ssu Nung	the Superintendancy of Agriculture
tai	Literally 'pockets' but here denoting Representatives in the House at Weimar. 'Owned' financially by the Seven, historically such *tai* have served a double function in the House, counterbalancing the strong mercantile tendencies of the House and serving as

a conduit for the views of the Seven. Traditionally they had been elderly, well-respected men, but more recently their replacements were young, brash and very corrupt, more like the hoppoes of the Opium Wars period.

t'ai chi — The Original, or One, from which the duality of all things (yin and yang) developed, according to Chinese cosmology. We generally associate the t'ai chi with the Taoist symbol, that swirling circle of dark and light supposedly representing an egg (perhaps the Hun Tun), the yolk and the white differentiated.

tai hsiao — a white wool flower, worn in the hair

Tai Huo — 'Great Fire'

T'ai Shan — Mount T'ai, the highest and most sacred of China's mountains, located in Shantung province. A stone pathway of 6293 steps leads to the summit and, for thousands of years the ruling emperor has made ritual sacrifices at its foot, accompanied by his full retinue, presenting evidence of his virtue. T'ai Shan is one of the five Taoist holy mountains, and symbolizes the very centre of Chaina. It is the mountain of the sun, symbolizing the bright male force (yang). 'As safe as T'ai Shan' is a popular saying, denoting the ultimate in solidity and certainty.

Tai Shih Lung — Court Astrologer, a title that goes back to the Han Dynasty

T'ang — Literally, 'beautiful and imposing'. It is the title chosen by the Seven, who were originally the chief advisors to Tsao Ch'un, the tyrant. Since overthrowing Tsao Ch'un, it has effectively had the meaning of 'emperor'.

Ta Ts'in — The Chinese name for the Roman Empire. They also knew Rome as Li Chien and as 'the land West of the Sea'. The Romans themselves they termed the 'Big Ts'in' – the Ts'in being the name the Chinese gave themselves during the Ts'in dynasty (AD 265–316).

te — 'spiritual power', 'true virtue' or 'virtuality', defined by Alan Watts as 'the realization or expression of the Tao in actual living'

t'e an tsan — 'Innocent westerners'. For 'innocent' perhaps read naïve.

ti tsu	a bamboo flute, used both as a solo instrument and as part of an ensemble, playing traditional Chinese music
ti yu	The 'earth prison' or underworld of Chinese legend. There are ten main Chinese Hells, the first being the courtroom in which the sinner is sentenced and the last being that place where they are reborn as human beings. In between are a vast number of sub-Hells, each with its own Judge and staff of cruel warders. In Hell, it is always dark, with no differentiation between night and day.
Tian	'Heaven', also, 'the dome of the sky'
tian-fang	literally 'to fill the place of the dead wife'; used to signify the upgrading of a concubine to the more respectable position of wife
tiao tuo	bracelets of gold and jade
T'ieh Lo-han	'Iron Goddess of Mercy', a ch'a
T'ieh Pi Pu Kai	Literally, 'the iron pen changes not', this is the final phrase used at the end of all Chinese government proclamations for the last three thousand years.
ting	An open-sided pavilion in a Chinese garden. Designed as a focal point in a garden, it is said to symbolize man's essential place in the natural order of things.
T'ing Wei	The Superintendancy of Trials, an institution that dates back to the T'ang dynasty. See Book Six, *The White Mountain*, for an instance of how this department of government – responsible for black propaganda – functions.
T'o	'camel-backed', a Chinese term for 'hunch-backed'
tong	A gang. In China and Europe these are usually smaller and thus subsidiary to the Triads, but in North America the term has generally taken the place of Triad.
tou chi	Glycine Max, or the black soybean, used in Chinese herbal medicine to cure insomnia
Tsai Chien!	'Until we meet again!'
Tsou Tsai Hei	'the Walker in the Darkness'
tsu	the north
tsu kuo	the motherland
ts'un	A Chinese 'inch' of approximately 1.4 Western inches. Ten ts'un form one ch'i.

Tu	Earth
tzu	'Elder Sister'
wan wu	literally 'the ten thousand things'; used generally to include everything in creation, or, as the Chinese say, 'all things in Heaven and Earth'
Wei	Commandant of Security
wei chi	'The surrounding game', known more commonly in the West by its Japanese name of Go. It is said that the game was invented by the legendary Chinese Emperor Yao in the year 2350 BC to train the mind of his son, Tan Chu, and teach him to think like an emperor.
wen ming	a term used to denote civilization, or written culture
wen ren	the scholar-artist; very much an ideal state, striven for by all creative Chinese
weng	'Old man'. Usually a term of respect.
Wu	A diviner; traditionally these were 'mediums' who claimed to have special pyshic powers. Wu could be either male or female.
Wu	'Non-being'. As Lao Tzu says: 'Once the block is carved, there are names.' But the Tao is unnameable (wu-ming) and before Being (yu) is Non-Being (wu). Not to have existence, or form, or a name, that is wu.
Wu ching	the 'Five Classics' studied by all Confucian scholars, comprising the Shu Ching (Book Of History), the Shih Ching (Book of Songs), the I Ching (Book of Changes), the Li Ching (Book of Rites, actually three books in all), and the Ch'un Chui (The Spring And Autumn Annals of the State of Lu).
wu fu	the five gods of good luck.
wu tu	the 'five noxious creatures – which are toad, scorpion, snake, centipede and gecko (wall lizard)
Wushu	The Chinese word for Martial Arts. It refers to any of several hundred schools. Kung fu is a school within this, meaning 'skill that transcends mere surface beauty'.
wuwei	Nonaction, an old Taoist concept. It means keeping harmony with the flow of things – doing nothing to break the flow.
ya	Homosexual. Sometimes the term 'a yellow eel' is used.
yamen	the official building in a Chinese community

yang	The 'male principle' of Chinese cosmology, which, with its complementary opposite, the female yin, forms the t'ai ch'i, derived from the Primeval One. From the union of yin and yang arise the 'five elements' (water, fire, earth, metal, wood) from which the 'ten thousand things' (the wan wu) are generated. Yang signifies Heaven and the South, the Sun and Warmth, Light, Vigor, Maleness, Penetration, odd numbers and the Dragon. Mountains are yang.
yang kuei tzu	Chinese name for foreigners, 'Ocean Devils'. It is also synonymous with 'Barbarians'.
yang mei ping	'willow plum sickness', the Chinese term for syphilis, provides an apt description of the male sexual organ in the extreme of this sickness
yi	the number one
yin	The 'female principle' of Chinese cosmology (see yang). Yin signifies Earth and the North, the Moon and Cold, Darkness, Quiescence, Femaleness, Absorption, even numbers and the Tiger. The yin lies in the shadow of the mountain.
yin mao	pubic hair
Ying kuo	English, the language
ying tao	'baby peach', a term of endearment here
ying tzu	'shadows' – trained specialists of various kinds, contracted out to gangland bosses
yu	Literally 'fish', but, because of its phonetic equivalence to the word for 'abundance', the fish symbolizes wealth. Yet there is also a saying that when the fish swim upriver it is a portent of social unrest and rebellion.
yu ko	a 'Jade Barge', here a type of luxury sedan
Yu Kung	'Foolish Old Man!'
yu ya	deep elegance
yuan	The basic currency of Chung Kuo (and modern-day China). Colloquially (though not here) it can also be termed kuai – 'piece' or 'lump'. Ten mao (or, formally, jiao) make up one yuan, while 100 fen (or 'cents') comprise one yuan.
yueh ch'in	a Chinese dulcimer, one of the principal instruments of the Chinese orchestra

Ywe Lung

Literally 'The Moon Dragon', the wheel of seven dragons that is the symbol of the ruling Seven throughout Chung Kuo: 'At its centre the snouts of the regal beasts met, forming a rose-like hub, huge rubics burning fiercely in each eye. Their lithe, powerful bodies curved outward like the spokes of a giant wheel while at the edge their tails were intertwined to form the rim.' (Chapter Four of *The Middle Kingdom*).

CHUNG KUO

AUTHOR'S NOTE

The transcription of standard Mandarin into a European alphabetical form was first achieved in the seventeenth century by the Italian Matteo Ricci, who founded and ran the first Jesuit Mission in China from 1583 until his death in 1610. Since then several dozen attempts have been made to reduce the original Chinese sounds, represented by some tens of thousands of separate pictograms, into readily understandable phonetics for Western use. For a long time, however, three systems dominated – those used by the three major Western powers vying for influence in the corrupt and crumbling Chinese empire of the nineteenth century: Great Britain; France; and Germany. These systems were the Wade-Giles (Great Britain and America – sometimes known as the Wade System), the *École Française de L'Extrême Orient* (France) and the Lessing (Germany). Since 1958, however, the Chinese themselves have sought to create one single phonetic form, based on the German system, which they termed the *hanyu pinyin fang'an* (Scheme for a Chinese Phonetic Alphabet), known more commonly as *pinyin*, and in all foreign language books published in China since 1 January 1979 *pinyin* has been used, as well as being taught now in schools alongside the standard Chinese characters. For this work, however, I have chosen to use the older, and, to my mind, far more elegant transcription system, the Wade-Giles (in modified form). For those now used to the harder forms of *pinyin* the following may serve as a basic conversion guide, the Wade-Giles first, the *pinyin* after.

p for b	ch' for q
ts' for c	j for r
ch' for ch	t' for t
t for d	hs for x
k for g	ts for z
ch for j	ch for zh

The effect is, I hope, to render the softer, more poetic side of the original Mandarin, ill served, I feel, by modern pinyin.

The translation of Meng Chiao's, 'Impromptu', is by A. C. Graham from his excellent Poems of the Late T'ang, published by Penguin Books, London, 1965. The translation of Po Chu-I's 'To Li Chien' is by Arthur Waley, from Chinese Poems, published by George Allen and Unwin, London, 1946.

The quotation from Sun Tzu's The Art of War is from the Samuel B. Griffith translation, published by the Oxford University Press in 1963. The quotation from Arthur Koestler's The Act of Creation is from the Hutchinson & Co. Edition, published in London, 1969, reprinted with their kind permission.

The translation from Nietzsche is by R. J. Hollingdale and is taken from Beyond Good and Evil (Prelude To A Philosophy Of The Future), published by Penguin Books, London, 1973.

A marvelous recipe for Yang Sen's 'Spring Wine' – mentioned in the opening to this volume – can be found on page 163 of Chinese Herbal Medicine by Daniel P. Reid, published by Thorsons, London in 1987.

Finally the game of wei chi mentioned throughout this volume is more commonly known by its Japanese name of Go, and is not merely the world's oldest game but its most elegant.

David Wingrove
April 1990/July 2011

CHUNG KUO

ACKNOWLEDGEMENTS

Thanks must go, once again, to all those who have read and criticized parts of Chung Kuo during its long gestation. To my editors – Nick Sayers, Brian DeFiore, John Pearce, Alyssa Diamond – for their patience as well as their enthusiasm; to my Writers Bloc companions Chris Evans, David Garnett, Rob Holdstock, Garry Kilworth, Geoff Ryman, Simon Ings, Bobbie Lamming and Lisa Tuttle; to Andy Sawyer for an outsider's view when it was needed; and, as ever, to my stalwart helper and first-line critic, Brian Griffin, for keeping me on the rails.

Thanks are also due to Rob Carter, Ritchie Smith, Paul Bougie, Mike Cobley, Linda Shaughnessy, Susan and the girls (Jessica, Amy and baby Georgia) and Is and the Lunatics (at Canterbury) for keeping my spirits up during the long, lonely business of writing this. And to 'Nan and Grandad' – Daisy and Percy Oudot – for helping out when things were tight... and for making the tea!

Finally, thanks to Magma, IQ and the Cardiacs for providing the soundtrack.